I t was dark and cold.
  The gloom surrounding
expected. Somehow, he though
that, a gigantic open area where the souls of the dead gathered
before they were called forth to face Lliania, Lady Justice, and
be judged by her ever-truthful Scales. He had certainly never
heard a priest speak about the Bailey Majestic as being a vast
emptiness.

"I felt those bastards shoot and stab me," Drangar said. "I'm
dead."

Of course, there was no reply, nor did he expect one.

It was cold and dark.

"Maybe even the gods don't want me," he muttered, his
voice fearful. "Don't I feel splendid now?"

He felt adrift, floating on a boat down some river. Sometimes
it was as if he could hear surf slapping against a wooden hull,
but neither did he sit on a bench, nor was he surrounded by
wood.

Someone touched his arm; he shrank away from the gentle
caress, all too aware of the nightmares that haunted his sleep.
Would he need to sleep here?

The touch lingered; escape was futile. Now he thought he
felt it more distinct, a rub, as if someone scrubbed him.

Drangar moved to take hold of the unseen cloth, but, as
expected, couldn't grab it. Nor could he touch his own arm. If
this was death, it was far more unpleasant than any being ever
imagined.

"All just lonely souls drifting away in nothingness. None
of us able to reach out to the others, none of us being heard,"
he muttered. "We came from nothing and leave for nothing. It's
pointless. Life is meaningless. There is no Round Hall, no grand
feasting chamber, and no glorious celebration. Nothing!"

DEDICATION

This novel deals primarily with fictional warriors; men and women who weather whatever life may throw at them. I would like to dedicate SHATTERED DREAMS to a young woman whose battle is very real: to Liz Chambers, you are a real fighter!

SHATTERED DREAMS

-Light in the Dark Book 1-

by ULFF LEHMANN

ACKNOWLEDGMENTS

My thanks to Katti Mattern who helped me hammer out the kinks, and Kathy Freuden, my friend and editor; to Kathleen Stammers, who gave me moral and artistic support from the get go; Anneke van Heusden and Ryan Ryker Lazslo for the inspiration, and David Dodd for giving the covers THE LOOK; to Faith McKee for bringing Dunthiochagh to life; to Riza Türker, for the first map; to Sayan Mukherjee for the second map and for helping me flesh out the Woods of Gathran; and to Robert Altbauer for taking all the stuff I, Riza, and Sayan had come up with and turning it into this baby. My deepest gratitude, however, goes out to Daniela Bockhorst, without whom I never would have discovered who I really am; and Susanne Fritsch, who never gave up and kicked me until I went and got better.

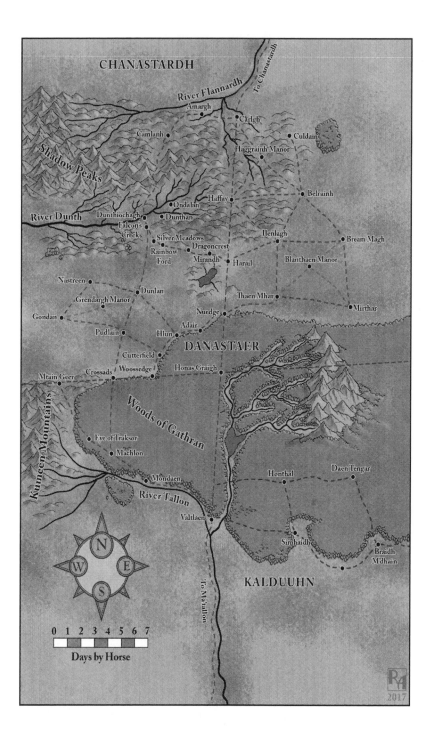

Dramatis Personae

Anneijhan Cirrain—Chanastardhian noble
Baron Cumaill Duasonh—lord of the city of Dunthiochagh
Braigh—a Caretaker
Coimharrin—a Lawspeaker
Drangar Ralgon—a mercenary
Ealisaid—a wizardess
Gail Caslin—a Caretaker
Jathain—Baron Duasonh's cousin
Jesgar Garinad—a thief
Kerral—Danastaerian General
Kildanor—a Chosen of Lesganagh
Lightbringer—a mysterious entity
Lloreanthoran—an elven mage
Nerran—friend and advisor to Baron Duasonh
Urgraith Mireynh—High General of Chanastardh

Pronunciation:

Some names, be it cities or persons, lean heavily on sounds not usually found in English.

For instance ch and gh in Dunthiochagh sound similar to the Welch consonant ch, think Johann Sebastian Bach; same goes for Carlgh, for example.

D o we humans ever learn from the past? No. Petty rivalries, greed, sometimes even, as ludicrous as it sounds, religion were and still are reason enough for one side to war on the other. I would like to say our age is enlightened enough for us not to re-enact the grand tragedies of the world. I would like to say peace is and will remain ours. But I am a scholar of history as much as I am Chief Librarian, highest of Traghnalach's priesthood, Keeper of Knowledge. In the most literal sense imaginable, my position allows me to delve deep into what has occurred before.

Complacency is the greatest foe of peace. Once the things our forebears have struggled and died for become as much a fixture in life as sleeping and waking, we take them for granted. Peace is something we have to strive for each and every day.

There are few things truer in life than the saying "war changes things." In our day and age that is as much a reality as it was in the centuries past. From war and blood the elven civilization rose to greatness, and they only prevented the same from happening to themselves by granting humanity its freedom before history could repeat itself.

In the waning years of Gathran, first and mightiest of the elven kingdoms, routine was the dominant factor in the behavior of that realm's people. It can be a good thing, but when the shepherd's attention turns inward the sheep fall prey.

After they taught us humans the secrets of magic and insured that the Phoenix Wizards, as the world-spanning order of mages was known in that age, could never become a threat to them, mighty Gathran closed its eyes, napping inhuman dreams. For a time, the trust they put in their human pupils was well placed. The Wizards, while being courted by every ruler of man, did rarely get involved in worldly affairs, preferring to further their own knowledge or lend aid in useful ways, such as construction.

As I have stated earlier, this journal is by no means an account of history. The capturing of events is, as always, a duty my brethren and I perform as part of our sacred rituals day in and day out.

I made it my task to review and interpret the events that led us to our enlightened age.

The year commonly known as Phoenix Unmade (1383 K.C.) denominates the end of that exclusive and reclusive order. The sudden death of High Master Kalaith, the Phoenix Wizards' last leader, and the absence of a preordained successor heralded a feud that destroyed wizardry, as we know it. As is usually the case when lust for power overrules common sense, everyone who deemed himself worthy fought for his right to call himself High Master. The struggle, in the following years called the Heir War or Wizard War, spread outward from the Shadowpeak Mountains, the Wizards' primary stronghold, drowning all lands in magical violence. Mighty Gathran and the small kingdoms Dargh and Janagast bore the brunt of the destruction, the rift torn into the Shadowpeaks a warning for generations to come. The elves in their complacency surged forward only at the last moment to end the fighting. By that time, however, Gathran's capital, proud Honas Graigh, lay in ruins.

For reasons only known to themselves, the elves withdrew from the world, thus leaving unguarded a door for an old woe to ravage the world.

With the presumable death of magic, the new age was heralded as the Age of Man. In my opinion this was a misnomer, for not only were there countless elves left in the world, but it was mainly the nobility, crafters and priesthoods that dominated the era immediately following the Heir Wars, not all of mankind.

Out of the ruins of Gathran, Dargh and Janagast grew

a new nation, Danastaer, led by Halmond the Great, former High General of powerful Chanastardh. Four years after Halmond's coronation, just as the people took a collective rest from rebuilding their lives; said door was opened in abandoned Honas Graigh. For the second time in a decade, war threatened the world; creatures born of nightmares ravaged the lands surrounding Gathran Forest and surged ahead to conquer the rest, for reasons that are yet unknown to us. It was only due to the timely intervention of the followers of Lesganagh All-Maker, God of Sun and War, that the threat was banished before too much harm could be done.

Reconstruction began anew, and this time the peoples were certain their troubles were at an end.

They were wrong...

CHAPTER 1

Fifteenth of Heat, 1472 K.C.

Liam held on to the leash, trying to hold the mastiff back, but the canine pulled on. "Beggar, stop!" the lad shouted.

"He's on the hunt, you can't control him like da," commented Erin.

Determined to prove his sister wrong, Liam turned his back to the tugging dog, clutched both hands around the leather and pulled. For a moment it seemed he would win the contest, but Beggar prevailed and dragged him a few steps deeper into the forest.

"Let him go," Erin said.

"Da will kill me if I return without him," he grunted. Dusk was already close, and their parents would be worried. Liam didn't want to think about the punishment that already awaited them for being late. How much worse would it be if they came back without the beloved mastiff? Maybe… "We should follow him until he's caught whatever got his attention."

"But no one goes deep into Gathran."

Erin made sense, but "You tell Beggar that. We can't come home without him!"

Erin grumbled, and he knew he'd won the argument. Beggar surely wouldn't drag them too far away from the path.

"I'm scared," Erin whined. Girls could be so annoying. This was just like any other forest, the same stupid trees, the same rustling when various vermin crept through underbrush and branches, nothing to worry about. "Can we go home?" she pleaded.

If Liam was honest with himself, he had never been in a forest at night, not deep anyway. He scowled, and pulled at Beggar's leash. "Scales!" he cursed.

"Ma says you mustn't swear," Erin scolded.

"Right now, I don't give a damn what ma says! We need to get out of this bloody forest!" His sister's prolonged wail told him he had been too harsh. He reached over and grasped her hand. "I'm sorry, don't cry, please."

Erin held onto him, but she said nothing. For a moment, he felt the leash slacken, and Liam rejoiced. Now they could go home. "Come, boy," he said and whistled. The mastiff, however, had other plans.

Neither of them knew how much time had passed, but if Liam had to guess, judging by how his feet felt, it should be midnight. "Look, sis," he whispered, pointing up to the sky. "The moon, the sun's little brother, he'll protect us."

"Really?" Erin asked. It was the first word she had said in a long while.

He was about to reply, when Beggar howled. At the same moment, a cloud pushed itself before the glimmering orb, plunging the forest into utter darkness. Beggar's howl changed into a whine that Liam had never heard from the mastiff before. The leash, still pulled taut, began to shake. There was an instant when he felt he could pull the dog back, and tried. The leather felt less stiff, it slackened, and the shuffling told him Beggar was coming back. Then the canine reversed again, and pulled brother and sister further into the darkness.

Scraping along thornleaves didn't even slow the dog's continuous tug. Liam sported more bruises, cuts, and punctures than he had ever imagined possible, he swallowed the pain, knowing little Erin felt even worse. Her arm was slack as he dragged her along, the only reassurance that she was still with him was her hand in his, and the occasional sob. Neither of them jumped when a new sound joined the cacophony already present in Gathran-Forest. Sure, by now he could see a little of the woods, but the looming shapes of oaks made him long for total darkness.

It was as if the trees were watching them. Every so often he felt a shiver running down his back. It was like when ma was looking at him, only worse. She merely scowled, but whatever was watching them put so much hatred into the glare that he could feel the eyes roaming his body.

"They're looking at me," Erin whispered. Her voice sounded so feeble.

"I know." He didn't know what else to say, wasn't even sure he'd said it at all.

"I gotta pee," she whined.

Liam snorted. "Think Beggar will stop for you?"

"Beggar!"

The mastiff didn't listen, and pulled on.

Thinking about something as normal as peeing, helped him to ignore the stares. "We'll stop soon," he said.

"Really?"

They trudged on.

"Eanaigh, Healthgiver, hear our prayer, protect us from this wicked forest," the siblings said. "Lesganagh, Lifegiver, send us your shining light to guide us."

"This is stupid," Erin grumbled. "The clouds won't go away. We should wait for dawn."

"And let Beggar go?"

"Stupid doggie. You should've let him go when he started pulling the first time. You wanted to take him with us in the first place!"

His shin smacked against... a stone. Liam cursed. "Damnation, da would've beaten us."

"No, he would've beaten you. You took Beggar," she insisted. "Ow! Stupid dog! Stupid stone!"

His feet touched paved ground, and the mastiff's paws scraped on rock as well. He was about to speak, when moonlight broke through the cloud cover. "What kind of idiot would build a city in this bloody forest?" he muttered, taking in the sight.

White marble seemed to seep up from the ground to cover trees. No, the trees were the stone! There: an archway looking like clingfern. Was the thing before it, looking like a felled tree, a bench?

Even Beggar had halted, growling at the ruins.

A glint of moonlight looked as if it was cascading down a stone waterfall. Was it just made of rock? Liam stumbled forward, and this time it was he who dragged the mastiff along. Erin followed tentatively. It looked like a waterfall; the shards of glass inlaid into the stone created the shine.

He whirled around. Beggar growled, and little Erin clung to him, whimpering. A shadow, it had crossed the wall, he was sure of it, but there was nothing, except... No, impossible, but he had to be certain. "Stay with the mutt. Don't follow me."

"Please don't go." Her voice was barely a whisper and he wished he could take her with him, protect her, but if what he'd seen was true, this was no place for Erin, or him. Slowly he inched toward the edifice; it must have been a house once. There, almost washed over by a wave of stone, he discerned a window. Unlike the waterfall this didn't look like a statue.

What could've melted stone, Liam wondered. The window was not the only thing the molten rock had covered. What was that? He squinted against the gloom, tried to discern what lay underneath the deformed marble. He gasped. Bones. A foot. No, two feet! Raising his head, tearing his eyes away from the wall's bottom, he saw the silhouette of a person. His mouth, wide open, was clearly visible, despite the obvious nest of some bird. He could also make out the eyes, or rather the empty holes where the eyes would have been.

"Liam," Erin said.

The calm in her voice brought him about. He could barely see his sister, or Beggar. Had he gone that far? "Don't come closer," he cautioned.

"I won't, Ethain said he'll protect us."

"Who?" Then he saw a greater shadow detach itself from the waterfall behind Erin. It placed a hand on her shoulder and leaned forward.

"Don't worry. All will be well, lad." The stranger's face, was it pale? No, it had to be a trick of the moonlight. Putting index finger against index finger, and thumb against thumb, the man made the orb of Lesganagh, and Liam felt better.

Maybe the Lord of Sun and War had sent Ethain to save

them! He hurried to his sister's side. "Thank you, kind sir."

"Think nothing of it, lad, it's just a happy coincidence we met, that's all," the man replied, and turned Erin about. "Let's go, you look cold. Are you hungry?"

"Aye," his little sister said. She sounded as if she were sleepwalking. They had been on their feet for a long time; she probably was just tired.

"Yea," he said.

"There's a fire and some sweetcakes waiting for you," Ethain said as he led them deeper into the ruins.

"Sweetcakes, yummy," Erin mumbled.

His stomach growled; sweetcakes did sound good. They rounded another bend, one that looked like the molten wall that had covered the body. This time he saw the relief more clearly. Here a family was buried! "What is this place?"

Without turning, Ethain said, "Honas Graigh, capital of Gathran."

Liam wanted to ask more, but was distracted by a choir which seemed to be singing from up ahead. Now he also saw the flicker of flames. When they had passed another hunk of molten stone, he saw the fire. Even though it looked small, it illuminated a wall that seemed to have been sunk into the floor. Before this wall the flames danced... with shadows! It looked as if motes of light spun around flecks of darkness.

Impossible. He blinked and rubbed his eyes, but the motes of light remained, as did the obsidian sparks. The song, something was wrong about it. The closer they came the more distorted the music sounded. Wailing, hushed whispers, screeches, and forming a delicate counterpoint to the deep, somewhat distorted voice of a second man.

"And this is the Aerant C'lain."

Liam wanted to run, get away from the two. He had to get Erin to safety! Da would be angry! The pair frightened him. His little sister walked alongside Ethain toward the fire, Beggar at her side.

"Welcome back, brother," the one standing with his back to the flames said. "This is the best you could find?"

"Does it matter?"

"Not really. They are frightened enough, it seems."

"And the dog will cause even more trouble," Ethain said.

Beggar! Beggar! Liam tried to scream, yell, drive the mastiff into action, but his father's trusted canine remained as still as Erin. *Erin! No! Leave her be!* Why couldn't he scream? Why didn't she run away?

"You're the older, the honor is yours," Ethain said and bowed. "Ganaedor, do it."

The other man's hand flashed forward. The boy thought he saw long claws at the tip of the man's fingers. Then blood spurted forth from Beggar's throat.

As the dog's life ended in slowly ceasing gasps and whines, Liam thought he saw something else leaving the mastiff's body. The red liquid flowed, first in a gush, then dwindling to a slow dribble, and with this surge came—he wasn't at all sure—Beggar's silhouette. The blood-shrouded reflection looked frantic. It seemed to growl. Was this the dog's soul? It bared its fangs, and the shine it had possessed just a moment ago vanished in darkness. Then the shadow shot for the roiling dance of struggling flecks, and immediately the luminescence of the dancing column dimmed.

"You take the girl, brother," he said, holding the dog at arm's length as it bled out.

"And the high honors to you," Ethain said, as he reached for Erin's throat. One hand held her by the neck, while the other, with similar claws, slashed over her jugular.

Liam wanted to holler, rage, scream, but no sound escaped his lips; he could hardly breathe. He wanted to turn his head, but his neck wouldn't move. His eyes remained open, and tears ran down his cheeks as he saw his baby sister bleed to death.

Again, the same thing he had seen with Beggar's spirit happened. Erin's soul, however, was more willful, dancing, snarling, and glaring with hate. For a moment it seemed her inner light would not be overwhelmed by shadows. Liam prayed she would go to the Bailey Majestic. Fear and weariness won the struggle, and Erin's spirit was swallowed by darkness, leaping for the column. Again, the dancing flecks lost some of their sheen. A voice inside tried to convince him this was all a bad dream, but as Ethain flung Erin's lifeless body away even that hopeful voice died.

The older, Ganaedor, walked toward him. Liam tried to run, put one foot before the other, get away, but like his eyes, neck, and voice his legs did not obey. As if he was taking a kitten, the man picked him up by the neck and carried him toward the screaming and howling motes of darkness and light. "Soon the soulward will fall," Ganaedor said as he slashed his claws across Liam's throat.

CHAPTER 2

The glow of the hooded lamp was enough to illuminate the book that the Hand was reading. This was the second time he had entered the house. Considering how scrupulous other merchants were regarding their property, the Hendard family estate was almost too easy to get into. The Hand didn't mind.

Initially he had wanted to confuse the two servants the timber merchant employed, but when he discovered that the man owned a sizable library he decided against the prank. Instead, he had begun to peruse the books standing in vast shelves in what he called the reading room.

That no other thief had hit the building before was surprising, especially if one considered the wealth lining the walls of this room. Maybe there was no market for books. He didn't know if Hendard owned jewelry, nor did he care, books were enough for him.

The Hand cast another glance around the room with its massive steeloak shelves, a brass chandelier, and the two other comfortable armchairs, before he returned to "Gathran: Rise and Decline of the Elves." Books like this had been popular before he'd been born, and given that few people knew what had really happened to the forest folk, the theories penned by some idiot proved vastly amusing.

"Sure, the gods called them back," he muttered, shaking his head. He was just about to adjust the lamp's glow yet again when he heard a noise.

It wasn't loud, not the groaning of the wooden stair or the creaking of hinges badly in need of an oiling. It sounded as if someone was trying to undo a window-latch with a piece of wire. A little scraping, the rattle as the metal noose was placed around the handle. To him it sounded like some apprentice was trying a bit too hard. Maybe there was a market for books, he concluded. Not that it mattered. The Hand fished around his belt pouch, a task made all the more difficult by the gloves, until he found a piece of string long enough to use as a bookmark. Let them wonder, he thought, barely able to suppress a chuckle. Then he put the tome back into its shelf and extinguished the light.

By now the other burglar had, judging from the sounds, managed to get into the house. He glanced out the window. Who in his right mind would try to steal from a place this close to dawn?

Sure, the stars were still shining, but beyond the tiled roofs of Dunthiochagh he could already see their light dimming. Good thing the burglar had made his entrance now; otherwise the rising sun would have caught him. He strained his hearing; the other thief was in the kitchen of all places.

The Hendards' pantry was well stocked, but nothing of worth was stashed there. Sure, the honeyed pastries were good—let the servants wonder how the plate got into the reading room—but of all the places to look for valuables, the kitchen was the last. There were still a few pastries left. He grinned and plopped another one into his mouth. Then he was out the window, booted toes finding purchase in the crevices between the quarry stones of the outer wall. He closed the window, pulled down the wire that shut the locking mechanism, and climbed down.

As he reached the ground, the Hand caught a glimpse of the other burglar. The boy seemed to be still trying to make up his mind which way to go. Poor sod. He was just about to head for the street when he heard the tread of heavy boots on cobblestone. A mischievous grin crept onto his face. Idiots had to be punished, he decided, and searched the ground for a pebble.

The watchmen were close now. His sooty face and black clothes hid him well, even in this false dawn, so he didn't worry about being seen, but the sound of a stone splintering through glass would catch the guards' attention. He found a suitable piece of rock and threw.

The moment the pane of glass shattered the Hand shuffled off, his boots making nary a sound. But stealth was hardly needed, already one of the guardsmen whistled for more watchmen to join them, while the other ran for the merchant's house. He almost made it into Cherkont Street when he heard the clattering of horseshoes on stone.

Riders? Why the Scales would they send riders after a burglar? Then he realized that the sounds were receding, the horseman was heading north, and he breathed a sigh of relief. The quick respite was over all too soon. Another pair of watchmen strolled up Cherkont from the west. The Hand grimaced, and sped onward. It wouldn't do to be caught in a burglar's attire in this street of well-to-do citizens. Not even the most daring of thieves got into trouble here. Cherkont Street was almost a town unto itself, with so many former warriors and their families living in houses surrounded by gardens and high shrubs. The people here didn't wait for the Watch and a Lawspeaker; they judged you then and there.

He could hide in one of the gardens, maybe. Now dawn was upon him, and for once he cursed the clear sky. What was that? The door of the timber-framed building next to the shrub where he hid stood ajar. Should he? Yes! He abandoned his hiding place and slipped in, leaving just a crack open lest the sound of the lock alert the inhabitants or the watchmen.

He waited and listened as the footsteps came closer.

"Maybe it attracts just peaceful folk," one of the guards muttered.

"What was that?" the other asked.

"Oh, you know, Cherkont being that quiet and all. Maybe it's because only peaceful folk live here."

The other chuckled. "There are more than enough warriors— former warriors mind you—living here, and I doubt you can call them a peaceful lot. Rather, I'd say because of so many people living there who know their weapons, any mugger would be insane to try anything."

The guy was right.

Both men stopped, right in front of the house, and spoke: "We hail thee Lord of Sun and War, may thy light greet us every morning."

A prayer now? He hardly dared to breathe.

"Think they'd kick us out if they knew of our little prayer each morning?" the first one said.

"More than half the lads do it, boy," the other replied.

"But the priests of Eanaigh say Lesganagh's evil."

What was this? Couldn't they have their philosophical discussion away from here?

"Evil, shmevil. All I know is that the sun warms us, makes the crops grow, and that a Chosen of Lesganagh is Baron Duasonh's friend." There was a short pause, then the man continued, "Listen, lad, would you want the sun to stop shining every day? I know I don't. Ever been up north? Bloody cold in the winter, sun barely comes up. With no sun at all, how could man or beast survive?"

The Hand knew if this went on the house's inhabitants would catch him. Maybe he could slip out back. He turned, and for the first time took in his surroundings.

There wasn't much to see, a small hallway, two doors leading to some rooms and a stairway up to the second floor. Nothing unusual... except. He swallowed.

There were bloody footprints and handprints on floor, stairs, and the door opposite him at the end of the corridor. Murder? Here in Cherkont? If he left now the watchmen would catch him, and think him the killer. What if the murderer was still here?

He saw that the footprints went up and grew fainter. Morbid curiosity got a hold of him and he inched toward the rear door. The tang of a butcher's shop permeated the air the closer he got to the room.

What had happened here? He pushed open the portal and stared.

The next thing he knew was that he was on his knees, vomiting. Little details burned into his mind. A severed finger, a tuft of hair, the shards of a wine bottle. Someone else had thrown up next to the fireplace. He stood, his knees shaking badly, and retched again. If the watch caught him he would be hanged as a killer, he was certain. Escape! There wasn't much else on his mind. He gingerly stepped past the gore but almost slipped on… was this part of a victim's gut?

The window opened without complaint and although he was out, the odor of death persisted. Every inch of him urged him to run, but whoever had been killed here deserved justice, deserved that the butcher paid for this brutality. The adjourning shrub was near; there even was a small stable for one or two horses. Had the killer stolen a horse as well? He didn't care. Looking at the charnel house one last time, he made up his mind and turned around. Glass shattered as he smashed the window, and without further thought he rushed through the shrubbery into the next plot, past the house, and into the next lane.

Later that week, the Hand heard people say that only one person had been murdered in Cherkont Street, and he knew no matter how much he drank, the image of that room would never leave him.

CHAPTER 3

Twenty-eighth of Leaves, 1475 K.C.

The strip of land between the fields to Ean's left and the orchards to his right was their favorite battleground. Usually he and Pudgy weren't fighting alone; it wasn't much fun attacking or defending against an enemy army of one. This Trannday, however, the other children were on the village square. Neither Ean nor Pudgy wanted to join the people of Carlgh in gawking at wares or haggling over some item or other.

Gawking was for children, and neither of them could be bothered with children's stuff. They were grown-ups. "Almost grown-ups," Ean's father always said, but to him the meager year until he came of age didn't matter.

The game of the day was "Ambush," and now it was his turn to patrol the footpath that ran north from their village, past Oak-Hill to where Little Stream joined Old Stream. Of course, the path went on, but aside from grassy knolls there was nothing there. Farther north, so old Jasper said, lay Chanastardh. Ean was still wondering about how far away Chanastardh really was, when Pudgy stomped through a bunch of ferns he had been hiding behind, screaming "Ambush!"

They spent a few moments trading blows with wooden swords; then Pudgy halted his assault and looked past Ean's shoulder. For a moment, he thought his friend was trying to fool him, but when Pudgy continued to stare, he finally turned his head and saw the shepherd. He looked even gaunter than the last time.

"He's got a beard," Pudgy remarked.

"Yea," Ean said.

The shepherd walked along the path, his boots still wet from fording Old Stream; on his back he carried a massive pack. Now he saw them and halted, stood up straight, slammed his right fist against his chest and smiled.

They dropped their weapons, waved, and grinned. Ean, who considered himself far more courageous than Pudgy, walked toward the shepherd, hoping to be the first child ever to exchange words with this man, and to tell that tale to their friends. Closing within a few yards of him, he saw the shepherd's features revert to his well-known sorrowful gaze, his eyes drifting toward Carlgh. He thought better of his plan, stopped, unwilling to disturb him.

The shepherd walked on.

After a few moments, Pudgy joined him. "Did you see that?" Ean exclaimed. "He almost talked to me."

The younger boy shook his head. "Nah, he don't talk to nobody much."

"But didn't you see him smile?"

"Something's changed, eh?" Pudgy suggested.

Ean's curiosity still nagging, he led the way, and the two lads followed the shepherd into town.

Today was market day in Carlgh, like every month's Trannday for as long as people could remember. On any other day, the younger boys would flock like proverbial sheep to old Jasper the guardsman to listen to his tales, but not on a Trannday like this. Traders came to the small town to sell cloth, pottery, animals, fruit and vegetables, to joke with old friends and haggle with their customers. Children played in the narrow lanes, dodging adult's legs, and peeking into the booths. Adults tried to move out of their offspring's way as they went about their business.

Ean really didn't care that it was the last market day before the coming of winter; there was adventure to be had. But his experienced eye noticed the lack of merchants traveling north to Chanastardh or south to Danastaer's capital, Harail. Normally the village was bursting with traders who traveled the Old Elven Road that gave direct access to Harail and Chanastardh's capital, but today he found the market's appeal strangely lacking.

The absence of Chanastardhian merchants was quite obvious; although he recognized a few familiar faces from Harail, native traders were not as strongly present either.

The two ignored this as they followed the shepherd to the merchant he regularly dealt with, keeping a safe distance. They saw him smile again. Something really had changed. Usually the man's face was blank.

Ean pointed out how the shepherd moved. "Think he's a warrior?"

Pudgy chuckled. "He's a shepherd, fool."

"Yea, but before that."

"Your ma told ya to quit dreamin', didn't she?" Pudgy glanced at his friend, a skeptical look on his face.

"Aye," admitted Ean, crestfallen.

"Then quit. He's a sheep herder, nothin' more!"

They stopped arguing when they saw the shepherd nod a greeting, this time at Pudgy's older sister who crossed his way as she headed to the Boar and Bustard.

"Oh no!" moaned the lad. "I'll hear about this for the next month!"

Ean smirked. "She couldn't stay quiet for days after the shepherd came here the last time?"

"You can't imagine," Pudgy grumbled.

It was business as usual for the shepherd. He sold his wool and mutton, and the two boys were only slightly distracted when the smell of fresh rolls wafted their way. Ean went off to gather lunch. When he reached the baker, his nose led him straight to the cooling bread and from there onward to the cheese-maker whose wares lured with their own smell. A quick detour past Farmer Melainh's pigsty to shake off the cheese-maker's dog, and Ean stood next to Pudgy again.

"That was close," he said between deep breaths.

"You wouldn't believe what I just saw," Pudgy almost shouted. The food Ean had brought was still untouched. This was more than unusual for his friend.

"What was it?" Ean broke off a chunk of bread and one of

cheese and began to eat.

"The shepherd."

"Yes? We both saw him, remember?"

"No, no. This was different."

Ean hated the way his friend spoke whenever he got too excited. "And what was different about it?"

"He… there… you know, this man from Harail who buys most of the stuff around here."

"Maddagh, the trader?"

"Yes, yes."

"What about him?"

"Well, the shepherd came to him and they talked." Now Pudgy realized food was near and he gathered his lunch before he continued.

"Well, they did talk for a long while and the shepherd pointed at various things he wanted. Maddagh nodded and the shepherd nodded and handed him a gold-piece."

"A gold-piece?" Ean hissed. He was stunned, how could Pudgy forget he had told his mother the same thing months before? How could his best friend forget the lashing he got for telling what ma saw as a blatant lie?

Pudgy must have seen his expression. "What?"

"You bastard!" the older boy snapped.

"What did I do?"

He glared at Pudgy. "You forgot already?"

"Forgot what?"

Ean forced the words out, "Four months ago I told you, my ma, and da that the shepherd had paid with gold! You didn't believe me. Ma and da didn't believe me, and I couldn't sit for a week or so after the thrashing she gave me."

Pudgy had stopped chewing. Pale, he looked at him. "Gods, mate, I'm sorry," he whispered.

"Ah, stow it!" He tore off another piece of bread. After a few bites he frowned at Pudgy. "So? What else?"

"Nothing. He paid with a gold piece."

"At least now you believe me," Ean snapped. "Damn, two gold pieces." He screwed up his face in concentration. "Think he got more?"

His friend shrugged. "I dunno. Why?"

"Because most folks are lucky if they own a couple silver leaves, my da said so."

"Aye," Pudgy halted his chewing, swallowed and added, "Think he's a robber? Or a thief?"

"I dunno. Could be. He sure ain't a noble; don't walk with a stick-in-his-ass."

"What're we gonna do?"

"Ask Jasper?" Ean shook his head as he spoke. "Éiran?"

"Yea, let's ask him."

Lliania's Lawspeaker would know about thieves, and nobles. Maybe he'd know whether the gaunt, brooding man was a robber.

"Where did the shepherd go? The Boar?" Ean asked as they headed to Éiran's house, located next to the Home of Law, Lliania's temple.

"Where else?" replied Pudgy. "He's gone there every time he's been here. And he always drinks the same."

"Warm milk," the boys said in unison, imitating their fathers' voices of disdain.

Ean liked milk, it made him feel calm, and warm milk was always the thing his mother gave him when he had trouble sleeping. "Maybe he has nightmares, you know," he said when this thought crossed his mind. "My ma gives me milk when I can't sleep 'cause I had a bad dream."

"What d'you dream of? The miller's daughter?"

Both of them shared the laughter of children who knew the place of others in their world, and the miller's daughter. "Aiden just looks strong, like a bull," Pudgy chuckled. "And his sister has the same looks, cowish my da always says."

Ean doubled over with laughter. "Cowish she is, aye!"

"Cows give milk," Pudgy reflected, his voice hinting at the mischievous humor hidden behind gentle brown eyes.

Ean glared at his friend. "You bastard! Now I can't drink another mug of milk without thinking of her! Cowish my ass."

Éiran wasn't at home, and soon the pair lost interest in chasing him from one peddler to the next where he was settling one dispute or another.

"He'll be near the well when the ceremony begins," Ean concluded.

The ceremony was custom, much like a prayer of thanks to Eanaigh after a thwarted illness. Every year the gods judged those who tread upon the world, and ruled whom the winter would treat harshest. Offerings were made, but it was more important to have a Lawspeaker of Lliania pass judgment on each individual. Generally, Éiran's rulings were mild, unlike other Lawspeakers', but about two winters ago Éiran had called upon old Mioroc, a man known for his cruelty. It was said Mioroc had beaten his wife until she was dead, and after Éiran had passed judgment, Mioroc had just laughed and gone back to his house, saying nothing could be proven. A few weeks later Mioroc's corpse was found frozen stiff in his barn. Ean had heard his father say it was Lliania's will, but old Jasper had chuckled and said it was the wife's family having their revenge, and justly so. Between Jasper and his da, Ean believed Jasper any day of the week.

"Think he'll pass judgment on that bastard Pol Haggrainh?" Pudgy asked as they trudged toward the market square, after filching a couple of sweet cakes from the baker.

Ean shook his head. "Father says that won't happen. He ain't the lord o' these lands, but a Lawspeaker won't rule over a noble nonetheless."

"But what he did to Brendan was wrong!"

"Aye, but what shall Éiran do? Pass judgment on the lord's nephew?"

"Sure, like he did with Mioroc," Pudgy grumbled. "He accused Brendan of the crime he himself committed, and had Brendan whipped bloody for it." Brendan was Pudgy's hero since they had been little, and Ean couldn't deny that he looked up to the big man himself. Brendan had a temper, yes, but he'd never treat a woman the way Pol Haggrainh claimed he had. It had been the woman's trembling finger that had accused Brendan, but only after looking fearfully at Haggrainh. Ean had seen the look between them, and Haggrainh had had the same glint in his eyes that Mioroc had always given them when he caught him and Pudgy stealing apples.

"No, he won't. Jasper said so, too." That settled the argument. Jasper was always right.

It was early afternoon when two men rode into town. Ean and Pudgy attended the ceremony on the market square and saw Lawspeaker Éiran and Eanaigh's Caretaker Bandh stop their sermons to look at the riders. Ean thought he saw a hint of resentment in Éiran's eyes. Prompted by the priest's reaction he took a closer look at the two men. They were clad in chain armor, half-helms protecting heads, swords belted at their sides, and shields on their backs. One of them cast a look of disdain upon the villagers, while the taller one scrutinized the people as if searching for someone. Both wore tabards with the royal colors, marking them King's warriors. "Warleaders," muttered Pudgy. "Only warleaders ride horses. And knights, knights also. Jasper said so."

"You forgot couriers," Ean added. "Could be couriers."

The taller of the two didn't wear any personal coat of arms on his shield or added to his surcoat, proof he was no knight. The second rider, however, had the banner of Carlgh's lord painted upon his shield and embroidered on his horse's blanket, marking him a relative of and therefore the voice of Lord Haggrainh.

Ean recognized the nobleman. "That's Pol Haggrainh," he whispered, poking his friend in the side. "Where's Brendan?"

"Probably in the Boar," his friend replied, still watching the pair of riders.

The warriors threaded their horses through the milling marketplace and headed for the tavern.

"We've gotta warn him," Pudgy said. "If he's there when Lord Pol is in a mood, he'll get flogged again."

Ean nodded, and the two rushed after the horsemen, and skipped into the Boar and Bustard through the backdoor. The cook, Suain, briefly looked up from chopping meat, recognized the two, and nodded before returning to his work. Pudgy rushed past Leese, the serving girl, into the taproom. Ean knew he was so familiar with the house he grew up in he could find the way blindfolded, like any other place in the tall building. The two boys arrived in the main room before the two riders entered. Pudgy inched his way toward Brendan who stood near the long bar, nursing a mug of ale. Ean followed.

"Brendan," Pudgy whispered. "Pol Haggrainh is here."

Normally the big man would have ignored his admirer, but at the mention of the name he stiffened, and glanced over his shoulder. Ean followed the man's glance and saw Leese, Brendan's sister, leaving the kitchen with a bowl of stew. He realized the big man was worried for her. "Get her out of here," Brendan said then tried to move into the shadows.

Pudgy didn't have to be asked twice, and hurried to Leese, took the bowl from her, and set it onto a nearby table. Ean took the girl's hand and pulled her back into the kitchen. He knew the house almost as well as any member of the family, and led the way up to the hideout Pudgy and he had discovered ages ago. Like nearly every building in Carlgh, the Boar was timber-frame, only a few buildings were of the brick and mortar variety. Higher stories were supported by beams of wood with a layer of boards making up the floor.

In the Boar's case the taproom's ceiling was an additional layer of planks; and with the beams as thick as trees, the space in-between was the ideal place to hide from annoyed parents. Also, it was the preferred nesting place for the mice that plagued Pudgy's ma and Suain to no end. Ean let go of Leese's hand, pulled away the loose part of wall, and crept into the hideout. He extended his hand and whispered, "Come on. Brendan said we should keep you away."

Further in he went until he reached a spot from which he could overlook almost the entire taproom. "Ean," Pudgy whispered. "I don't fit anymore."

He was about to tell his friend to shut up, when Pol Haggrainh strutted into the room, proud like a rooster. The other man looked about the room before following the noble. Haggrainh headed for an occupied table, gave one challenging look, and waved his hand in a shooing motion. The occupants didn't wait for a spoken order and left. The men sat down, removed their half-helms, and dropped them on the table.

A few patrons were still engrossed in a heated discussion, but now everyone looked up, even, Ean noticed, the shepherd who sat next to the fireplace, holding a mug in both his hands, his boots drying near the flames. He thought he saw a glint of recognition flash across the man's eyes. Then the shepherd shook his head and quickly averted his gaze, staring again into the hearth.

Everyone's attention was on the Lord and the warrior, but Ean's eyes were on the shepherd, whose demeanor seemed to have changed again. It was as if he was trying to avoid attention.

"Publican! Mead!" the tall warrior yelled, despite the attentive silence. He glared at the bar, brushing his hands over the blond stubble on his scalp. The shepherd smirked, shaking his head.

Ean heard the familiar cough Pudgy's father made whenever he was nervous. He glanced to his right and saw the innkeeper cast a frightened look at his new guests. He then hurried to comply, yelling for Leese.

"Please, you mustn't go!" Pudgy pleaded.

"Let go of me!" Leese snapped. "What do you two want to do with me up here anyway?"

"Brendan said to get you away," Pudgy whined.

"Leese!" Pudgy's father shouted again.

"Let me go!" Following the girl's feral growl was a resounding slap and a moment later the disheveled serving girl stood before her employer.

"Hurry up, wench, the noblemen want ale!"

"Mead, you oaf!" the warrior barked.

Some patrons chuckled.

"Dubhan, them lords want mead, not ale," several of his regulars shouted in unison.

"Leese!" the publican pleaded, harvesting more laughter.

This was the first time Ean had seen the big man so nervous. "Probably because of Brendan," he muttered, glancing at the man who stood in the shadows, hands in his pockets and trembling with... was that fear in his eyes?

The girl hurried out of the taproom.

Again, Ean heard Pudgy's plea, he couldn't make out any

words, only that his friend was truly distressed. Leese's reply sounded as fierce as before. A few moments later, she returned to the bar, carrying a bottle of honey wine. "Sorry, had to go to the cellar. I came back as fast as I could," she panted.

"Thanks, girl," Dubhan said, fumbling with two tankards that the young woman took from him.

Her employer's nervousness reflected on Leese as she walked to the newcomers' table. As she closed the distance, Pol Haggrainh looked up and inspected her much like the merchants who appraised horses. Ean couldn't hear what passed between noble and warrior, but he saw the warrior shake his head energetically. Whatever advice he'd been given, Lord Pol ignored it and leered at Leese. "What a lovely lass you have working for you, Dubhan!" he shouted. "How much?"

Ean saw how fear replaced Brendan's rage.

"She's not for sale, milord."

Haggrainh shook his head. "I was merely being polite." He took the mugs and bottle and placed them on the table. Before Leese had half turned away, he grabbed her by the wrist and pulled her into his lap. "A nice fit, I daresay."

"Please, Milord, no!" Now she sounded almost like Pudgy had done only a little while earlier.

"You want my uncle to think kindly of you and yours, eh?"

"Young Lord Haggrainh," the warrior said in a soothing but determined voice. "May I suggest you don't offend the villagers; we do need them."

The noble turned to look at the warrior while he worked his left hand into Leese's bodice. "General Kerral, you need my uncle's good will, the villeins will do as they're told!" The young woman began to cry. To her, Haggrainh said, "Stop your whining girl, you'll enjoy it."

Ean saw Kellen the butcher standing next to Brendan; hand on the young man's shoulder, talking intently. How Brendan felt, he could barely imagine, but he knew what he'd do if someone would touch his sister or ma. He also knew what would happen to anyone raising a hand against a noble. Brendan had already felt the whip. The man was trembling with rage, and fear.

"I told you to stop whining!"

General Kerral shook his head. Ean figured the warrior also knew that nobles couldn't be denied their desires.

"You give lecherous nobles a bad name," someone said into the ensuing silence. Ean tried to identify the speaker but the patrons were as shocked as he.

"Who said that?" Pol Haggrainh snarled. "I am nephew to the Lord Haggrainh; I'll do as I please!"

"You should be gelded and fed your testicles." The shepherd had turned his head and spoke over his shoulder!

The noble shoved Leese off his lap and stood. At the same moment Ean saw General Kerral's eyes grow wide. The warlord placed a hand on Lord Pol's arm, saying, "Careful now."

Haggrainh shook the warrior's hand off. "Don't ever presume to tell me what to do, upstart!"

The general raised both his hands in defense. "As you wish," he replied with a courteous bow, but Ean could hear both mocking and pity in the man's voice.

"Who are you, vermin?" Haggrainh snapped. "No villein speaks to his lord this way!"

The shepherd had turned his head and was staring into the flames once more. "I am no villein, and you are no lord," he said, pulling some straw away from the fireplace with his feet. Ean's eyes were fixed on the man; no one defied a noble this way. He didn't see what Lord Pol was doing, but the hiss of steel on leather told him enough.

He had never before seen a man drawing a sword, a dagger certainly, usually to gut a pig or cow, but never a blade that was as long as the back of a chair was high. "You'll pay for this insult, swine!"

As Lord Pol approached him, the shepherd stood and turned to face the noble. Ean couldn't see the man's eyes, but those who did took a step back, even Pol Haggrainh. The only man who barely moved was General Kerral who looked straight at the man. "Behave," the shepherd said, then dug into his pouch, and retrieved a coin. Haggrainh's sword clattered to the ground.

"Inhuman," one patron whispered, his voice shaking with fear.

"Impossible," said another.

"A Chosen," Brendan muttered, his shaky hands clutching his tunic while he knelt down, still shivering all over.

"Drangar? Drangar Ralgon?" General Kerral looked at the shepherd, his voice full of astonishment and wonder. "I didn't recognize you with the beard. What in Lesganagh's name are you doing here?"

The confusion was complete. Ean gawked at the scene unfolding below him. As the shepherd, Drangar, turned back to the nobleman, the tavern's guests avoided looking into his eyes as they came to rest on Kerral.

"Too much," he muttered as he pulled on his boots. Then the shepherd tossed Dubhan the coin. "Thanks." Without uttering another word, he quit the place, slamming the door behind him.

CHAPTER 4

Drangar left Carlgh, provisions on his back. As expected, word of his challenging the idiot noble had traveled fast, and now even the children looked at him through wondering eyes. No longer was he the quiet, unassuming shepherd. He growled, shook his head, and ran a hand through his long hair. Lesganagh's blessing was his curse. Now, as always, he was treated as a pack leader no one dared to challenge. What people didn't know frightened them; the same game in a different place. "They'll learn, same as I have," he said, shrugged, and headed north.

The shepherd had just forded Old Stream when he heard two horses whinny behind him. A quick glance over his shoulder confirmed his suspicion: Kerral and the fool Haggrainh.

"You dare insult me!" the noble shouted as the pair rode up next to him.

Drangar walked on. "Didn't you warn him?"

"Aye, I did."

"Then get lost."

"No villein will treat me this way!"

"I'm no villein," Drangar muttered.

"I order you to stop," Haggrainh shrieked.

"Lord Pol, I urge you to reconsider," Kerral said with a much calmer demeanor than Drangar remembered of the warleader.

"The day I consider what some upstart has to say, will be the day I die."

"Get lost, boy."

"I am no boy, and I command you to stop."

Kerral, who was riding to Drangar's left, abruptly brought

his horse to a stand. "I warned you."

The shepherd took a few more steps, which Haggrainh's horse matched, then halted and glanced at the idiot noble. "I want no trouble, boy, get lost now and I won't get any."

"You will address me by my title and name, peasant!"

For a moment he wondered what he could do that would not incur Lord Haggrainh's wrath on the folks at Carlgh. He had heard people talk about this idiot's uncle and knew he was a rather benign landowner. To spare the villagers he'd have to take a beating, but by Lliania's bloody Scales, if he were to take a beating it would be for something other than protecting the lass. "Who'll mourn you?"

"What? You threaten me!" Drangar heard a trace of fear tainting Lord Pol's voice.

"I don't threaten."

"How dare you!" the idiot shrieked, drawing his sword.

Years had passed since Drangar had last been in such a situation, but endless practice didn't go away no matter how much he wished it. As rider turned horse, a maneuver any trained charger would have performed with ease, he had ample time to drop his pack. When the noble finally was in a decent position to strike, a flash of anger surged through him. For a moment Drangar felt the Fiend roar. No matter the pain, the hurt, the revulsion, the monster within was only a breath away from breaking through. This time he barely held it back. Was he really blessed by the Lord of Sun and War? The ever-present Fiend shouted a different story. His hand balled, fist flashing forward, punching the horse's throat. The steed collapsed, wheezing for air, trapping Haggrainh. "I will defend myself!" Drangar growled the snarling furor into submission. He had sworn never to kill again, but this was different.

"Please, kind sir, don't hurt me," Lord Pol whimpered.

The Fiend pounded; he felt its anger. *Pitiful oaf,* it screamed. Two years of meditation, and still he could barely contain the red fury. "Like you didn't want to hurt the girl?" Drangar bellowed. This man was not true. He felt it. Injustice followed Pol Haggrainh, visible through the badly applied mask of nobility. How he hated such falseness.

"I swear I won't do it again!" By now the young man was weeping freely.

Drangar cursed his sense of justice, knew the villagers would never be safe from the bastard. Even though the Fiend roared in triumph, he made the decision without its furor. "Let her Scales judge you," he muttered, stepped over the struggling horse, and broke the man's neck. This was no murder; it was justice, plain and simple.

Then, without looking back at Kerral who gaped at the scene, Drangar shouldered his pack and continued his walk north. He had overstayed his welcome; it was only a matter of time before Pol Haggrainh would be missed.

From the next hill, he looked west. Lesganagh's glowing orb crowned the distant wooded hills; night would come soon. He'd never bothered to find out exactly how far it was from Carlgh to his hut. The fields ended a mile or two from the village, and beyond only grassy plain and tree-topped knolls awaited him. He had seen it all before, and aside from a few wood gatherers not many people traveled off the dirt road that stretched its way along the River Flannardh coming from the west.

His boots were wet, thanks to the fording of Old Stream. Best he got a few more miles behind him before he camped. As he trudged on, he heard a horse's steady hoof beat coming up from behind. Kerral.

"I want no company! Get lost!" he flung at the rider when the warleader—who the Scales had made him general?—had closed the distance.

"You killed him!"

"Better me than the villagers, eh?"

"He was the Lord's nephew," Kerral said.

"Probably was for the best," he replied.

"Mate, you killed a noble."

"Not the first. And I ain't your mate." He picked up the pace; fell back into a warrior's march. "Besides, he would've threatened others with that sword of his."

Kerral talked on, but Drangar ignored the prattling. He focused on his breathing, his steps, and soon the chill in his feet was gone. A few hills later he had to pass a small lake, soon the frost would make fishing impossible. He chuckled, when would he have the chance to fish here considering Haggrainh's men would definitely come looking for Pol's murderer within the next week. At least the villagers wouldn't be blamed for the killing.

He jumped across the small stream that fed the lake, and moments later heard water splashing. A quick turn of the head told him Kerral was still following. "Want to avenge the oaf's death?" he asked.

"No, he had it coming."

"Aye." He continued his march.

"I need to talk to you, my friend."

Drangar snorted. "We haven't been friends since your show of integrity."

"You wanted me to fall with you?" said Kerral.

"That's what friends do for each other."

"You did what you thought was right, and I did the same. We were both younger then. You never gave me a chance to explain."

"Treason can't be reasoned away."

"I've changed, look what I am now."

The shepherd cast a sideways look and shook his head. "Offal stays offal, no matter the coat it's dressed in, think of that idiot Haggrainh."

"I didn't follow you to be insulted, Drangar. I wanted to renew our friendship," Kerral snapped.

"You want a hug? Sure," he murmured and then ignored the warrior. After a few steps with Kerral still riding beside him, Drangar turned again. "You are deaf and stupid, obviously. Get lost!" he snarled and forced himself away from the warrior, continuing his way home.

In silence the two went on, Kerral, the man he had once called brother, whom he had, in fact, admired as a warleader, rode beside him. Drangar glared at him every once in a while, hoping he would leave, but the rider didn't.

Kerral had changed. Gone was the carelessness in his brown eyes, and although his pose was still arrogant, it was proof that the man had learned to carry the burden of commanding more than just a warband. Straight and alert he sat on his charger. Drangar noted the scar on the right cheek and remembered how the man had almost lost his eye in the bloody melee that had ensued when their shield wall had broken.

Whenever Kerral saw him looking, he tried to strike up a conversation, only to be ignored. Drangar kept going north, marching, and putting one foot before the other. Left, right, left, as if following the silent beat of a drummer. He walked the warrior's disciplined pace, burned into his body by a life as unforgiving as Lliania's Scales. Eyes straight, always on the horizon.

He didn't mind the silence, had lived with silence for two years. Only the march mattered, and the longer it went on, the less important Kerral's presence became. He was part of Drangar's past, yet another part he yearned to forget.

Still Kerral followed.

Something was driving the general; why else would he follow him through the night? It mattered little. Drangar shook his head, trying to dislodge the memories climbing to the forefront of his thoughts. The old Kerral, the young warleader, had been impatient. This new Kerral was not, and would not turn his horse south.

They walked through the cold night, their breath creating clouds before mingling with the frosty mist that rose from the plain. The silence only disturbed by the sound of feet and hooves crunching on frozen grass.

Why had he come? Was he going to turn him in? The questions ran through Drangar's mind repeatedly. He had tried so hard to get away from his past, now he had killed, again, and here was Kerral, his former brother-in-arms, his one-time friend, his captain, bringing back what he'd rather forget. They hadn't seen each other since his disgraced departure many years ago. That they had recognized each other in the Boar at all showed him that those years were not enough.

Would any amount of time be enough?

As the sun rose, they neared his small hut, the huddled shape angular against the hill. Had this ever been his home, he wondered. Sure, he knew the place, could have found his way here blindfolded, but did this return feel like a homecoming? No.

In the morning's stillness Kerral's gasp sounded louder than it probably was. Why had he followed him here? Certainly not to gloat. His curiosity overcoming resentment, Drangar turned. "What do you want? You've been pacing me all night, without a reason. Were you looking for me?"

"No."

The shepherd shrugged, surrendering to the other's persistence. Maybe the company would do some good, though he doubted it. "Guess I can be polite and ask you in." He pointed to the corral behind the hut. "Put your mare there."

While Kerral took care of his horse, Drangar slipped his provisions from his back. When the general returned from the corral, they entered.

Drangar glanced at Kerral. What did he want? The general looked about the cluttered dwelling, in all likelihood curious of the simple life he led. It mattered little what the other thought, and he began to unpack, ignoring his former friend.

That Kerral had followed him all the way from Carlgh showed that the mercenary-warleader had become even more determined than Drangar remembered. He was like a bloodhound. The thought reminded him of something, something he had almost forgotten in the solitude.

He looked up from his opened pack, leaving the provisions alone for a moment. "Did anyone follow you to the village? Aside from that fool, I mean." There already were enough people chasing him, and Haggrainh would add his own to the lot. Maybe it was time to move on. The sheep would take care of themselves, and some lucky bastard might find them before the wolves did.

Surprised, Kerral chuckled. "Apart from two hundred men, who still camp south of the town? No."

"Two hundred men?"

"Not all men," said Kerral, grinning. "Women, too."

"What for?"

"War. Rumor has it Chanastardh is expanding."

Drangar winced. "I wondered about the lack of merchants at the market."

"Carlgh is the first town on this side of the frontier. It's right in the Chanastardhians' path."

"When?"

Shrugging his shoulders, Kerral said, "No idea. I came here to draft warriors. Most of the army is supposedly gathered around Harail, and they aren't ready. I've heard the call to arms has gone out, but I think it's too late."

"Who's in charge of this nonsense?"

"The Lord High Marshall."

"He sent you north?"

"No, I got my orders a while ago."

Drangar walked to the fireplace, fumbling in his pocket for a flint. Kneeling, he struck it against one of the stones lining the wood, igniting a fire. "Don't ask me to fight," he said. "I'm done fighting other people's wars." He got up and retrieved some provisions from a chest standing in the corner. Then he cut dried meat, cheese, and several slices of bread.

"But this is your home too, isn't it?" Kerral sat down on one of the stools near the table.

Drangar shook his head. "I'm from Kalduuhn, and the Chanastardhians won't fuck with them." He frowned and removed two wooden tankards from the chest, filling them with milk. He handed Kerral one, and sat on the opposite stool.

Kerral looked at him, into his mug and grimaced. "Milk? Still no alcohol in your life?"

"No." He shoved food into his mouth, pointedly ignoring Kerral.

The general took a swig. Then, after a few moments of trying in vain to get Drangar's attention, he broke his fast as well.

They ate in silence. Drangar stared at the wall beyond Kerral, chewing his food and washing it down with milk. Why the Scales did war follow him wherever he went? Had all the years not been enough? He felt a wave of hidden memories threaten to swallow him again. He cursed his sense of fairness and thanked Lliania, the Lawmaker, for this questionable blessing. Where had she been when he had needed her?

Drangar stared at his former friend, watched him munching his bread. Confusion was plain on the other's face. Had he truly changed that much? The thought crossed his mind briefly; he grimaced and shook his head. Of course he had. Who wouldn't have?

Once, people had called him Scythe, the wall breaker. Now he was just a shepherd, but even that life seemed at an end. Like every life before, this one came to an end with blood on his hands. Even now Haggrainh's face was obliterated by the faces of all the others he had killed.

He didn't want to remember! These memories were better left untouched, but what choice had he, having Kerral opposite him? Was he really blessed by the God of Sun and War?

He remembered his father saying the god Lesganagh had blessed him upon his birth. Lesganagh, God of Sun and War. Lesganagh, the Forbidden God, whose cult had been outlawed for decades, due to the scheming of its priests. The god still had influence over the world, though, for the sun still shone and wars were still fought. Given how death haunted every step of his life, Drangar doubted Lesganagh was responsible for the blessing. Too much death. Far too much death.

Yet another thing he tried to forget.

Kerral broke the silence. "What happened to you, friend?"

Drangar glared at him. "We haven't been friends in a long time."

He shrugged. "Still, what happened?"

Drangar gulped down the last bits of cheese and stood. "Life happened." He knew that if he opened up to Kerral now all the effort of the past years would be even more wasted than they already had been. "Leave, please! You have overstayed your welcome."

"But…"

"I invited you into my house, gave you food, knowing no good would come from it. Damnation, my old self would have killed you the instant you followed me! Consider yourself lucky, but don't count on guest right any more. I've done my duty. Get out; go back to your war. I want no part of it!"

Kerral winced. Turning toward the door, he said, "It was good seeing you again." Leaving the house, he mounted his mare. "I won't tell them where to find the body." Nodding to Drangar, he turned the horse and rode southward, back toward Carlgh.

He stepped out and watched him. "Thank you."

CHAPTER 5

Twenty-ninth of Leaves, 1475 K.C.

He liked this vista: the grassy plain, the few wooded hills. Sure, it was different from the Eye of Traksor in Kalduuhn with the far reaches of Gathran surrounding the stronghold, but it was peaceful. Drangar looked south until the receding Kerral was an indiscernible dot against the horizon.

"I don't want to fight," he muttered, his right hand resting on the doorframe. But what did he want? This question hadn't occurred to him before. Until now he had been content with his attempts to forget the past, the pain, and the loss. Certainly, the time up here in the border region of Danastaer had helped, but now that he considered it, he wasn't sure it had truly done much good.

The screams, the blood, the faces, they were still clear in his mind. "The bastard Pol Haggrainh would've let the villagers feel his anger, better me being hunted than them being tortured." Unlike his nephew, Lord Haggrainh was lenient, but the death of a noble, especially a relative, wasn't something that one could just overlook.

Now he had to decide where to go. Drangar ran both his hands through his hair; it clung to his scalp, plastered there by dust and sweat. "Haven't taken a bath in a while," he mumbled, berating himself. There had been times in the past two years when he had washed in the pool on the western side of his hill daily. Now he couldn't even remember the last time. Dirt was a breeding ground for all sorts of vermin, and in the past he'd seen his share of the little buggers on people who did not see to their hygiene.

"I've seen animals take better care of their pelts than some folks," he scoffed. Something itched on his chin. He scratched, and for the first time realized he had let the stubble grow into a beard. Dunthiochagh, he'd had a beard then.

Unbidden, the memories surged up and he beat them back down, focusing on better things; there were so few that weren't linked to something he longed to forget, even his training with Anya, the Eye's master-at-arms, was tainted by the sneers and grimaces of the other children. Anya had been one of the few who could match his strength for a while, until he had turned ten. "Why is every good memory chased away by a bad one?" he wondered aloud.

A whinny, a bark, and the bleating of sheep came from the north. How did the animals know when to return? He scarcely had to look for his herd; Dog and Hiljarr watched over the little buggers better than he'd have ever been able to. It still fascinated Drangar how the charger had picked up the skills of a shepherd's dog in a few months. "Maybe Dog's shown him," he said, repeating the conclusion he'd come to almost two years ago. How canine and horse communicated at all was a mystery he dared not consider.

The bleating came closer and Drangar walked around the hut to check if Kerral had left the gate open. He had, and now the shepherd observed Dog and Hiljarr chasing the sheep into the enclosed area. When the last animal was inside, he hurried over to close the opening. "I'm good for something, at least," he told both charger and the canine. Hiljarr whinnied and Dog barked, as they always did, and he was not sure if the pair merely reacted to his voice, or if they understood his words. "How've you two been?"

Hiljarr cantered toward him, halted, and pushed his snout against his face. He scratched the stallion behind the ears and received a satisfied snort. The horse had been a grateful noble's gift, after Drangar had rescued his foolish daughter from a competing House. They had been companions ever since. Now, after almost five years, Hiljarr had become as a brother to him. The stallion was loyal and well trained. He had carried Drangar to many battles, had even fought in a few of them when there was no time to form a wall, and had defended his rider against enemies when he was prone on the ground. After that fateful day two years ago, Hiljarr had traveled with him all the way to the Chanastardhian border, and since then he had enjoyed being a sheep-horse.

Dog, on the other hand, remained where she sat and looked at him. Was she arching her right brow? He shook his head and said, "Things are changing, you two. We need to go." Where to? If war was coming to Danastaer, the entire area would be crawling with warbands of one country or another. And some other warleader might not be as decent as Kerral and draft him into an army.

"East there's Dhomac, another puppet to Herascor," he said. "West to Madain?" He thought a moment and then shook his head. "No, they're with Chanastardh as well, and I really doubt Drammoch'll leave me be." Hiljarr snorted. He scratched the charger's nostrils. "You damn well know there's still a price on my head." He barked a grim laugh. "Just how much past can I run away from?" Sunlight broke through the gathering clouds and illuminated the ground. Drangar knew how painful it was to look straight into Lesganagh's glowing orb, so he averted his gaze. "If you really blessed me, Lord of Sun and War, couldn't you have given me a clear path to follow?"

As expected, there was no reply. None of the gods ever did, no matter how much he begged, pleaded, and prayed.

Drangar turned south and west and looked toward the cloud-enshrouded Shadowpeak Mountains. *You had a path once.* What was this? He'd heard the voice, but he saw no speaker. Hiljarr snorted and he let go of the stallion. "Go eat, mate."

As the horse cantered away, the shepherd headed back into his hut and began to rummage in his chest. "Where is the bloody thing?" he muttered. "I know I put it in here."

Instead of the knife, the first thing he retrieved was a wooden box wrapped in oilcloth. Carefully, he peeled away the layer of fabric and cast a wistful glance at the small container. It was a memento of Dunthiochagh, but then, so was his reflection whenever he looked into a mirror or a pond of water. Why had he taken this thing with him? He scoffed. "Because you're a fool, Drangar Ralgon," he said. "You've always been a fool."

A flick of his wrist and the box bounced off the wall. It laid there, lid open, and the emptiness inside glaring back at him. Where were the rings? For a moment he was shocked at the thought, also trying to suppress the memory that threatened to surge up. Drangar balled his hands into fists, forcing the images back, away from his conscience. There! The golden loop was still on his finger. "I forgot it was there," he said. "I actually forgot something!" The ring's counterpart would still be in Dunthiochagh.

There was a shuffle behind him, and he turned to see Dog sitting in the doorway. "Why can't I just get rid of this stuff?" he asked. "Why can't I only remember the good parts? Why is everything tainted by bad memories?"

The canine looked at him, sympathy edged into her face. She padded forward and placed one paw on his shoulder.

"I could toss away this band, you know," he went on. "But that won't change a bleeding thing! Her face, her laughter, all would still be here with me!" Drangar swallowed back tears. "Gods, why can't I forget?"

You can't. No one could.

Drangar swallowed. "Who's there?" he tried to shout, but his voice broke with the sorrow that threatened to overwhelm him. The gurgle that sounded through the hut made him laugh, despite his pain. He grabbed a rag and blew his nose. "I sound like a stupid boy." Still, the question of whose voice he had heard remained.

"Stop your weeping," he growled. "Find the bloody knife and shave!" The sound of his voice, so like Anya's, like a drill-warden's, brought some semblance of calm, and he focused on finding the blade.

It wasn't in the chest, although Drangar remembered putting it there. "Where's the damn thing?" Before he reached the bottom of the container, he stopped. Some things he was not ready to look upon again. The only place left for the knife was the cluttered hut itself. The makeshift table he dismissed, after all he'd just sat there with Kerral. Lifting dirty plates, rags and blankets, the shepherd talked. "Stupid chest, I know I put it there!" "Gods, this place is a mess." "Damned knife, where are you!" "When she gets back I get an earful." He stopped, realized what he'd just said, dropped the mugs he was holding, and stared at his hands as they began to tremble. Without him noticing, his mind had drifted back, again. "Bleeding Scales! Why? Why can't I forget?"

He half expected to be berated again, but this time the voice remained silent. Drangar bent down and picked up the mugs. That was when he saw the knife's wooden handle underneath a pile of dirty clothes. "There you are." Testing the edge, he realized it needed sharpening. As he placed the knife on the table, he looked around for the whetstone.

At least the stone was where he remembered it to be.

He retrieved the item from the makeshift shelf, and as he stepped back, he caught sight of the small box again. The belt-knife had been a gift of hers. It was as tightly bound to the past as the ring on his hand and the box. Feeling tears well up again, he scrunched up his face and shook his head. "No more!"

The blade was in his left hand before he had fully taken seat on the stool. His hand moved the stone steadily back and forth. He was used to this motion, had sharpened weapons often enough in his life. Always at the eve of battle. Was battle all he knew, he wondered. Sure, he knew history, legends, but he had never finished his schooling. Only a jumble of fragments remained of what the Sons had taught him. Yet, despite the sting those memories brought forth, the steady motion of his hand, the sound of stone on steel calmed him. "Strange thing, this," he muttered. "Why does this relax me more than the silly prayers and meditations?" He continued his task.

He had no idea how long he had sat there sharpening the knife when he finally checked the blade. Satisfied, Drangar got out of the hut and headed for the spring. Upon his arrival at the bottom of the hill, he knelt on the cold rock surrounding the little pond and bent to wet his beard.

Upon seeing his bearded face again, his inner peace evaporated as the ghosts of his past surged up again. For a moment he was tempted to retrieve the whetstone and start on the blade once again. "What's the point?"

The past is the past, live with it.

"Who's there?" Drangar's head snapped up and he looked for the unseen speaker. The only other being close to him was Dog, and for a moment she looked sad.

"I am trying," he said.

No, you're running, like you've always done, the voice scolded.

Was he hearing things again? It wouldn't have been the first time; he'd heard things before, not only in Dunthiochagh. They had taunted him, mocked him. What was the name of the village? Gods, he remembered the villager's faces, every single one, men, women, children, the old, the infirm, all were as visible to him as the bearded mask of loathing that looked back at him from the pond.

"Damn you!" he snarled and punched his reflection. "I need to wash."

There was still some soap left, he knew, inside the chest. He had caught sight of it when looking for the knife. The jog to his hut and back again dried the tears, and as he returned, Drangar saw Dog was still sitting where he had left her.

Take a bath, the voice commanded.

At least it didn't tell him to kill anyone, he thought, smirking; then he undressed. He piled his boots and clothes against an outcrop and jumped into the pond.

The chill stole his breath. "I thank thee, Broggagh, Weatherlord. Thank thee for this well. Thy rain feeds it. I thank thee, Eanaigh, thy soil nourishes it," he wheezed out the old prayer while splashing about.

Soon he was lathered in soap, rubbing and scrubbing. He dropped to his knees, submerged his body. Then the soap was back in his hand and he washed his beard anew. When he was satisfied, Drangar stepped out of the pool and grabbed the belt-knife once again. Even though the blade was a memento, the water's cold prevented any memory of Dunthiochagh to rise to the forefront of his mind. He waited until the ripples of his passing had faded and he could see himself in the water again, then set knife to whiskers and began to shave. One stroke and part of his left cheek was free. Drangar glanced at his reflection in the water. He looked abominable, he thought, bringing the knife up to his cheek again. He had looked like that two years ago, a ragged shell, empty and hollow.

His thoughts drifted back to the little box, and he wondered why he had taken it with him. "I can't forget you," he whispered.

Swallowing back the tears, Drangar let the knife slide down his chin. There the motion stopped. The blade lingered on his throat. One thrust, just one thrust.

It would be a slow death, but what was the agony of bleeding to death compared to his misery? "No death is as slow as life," Drangar muttered.

One thrust.

He had seen people die from such wounds. A gurgling struggle for breath as the lifeblood flooded out the throat. First it was frantic, but with the loss of blood the gurgling, wheezing, and moaning became slower and slower. Hands that had once been able to lift a sword or a loved one were now weaker than any grandfather's. And as the gasping for air subsided the body convulsed.

One single thrust.

It was as if he heard a teacher preach to him: *"Taking one's own life condemns you. When you approach the Bailey Majestic, the doors will be barred. You will drift alone, suffering for your folly for all eternity."*

More suffering? Could there be more than the guilt and pain that already weighed him down so much that he could hardly breathe? The Gods were real, just as real as his nightmares. He didn't want to be shut out from the afterlife. He didn't want to suffer eternally, a lost soul haunting whatever oblivion awaited those who killed themselves.

The doom that awaited those who took their own lives made him shiver. "I can endure this pain, I have to. No eternity of nothing for me," he muttered as tears ran down his newly bare cheeks.

Carelessly, he let go of the knife, trembling. How often had he tried to take his life? To just be done with it all? He was afraid, he realized. A few years ago, he would have scoffed at the idea, but here, out in the nothingness between two countries, he could only look at the truth. He was frightened of himself. As the thought crossed his mind, the image of the village, he'd forgotten the name, rose up again. Senseless deaths born of his furor, but he could still remember the slaughter, could remember it had been his hand that had held the blade and killed the villagers. What was the name of that place? Like the names of his so-called friends, people long gone, he couldn't remember what the village was called. Oh, he could recall his anger, and how he struck down old and young, but not the name!

You can't wash away the past.

There! The voice! Drangar turned and glared at his surroundings. Aside from the hill, pond, and the wide, grassy plain, and Dog, no one was there. Was it beginning again? He'd heard voices in Dunthiochagh; at least he thought he had. His nightmares were full of them, and if it wasn't the one with the village it was the one where he killed...

No, he didn't want to remember!

You have to see what really happened, the voice urged.

"I know what happened," he said hoarsely. "I killed." Drangar slumped onto the floor and looked at Dog. "I killed so many, and for what? Look at me, will you? Scythe," he growled, "they called me. Wall breaker. I want to forget."

The canine remained still and gazed at him.

"I'm afraid of myself, afraid of the world, afraid of what the world will do when they know. On the field it's easy, you know. There's the enemy, that's whom you have to kill, but how many left behind people who loved them? How many widowers and widows did I leave behind? How many lost their brothers, sisters, fathers, mothers? I never stopped to consider them." He paused and grasped knife and whetstone. He began to sharpen the blade again, and again it calmed him. "What if this is all I have?" he muttered. "What if I stand on Lliania's Scales and my life is weighed and all I have to show is that I was good at killing people? Enriching the world with those who were left behind?"

The past is what it is.

"Yes, I know I can't change what was, but I'm afraid to look ahead when all I see is what was, how I was. How can I look onto the path when all I see is her, when all I want is to turn back and prevent what happened? I can't even stand the sight of my own face. I want to focus on the good, but all of it is smudged by the bad. The Eye, the village, Dunthiochagh. Like all the gold at the rainbow's end has been replaced by offal!"

Retrace your steps.

"I can't go back!"

You don't want to go back.

Who was talking to him? Had he gone mad and was now talking to his conscience? Astonished, Drangar looked at Dog. He had a conscience. "When did this happen? The Scythe feels remorse," he gave a sad laugh. "What do you think, Dog? Should I go back?"

A bark was her reply.

"Aye, I should have never left."

You can't run away from pain.

"But I tried," he stated.

How could you do otherwise? You never learned to feel.

"It's a small wonder I ever loved."

Dog barked again.

"Thanks for confirming it."

Drangar stood, gathered clothes and boots, and headed for the hut. "Dunthiochagh it is, then," he said and Dog yapped her agreement from beside him.

For a moment, as he entered the hovel he'd lived in for the past two years, Drangar stood, unsure of what to do. The decision to head south and west had come somewhat easily, but now he faced the dilemma of what to take with him. Most of his belongings, no matter how meager they were to begin with, he dismissed right away, others he wasn't sure about. He got dressed and looked about the cluttered room. The knife, he needed to shave. Some clothes, although he doubted he'd need them once he reached the city beyond the Shadowpeaks. Food; there were inns along the way to the wizard-wrought canyon, certainly, but it was best to be prepared.

As he pondered his departure, so unlike the one from his

home in Dunthiochagh, the despair and frustration, even the pain receded. Good, he didn't want to relive it all. He'd always kept busy before, whenever the hurt became too much.

You're running again, the voice scolded.

"What do you want me to do?" Drangar asked aloud. "If I go and face a Lawspeaker, I'll do so upright, on my own terms." He realized he really wanted to be judged. "I can't carry on like this, no more running, I'm tired of it." No, not only tired, fleeing from the past would not turn it aside. He didn't know what he wanted. "I never actually paused to consider what I want," he told Dog.

With renewed vigor he stuffed a few spare clothes into his pack, added some dried meat and cheese, and then began to search for the bridle. It had been a long time since he'd ridden Hiljarr.

When all the necessities were stacked against the hut's outer wall next to the door, Drangar went back inside and stood there, staring at the chest. War was coming, and only the gods knew what kind of people were traveling the countryside. A sword might give pause to the lone highwayman or group of bandits. Part of him began to simmer with renewed self-loathing, as he retrieved the weapon from the bottom of the trunk. It was only sensible, he told himself. When he held the scabbard in his hands, his thoughts returned to Dunthiochagh. "No! I don't want to remember," he growled.

You must.

"I can't," he pleaded with the unseen speaker.

Dog barked.

"No, I take this with me for protection," he insisted. "Nothing more." Drangar tried to pull the blade out of its sheath. "No," he groaned. "Gods piss on me!" He hadn't cleaned the steel! Maybe it was for the best, he thought then tugged again. Offering some resistance, the weapon slid free. "This is just a tool," he snarled, found the mercenary within, and began to scrub and oil the blade, his mind focused on the task, not the circumstances. Why he'd taken the sword with him in the first place, he could not remember.

It was ironic how some actions stood out, no matter how

hard one tried to rid his mind of them, whereas others possibly as important just vanished. He poured oil into the scabbard and slid the weapon back into place; it would be pointless to carry a sword and not be able to draw, much less wield it.

When Drangar left the hut for the last time, he walked to the corral and opened the gate. Hiljarr's head perked up, and the stallion moved to intercept the sheep. He stopped the charger with a quick whistle. "Leave them be, mate," he said. The horse looked at him, then at the sheep, and finally back at him, obviously confused. Drangar shrugged and went to fetch his gear; another quick whistle and Hiljarr cantered up beside him. For a moment the steed seemed to hesitate when Drangar tried to put the bridle on, then relented.

"Yea, we're leaving, time to..." Drangar paused. What was it time for, he wondered. Look the truth in the eye? He couldn't even stand his own reflection, much less turn to face the past. "We're leaving."

Hiljarr saddled, and blankets bundled at the rear lip of the saddle, the shepherd slipped the scabbard into the leather hoop, and checked his purse one last time. It was enough to get him to Dunthiochagh. "No need to plan for more," he muttered and swung onto the horse's back. He clicked his tongue twice, turned the stallion, and whistled for Dog. The canine barked once. Then the three headed south and west toward the cloud-dimmed sun. "Let's get some miles behind us," Drangar said, "before the rain comes."

CHAPTER 6

It was early evening when five hooded figures entered the Laughing Horse Inn. It was the better of the two inns in Carlgh; hence it was more expensive. Only some merchants could afford to stay here.

All five wore long, black cloaks and boots, and aside from the belted swords that poked out from under their cloaks they were indistinguishable. Morna, the proprietress of the Laughing Horse, looked up from her knitting and stood, ready to greet the newcomers.

One of the five approached the table that served the innkeeper as counter and desk. Morna suppressed a smirk as she regarded the dark clad people. They could not be as remarkable as the shepherd, Drangar Ralgon. Every step the person took was accompanied by a jingle, telling Morna he wore some sort of mail armor as well.

The stranger removed his hood, and smiled as he regarded her. It was a smile she was very familiar with; only a day before Pol Haggrainh had reminded the people of Carlgh of their status. It spoke of power and wealth, and arrogance. The stranger was about five feet six inches, had jet-black hair, and was well groomed. In spite of his thin smile, his eyes showed no emotion.

Nobles, Morna thought derisively, always considered themselves more important than they really were. "What can I do for you, good sirs?" she asked aloud, hiding her annoyance behind a well-practiced veil of reverence appropriate to one of her station.

Without changing expressions, the man replied, "We need

rooms for the next few days, and stabling for our horses. Can you give us both? At a reasonable price, of course."

Morna smiled. "Certainly. Stabling for... five horses?" The man nodded. "And rooms?"

"Yes."

She looked at her customer and did a quick, and in her mind very generous, calculation and said, "Well, that would make two leaves. Does this suit you?"

"Yes."

Startled by the stranger's ready acceptance, she added, "Supper and breakfast?"

"Yes."

The other four hadn't moved since entering, but Morna guessed that they were watching the room and the street. She frowned. "For how long?"

"Until we leave."

The answer was almost as haughty as the man's behavior, Morna thought, resisting the urge to shake her head. She wiped a strand of graying hair out of her face and said, "Well that would make three leaves for a night and two meals. It's best if you pay at the beginning of each new day."

"Agreed." He poured out some coins from his moneybag and, sorting through them, asked, "Where are the rooms?"

"Upstairs. Pick any you want, except for the last one on the left. Supper is after sunset. Stables are in the back."

"Thank you," the man said, handing her the coins. He turned around and nodded to his men.

Following the silent order, the four strode out. Two returned shortly afterward, carrying several large bundles.

The leader walked to the stairs and climbed them at a brisk pace. The two followed.

Morna heard doors opening, and closing. A little while later, the last two hooded men came back from the stables. There was straw marring their black clothes and their boots were dirtier than before. "I will have the boy sweep the stables," she said, nodding at the two, only to be ignored as the men followed their companions upstairs.

Nobles, Morna thought with scorn, and headed for the

kitchen to tell her husband to prepare more food.

Later that night, the association of local businessmen gathered in the Boar and Bustard to pass some time. Morna was one of the last to arrive. She was greeted by her friends and quickly joined one of the larger groups, drinking ale and joking in the way folk around the world behave in well-liked company. After those five strangers had appeared at her inn, she badly needed the relaxation a good drink offered.

"How was business, Morna?" Kellen, the butcher, grinned.

Adjusting her leather apron, Morna replied, "Got some more guests. Rich customers."

"Guess you can pay your bill soon." The butcher laughed, and was joined by several others.

"Aye," she replied.

"Know why they're here? And what the warrior's doin' here?" another asked.

The innkeeper shrugged. "No. You know I don't question my customers, Will."

Grinning sheepishly, Will said, "One still can ask, eh?"

"Sure. Jus' don't expect an answer."

The next day Pol Haggrainh's body was discovered. Amidst the trouble caused by Lord Haggrainh's steward conducting an investigation, General Kerral began to levy troops like he had already done in a few other villages. All of the young men and a few womenfolk soon were in arms, training to fight in a shield wall with the King's warriors and the other draftees. The army moved into town from their camp outside Carlgh, and soon armed folk crowded the inns and the tavern. The citizens were forced to clear an old barn and set up a makeshift tavern. More ale was brewed, but it didn't suffice, leading the townsfolk to buy some from neighboring villages that had hardly suffered, since General Kerral had merely added people to the ranks and moved on. Carlgh, he explained, was the first line of defense.

The five men, on the other hand, inquired about a stranger, a tall man who must have come through Carlgh in the last two years. They said he was wanted for crimes in several countries.

It was urgent that this fugitive be captured.

It wasn't long before someone guessed they might be looking for the shepherd. As soon as this speculation aired, the five strangers left the village, despite the threatening thunderclouds.

The sun went down over the desolate plain north of Carlgh, when five black-clad riders closed on the lonely shepherd's hut. Wind had come up during the afternoon, and its steady rush blew leaves across the hills, masking the horses' steady hoof beats.

The sky had darkened at a frightening rate; clouds covered it from horizon to horizon, threatening a downpour of immense proportions. When the rain started, the grassland around the hills would quickly turn into marshland, but the riders were unconcerned with the threatening weather.

They closed the distance between themselves and the hut to about fifty feet. The leader gave a sign, and the riders fanned out, covering as much ground as possible, positioning themselves around the hut so their prey could not escape.

Twenty feet from the building the horses came to a halt, their riders dismounted and approached the hut. Lightning flashed across the dark sky, illuminating the scene.

The leader stared at the building, which for the blink of an eye was discernible. His hand flashed up.

Carefully the leader edged forward.

Reaching the door, the man charged. He kicked the door. Behind him, his four companions froze, hands on their weapons.

Nothing happened.

Another flash of lighting lit the area.

"Damnation! Curse his bloody carcass!" roared the leader above the deafening thunderclap that followed. "He's gone!"

CHAPTER 7

Eighth of Chill, 1475 K.C.

Passion was an apt name for the place, and Jesgar Garinad was enjoying every moment of it. Sure, some folks knew him as the little brother to one of the best smiths in Dunthiochagh, but only one person, other than himself of course, knew who he really was. Right now, that person was teasing his neck with little bites. They were alone in the steam bath, lounging on one of the wooden couches, usually meant for only one.

"And then, dear?" Evlin breathed into his ear. "What happened?"

A content sigh escaped his lips, and he turned and looked the pretty blond lass in those gorgeous green eyes. Indeed, he was a happy man. "Oh, I ate some of the leftover roast, had a nip of wine, and was off again."

"To see me?" The wicked gleam in her eyes left little doubt of what she had in mind.

Jesgar didn't mind the thought either. "Of course, dove," he said as he leaned forward and kissed her.

Their kiss didn't last long.

The door to the steam room was shoved open, Evlin pulled back, and he turned to the intruder. "Private party, get out."

The man in the doorway, Jesgar noticed against the backdrop of the corridor lights, was dressed, hardly the right attire for the hot vapor. "We need to talk, Hand."

"No idea what you're talking about," he replied. How could anyone except Evlin and him know? A quick glance at the girl showed that she was as confused as he. No, she hadn't told anyone, he decided.

"Listen, boy, I have not time for your games," the man said. Now that Jesgar's eyes had adjusted to the murk caused by the steam, he saw the intruder wore some kind of armor, possibly even a surcoat, a hooded cloak, and most definitely a sword. "If you want to, we can go see Upholder Coimharrin right now to verify if you're telling the truth."

"Close the door, if you please." This answer was no ready admission of guilt, but what was he to do? The stranger did as requested. "How did you know?"

A few steps brought the man forward and he settled on the other couch. "Overheard you a while ago." He nodded toward Evlin. "She didn't sell your secret to me, but I have to warn you, boy, some walls are thinner than you think. Be wary of pillow talk." He gestured toward his groin and smirked. "Shall I fetch some ice water?"

Jesgar felt himself blush; Evlin giggled as she stood up and wrapped a towel around her. He covered himself with the cloth they had been sharing. "No need."

"Very well. Lass, be so kind and leave us." So far, the stranger had not revealed his face.

"As you wish," Evlin replied and hurried out, closing the door behind her.

"Now to business," the man said. "From what I've gathered, you're neither a thief nor a killer, correct?"

"Yes, sir." Jesgar didn't know why he gave the unexpected visitor an honorific; it just felt right.

"You're Bennath Garinad's little brother, aren't you?"

"Yes, sir." What was wrong with him? He didn't have that much respect for most priests; then again, it was sort of difficult to remain aloof when the person you were talking to was dressed—and armed—and you weren't.

"And why do you break into houses?"

"Because I can." There, that was more like the defiant man he was.

"And you think it right for anyone who can do something to do it?"

He shrugged one shoulder. "As long as no one gets hurt."

His opposite was about to voice another question, when Jesgar blurted out, "Right, you know my name. Obviously, you are not here to put me in chains. This is about as secret as you can get. Evlin won't talk. Before this little interrogation continues, tell me: who are you?" The stranger removed his hood, and Jesgar sat up. "I'll be damned!"

"Pleasure to meet you, Jesgar Garinad," Kildanor, Chosen of Lesganagh, friend and advisor to Baron Duasonh, said.

He couldn't believe it, a Chosen. Rumor had it that the God of Sun and War had blessed them at the time of the Wizard War, or Heir War as folk called it. They were the king's elite guard in Harail. And one of them was sitting here! For a moment, he was unsure what to do: worry, be elated, or worry some more. The little he knew about the Chosen made up his mind for worry, it was never good to meet an experienced… was killer the right term? After all, Lesganagh's faith had been prohibited years before he was born, and from what Ben had told him, the Lesganaghists had been a violent bunch at the best of times.

"What do you want?" Jesgar blurted out.

The warrior nodded. "Right to the point, I like that." He took a deep breath and continued, "You like the Baron?"

"Aye," the Hand answered.

"Why?"

Jesgar raised fingers for the points he wanted to make. "He's no toad, for starters." Where was this Kildanor going with these questions anyway? "He doesn't have any kind of stick in his ass, unlike a whole bunch of other folks. Unlike what I've heard from other places, he actually is a lord, and no bastard. And if the people have complaints he listens." As an afterthought he added, "Unlike that cousin of his, that Jathain fellow."

He must have said something right, because for an instant Lord Kildanor's eyes flashed in approval. "Splendid." The Chosen poured himself some of the wine Jesgar had arranged for Evlin and himself to drink. It was just as she liked it, sweet as an overripe berry. Kildanor spat out the first pull almost as soon as it passed his lips. "Gods, what's this?" He shook his head and finally continued. "Never mind. So, how long has your family lived in Dunthiochagh?"

Jesgar thought for a moment then said, "One of my great-granddas fought for the old Baron in the Heir War. Got his wife pregnant and died."

Kildanor's look grew distant for a moment then he shook his head. "So, your folks have been here a long time?"

"Yea."

"If I were to tell you the city is threatened from within, what would you do?"

Before the Chosen had finished his question, Jesgar blurted out the answer, "Try to nail the bastard, of course."

The warrior nodded, apparently satisfied with the reply. This was where the entire affair was leading, the young man realized. Kildanor was asking him to help.

"Would you also go to jail for it?"

Jesgar was still pondering Lord Kildanor's plan when he left the Passion. Thanks to his ample allowance he could afford to frequent the establishment at least once a week and still have enough left to spend carousing. Sure, he had to help his brother in the smithy every once in a while, but most of his time he had to himself.

Now that he'd agreed to the Chosen's plan, all of this would change. Provided he survived the night. The gong-strike heralding sunset, one of the few customs carried over from the now-banned religion of Lesganagh, signaled the sinking of the sun; slowly the late evening's gloom was replaced by lengthening shadows, Jesgar's favorite time. Not yet utter blackness, but closer to it than the brightness of day.

The Passion was at the western end of Boughaighr Alley. The way might have been aptly named many years ago when only a few streets had made up the keep at the Dunth. Nowadays there were very few people left who could remember the ruinous fire that had swept this alley clean of all buildings save Eanaigh's Temple. What had once been a narrow dirt lane with wooden houses on each side was now a stone-paved street two cart widths in breadth. Shingle-roofed stone houses that contained well-to-do inhabitants had replaced the timber buildings. Although Trade Road in the center of the triangle between the two temples and the Palace still was host to the open-air market, Boughaighr Alley was home to some of the finest craftsmen, and they had profited from their proximity to the market. Yet many people, including Jesgar, called the street Beggar's Alley: in the old days before the fire, beggars had lined up in front of the Temple of Eanaigh to receive alms. Beggars were still a common sight here, but the giving of alms was now in the hands of the people who walked the streets.

Jesgar observed the last of the drifters slipping away into the night as the street emptied itself of potential marks. Even though the smell that surrounded the beggars went with them, the pungent odor of the first canal, into which every connected household dumped their refuse, remained. It wasn't as bad as the smell of the slum near the West Gate, or other areas not near a canal or the river, but it was ever-present. Also ever-present was the watchmen who patrolled this part of town and went to the non-canal spots only when needed, a fact that Jesgar had begun to appreciate ever since he had started his trips into other houses.

As he turned right onto Trade Road, he saw what he'd come to expect; the Palace's drawbridge was raised. And as Lord Kildanor had pointed out, the battlements were strangely devoid of warriors. On his nightly trips, Jesgar had made it a point to avoid the Palace's vicinity because of the sentinels, but when he focused on the merlons and what went on behind them he barely saw any movement.

The Hand was of a mind to walk right up to the moat and look for the spot Lesganagh's Chosen had mentioned earlier, but caution prevailed. Instead he kept to the shadows; a relatively easy task considering that with the cloudy sky there was nary a well-lit place. He reached the northwestern corner of the moat and stared into the splashing and gurgling waters. Sure enough, there was a lot of junk in the moat. It almost seemed as if the canal waters had stopped flowing south entirely and that the only way fresh water came into the ditch was from the river. This current was not enough to dislodge whatever was forming a second bridge to the outer walls.

How the Scales could any diligent guard miss this crossing,

Jesgar wondered. It certainly confirmed what Lord Kildanor had mentioned earlier. Baron Duasonh's cousin, Lord Jathain, was not acting in the city's best interest. If the wall was in the same state of repair as the moat, climbing the Palace's outer fortification would be very easy.

For a moment Jesgar questioned his decision. Was it really wise to get involved in the intrigues of Lords? He was a citizen of Dunthiochagh, freeborn. His loyalty lay with Cumaill Duasonh, who was a rarity himself, if visitors to the city could be believed. Other nobles mistreated the villeins, even the freeborn, with high taxes and the unjust overruling of Lawspeakers' judgments. All this was nonexistent where the Baron was concerned. But the city and the Palace's safety were Lord Jathain's responsibility. The watch inside was still doing its duty as far as Jesgar could tell, but the patrols on Dunthiochagh's outer wall were not what they should have been.

There was movement. Jesgar remained still, his eyes focused on the battlement. A lone, lantern-bearing warrior trudged toward him. The woman—upon closer inspection he realized he knew her—held her spear in the cradle of her right arm, while her left swung the lantern lazily back and forth. The Hand couldn't believe his eyes when the woman stopped and undid her braid only to plait the blond curls anew. When she was done, the Spear took a long pull from an earthenware bottle, wiped foam from her lips and, after replacing the cork, resumed her patrol.

He decided to check how aware she was of her surroundings. The canal's current was not as strong as the Dunth, yet there was enough gurgling and splashing to mask a lot of sound. A stone, tossed into the waters with sufficient force, was enough of an irregularity to register to even a casual listener.

Jesgar's hands searched the ground for an adequate rock, decided to lob it eastward along the sentinel's way, stood, and threw. The pebble hit the stream with a good plop, and Jesgar crouched to keep out of sight while observing the warrior.

She barely turned her head! Her lantern still swinging back and forth, the woman continued on her way.

Her gait was too upright for her to be drunk, he decided.

Lord Kildanor was right, and any reservations he'd had vanished when Jesgar understood what sort of influence this night's actions might have on his and everyone else's life. If he didn't do as the Chosen asked, a right bastard would make his bid for power. There really was no other choice. He scuttled back onto Trade Road and crossed Old Bridge, then headed west toward the slums and the big warehouses.

Glancing back at his pursuers, Jesgar sprinted for the dark alley. At the last possible moment his left hand shot out and gripped one of the slender, but strong trees lining the main street. Using his own momentum, he swung around, continuing his sprint along the dark road.

"Idiots," he huffed, trying to gain greater lead on the two men who pounded into the side road to follow him.

Cursing and shouting, the pair skidded to a halt and looked to the left and right, trying to catch sight of him again. "There," wheezed one, pointing. They continued the chase. In a matter of moments, he was lost in the shadows, and the pursuers halted.

"Damn," panted the taller of the two. "That one's fast."

Peering into the darkness, the second man mumbled, "You should have paid more attention. Now we gotta move all the bloody contraband."

"Boss ain't gonna like this."

"You damn right... he ain't gonna like this at all."

The two looked at each other, shrugged, and turned around.

Hidden in the shadow of a large building, Jesgar smiled. What he had seen, heard, and taken would be enough, especially since he'd seen Lord Jathain in the warehouse. He waited until the two smugglers had gone back into the alley leading onto Dunth Street, then he hurried on. He had an appointment to keep at the dungeons.

Dunthiochagh was quiet, but the Hand knew he was not the only one who went about business other than the usual. The two smugglers were not the only people, apart from himself, who stalked the night. He knew he was walking the razor's edge; if Kildanor knew he was the Hand, someone of the Thieves' Guild might know as well. So far nothing had ever happened, but one could never be too sure. If the Guild knew of him, he'd be a target to be taken down, and right now he could not afford any trouble.

According to Lord Kildanor's instructions he had made sure he would be seen when Lord Jathain had glanced his way. Now there were not only Guild members to watch for, but also whatever goons Jathain might send out to intercept him. It had only been a moment, nothing to identify him properly, just as he'd been told to do, but still. If the Baron's cousin knew his face, he'd also know who his brother was. Making sure Bennath and Maire were safe would have to come before his supposed entry into the Palace.

The Guild had enough reason to take him out as it was; he hadn't learned thieving from anybody affiliated with it, had never even bothered to tell the masters about his night work. Then again, he never even cared about stealing jewels, money and the like. It was the exhilaration of breaking into another person's house. He loved the thrill.

Looking about, Jesgar tried to get his bearings. The warehouse stood near the West Gate slums, just off of Dunth Street. It would be easiest to head for the river and go toward the Trade Road due east. From there it was just a quick walk north across Old Bridge and then into the Palace, but was this wise? By now Lord Jathain should have people looking for him. The Chosen had made it perfectly clear that until he was in the dungeon he was on his own.

Best to take the long way around, he decided. Sure, Old Bridge played host to booths and stalls, even some ramshackle storage buildings, but the hodgepodge of structures provided ample cover for anyone trying to stay out of sight. It was best to cross the Dunth at New Bridge, take the shortcut across Miller's Strip, and then cross the old canal close to the Palace. The bridges leading onto Shadowpeak Street were wide enough for grain carts and were unobstructed.

Jesgar looked up. The moon already was in decline, but there'd still be enough time to get back. Dunthiochagh wasn't that big after all. Most tradesmen would still be asleep, with only the bakers heating their ovens, and the occasional smith firing up the forges. His brother usually was up well before dawn to prepare for the day. The thought of his family reminded Jesgar to make sure they were safe. The slightly longer way through the merchant district it was. He knew that he couldn't actually contact Ben and Maire, but to see all was well would ease his mind a little.

He quickened his pace and wound his way down an alley running parallel to Dunth Street. If he remembered correctly, this way, with its wattle and daub buildings leaning together across the cart-wide lane, would lead into Halmond. From there it would be easy to get to his home.

A short while later Jesgar halted and peered around the bend, glancing up and down Trade Road. Garinad's Metal Works was at the end of Halmond Street due east, a few hundred yards away from his current position. The passage was clear and he made his way across slowly, assuming the pose of a man too into his cups to avoid being heard. Before now the muddy lanes had muffled his footfall, but this changed at Trade Road. Everything east of here, including the big street that split the city in two, was laid with paving stones, courtesy of the merchants and petty nobles who adamantly refused to tread in mud. Also, here in the well-to-do quarter, construction of the houses changed. Whereas most of the city consisted of timber and waddle and daub buildings, the dwellings here were either a combination of quarry stone and timber frame, or entirely constructed of stone. Jesgar was at home here. He'd entered most of the buildings here at one time or another, but he knew that if he failed now, he would never see this place again.

Soon he reached the smithy, nestled against an arm of the new canal. There was already light in the kitchen, but he resisted the urge to peek through the window. Instead he tried to discern if Lord Jathain already had people in place. A few nooks and crannies and little paths that led between the houses into gardens or to the canal offered good shelter against searching eyes, and as far as Jesgar could tell they were empty.

The door of his home opened, and out came Maire carrying a lantern in one hand and a jug of water in the other. She headed for the workshop, and soon Jesgar heard her working the bellows.

He remembered an argument she'd had with his brother when she'd insisted on working side by side with him in the smithy so she could take over the business should Ben fall ill. After she had won the fight, husband and wife had alternated firing the forge every morning and sharing the workload of each day. By now Maire, despite her still-slender figure, was as corded and muscled as Ben and could work most items almost as well as her husband.

The light in the kitchen went out, and when Jesgar caught a glimpse of his brother heading for the workshop, he mouthed a silent good-bye and was off again, heading up Hill's Road. With luck he'd see them again soon. Lord Kildanor's plan might still fail. Yet it was worth the risk.

The moon had almost vanished, soon vendors would open their booths, craftspeople would begin to lay out their goods, and any chance to get into the Palace would be gone. The Hand doubled back onto Dunth Street, crossed the bridge onto Miller's Strip, and was well down Shadowpeak when the first sliver of dawn appeared in the east. At dawn the Palace had its change of guards; now it was a race.

Part of him reveled in the exhilaration; another part dreaded the consequences of discovery by the wrong people. Jesgar rushed to the spot he'd discovered earlier and made his way across the moat as quickly as he could. His boots were wet and his feet cold, but he stood securely on the small outcrop of stone that was part of the curtain-wall's foundation. Despite his frozen feet it was up the wall, his fingers, and toes searching for and finding purchase in the cracks of splintered mortar. How could anyone leave the wall in this condition, he wondered. Then again, Lord Kildanor had voiced his suspicions, albeit vaguely, and with Jathain's presence at the smuggler's warehouse the disrepair of the fortification was understandable.

Now he was on the battlement, hunching between the merlons. A quick glance across, then to the left and right. He sprinted for the ladder some guard had, to Jesgar's amazement, left to connect the inner with the outer bailey. Just as the Chosen had told him. He climbed and hid once again in the deep shadow of the battlement. Up here the sentinels were more numerous, but still too few and too sleepy after a supposedly long night to cover properly every possible angle. Again, the Chosen's professed suspicions came to mind.

After an approaching guard passed the spot he was hiding in, Jesgar darted across the walkway and down the stairs. At the bottom of the steps he lurked in the deep shadows of the wall, dreading the ring of the gong that signaled dawn. The change of guards was bound to lead to even more lack of attention.

He waited until a barrack's door opened and a score of warriors emerged. They headed for the kitchen. Did they postpone the changing of the watch until after breakfast? Indeed, the men and women waited patiently for a scullion to bring them a steaming kettle. Jesgar was flummoxed. There was rumor that Chanastardh was preparing for war. He wasn't quite sure where Chanastardh was, but if that kingdom intended to invade Danastaer shouldn't the warriors be more alert? No wonder the Chosen was so upset!

Some warleaders emerged from the keep, leaving the gate open for those they were to replace. Now was his chance! Keeping to the shadows, Jesgar hurried to the corner that connected curtain-wall with the main building, and from there to the gate. A quick survey of his surroundings, no one bothered to check the entrance, the guards were probably off to grab breakfast as well. Inside was only empty darkness. He rushed in, and, keeping to his right, headed for the corridor leading to the chamber in which Kildanor was supposed to wait for him.

On his way he had to hide behind tapestries in the shadows of alcoves, while servants rushed to and fro on their errands. Once he even had to dodge a patrol of Swords, but aside from this too close encounter, he saw no guardsmen. Last night he would have thought the lack of sentinels strange, would have expected more of a challenge breaking into the Palace. Now, as Jesgar remembered Lord Kildanor's anger and worry, he felt this anxiety also influencing him. He knew too little of courtly matters and machinations to come to any conclusion, but something was amiss.

At the next intersection he turned left and crept along a deserted corridor. Here was supposed to be the door that the

Baron's friend had mentioned. Ah, there it was. Out of habit the Hand checked the hinges and found them well oiled. He pushed down the handle and against the wood.

As predicted, it was locked.

Now he had to wait for the right moment: the dawn gong strike, the agreed signal. Jesgar waited, hidden in the shadows of a nearby suit of armor.

A pair of warriors walked down the corridor, their steps definitely not as sleepy as their counterparts outside on the walls. They came his way, the Hand realized. In a matter of heartbeats, the pair stopped in front of Jathain's door. One of them, a woman with short-cropped hair and a mean streak to her face, checked the handle, found it locked and turned to her companion.

"Seems he's too cautious. Why should that thief try to get in here?" she asked.

The other warrior shrugged. "With all that's going on, can you blame him? If the Guild knows who their secret sponsor is they might try to blackmail him."

The Guild was in on this as well? Jesgar forced himself not to breathe too deeply. He sent a quick prayer to whatever god might hear, wishing for luck the pair might not discover him. Far too much was at stake.

It was bitter irony when, as the two guards walked off, the gong struck the coming of dawn. There was no time left! He had to open the door now, or all of this would be an exercise in futility. He slithered toward the door, inserted a slender wire into the lock, and began to probe. No matter what happened now, he was committed to the Baron's cause.

CHAPTER 8

"And you're certain you can trust this man?" Cumaill Duasonh, Baron of Higher Cherkont and Boughaighr, looked up from his desk and frowned at Kildanor.

Duasonh always wore this stern, searching look when things did not go his way. Kildanor had seen it a lot these past few days. Somehow, someone had managed to infiltrate the Baron's Palace. So far, the thief had eluded capture, but if this trap worked the man he suspected would be forced to show his hand. "If he shows up at the appointed time, yes."

"It's far too risky, I won't hear of it!" Duasonh slammed his hands on the table, thus ending the discussion in his usual, direct manner.

Kildanor was tempted to correct his former student, but held back. One couldn't order a fifty-year-old man around as if he still was a young lad. "Lesganagh grant me patience," he sent a quick prayer to the god whose orders he had followed for almost a century now. He was a Chosen.

Sometimes he regretted volunteering. He hated seeing friends like Duasonh grow old while he remained as young as he had been during The Choosing.

"You can't be sure it's not him, Cumaill."

"Jathain is my cousin, and he has been my advisor for almost as long as you," Duasonh said. With a sigh he leaned back and closed his eyes. "Think of something. I hope my faith in him isn't misplaced."

A knock on the door prevented Kildanor from replying.

"Yes? What is it?" the Baron shouted, annoyed.

The study door opened and one of the scouts Duasonh

had sent out almost a week ago entered. The man approached on muddy boots; his other attire was as dirty. In other palaces this sort of behavior would have seemed rude, but not in Dunthiochagh. Cumaill Duasonh was an unusual noble, and etiquette mattered little to him, especially when it came to one of his own warriors. His friend's behavior made Kildanor proud.

The scout halted next to the Chosen, bowed, and handed the Baron a scroll.

"What's this?" Duasonh took the parchment, frowning at the mud-covered man. "This couldn't wait?"

"No, sir. Found this in the saddlebags on some mare close to the Old Elven Road."

Kildanor arched a brow. "Horse? What of the rider?"

"Poor chap. His horse was prancing along some mud hole, as if trying to get to something. I went in and found him. Had his throat slit and then was thrown into that stinking hole. Whoever dumped him there had no clue about such things. If a chap is dead and not moving, well, he won't sink much."

"Did he bear any coat of arms? Anything?" Duasonh frowned at the waxed shut scroll. "There is no seal imprinted here."

"No, sir, but judging by his clothes, whoever attacked him removed any trace of where the lad came from."

"Tracks?" Kildanor asked.

"Aye. Seems that the lad had been making his camp near where they dumped him. Also found splashes of blood and a covered-up campfire. Seems like his horse had not been bound to anything and when the robber came the mare bolted."

"Were the tracks covered up?" Duasonh shot Kildanor a warning glance.

"Aye, sir. But any chap with two eyes in his head would've found them. Really sloppy work."

The Baron nodded and scratched his scalp. "Thanks. Dismissed."

"By your leave," the scout said and bowed. He hurried out, closing the door behind him.

"Curious," Kildanor muttered and stepped closer to look at the scroll.

The Baron broke the seal, unrolled the parchment, and began to read. He kept the letter tilted back to catch more of the candle's light. After all, it was well past midnight.

Unable to read the parchment from his position, the Chosen walked over to the imposing bookshelf on the room's far wall. He had read those books, all of them. In some cases, he had even known the author. A few of the books had been gifts to Duasonh's family well before the Heir War. Well before the destruction of Gathran, Dargh and Janagast. The three realms he had known so well.

How futile it seemed to remember the past glory of kingdoms and people long gone. He remembered visiting Dunthiochagh as a boy, how awed he had been by the imposing walls and the sights and sounds so alien to his young mind that his father had told him to close his mouth lest a bird would nest in it.

Back then the world had seemed so large and bright. Now, after more than a century, after seeing all his family grow old and die, a big part of him resented having pledged his life to Lesganagh, having volunteered for The Choosing. He had talked about this with Orkeanas, First of the Chosen. Like himself, Orkeanas was of the original twenty-four that had sacrificed their mortality to serve Lesganagh, Lord of Sun and War. Like Orkeanas, he would never know what it meant to die of old age.

Kildanor smiled as his fingers traced the spine of an old folio. "History of the Elves of Gathran," a book few Houses of Knowledge owned. As with everything else concerning the Heir War, the true reason for the disappearance of the elves was unknown to man. Many scholars of recent times were convinced that with the elves, magic had also vanished. Some even claimed that mankind had driven them off.

They were wrong.

Was it any use to tell people that they erred? It hadn't helped when the church of Eanaigh had declared the faith of Lesganagh heretic, supposedly because the priests had summoned demons to fight demons during the Demon War. Opposing the destruction of the temples had only resulted in more bloodshed. Thus, the Chosen and others of Lesganagh's faithful had kept quiet. There had been enough killing already.

"Jathain has been to Kalduuhn recently, hasn't he?" Duasonh interrupted Kildanor's musings.

"Aye." He turned away from the books and looked at his friend. Some decades ago he would have called him "lad" but that was quite inappropriate now. The once trim figure of Cumaill Duasonh had lost the fight with the courtly lifestyle, despite the weekly practice bouts the Baron still went through. "What of it?"

Duasonh shook his head. "Nothing... I think."

"You think?" echoed Kildanor, a slight smile curling his lips. He had known the Baron since the man's childhood, and knew when he was in such a thoughtful mood, something was most definitely wrong.

The Baron cleared his throat. "Maybe you are right."

Kildanor arched a brow. "Really?"

"Aye."

"Oh?"

"Aye," the Baron said. "Look at this."

He walked over to the ornately carved desk and took the letter Cumaill was holding out to him. The writing was simple yet elaborate. "Someone really knows how to handle a feather," he muttered as he read on. "Whoever wrote this knew Chanastardh was planning to invade. Look at the date!" He was well aware that his voice had taken on an angry pitch by the time his sentence was finished.

"So it seems," Duasonh replied. "And that other threat? What do you make of it?"

Despite being away from Harail, Kildanor's mandate was clear, and no one except the King was to know what other dangers lay hidden in the country. Was this what the writer of the letter was referring to? It could be a multitude of things, he argued. Besides, if these Sons of Traksor were to fight against demons, why would they bother with the Chosen's mandate? That didn't make sense.

"Kildanor?" the Baron's voice pierced his thoughts.

He looked up. "Aye?"

"Something wrong?"

"No, just thinking."

"Speak your mind, mate."

"Well," the Chosen replied. "I've no idea what that other threat might be, unless you count your cousin as yet another threat." Duasonh raised a hand as if to wave him off, but Kildanor continued. "No, listen. Jathain was in Kalduuhn just a fortnight ago." He counted down fingers as he made his arguments. "Those lands south of Gathran Forest are the most direct route to take if you want to get back here. Jathain's escort was missing a couple of men and he said they were ambushed, yet all the stuff he wanted to purchase was still with him." He paused to catch Cumaill's attention anew since his friend had that faraway look of one who was already pondering the issue. When the Baron looked his way again, he went on, "Suppose, Jathain's expedition was ambushed, and these Sons of Traksor saved them. Then he was warned about the Chanastardhians, but instead of coming to you so we might levy troops and warn Harail, he keeps silent." Duasonh nodded in understanding. "And he also has people watching the south road in case these Sons decide to put more emphasis on their warning. But the murderer blunders, the horse with the missive bolts and we get the letter nonetheless."

For a moment the Baron remained silent. Then he shook his head. "I don't believe my cousin would do such a thing."

"And what of the sentinels? The state of disrepair of the walls? Jathain is responsible for the city and he isn't doing his job, Cumaill!"

"And this Jesgar Garinad?"

Kildanor allowed himself to grin. "Oh, he's the bait."

"Can you trust him?"

"He dislikes Jathain."

"You think this is the threat the Sons speak of?" Duasonh leaned back in his chair, rubbed his hands over his face, and yawned.

"If it is, it wasn't part of the oral message Jathain might have been carrying."

"So, what shall we do now?"

"Easy. We catch young Garinad as he tries to enter Jathain's chambers at the stroke of dawn. Provided he lives of course," he said. If the youth was as good as he seemed, Kildanor was confident Jesgar would make it.

"And if he does not?" the Baron asked.

"Then we've lost nothing and are none the wiser."

"Guess we'll have to wait until dawn?"

So many things could go wrong, Kildanor knew the risks, but he had made sure the Garinad boy was aware of most of them. There wasn't much else to say on the matter. "Aye, and hopefully we're going to be able to bait your cousin."

The first glint of light broke the darkness to the east. As Kildanor stood at his window looking out, he snorted in amusement at the antics of Eanaigh's church. They had brought down Lesganagh's church, but they still kept to the tradition of ringing the sun gong. To him this act was the epitome of hypocrisy; killing the messenger did not kill the message. Sure, he had goaded Caretaker Braigh more than enough times on the matter, and it amused him how the priest began to doubt his own church's dogma, but in the end he knew Lesganagh's faith could not stay banned.

There was a knock on the door. The Chosen turned and went to open. As expected, Cumaill Duasonh stood before him. The Baron looked as if he hadn't gotten any sleep. Kildanor couldn't blame him.

"Jathain has not returned," Duasonh said as he adjusted his belt.

"I was hoping he wouldn't," Kildanor replied.

"You want to take in Garinad alone?"

He nodded. "Best you not get involved directly." There was no point in revealing Cumaill's involvement until it became necessary. This, the direct involvement in politics, was what had forced him to leave his brethren in Harail. The others followed Orkeanas' lead; they remained firm and did not take sides. Kildanor refused to be bogged down by stupid traditions.

"Very well," Duasonh said. "Good luck."

The Chosen gave his friend a wink and rushed off, down the

corridor and stairs. With the strike of the gong, he was on the landing that directly led to Jathain's quarters. A quick survey of his surroundings showed him the path was clear, and Kildanor sprinted due north.

He heard muted conversation right ahead of him, but footsteps along with voices receded. Were those two of Jathain's men? Why else would they patrol this section? Had young Garinad been detected? Cautiously, Kildanor glanced around the corner.

Aside from one kneeling person, the corridor was empty.

The Chosen walked toward the hunched figure. "Found something?" he asked.

"Aye," the youth replied.

"Good, were you seen?" That Jesgar could be identified was necessary to lure Jathain into the trap.

"Aye," young Garinad replied as he retrieved a bunch of papers from his shirt. "By none other than the Baron's cousin." Turning back to the lock, Garinad gave the wire a twist, and the mechanism clicked open. Then the young man pulled the wire out, drew a dagger, and gave the lock a good scraping. "Don't want anyone to think the door wasn't opened, eh?" he asked with a smirk.

Kildanor chuckled. He liked this youth. "Aye. Ready?"

Garinad gave a curt nod, and whispered, "Gut if you please. Not the head."

"Never thought otherwise, son," he replied and kicked the false thief's dagger away. "What have we here?" he shouted. "Trying to break in, weasel, eh?" A resounding blow to young Garinad's stomach accentuated his second question. The burglar folded like a pair of scissors. "Guards!" Another punch made sure Garinad was out cold.

A pair of warriors trotted into sight.

"This lout has tried to gain access to Lord Jathain's quarters," he told the new arrivals. Was there shock in their eyes? Or was it worry? It didn't matter, but their reaction reconfirmed Kildanor's decision to take the boy to the dungeons personally. "You." He pointed at the female warrior. "Help me carry this lout. And you, fetch a Lawspeaker." It was no court day and the priests of Lliania would be about the city or countryside to judge disputes, so it might take a longer time to procure one. Sure, Cumaill could preside over the thing but as arranged, the Baron would not be interested in a thief who had not stolen a single thing. Procedure was bound to be drawn out for days.

CHAPTER 9

Ninth of Chill, 1475 K.C.

"I called a meeting with Jathain and Braigh," Duasonh said with a straight face, to offset any spies among the attending servants. He wiped his mouth with a napkin and stood. "Shall we?"

"Sure," the Chosen said then added, "What about the Paladin?" Kildanor stood and walked beside the Baron. They headed for the door.

"Nerran? Off to the Shadowpeaks. You know how he is."

Kildanor grinned. "You two could be brothers if one was to judge by your stubbornness."

"And that would make you what? Our father?"

"Hardly," the Chosen said with a chuckle. "But with the invasion looming one would expect he'd put his hunting trips on hold."

"You really think Nerran would let a war spoil his mood? Or his schedule for the hunt? His Riders are the same, and you know how they are." Duasonh rolled his eyes at him. It was as much a joke as it was a show for the servant who opened the door and bowed.

As he walked into the hallway, the two guards left and right of the door snapped to attention, and Kildanor's amused look changed to the stern face that the Palace's inhabitants had come to expect of him. He turned and walked toward the main audience chamber, slowing his pace until Duasonh and his escort caught up.

When they arrived, a small crowd had already gathered.

Kildanor recognized the usual suspects. Veteran sycophants who looked more at home in Harail's Royal Palace than in the rustic castle of Dunthiochagh. A few priests waited their turn to speak with the Baron.

Although Kildanor himself represented a faith, albeit a banned one, he had never become used to churchly matters influencing so many monarchs and nobles in whatever way struck their fancy. Most of them had never even heard their deity's voice, and even fewer were given the blessing of performing miracles in the name of their god. These were the people who had brought the downfall and banishment of Lesganagh's church. He sighed inwardly and nodded a polite greeting to those men and women who dared meet his gaze.

The petitioners' murmurs swelled to a steady buzz from which only individual voices escaped. "My Liege!" and "Lord Baron!" were shouts accompanied by a waved parchment. Duasonh ignored the persistent petitioners and walked on.

"I won't see anyone today!" the Baron announced, his voice booming over the collective mutterings. "Tomorrow anyone whose needs supersede those of King and country may come before me!" The drone quieted as astonished minor nobles and merchants gaped at their liege. "Now be gone!"

As they reached the door, Duasonh waved the single guard to his side. "No one but Lord Jathain and Caretaker Braigh may enter."

"They are already here," the man replied and opened the door.

Duasonh and Kildanor stepped through, leaving the mumbling assembly of disgruntled petitioners behind.

When they entered the main audience chamber, Kildanor saw Baron Duasonh's two other advisors: Braigh, Caretaker of Eanaigh's church, stooped over the table, ignoring his fellow advisor, Jathain, as he always did when they were called to attend Duasonh. Despite his youth, Braigh's hairline receded at the rate the man climbed the church's hierarchy, and his shoulders seemed bent by the weight of his many obligations.

Kildanor saw the priest grasp the tabletop, and then stiffen as he and Duasonh approached. It was the man's usual reaction when meeting him. After all, it was Eanaigh's church that had most fervently persecuted the followers of Lesganagh. Kildanor grimaced as he stepped closer.

Jathain stood opposite Braigh. Lean and tall, Duasonh's cousin towered over most people. His gaunt features gave him a vulture-like look, the long thin neck supporting a head that resembled a skull, with a face that rarely smiled. Today, he looked even more tired, accentuating the skull. Ever since Kildanor had taught the two cousins he disliked Jathain.

Both advisors bowed before the Baron.

"Cumaill," Jathain began as expected. "I've been told you have arrested the scoundrel who broke into my chambers."

"Kildanor caught him."

The Chosen wasn't sure what the glimmer in Jathain's eyes meant. "Cousin, I demand the thief be tried at once!"

"He stole nothing," Duasonh stated. "He can wait." The Baron glowered at Jathain. "And never demand anything from me! I am the lord and the law here! Demand something of servants, villeins, freeborn or warriors, cousin, but don't demand a bloody thing from me! Understood?"

Jathain grew even paler, gulped, and said, "Yes, milord."

"So, now that this is settled," Duasonh said as he sat down on his massive chair. "Any word from our spies?"

"No, Cumaill," Jathain replied crisply. "Nothing."

The Baron frowned. "How can this be? We should have heard something by now."

"I am certain Eanaigh will guide their steps safely," Braigh quipped. "As long as they have faith in the All-Mother everything will be all right."

Kildanor snorted. "Sure," he muttered.

The priest glared at him. "You should be aware of the goddess looking out after everyone, after all she is the Lady of Health and Fertility."

The Chosen glanced at Duasonh, saw the Baron slightly shake his head, and said, "Aye. That I know."

"What is going on in Herascor?" Duasonh snapped.

"We're awaiting our spy's report daily, you know that," Jathain said.

"And by the time we're done playing 'who and why' the Chanastardhians are laying siege to my city!" Kildanor hadn't seen his friend this angry in a long time, and he hoped Cumaill wouldn't betray their ruse. "I want scouts out there now! I want spies in every blasted city, every village from here to Herascor! If that fool king of ours is too inept to do anything, we will have to do the work!"

"At once, my Lord Baron." Jathain bowed and hurried out.

"Now," Cumaill Duasonh said. He glanced at the letter he had received last night, and turned to Braigh. "Ever heard of the Sons of Traksor?"

The priest shook his head.

"They claim that the lands south of Honas Graigh are their fief," the Baron said. "I made some inquiries." This statement explained why Cumaill looked so tired. Kildanor listened attentively. "Merchants coming in from Ma'tallon reported that the lands south and west of Honas Graigh have been unusually free of robbers for some time now, however." Duasonh scratched his neck and yawned.

"Braigh?" the Baron mumbled.

"I don't think so, my Lord. What letter is this?"

"It was brought to me last night." Duasonh passed the parchment to the priest. "Have a look."

"It's dated from four weeks ago. Why did it take so long?" Braigh mumbled. He looked up at the Baron and frowned. "It takes less than two weeks to travel from the Kalduuhnean border-regions to us. Less on horse. This man should have arrived here at least two weeks ago."

The Baron nodded. "Agreed." He looked at Kildanor. "When did Jathain return from Kalduuhn?" he asked with a frown.

"Three weeks ago," Kildanor said.

"And he must have passed through the area these Sons of Traksor claim to protect," Braigh added.

Kildanor arched a brow and looked at the priest. He didn't like the man, or the church he represented, but he had to admit that Braigh had his wits about him. "Indeed."

"When Jathain returns none of this will be spoken of, understood?" hissed Duasonh.

"Certainly," both men said in unison.

"So, it is entirely possible that Jathain met this order, these Sons of Traksor?" Duasonh asked for confirmation.

"If the area around the forest is their fief, I'd say so," Braigh said.

Kildanor smiled in surprise. Braigh and Jathain were known for their strong friendship, but maybe the priest had been suspicious far longer than he. He thought on it for a moment.

He had also taken a long time to resent the King he had been charged to protect. He'd lived in denial up to the point when he'd discovered Harail's biggest and bloodiest secret. Even after that he'd tried to find excuses, tried to rationalize the cruelty he had witnessed. Until it had been too much. Maybe Braigh had gone through something similar.

"So," Cumaill Duasonh said, pulling Kildanor's thoughts back to the present. "These Sons knew of Chanastardh's invasion plans well before we did. And they tried to warn us. Not only of that, but of this other danger as well. Whatever it may be. Somebody who has been in contact with them didn't want us warned about the invasion."

"Why do you think they wanted to prevent this news from getting here and not the other warning?" Braigh said.

"Because the Chanastardhian threat has been named, this other one hasn't." Duasonh looked at them and was about to continue when the door opened and Jathain strode in. "As I was saying," he changed the topic without missing a beat. "I think the Chanastardhian army will lay siege to Harail first before it bothers with other cities."

"I agree," said Kildanor, and Braigh nodded sagely.

"That is to be assumed, cousin." Jathain took his place at the table. "Your order is being carried out."

"Good." Duasonh smiled.

"I also took the liberty of sending new commands to our outposts," Jathain went on.

Kildanor glanced at Duasonh and saw him shaking with rage. He knew that to voice his suspicions to Jathain now would accomplish nothing except to make the man even more guarded. Jathain assumed too much, he thought grimly and was surprised when Cumaill spoke.

"Jathain, dear cousin," Duasonh drawled. "Who the bloody Scales do you think you are? As far as I know, you are not responsible for the outposts. Nerran is the commander of our field forces."

"Cumaill," Jathain protested. "Nerran isn't available. Decisions have to be made in his absence."

Kildanor couldn't deny the noble's logic, but based on his suspicions he doubted Duasonh's cousin gave his orders in the best interest of Higher Cherkont and Boughaighr.

"Regarding that thief you caught," the gaunt man went on. "I demand his immediate execution. He broke into my office, the gods only know if he wanted to spy, and if he actually succeeded."

The Chosen didn't like the man, but he had to admit this accusation was a very nicely performed ruse. Even he might have bought it, hadn't he been the one who had organized young Garinad's entry into the Palace in the first place. "We found nothing on him," Kildanor said, keeping his face as emotionless as a Deathmask.

"I'll have him interrogated by Upholder Coimharrin tomorrow," Duasonh added. Before Jathain could interject, the Baron went on, "So, what orders did you dispatch to the forts?"

Jathain's orders sounded plausible, but as Kildanor looked at the other men's faces, he saw Cumaill's features darken ever so slightly. Braigh frowned, perhaps because of his lack of knowledge of anything military. If the Caretaker suspected Jathain of treason, this frown could mean anything.

When Jathain had completed his report, Duasonh rose. "That'll be all for today. Cousin, see to it that the patrols are tripled, we wouldn't want anyone getting into the Palace again. Also, double the watch around the gates."

Jathain bowed, and muttered, "As you wish." Then the noble stalked out the room.

When the door had closed behind his relative, Cumaill turned to Kildanor. "I want you to guard our intrepid thief." The Chosen nodded.

To Braigh, Duasonh said, "You know Gail Caslin?"

The Caretaker nodded after a moment's hesitation. "She is one of Nerran's riders, isn't she?"

"Aye," the Baron replied. "Find her and bring her to me."

CHAPTER 10

Despite the cold, Drangar refused to hurry. He took his time, avoided the dirt road that wound its way through the hills of Higher Cherkont, kept to the Flannardh, and only headed south when he deemed he was farther west than Camlanh. As chance would have it, he encountered no one and saw only the occasional fisherman trying his luck on the banks of the river. He avoided those as well. It seemed best to stay clear of people.

At the end of the eleventh day, the dark clouds that had remained to the east finally caught up with him. It was still too warm for snow, even this close to the Shadowpeaks, and he was loath to camp in the torrent that was bound to come down.

The memory of his journey through the area two years before was a blur; he recalled only the desire to flee. A rather new sign by the path took him by surprise. He didn't remember an inn being here, but then he barely recalled anything, especially not landmarks.

"Am I doing the right thing?" Drangar muttered as he dismounted. The building didn't look that inviting. He could tell that over the past few years the structure had seen only the barest minimum of repairs. Was he fleeing again? Was it right for him to do so? Kerral's words still rung in his mind and part of him longed for battle. Maybe it would have been better to defend his home. It hadn't been Carlgh, and the only place he'd called home, aside from the Eye, was Dunthiochagh. To him both were gone now.

Tying Hiljarr to a pole, he looked around in a vain attempt to discern how many people stayed here tonight. Since the wind and thunder covered most sounds, nothing could be heard from either inn or stables.

The shutters were closed for the night, but the light that escaped the slits of door and shutters showed the Sparrow Inn was still open. The sign "Welcome Weary Traveler" from a few hundred yards down the path had left its impression; there were a few other travelers in the common room.

He ignored the stares. From the smell in the room, he guessed they were serving some sort of roast. Not bothering to shut the door, Drangar looked at the balding innkeeper who stood behind the bar wiping a tankard with a rag as grimy as his apron. "Stables open?"

The man nodded. "Somethin' t'eat?"

"Roast, bread, and a mug of milk." Again, he ignored the stares, and turned to head out. "Got a free bed?"

"Aye," the innkeeper replied.

"I take it."

"Two coppers a night."

Drangar nodded and left the taproom. Outside, he untied Hiljarr's rein, and led the horse to the stable. Dog followed. The charger trotted into the one free box, and Drangar removed saddle and bags, tossed the containers into a corner, and hung the saddle over a bar. Filling the trough with oat and scattering some hay about the chamber, his thoughts returned to the looming threat.

War. He knew war would come eventually, it always had, but he hadn't anticipated that the herald of this conflict would be connected to his past. He shook his head, tried to keep the resurging memories at bay. "Why can't I leave it all behind?" he growled, choking back tears.

Dog barked.

Because it is your past and you have to deal with it.

"No, I don't."

He had grown used to the voice in his head. It was like a constant reminder nagging inside whenever he tried to force his memories back.

You have to remember, and you have to deal with it.

"No!" Abruptly he turned around, grabbed his pack and

sword, and closed the gate. Neither Hiljarr nor Dog would mind spending one night in a confined space. He headed back toward the inn. "I don't want to remember. It just hurts."

The noises inside the taproom led his thoughts to other matters. The customers had returned to their conversations as the first moment of idle curiosity about the lone traveler had passed. Now, as he entered again, sheathed bastard sword in hand, his pack thrown across his right shoulder, some of the patrons halted their conversations to size him up. He gave them no thought.

Despite the already crowded room, Drangar discovered an empty, shadowy table and headed for it. He sat down, back against the wall, his weapon placed for easy reach next to him. The weariness of his journey so far had not dulled his instincts. Strangely enough, much like his sharpening of the knife, he felt calmer as he waited for his food and observed the people who occupied the other tables.

From the look of their clothes most of the men and women came from the south, probably from Dunthiochagh or even the capital. Some appeared to be merchants, while others were either guardsmen or warriors. Drangar withdrew deeper into the shadows, not willing to meet another of his former "friends". Encountering Kerral had stirred up enough bad memories. He had no desire for more.

Some of the warriors talked about battles they had fought, boasting about their heroics, about the enemies they had slain. Drangar let out the breath he hadn't even been aware he was holding. More cattle to the slaughter.

Listening to the glorification of self-proclaimed dragon slayers was tiring business, he realized. There were only so many hardheads one could endure, and it wasn't long before he found himself growing restless. Without thinking, Drangar reached over, unsheathed his sword, and fished for the whetstone inside his belt pouch. He ran the stone up and down one side of the blade several times; then repeated the process at the other side of the edge. People always assumed the weapon had cost a fortune, and in a way, it had. People always thought in terms of money, but the dwarves cared not for wealth. They wanted dedication, honesty, not greed and pride. In a world so dominated by the latter, those who lusted after such artwork were disappointed to find out their money was useless. Legend had it that the stone-lords had supplied the gods with arms to battle the dragons and now that he thought about it, he realized that even after sitting grimy for two years in its sheath, there was not a spot of rust on the metal. Even the fullers were pristine.

His doubt concerning a return to Dunthiochagh and standing trial for his crime evaporated as he let the whetstone glide down the sword's opposite edge.

Someone was humming an old war song, the tune's rhythm accentuated by the swish of the sharpening stone. For a moment Drangar was unsure who or rather why he heard the humming at all. Then he realized it was him.

The room had fallen silent. He looked up from the sword, his hand halted in mid-stroke as he beheld an entire room of people, their faces scrunched up in either concern or fear. In the back, half-covered by a door that presumably led to the kitchen, he made out the innkeeper holding a butcher's knife and looking fearful.

Only then did he grasp how threatening his behavior must seem. Was that embarrassment? His face felt hot, and he managed a weak grin, feeling rather stupid. Sharpening four feet of tempered steel inside an inn was definitely not a common sight. "Sorry," he mumbled and slid the sword back into its sheath. There were still cautious glances thrown his way, but the barely suppressed worry was gone.

"One does not go about sharpening one's weapon inside a bleeding inn!" he growled. "Idiot!" He had lived alone far too long.

Despite the embarrassing incident, things quickly returned to normal, although the patrons heading for their rooms gave him a wide berth, something Drangar didn't mind at all. Finally, his long wait was rewarded. A young, snub-nosed woman with dark brown hair, hardly of age, walked to his table and set down a tray laden with a huge chunk of roast, a tankard of milk, and some slices of bread. Her bright brown eyes shone at him as he said, "Thank you," and gave her two silver-leaves. "One is for you, the other for the publican, tell him I mean no harm." For a moment, she stared at the two coins then darted back into the kitchen.

Drangar ran both his hands down his face. The girl's shining brown eyes reminded him of...

He shook his head, raked his fingers through his tresses, and bound the hair with a strip of leather he fished out of his pocket. "No! I must not remember. Never! The past is past!"

Fiercely, he began shoving bread into his mouth, gulped it down with milk, and then checked the roast. It was edible, barely. He breathed deeply, this would have to do. Right at this moment the would-be warriors raised their voices in a marching song. Soon the entire tavern joined the tune.

Groaning inwardly, Drangar resigned himself to eat despite the noise that surrounded him. Hearing a song he knew so well, made it so much harder to push back memories and sharpening his sword, or any other blade, wasn't an option.

The singing became louder, bolder. Some of the would-be warriors began to stomp their feet in rhythm, others slammed half-full tankards onto tables. Although Drangar tried to ignore them and eat his supper in peace, he found his toes tapping along with the general merrymaking. "Gods, is every part of me bound to war?" he mumbled, his mouth full of bread and roast.

Soon the room quieted down to its former level of muttered conversations. From time to time he couldn't help but listen to the talk of his fellow travelers, and what he heard confirmed that his decision to leave was a good one. It seemed as if the kingdom's army was in such disarray and poor training that all the Chanastardhians had to do to win the war was to appear before Harail's walls. Though it was none of his concern, he wished Kerral the best of luck against a foe that was superior in numbers, training, arms, and readiness. In silence he finished his supper, grabbed a lit candle, and went to bed. He didn't care about the strange looks the other guests threw his way as he crossed the room and headed up the far stairs.

For the ridiculously low amount the room had cost Drangar had expected nothing fancier than a straw mattress on a squeaky wooden frame, but this was worse, not that he cared much. He dropped his gear into one corner of the room and locked the door. Then, too tired to check the bedding, he blew out the candle and lay down, immediately regretting his decision.

The stench was terrible. He had been in mud-holes that smelled better. His senses recoiled from the tang of sweat and urine, paired with something he really didn't want to know about. As matters were, he didn't care enough to walk to the innkeeper and demand his money back, or at least fresh linen.

Despite the smell, sleep came quickly, and as he drifted off into a deep slumber he again saw the maid's brown eyes.

Hesmera's eyes...

This wasn't a banquet. This wasn't even the huge hall.

He is alone. Lost. In a dark corridor. Unseen hands grasp his boots, his trousers. Voices, hideous and hoarse, call out his name, echoing in a wind that reeks of death. Fear. Never before has he been so afraid. His shirt is soaking wet. It sticks to his body as the voices cling to his soul.

Drangar... Drangar...

"No!" he howls, turning around, stepping on invisible arms, crushing them. He shakes his legs, forcing the grasping hands away. Still, the clawing goes on.

The hands are everywhere. They claw at his hair, his beard, his legs, and his face. No matter what he does, they always come back. He twists and turns, crushes more hands beneath his boots. To no avail.

Fighting down panic, he rushes forward, and halts again. The hands hold him in place. Something moves beneath his shirt. He rips the cloth away and gazes at the maggots that are wiggling over his sweat-soaked body.

Frantically, he tries to brush them away. They dig into his flesh, eating away his body. His fingernails claw away his skin as he tries to reach the maggots inside.

Then he hears her voice. Calling him, pleading to him.

"Hesmera!" His clothes soaked with sweat, Drangar sat up.

Her eyes.

Her voice.

Tears welled up in his eyes. "Forgive me, my heart. Please forgive me," he whispered. Viciously, he wiped the tears away and looked out the window. Dawn was near and he got up. Grasping his pack, he gave his body a casual check for insects larger than fleas. There were none.

He opened the door, descended the squeaking stairs, and left the building in search of a basin of water. His busy quest was accompanied by the sound of the first birds. He wistfully thought their song was a welcome, but why would any creature sing for him? Finally, he found a horse trough that had definitely seen better days. Then again, so had he. He cleared the grub and leaves out of the makeshift bathtub and then proceeded to fill the thing with water from the well. This wash, although part of his ritual, was necessary; the bed's stench penetrated everything. He dropped his pack and, with a pang of regret, removed his leather pants and linen shirt and tossed them away. They landed in a distant shrub.

Better the thicket than the rest of his stuff, Drangar thought as he slid into the chilly water. He suppressed a howl and began to clean his body methodically.

At least some things he had learned as a child were useful; he remembered how his knowledge of dialects had helped him on his travels, and the knowledge of water and soap had prevented many a disease.

As with so many things in the past fourteen years, his childhood was something he tried not to remember. But that was as vain an attempt as trying to forget…

He plunged into the cold wet.

After long, painful moments of washing he emerged from the water, feeling much better. He bent down to fetch some cloth to dry himself when he heard a rustle in the leaves.

Stopping in mid-motion, he strained to hear.

Nothing.

"Nerves," he muttered and went back to his pack. He heard the rustle again. Followed by giggles.

Grinning, he straightened and said, "Early, isn't it?"

"You're n-n-n-naked," a female voice stuttered, accompanied by more giggles.

He frowned. "So?"

"It ain't proper t' see a man n-n-n-naked," said the voice.

It took him a moment to realize the absurdity of the situation. "Then stop looking."

There were more giggles.

Drangar shrugged and resumed dressing himself, ignoring his audience. He laced up his shirt, pulled on his trousers, and slipped into his boots. "I'm done, happy?" he said at the shrub the girls were hiding in.

Out of the thicket came three young women. One of them he recognized as the maid. He remembered her dark hair, but her brown eyes were burned into his mind. Hesmera's eyes. The well-known sorrow gripped him again. He growled, causing the girls to step back. Trying to hide his pain, he forced a smile. "You have nothing better to do?" he mumbled, as he regarded his audience. The young women approached again.

They seemed to be about the same age and, judging by their clothes, were daughters of locals.

He sized them up and smiled. "Morning." He nodded. "No chores to do?"

The giggles abated.

The redhead of the group stepped forward. "No chores to do yet, sir."

Drangar smirked. "Instead you peep at washing men?"

"It was unintentional," the redhead replied.

"Too long for it not to be on purpose."

The girls blushed and giggled again.

Drangar shook his head, grabbed his pack, and headed back to the awakening inn. "Don't make it a habit."

When he reached his room, he stuffed his belongings into his backpack. The girls forgotten, he busied himself with his pack. As he pulled out his knife to shave, something tender touched the back of his hand. Frowning, he looked into the container. Something stringy stood out from the backside. Drangar took a closer look and saw a silk patch sewn to the leather. His frown deepening, he grasped the patch. Its touch felt soft to the skin, but it wasn't what had brushed his hands a few heartbeats ago. Finally, he removed the patch and looked at it.

In his hand were not only silk, but also a braid of black hair and a small piece of parchment.

He remembered. Her hair.

"No," he moaned.

His hands shook as he pulled the parchment from beneath the braid and opened it.

He remembered the writing. Her tender, loving hand.

Before he could even begin to read, he wiped away the tears from his eyes. "Why now? I don't want to remember."

But now the spell had been cast and he couldn't take his eyes from the note, her note.

Beloved, remember what we promised each other the day we first went into battle together? That if one of us should die the other will have something to remind him of the person gone. You gave me your lucky charm. I didn't have anything then. But now I do.

I love you, remember this
Your wife in heart and soul, forever

Stunned he looked at the braid, her hair.

He didn't believe in fate. He never had and never would believe in anything again, but why did he stumble upon her note and her hair now? Shaky hands thrust everything into the pouch and tied the opening shut.

"The past is past," he reminded himself.

But now it had caught up with him again, as if it had followed him all the way from Dunthiochagh. Stunned, he gazed at the backpack. It had followed him indeed! Unlike his sword, her hair seemed something more than a reminder, something worse. The meeting with Kerral had only been the beginning.

"No, I don't want to remember."

I love you, remember this.

"I love you, too, Hesmera," Drangar said softly. "Forgive me."

Without noticing anything in the common room, he ate and left the inn. Quietly he saddled Hiljarr and then, not looking back, headed south, toward Dunthiochagh.

CHAPTER 11

The sound that reached Jesgar's ears was unlike the door hinges to the dungeon's guard chamber. It sounded almost as if stone was grating very gently on stone. Then a light shone into the corridor. From the opposite end. He hadn't seen much of the place when the warriors threw him into his cell, but he was certain that there was no other entrance on the far side. Yet the light came from that direction. The bars didn't allow inmates to poke out their heads, so all Jesgar could do was wait. Lord Kildanor had made clear he was in danger, but unarmed in this bare cell there was nothing else he could do.

Footsteps echoed ever so slightly toward him, but as far as the Hand could tell they belonged to one person. Yet, one person was enough to kill him.

Jesgar retreated into the corner where the light would reach last. It was a flawed hiding spot, considering the confines of the cell, but he decided to live as long as he could. This wouldn't be all that long, if the intruder actually wanted to kill him. Closer the footsteps came.

The light wedged its way into his cell. Now he heard an unmistakable clatter of metal against leather and in addition to that, the slap of a sheathed sword against a cloth-covered thigh. In an instant the stench of rotting straw was forgotten. Whoever was walking down the corridor was coming for him.

"So, this is how it ends," Jesgar muttered grimly.

Then, deciding he'd rather meet his murderer head on, he stepped into the middle of his cell and waited.

As the steps closed in, his eyes slowly adjusted to the light's glare, and he discerned the intruder to be the Chosen. Lord Kildanor's eyes lit up as he approached with a covered basket in his left hand and an additional sword in the other hand next to the small lantern.

"Good day," the warrior said.

"How did you get in here?" Jesgar blurted out.

"Secret passage," the Chosen replied. "The Baron uses it to spend time with specific prisoners. He likes to question them himself. Usually involves hot pokers and needles. Hungry?"

He hadn't eaten since being captured, and before he could give a verbal reply his stomach grumbled, louder than it had all day long. "Aye," he said. A spark of defiance born of boredom urged him to continue. "What took you so long? What's with the sword? Your old one broken? And what's in that?" He pointed at the container.

How long he had been in the dungeon, he did not know. Time had no meaning in this place of no light and smells that he rarely encountered. Lord Kildanor had locked him into the cell just after dawn. He had slept little, the pallet's straw as moldy as that on the floor of the slum's most disreputable tavern. After the not so restful sleep, with gods know what crawling across his skin, Jesgar the Hand had merely sat in the dark fearing the worst.

"Business. The blade is for emergencies. No. Food." Kildanor unlocked the door. "Can you handle it?" The extra sword rattled in its scabbard as the Chosen shook it.

"No," he replied, and wondered if the scheme he had agreed to would entail more than just setting up a possible traitor. "Am I in danger?"

"Jathain wants you dead."

Something crawled across his back, and Jesgar scratched vigorously. "Excuse me?" he asked, feeling faint.

"You definitely rattled his cage," Kildanor said, his face hardening into a steely mask as he put the sword against the wall adjacent to the cell door. Then Lesganagh's warrior sat and opened the basket.

"I didn't even take a thing!" the Hand protested.

"No, but I did, after you were locked away." He retrieved half a loaf of bread, cut a slice, and handed it to Jesgar. "It had to look real."

"You didn't tell me about that part!" Jesgar hissed, his hand clenched into a fist around the bread.

"The traitor needs to be gone, boy, and you are the bait." The Chosen handed him some smoked ham. "What do you think the sword is for? I got you into this and I'll make damn sure I get you out of it."

Jesgar's anger and fear ebbed away. There was no doubting the warrior's sincerity. He tore into the bread. After a few bites he asked, "What about the guards?"

Lord Kildanor produced a water skin and handed it over. Jesgar took a sip, and the Chosen said, "You got in too easily, boy. I fear a whole bunch of guards are in league with Jathain."

"So, you're here to make sure I don't get offed by them?" he mumbled as he bit into the ham.

A brief nod was all he got as a reply.

First bait, now potential victim. He realized he didn't have much choice in the matter. After all, he had agreed to the ploy. There wasn't much point in blaming anyone except himself, and he'd been in the quandary before he even knew of it. "What're we going to do?"

"First, we eat, then..." Kildanor trailed off and looked into the distance. His eyes widened with surprise.

"Something wrong?"

"Aye," the Chosen replied. Then he stood, handed him weapon and basket, and pulled the door shut without locking it again. "I will be back," he muttered. "If someone tries to poke you, poke him back." The warrior patted his sword's pommel and hurried off, taking the lamp with him.

Jesgar frowned, then cleared the floor of some rotten straw to make room for the basket, and then, with the weapon lying next to him, settled on the pallet and resumed his meal.

Jesgar had finished the apples by the time The Chosen returned. Lord Kildanor was restless, the light from his lantern bouncing back and forth as he hurried down the corridor. Jesgar stood and bowed when the warrior stood before his cell.

"I see no one's poked you, eh?" the Chosen remarked. "And stop that bowing nonsense. Done eating? Good."

"What was this all about?" Jesgar asked.

A stern mask replaced the warrior's anxiety so quickly that the Hand wasn't quite sure if it had been there in the first place. A quick shake of his head seemed to dismiss the thoughts Kildanor must have been occupied with. "Chanastardh's army has captured Harail."

Taken aback, Jesgar thought for a moment then frowned. "Impossible! I heard it said that her walls are as impressive as ours."

"Quick, don't you think?" Kildanor opened the door and rummaged in the basket. He retrieved a stoneware bottle, took a long pull and then began to investigate the basket's other contents.

"Aye."

"Don't you wonder how this was possible?"

Jesgar hadn't really bothered with the news of the war. Why should he? Until a day ago he had been a burglar by night and a smith by day, if he didn't sleep too long. "Well, I don't know. Never really thought much about wars and how they concern me. Chanastardh is far away and even if they succeed at first, I was sure they'd be stopped when they reached Harail."

"Which didn't happen."

Before Jesgar could reply, Lord Kildanor said, "Why do you think Harail fell without even the beginning of a siege?"

"I don't know."

The Chosen drank some more and looked at him. "Thus begins our first lesson. It's called how do I stop being so damn ignorant about the state of my own country."

Jesgar groaned. This was the sort of lecture he had always received from his brother. He had never cared for politics, intrigues, and the like. Then he stood straight, alert. "I thought I was out of here when this ends!"

Lord Kildanor looked at him, a chicken leg almost touching his lips. "A spy needs not know about politics." He took a bite off the leg and rinsed it down with some ale.

"Spy?" the Hand echoed dumbly.

"Aye, should we get through this mess, you'll be taught."

"Taught?" What the Scales was going on? He was a thrill

seeker, not a secret seeker.

"Aye." The chicken leg finished, he tossed the bone aside. "Sit down, son."

He did as he was told, still staring at the Chosen.

Rubbing his eyes, the warrior drew in a deep breath and exhaled. "You're loyal, that you have proven," he began. "Considering what has transpired in Harail, loyalty is an even more valued trait now." He looked Jesgar in the eye and went on, "We need a set of eyes and ears that are not attached to the Palace."

"I know how to get into places unseen, what other teaching do I need?" the Hand interjected.

"You think being a spy only means you slip into the enemy's stronghold, steal some papers, and be off again?"

"Um..." was all Jesgar could say, and he felt embarrassed.

"Does Jathain look like a spy to you?"

He shook his head, afraid to reply.

"Did the folks in that warehouse look like spies to you? Or smugglers?"

Again, he merely shook his head.

"Well, we can be reasonably sure that Jathain and those smugglers are spies and traitors." Kildanor took another drought of ale, wiped his mouth, and looked at him. "Aye?"

He felt stupid, like a child who was lost in a much larger world. "Aye," Jesgar finally managed to say.

"A spy needs not only to know how to slip into a building and steal papers. He also needs to know how to become a part of the world he is to steal from. And he needs to think!"

"But I do think!" Jesgar protested.

"Really?" Lord Kildanor asked, grinning slyly. "So, tell me, oh great thinker, how could the Chanastardhian army take our capital so swiftly?"

Jesgar thought for a moment. He had heard rumors, tavern talk really, about how the King was a decadent, weak willed man who preferred to strut around like a peacock letting others rule Danastaer. He said as much.

"So, the King let others rule?"

He nodded. Then he had an idea. "The ministers wanted

Chanastardh to win."

The Chosen looked him in the eye, and nodded. "So, you can think, young man. At least some of the ministers wanted Chanastardh's army to win, but that hardly matters now." He paused, retrieved another chicken leg, took a bite, and then continued with his mouth still half-full. "How can such a feat be accomplished?"

Jesgar thought for a moment, then replied, "Have people of importance that could prevent such a grasp for power assassinated. Place your own men in those positions and then wait. Is that what's going on here, Lord Kildanor?"

The Chosen nodded. "You think indeed. But there's more to the art of spying than having a bright mind and nimble fingers." He stared at him, and Jesgar cringed under the Chosen's gaze. "You need to learn how to tread the paths of nobility. Courtiers and the like."

He was appalled. "I am no peacock!"

Lord Kildanor frowned. "I can't remember saying thus. You are no fop, but you need to learn the patterns of guards und such when you want to break into a house, do you not?"

He understood where the Chosen was going with that line of thought, and although it pained him he nodded. "I guess so. But how can I fit in?"

"By learning, boy, by learning. This is why you will be tutored in etiquette and dance in addition to swordsmanship, once we get through the night." He paused, frowned, and then got up. "Your lessons will begin when the city is safe." The Chosen left the cell and sat on the floor, his back to the wall.

Jesgar groaned. He had not expected this sort of foolishness when he'd agreed to get captured. He should have known better; getting involved in politics usually turned anyone's plans upside down.

CHAPTER 12

"What the bleeding Scales?" Kildanor hissed. The noise was barely audible, but he had been in so many battles he could identify the rhythmic ringing of blades slamming into each other any day of the week.

"What is it?"

Instead of answering, the Chosen pointed at the sword he had brought for exactly this occasion. "Take it."

"What's this for?" the young man asked.

"Protection," he replied. The sounds of fighting seemed distant, as if the battleground was not inside the guard chamber. Were Jathain's goons battling through the entire Palace to get to young Garinad? No, that seemed wrong. It was easier to get one's own men assigned for guard duty in the dungeons. Something else was going on. "I need to find out," he said, more to himself than to his charge.

"Find out what?" Garinad echoed. "Can it be that the Chanastardhians are already here?"

"It's a one-week trip from here to Harail, and nothing is in Shadow Pass," he replied. The thief had a point; this sounded more like a full-scale engagement. Someone was trying to— Jathain! "Damn him!" Cumaill was in danger! "Listen, you are coming with me, stay behind me, and follow my every order. Understood, boy?"

Jesgar nodded, uncertainly.

"Good, get a good grip on that sword, we're leaving."

In the lantern's light the pair hurried down the corridor to the hidden doorway, up the stairs, and into the Baron's private office. They were barely inside when the door opened and two warriors, in Duasonh's colors, entered with drawn swords. For a moment Kildanor was unsure which side they were on, but when they charged their allegiance became obvious.

A burst of speed brought the Chosen close. An instant before he reached his opponents he whipped out his sword, let one blow deflect to his left and parried the other warrior's slash. A quick glance showed young Garinad with drawn steel in both hands, looking at the combatants with more fright than attentiveness. Kildanor had no time to spare; the warriors now attacked in unison. He caught one blow on his blade, let the enemy's steel slide onto his weapon's crossbar, and kicked the other one in the stomach.

With the second man winded, and he was free to deal with his partner. Unfortunately, the pair was well trained, and the warrior retreated a few steps to cover his gasping companion. The Chosen resorted to a risky trick, especially since Garinad seemed a threat to the foes now. The marble floor was polished to a dull sheen; he remembered the times he had caught young Cumaill and his cousin using the floor as a slide. Maybe he could use it in just the same way.

The first assailant went down in a bloody gasp; Kildanor continued his slide, rolled to the side, and came up on his feet, facing the reinvigorated second man. The Chosen's blade flashed up to deflect the attacker's overhead blow. From outside—it must have come from the Baron's room—came a muffled yell, followed by a crash.

When the Chosen heard his friend's battle roar, he knew Duasonh was still in the fight. The slayer he faced came in for another swing. Kildanor batted the sword aside and stepped into the man's reach. Sword-arm wide, the would-be murderer tried to get away. Unfortunately, the man had dismissed young Garinad, and he did not live to rectify that mistake. The spy-in-training stepped forward and plunged his sword into the warrior's side.

With a gurgling moan the assassin went down.

"Just don't get yourself killed," the Chosen ordered. "Follow me!"

The pair hurried out of the office and headed for Duasonh's

room. They met no resistance, and reached the open door a few heartbeats later. As Kildanor charged into the room, the Baron drove his blade into the last man.

"Jathain is getting nervous, eh," he said, as Jesgar stumbled in.

Duasonh shook his head, bent down to one of the masked men, and pulled off the hood. "I guess Jathain has been busy for quite a while," he panted, nodding at the revealed face. "I have seen this man before, guarding my home!" he growled.

"We fought another pair of warriors who went for your office," Kildanor said. He disliked Jathain, but to think him capable of murdering his cousin... Had they been so deceived?

"Who's this?" Duasonh asked as he bent down and removed the second man's hood.

"This is the man who got your cousin's blood all up and running." When Jesgar began to kneel, he put a hand on the young man's shoulder. "No time for courtly antics, boy. Guard the door."

Jesgar obeyed.

"And another!" Cumaill growled and looked at him. "How many men did Jathain hire for the guard?"

Kildanor kneeled and pulled off the hood of a third. "Too many it seems." Duasonh's pained groan made him to look up.

The Baron held his side, blood welling from beneath his tunic. Immediately the Chosen jumped to his friend's side.

"Let me look at that," he ordered, pried bloodstained fingers from the side and began to tear the cloth. Duasonh sat down on his bed, trembling.

"You shouldn't put yourself into such danger, oaf!" He knelt next to the Baron and examined the wound.

"Is it bad?" Duasonh asked through clenched teeth.

"You'll live. Too much fat in the way." Kildanor shook his head. "I'll fetch Braigh."

He stood and grabbed Jesgar by the collar. "You will stay with him, understood?" The thief bobbed his head. Then he knelt briefly and prayed, "Lesganagh, I beseech thee, protect this man. I beg thee." He remained thus until he felt the god's power wash through him.

Looking at Duasonh, he smiled. "Well, now I fetch him."

Kildanor arrived at the small shrine to Eanaigh that preceded Braigh's chambers, and heard the sound of battle. Again. Sword in hand, he rushed through the chapel, nodding to the goddess's statue in acknowledgment.

He hurried through the open doorway, and stumbled over an assassin lying on the floor, a gaping wound crowning his forehead. Kildanor struggled to keep his footing, finally dropped forward and rolled into a crouch, sword at the ready. Again, the ring of weapons echoed through the high-ceilinged room.

He had never been to Braigh's quarters, but judging from the trail of blood on the floor, only the initial engagement had been fought here.

Braigh's steel reinforced quarterstaff bashed into an opponent's skull as Kildanor entered the bedroom. The priest didn't stop with his forward movement, used the staff's velocity to swing around, and hammered the bloodied weapon into the second man's crotch.

Kildanor winced despite himself, and, thinking Braigh done with the battle, moved forward. The priest, however, was far from finished. As the second assassin went to his knees in a whimper, holding his groin, the Eanaighist whirled around again. The clean end of the quarterstaff drove into the man's head with a sickening crunch.

"Praise the Lady of Health and Fertility," Kildanor said with a chuckle and immediately brought his blade up to fend off Braigh's instinctive thrust.

"Damn you, Lesganagh-spawn," spat the priest, glowering. Then he relaxed. "What is it?"

"All this killing in her name and now back to business, eh?" Kildanor shook his head in amusement. Then the mirth left his face. "Cumaill needs you. This wasn't the only attack!"

Braigh didn't even bother to reply. Instead, he rushed out the room, gathering his herb-bag on the way out.

When they left Eanaigh's chapel, sounds of battle reached their ears. The Chosen drew his sword anew and Braigh's stance showed that he was ready to fight as well.

Kildanor shook his head. "See to the Baron first."

The priest nodded and hurried off.

How many people were on Jathain's side? Kildanor rushed toward the sound of the fierce melee. He passed several confused and frightened servants whose pleading eyes almost ground his run to a halt. A quick gesture, a few snapped words sufficed to send them to their quarters.

As he reached the grand staircase, the clash of arms grew cacophonous. Kildanor stopped and surveyed the melee. Below him, two score of warriors were fighting each other, several more lay bleeding or dead on steps and floor. The Chosen's impulse to immediately rush down and join the skirmish was halted by his inability to distinguish the combatants. All of them wore Dunthiochagh's coat of arms over chain mail, two score of tabards adorned with House Duasonh's falcon.

Some combatants seemed as confused as Kildanor. How could he help those loyal to the Baron? How could he tell friend from foe? Just how many were merely following orders? Certainly, the traitorous Jathain had not subverted half the Palace guard. Warriors were drilled to obey. Some might be directly in league with Duasonh's cousin, but who was merely following their superiors?

"Only one way," he muttered. Pushing the noise to the back of his conscience, Kildanor reversed his sword, turned east, knelt, and placed his right hand around on the hilt.

Then, eyes closed, he began to pray, "I hail thee, Lord of Sun and War. Here on the field I stand, to fight for thy glory. To rise in battle like thy glowing orb doest above the ravages of the world. I beseech thee; show me innocent from foe, to fulfill the duty thou hast bestowed upon me."

For a brief moment he felt the deity's infinite power touch his soul. Fire coursed through his sword into his hands and arms. His lids were forced up.

The prayer finished, Kildanor stood and turned back to the battle, in time to see a shadow-shrouded man go down. As the guard died the gloom lifted off him. It took Kildanor a moment to orient himself. He saw shadowed guardsmen battling, hesitantly, opponents who shone like blazing fires while others glimmered in a subdued halo. Lesganagh illuminated Jathain's followers, outlined the warriors simply following orders, and clouded those on Duasonh's side.

The Chosen jumped into action. A single leap brought him the fifteen feet down into the melee, straight onto one of the blazing traitors. With his sword still in a reversed two-handed grip, Kildanor punched his blade through the man's helmet, pierced skull and spine, and pushed until three feet of steel were firmly embedded. Jathain's follower didn't even have time to scream before he smashed to the floor.

All three sides took a shocked step away from the Chosen. "Stop this nonsense now!" he barked, eyes boring into the combatants as his sword came free with a sickening crunch.

"I rescind your orders!" Kildanor bellowed. "Drop your weapons and stand back!"

All of the dimly lit warriors obey, and a handful of illuminated ones complied, but several of the blazing warriors did not. The occasional clang of metal on stone told the Chosen that some turncoats weren't firm in their support of Jathain. After a short, hesitant moment the men and women turned toward the reformed, unarmed warriors.

This he could not allow!

With a grunt the Chosen began his bloody work. Honor demanded he confront the traitors frontally, but there never was honor in betraying one's liege; he was Chosen, his was the God of Sun and War. As unforgiving as the blazing sun, he waded into the melee, cutting throats and stabbing unprotected backs before Jathain's agents could slay anyone else. Then he made his way to the gateway that led to the inner bailey. The ones he despised most were those who betrayed.

Kildanor slaughtered the guardsmen loyal to Jathain. With each strike he recounted those of the Choosing that were lost. With each deserter he slew he also finished off those whom he had never been able to kill, those he wanted to kill, had wanted to kill for almost one century.

"Ethain! Ganaedor! Traitors! Liars! Murderers!" His grunts

accompanied each sword stroke.

He began to weep as he struck the fighters. All the pent up, repressed emotions welled up. "Ethain! Ganaedor!" He thrust his sword into the back of another. Chosen they had been! Chosen! And they had fallen! "Damn you on the Scales!"

CHAPTER 13

Tenth of Chill, 1475 K.C.

"Any word from the seekers?" The old man bent forward in his chair.

"Yes, sir, they returned this morning," the younger man said as he bowed low.

"Were they successful?"

"No, he left before they arrived."

"An unfortunate accident." The old man paused, closed his eyes, and took a deep breath. "Send them to Shadow Valley, he will be there," he finally said. "Tell them that the punishment for failure is, as always, death."

"They know, sir."

"Of course they do."

The young man thought he heard a sigh accompanying this last statement. He bowed to his superior, left the cluttered study, and didn't see the Priest High bow his head in resignation. He also did not see the older man open the highest drawer of the cupboard behind the high-backed chair and withdraw a sheet of parchment.

The old priest looked at the painting so meticulously drawn by a child's hand. He shook his head and sighed yet again. "I am so tired of this," he whispered.

Anne Cirrain rode at the head of the small column of warriors. Although she had never been this far south, she certainly had heard of Danastaer; its wine was one of her favorites. The country's short but intense past was also well known. Her teacher, Tomrinh, had been one of those who had fled the Lesganagh Purge a few decades ago.

Tomrinh had been a friend of her great-grandfather, a man whom Anne had only heard of in tales told by both her father and her granny. He had been a Paladin, appointed and led by the Sunmaster of Lesganagh himself. Sometimes she wished she lived in those days. She dreamed of it at night: a lady knight in shining armor doing Lesganagh's bidding.

Instead, she now rode to war for an aging king, for a cause she didn't fully comprehend but great-grandpa's legacy lived on: duty and honor 'til you die. There was no one of House Cirrain who did not live by this motto; it was embroidered on the coat of arms that crowned the mountain, plow, and sword. Anne smirked when she recalled her pitiful skill at needlework, how she had failed to stitch properly the thread into the words she knew so well.

"I was born a warrior, not a housewife," she muttered.

"Uncle Wadram always told Aunt Rose so, I remember," said her cousin, Padraigh.

Anne looked at the older man riding next to her. She nodded. "Mother should have known it as well, with me suiting up my dolls in coin-armor, Paddy."

Padraigh chuckled. "She blamed me for years, you know."

"And falsely so, for it was father who hammered the copper himself."

"The ass never said a word in my defense!"

Anne shot him a vicious look. "Don't insult our Lord!"

Padraigh raised his hands in defense, letting go of the reins. "I meant no slight, Anneijhan. I was merely expressing my dismay at being accused the culprit."

Anne chuckled. "He gave you that sword, you know." She pointed at the weapon at Paddy's side.

"Aye," Padraigh nodded and started to say more when he caught sight of their forward scout galloping toward them. "Looks like Janh found something."

"Someone, more like it," said Anne, pointing at the rider in pursuit of their own warrior.

At Anne's signal House Cirrain's small warband halted, the

handful of bowmen stringing and readying their weapons. It was a standard procedure for the warriors from Chanastardh's mountain region. Fighting skirmishes with the highland barbarians every day, the men and women were so accustomed to warfare that their war leader needn't order them into defensive formation.

As Janh and the other rider closed in, Anne discerned the King's coat of arms emblazoned on the second man's tabard. A small motion of her hand sufficed to let her archers lower their weapons. They relaxed; a few of the veterans voiced their disappointment. So far, this trek had been nothing but riding, camping, and riding again. The warriors were unused to the dullness, had expected more from the invasion.

"Another dandy," murmured Dubhan, Anne's former weapon's master, much to the amusement of the entire group.

Anne glanced back at the scarred man and shook her head in mock anger. "You don't know your betters, Dubhan," she scolded. "Then again," she said after a moment, "none of the fools from Herascor can be considered thus."

The warriors roared with laughter.

"Some people would consider your words treason," Paddy said, a broad grin distorting his face.

Anne stuck her tongue out at her cousin then said, "Some people might consider your face treason."

When the two riders arrived, they were still laughing. Seeing her mien revert to her official, stern face, they quieted and stood at attention. Anne glanced at Paddy and winked; she hated the superficial behavior of her peers and enjoyed making fools of them.

"Forgive me if I don't bow as is appropriate," she said, ignoring her warriors' suppressed laughter. "What is it your lord bids us do?"

"Lady Cirrain," the rider said after a quick bow. "High General Mireynh bids you to make haste for Harail."

"They've taken the city already?" Paddy gasped.

"Aye, sir."

"What about my warriors?" Anne frowned at the messenger.

The messenger bowed again. "They are to meet the main

army on the road leading from Harail to Dunthiochagh."

"Why not head to Dunthiochagh directly?" Janh interrupted.

"To go south first will cost us several days."

Anne turned to the scout, her face grim. "We have our orders." To her entire band she said, "I'll meet you on the road in a few days."

The messenger turned his horse and headed south a few yards, granting Anne a few moments of privacy with her people. She appreciated the gesture.

"We're now part of a larger army, folks," she said. "Things are run differently."

"What about you?" Paddy asked.

"I've no idea."

"Why not go through the Shadowpeaks?" Janh insisted.

"Because Mireynh ordered us," Anne snapped. "Would you question my father or me?"

"No, of course not."

"I expect you to afford Mireynh the same honor; he is High General."

"Yes, ma'am," Janh said.

"Now that this is settled," Anne sighed, "Paddy, lead them well, and remember our motto."

Paddy winked and saluted her. "Duty and honor 'til you die," he said, the others following suit.

Clasping her cousin's arm, she nodded at him. "Be well," she muttered, then turned her horse and followed the messenger who trotted a few score yards ahead of her.

Their ride along the Old Elven Road to Harail was fast, faster than she had expected, and over the next few days they changed horses several times. Anne noted that Mireynh kept a tight leash on his army. She was unaccustomed to seeing the other noble houses' warbands behaving in such an orderly fashion. On the few occasions she had been to Herascor and had seen house warriors, they were either boisterous know-it-alls or no better than common thugs.

The men and women she now saw did their duty, refrained from harassing the locals, and were far more disciplined than she expected. There even were constables enforcing order.

Anne had heard about High General Urgraith Mireynh only in gossip. Rumor had it Mireynh was a mercenary with quite a reputation: short tempered, yet cunning in battle. He had only recently accepted the position of High General, a post that had been vacant ever since Halmond had been crowned first king of Danastaer.

When Anne looked back at Chanastardh's and Danastaer's history, it surprised her that King Drammoch had ordered the invasion. Why conquer a country that was strongly connected by heritage to its neighbor? It made no sense. Had Drammoch ordered Mireynh to quell the highland tribes she would have understood, but this campaign confused her. Not that it mattered. Drammoch had made the call to arms, and House Cirrain, like every other noble family, had answered.

Glum thoughts of the situation with the highland tribes and the reduction of her father's forces filled Anne's thoughts as they rode on. At dusk they finally reached Harail. By that time, she was not only exhausted but weary of soon being in the company of nobles she regarded with more disdain than the highlanders. At least the tribes had honor.

Then Anne grew excited. She had never been in the city that had been built by Chanastardhian warriors who had remained loyal to their leader, Halmond, High General and first King of Danastaer. Back at the time of the Wizard War they had fought for Halmond and had followed him to his new kingdom. She saw houses that featured the same architectural style as many buildings in Herascor. Harail seemed quiet, almost peaceful, if one ignored the scores of Pikes and Swords patrolling the city. Each of the various groups sported the tabards of one House or another, an exception being the groups of constables who wore tabards bearing Drammoch's royal crest: a roaring mountain lion holding bow and sword above a blue and red shield. These were the King's Men. Here in Danastaer, if the rumors were true, that appellation had an entirely different meaning than in other kingdoms.

Anne grimaced. The gossip had even reached House Cirrain, which in itself was surprising enough, if one considered that news from the court in Herascor reached them several weeks later, if at all.

As her way took her closer to Harail's palace, excitement gave way to anxiety. Warfare was nothing new to her, she had grown up among warriors, had hardly ever seen her father or any other member of the household unarmed. Still, having seen combat ever since she could fight, Anne did not know why Mireynh had requested her presence and ordered Paddy and the others ahead. All she could do was to wait.

CHAPTER 14

There were still skirmishes in the streets. Pockets of guardsmen loyal to Jathain had not yet given up the fight, but most of the city was secure.

Kildanor leaned against a merlon on the battlement of the outer bailey. After a night and half a day of constant fighting he was so exhausted that sleep threatened to overwhelm him. At his side, strangely enough, was Braigh, whose bloodied staff seemed to support his entire weight.

The Chosen glanced at his unlikely battle companion and shook his head weakly. "Who would've thought?"

"Aye," the priest whispered, a scowl distorting his face.

The two men fell silent again, and left each other to their own musings. It had been a long night indeed. A long and bloody night. In less than a day, about one third of Dunthiochagh's defenders had died.

"We don't need the Chanastardhians," Kildanor grumbled. "We can take care of our own killings."

Braigh looked at him and managed a smirk. "We always could, unfortunately."

"Aye," Kildanor grunted. "You fight well."

"Who would have thought?"

"Indeed." The Chosen turned to look across the city.

"You fight better."

Kildanor shook his head. "Decades of practice." Despite his dislike for the man, and the church he represented, he had to admit that Braigh was a worthy brother in arms. Despite his misgivings about Eanaigh's church, he could not help but respect him.

"Surprised?" Braigh looked back at the Palace where survivors took care of the dead and wounded.

"A little."

"So am I, my... So am I."

Kildanor arched a brow. "Friend? Hardly."

"I can see another reason for... the..."

"What?"

"The banishment." Braigh breathed deeply and shook his head.

"Oh?" What was the man on to now?

"Fear."

Kildanor had expected any other reply, but not this. It seemed as if the battle had pushed some of Braigh's usual hostility aside. There was no aggression in his voice now, only exhaustion, mixed with anxiety.

"Of?"

"You and your kind."

"The priests and paladins were never my kind." This flash of insight was as confusing for Kildanor as it seemed for Braigh.

"No. That's not what I meant."

"Speak plainly, priest!" the Chosen demanded.

"Give me a moment, please."

Kildanor snorted, shook his head, and let his gaze return to the city, wishing he was out there hunting. In this, he had to admit grudgingly, Braigh had been correct. They had done a lot, and there were fresher combatants than themselves, or anyone else who had liberated the Palace. In Dunthiochagh, Jathain's followers were few, compared to the people who had tried to gain control of Castle Duasonh. How he hated to agree with a priest of Eanaigh, especially Braigh. It angered him to see this man fight alongside him and guard his back, even as he treated the wounded.

More than that, he hated to see this bigoted man wield the power of his goddess with a certainty that astonished him. Too much was unresolved between the Chosen and Eanaigh's church, too many years of suspicion and hatred on both sides. And...

"Fear," he whispered. He turned to find Braigh with his

eyes closed. "You fear us."

Braigh blinked and looked at him. "Aye... the fervor with which your brethren fought, with which you still fight, it is frightening."

"And your healing words are not?" Kildanor looked at him, incredulous. "You fight with as much zeal as any of the true priests of Lesganagh."

"Aye. Yet there was a difference, and I now see what might have caused the church to turn against your faith in the past."

"And that be?"

"Fear of your power, the power Lesganagh granted your priests."

"Everyone else stood back during the Demon War!" Kildanor grew furious. "Who else was willing to fight? Your church was more worried about crops and the wounded, not at beating back a threat that made the Heir War seem insignificant."

"We all have our duties," Braigh said, his confusion showing.

"Yet now you are out here, bashing in skulls by the score."

"I did what needed to be done," Braigh said with a quivering voice.

"And Lesganagh's priests did not when the demons fell upon us?" snarled the Chosen.

"I see that now," the priest whispered. "I see that now."

Kildanor watched as Braigh turned and staggered away. He shook his head in wonder, surprised at how a battle could lead to new insights. To him, Braigh had always been a devout, some would say zealous, follower of Eanaigh. That he was high in the goddess's favor was evident by his ability to perform healing miracles, whereas clergy members who outranked Braigh could pray all they wished and still receive none of Eanaigh's blessings. Kildanor knew Braigh was not responsible for the Cleansing some thirty years ago, but the priest believed the tenets the church's elders put forth. Yet despite his naiveté, Braigh had found the ear of his goddess, and she answered his prayers.

"Maybe he wakes up now," the Chosen muttered. He looked to the noon sun. "It's past time your wife's followers see the truth." He nodded his head in reverence. "I hail thee, Lord of Sun and War. Sometimes thy paths aren't as straight as we believe them to be."

The repeated sound of wood smacking on wood turned his attention away from the sun. Until now he hadn't paid attention to most sounds, but these intrigued him. He walked down a flight of stairs and crossed the outer bailey. The sounds were closer now, but none of the nearby warriors seemed concerned. Despite his desire to chide the men and women, he ignored their lack of interest. The enemy had been defeated and everyone who could still put one foot before the other without falling asleep was doing their duty.

After he had left the inner gate behind he saw the unfolding spectacle, which had already drawn a small audience. A Sword-Captain was teaching that pickpocket Garinad how to use a sword, and judging by the sweat that drenched young Garinad's clothes, they had been at it for a while.

"How's the boy holding up, captain?" Kildanor asked as he approached.

The pair stopped the melee, and the Sword-Captain turned and saluted. "Lord Kildanor, sir. Lord Duasonh commanded me to train him."

"And how is he holding up?" He looked from the woman to young Garinad who barely stood upright, huffing and puffing.

"If he's of a mind, he does well enough, sir," the woman replied, her voice tinted with a slight Kalduuhnean accent.

"Good, keep at it, but don't let your other duties lag, there's more to do here than train this boy."

The Sword-Captain snapped to attention. "Yes, sir."

"Then get back to your duties, woman," the Chosen said with a wink. "We still have some rebels in the city."

The steady tattoo of shod hooves beating pavement, made Kildanor turn his head. For a moment he thought yet another rider-less horse had made his way back to the stables, but when he looked closer, he saw a figure slumped across the steed's neck. He hardly recognized Gail Caslin, and with renewed vigor hurried toward the skittish charger.

"Fetch Braigh!" he commanded the nearest warrior. The reins were in his hand before the guard sprinted for the keep.

"Ho, boy," the Chosen said, trying to calm the nervous beast.

The rider stirred, barely. She looked up, seemed to recognize him, and said in a strained voice, "Tried to find the old fool, Sunsword."

Kildanor's head snapped up when he heard the formal title used only by members of Lesganagh's clergy. He had heard rumors that there were Lesganaghists among Nerran's riders, but he had never known who they were. Secrecy was of utmost importance in this time of persecution. "What happened?"

"Got ambushed. City guards. Took a couple with me, but made it out just barely. They're after the Paladin. Find him, Sunsword. You have to find him!"

"I will," he replied.

Braigh stumbled back into the inner bailey. He looked wearier than before, but the sight of the badly wounded woman brought forth his last reserves.

"Take good care of her," Kildanor said.

A warrior ran up to him, saluted and said, "Lord Jathain has fled the city, sir."

"Anyone after him?" he asked distractedly. Yes, Jathain was a major concern, but he had Nerran to worry about now as well.

"Some of the Riders volunteered, sir."

"Then get to the Horse-Mistress's altar and make an offering to her so that she will bless them," Kildanor ordered. He gave a silent prayer of thanks to the gods. Nerran's Riders were without doubt the best for such a chase.

"Already done, sir."

"Then why do you bother me with this?" he snapped.

"No one is to disturb Baron Duasonh, sir, and my captain told me to report, sir."

For a moment Kildanor was lost for words. Who would be foolish enough to forbid Cumaill from seeing his people and giving orders? He looked at Braigh and knew the answer. The man was a priest of Eanaigh, practicality in matters of war and politics came as natural to him as flying came to a rock. "I'll tell him," he growled.

CHAPTER 15

Why? This question had haunted Drangar the entire day. Ever since leaving the inn, he'd pondered this one question. *Why?*

Could it be coincidence that first Kerral, then a lock of Hesmera's hair swept into his life, making obsolete the attempts to rid himself of his past? Both forced him to remember. He longed to forget, but no matter what he did, it never vanished completely. Now, even as he tried to force the past away again, he headed straight toward it.

Dunthiochagh. Their house. He couldn't forget. Everything was burned into his mind, his memory, haunting his sleep and every waking moment. He had to find forgiveness... and judgment.

Looking at the horizon, he realized he could either ride on through the night or find shelter from the rain that was bound to come forth from the looming clouds. The animals had been on the road for the entire day, and though he could have pushed Hiljarr farther, knowing the charger could easily manage the additional stress, he decided against it. Besides, here in Shadow-Pass, without light, the only thing that was certain, if he carried on, was that Hiljarr was bound to stumble and break something. The horse was too much a part of his life to deserve such an end. Even though he rode to meet his past, he didn't want to live in it again. He had changed.

Some, he thought grimly, caressing the jet-black lock of hair he had stuffed into his shirt, into the pocket right above the heart.

With a growl he brought Hiljarr to a stop, jumped out of

the saddle, and removed it. Before them was a small cave, high enough to let a full-grown man stand upright and deep enough to allow a medium sized cart in, too. A small stopover provided by merchants for travelers. "This'll do," Drangar muttered, while he gathered brushwood to use as a mattress. Someone had forgotten to restock the usual commodities. Like firewood. He laid his old winter cloak onto the makeshift-bed, added a blanket, and managed a weak smile, satisfied.

After Hiljarr was fed and tied to the hook in the wall, he ate some cold meat and bread for supper, leaving the bones for Dog. When he was done, he wrapped himself into the blanket and lay down to sleep.

Hesmera. As always, her name was there, brushing against his sleepy consciousness. It caressed him, threatened to trigger his memory until slumber claimed him.

He remembers the music. Slowly the cymbals prepare the audience for the dancers' great entry, and then they finally come into the grand chamber, like a second sunrise. Beaming at her, he refills both their glasses with wine as excellent as the supper
.

Gracefully gliding across the floor, the dancers join the music, which caresses them, encouraging them to wilder, and more enraptured moves. Arching left and right, the rhythm guides their way, leads their steps, moves their bodies.

The drums pick up the pace, are followed by the harps and cymbals, until the crescendo of sounds reaches its climax. He smiles at her, heated by the sweating bodies of the now departing dancers.

She isn't there.

The room isn't there.

He is alone. Turning left and right, he tries to get his bearings. His vision blurs as if he is weeping. Something wet runs down his cheeks, gathers in his moustache, and then drips onto his lips. A coppery taste. Blood.

He hears screams and low moans, echoing through the darkened corridor, beckoning him. He feels a cold breeze touching his hot skin, chilling it to the point where he shivers uncontrollably.

Calm, *he tells himself.* Stay calm.

But he can't.

Now voices can be heard from within the walls, screaming at him. "You are cursed! Cursed!"

"No!" *he yells, running heedlessly in one direction, not caring where it leads, trying to escape the voices.*

"Cursed!"

Running! I must keep running! *His breath thunders in his lungs and his heartbeat roars through his ears, but he can still hear them, following him, taunting him.* "You can't touch me! Nothing can!" *he shouts.*

"Cursed!"

Cursed.

Incorporeal hands grasp at his legs, clutching his pants, tearing his flesh. He screams, his voice echoes through the corridor but the hands keep clawing, tearing his legs to shreds. He fingers for his sword, but instead pulls at something wet, flexible.

Another tug. He screams. Pain in his gut!

A look.

His guts are in his hand, both crawling with maggots. He shrieks, scratches his own flesh, realizing that the larvae are under his skin, eating him alive.

"Cursed!"

He hears her voice, her tender voice screaming in terror. Slashing his sword to the left and right he fights his way toward her. Hold out, my love, I'm coming!

There are no foes, no sword, and no corridor.

He is standing in a great chamber, surrounded by rotting dancers who feast on a corpse. He looks more closely at the corpse, dreading what he will see. Her hair is black. What remains of her skin is pale as only death can make it. On her left hand the golden ring he has given her when he asked her to marry him.

A gigantic figure stands behind her, grinning at him the toothless grin of death. "Join the feast, the main course is rather delicious."

"No!" he shouts, drawing his sword. All he can hear now are her screams, her plea for help, her cries to him.

Viciously he drives the sword home, slashing at the monstrosity. The fury inside him extinguishes all sense, all reason.

He wants to kill this monster.

Again and again he hacks at the beast, and finally when all that remains is a withered torso and a neck connecting it to the head, he defiantly screams at the fiend, raises his sword in a wide arc and beheads her...

"No!" Drangar all but stood on his makeshift bed before he collapsed again. He could smell her perfume intermingled with blood and looked at his sword.

Peacefully lay the blade, wrapped within the rough skin of a goat next to his saddlebags, a vengeful reminder of the deed. He looked at the weapon, felt madness fueled by fear, anger, and regret rise inside him.

"I have seen what I've done again and again. I am tired of you, tired of the blood on my hands. Cursed weapon! I'm going to atone for my deed!" he shouted at the sword. "But I don't need you to remind me any longer!"

As if the piece of metal was ready to escape, Drangar jumped it, grabbed the hilt, and unsheathed it. "Time to go."

Raising his sword, he looked at Dog. She seemed sad, as if to say, "No, you're doing the wrong thing." But at this moment it felt like the only thing that was right, the only thing he could do.

Silently, with every ounce of strength he possessed he swung the weapon onto the cold, uncaring stone. The sound of steel on rock reverberated through the cave, up Drangar's arms and down his spine, but the dwarf-forged blade showed not a scratch. "Bloody mountains," he snarled, and swung at the stone again. The result was the same. Nothing happened.

Utterly frustrated, he tossed the blade aside. "I hope some bastard has more luck with you than I!"

Dog padded over to the sword, put a paw on its hilt, and looked at him reproachfully. "I'm tired of this thing, can't you see that?" Drangar complained. "Even without it my nights are full of nightmares." He rubbed his eyes and fell to his knees, as if pleading with the canine. "Can't you see it's already bad enough for me as it is? I just want to be free of the pain!"

No one can escape bad memories.

"Oh, and what am I supposed to do?"

Live with them.

"I don't want to," Drangar said, and turned to move on. Tomorrow noon he would reach Dunthiochagh.

CHAPTER 16

Nerran! He should have remembered before the Rider had brought news. He should have remembered the moment young Garinad had enumerated the actions preceding any uprising! A fresh surge of energy coursed through his body. Kildanor ran across the inner bailey toward the stables. Dodging the busy guardsmen, he looked for a stable hand. After a few moments he discovered one. The lad helped with the disposal of corpses.

"You! Garranth! Ready my horse! Immediately!" he hollered across the courtyard as he continued toward the Palace.

"At once, Lord Kildanor," the youth replied, but he was already through the gate.

Many had seen him up and about throughout the night, and he surprised them now as they stepped quickly out of his way. He ignored their stares as he rushed down the hall to the grand stairway that led to the second floor. He bumped into a maid who was too slow to step out of his way. While the young woman stammered apologies, he righted himself, pulled the lass back to her feet, and was on his way again.

He was at Duasonh's room a few heartbeats later, and ground to a halt. The two guards left and right of the door crossed their short spears to block his passage.

"Terribly sorry, sir. Baron's resting and the priest said he isn't to be disturbed," the taller one said.

"Let me pass," panted the Chosen.

"No one may pass, except on Caretaker Braigh's explicit order, sir."

"I have no time for this," Kildanor growled, grasped the spears by their shafts, and pushed weapons and bearers aside.

The two could only watch in stunned surprise when he let go and opened the door. Some people, it seemed, still knew nothing of him.

"You're supposed to be at rest, Cumaill," Kildanor said when he saw his friend hunched over a pile of parchments, with more of them littered around his bed.

The Baron looked up and yawned. "Could you?"

He shook his head. "No, and you damn well know it."

"You see my point. I couldn't stand Braigh fussing over me and ordering me to stay put while my warriors were fighting Jathain's goons."

"You did your share of hurt early on," Kildanor smirked. He pointed toward the papers. "What are these?"

"All of what could be saved from Jathain's rooms. Damn bastard decided to put his place to the torch before he fled."

"I heard he escaped—Nerran's Riders are on his tail—but nothing about the fire. Then again, I was busy cleaning up after your beloved cousin."

"Rub it in, I beg you." Duasonh shook his head.

Kildanor slumped against the wall. "Sorry, didn't mean to let this weigh on you even more." He hesitated. "After all..."

"You know how the betrayal of your own blood feels, I know, old friend."

Ethain. Ganaedor. Even after ninety-six years the hurt of their treason stung as if it had happened moments ago. He forced the memories aside. "I'm off to find Nerran."

"Caslin didn't find him?"

"Almost got killed by Jathain's creatures," Kildanor replied. "Do you know how many in our garrisons were not recruited by Nerran?"

"No, but judging by how many turned against us here, it's likely he will have his men in the fortresses as well."

"We need him back and weeding out the good from the bad in the castles. Despite Jathain having lost here, if he manages to find Nerran before we do, our fortresses will be in Chanastardhian hands with close to no battle."

Duasonh cast his friend a tired smile. "It's good that you're here. Thank you."

"Wish me luck," Kildanor said and hurried out.

When he returned to the inner bailey his horse, Dawntreader, stood ready. Sensing his rider's tension, the stallion's capricious temper grew even worse. Dawntreader danced on the spot, pulled on the reins the stable boy clung to and neighed impatiently. Kildanor approached his steed and took hold of the reins. "Calm," he whispered. The horse quieted immediately. "Thanks, lad," the Chosen muttered as he mounted, turned his charger around and guided Dawntreader out of the Palace at a light trot.

He reached Trade Road and urged Dawntreader north. Since the uprising, the streets had become unusually empty. People were afraid to be caught in the middle of skirmishes and stayed at home. Only patrols of Duasonh's warriors marched the streets, and those moved aside the moment they heard horseshoes on cobblestone.

Jathain's assassins already had a head start, but he knew the aging warrior hadn't lost his guile. On his hunting trips Nerran insisted on traveling alone. The only thing that worked for the Paladin now was his erratic track through the Shadowpeaks. It also worked against Kildanor; he had to rely on chance to find him.

He reached the North Gate, and, once outside, he dug his spurs into Dawntreader's flanks and galloped toward the shattered silhouette of the Shadowpeaks.

Now with Dunthiochagh behind him, Kildanor finally had the time to reflect on last night's events. The traces were still evident on his surcoat and armor. There had been no time to change, not that he cared. Appearances were for people who had nothing else to prove their worth. Jathain had been the only one from Duasonh's inner circle who had favored opulent clothes, a perfect example for clothes not making a man.

Jathain! Kildanor gritted his teeth. He missed the old days, before the ban. Back then the appointed of Lesganagh were like the purifying sun, they had acted without mercy to do what needed to be done. Jathain would have died years ago. So would have the king. With all their actions being scrutinized by the other faiths, how could any Chosen do what was necessary? He took a deep breath and shook his head. Times, like people, changed.

The sight of the wizard-wrought scars that marred the foothills of the Shadowpeaks was the first reminder of that terrible time almost one hundred years ago. Since then nature had tried to reclaim the ground lost to the battle magic that the Phoenix Wizards had unleashed. In some places Kildanor saw shrubs and ferns clinging to remnants of once rich soil that the Wizards' spells had blasted away. Those parts of terrain that had survived the spell-battles had suffered under the lack of snowfall in the mountains itself.

Several centuries ago the Phoenix Wizards had enchanted their stronghold and its surroundings to maintain a spring-like climate even in the depths of winter. Then, when Wizard fought Wizard during the Heir War, some spell-battle had caused the entire mountain range to suffer from the enchantment.

Now that the last remnants of snow had melted a few decades ago, dark rainclouds enveloped the shattered mountaintops. The steady drizzle only vanished during the hottest summer days. The farmlands surrounding the Shadowpeaks began to vanish into an ever-increasing marshland. Beyond and between the foothills, the Shadowmarshes surrounded the mountains, and no matter how hard people worked to drain parts of the bog, the rain did its part to ravage more and more habitable land. Given time, the bog would claim Dunthiochagh.

"We should have left some of them alive," Kildanor muttered as he guided his horse across one of the many stilted pathways that crisscrossed the marshland on each side of the Shadowpeaks.

At dusk he halted, dismounted, and knelt, facing west. It was time for the evening prayer. Last night he hardly had the time for worship; Lesganagh understood. During the Demon War none of the Chosen had found a moment of quiet to recite the traditional rites at the appropriate times. Some things were more important.

Although it was urgent to get to Nerran before Jathain's henchmen tracked him down, Kildanor doubted the aging warrior would be easy to find. Nerran's hunts took him across the entire range; he had no clear pattern, nor any preferred area. Maybe Lesganagh would grant him insight. He bowed his head and formed Lesganagh's orb with hands, fingers and thumbs touching. "I hail thee, Lord of Sun and War. Thy day hast ended, thy light almost spent on us, as thou follow thy path along the sky. I beg thy blessing for the coming dark 'ere I see thy light again in the coming morn. Grant me sight to find my friend, guide my hand to slay my foes, and bless my heart with courage, to do what needs to be done. Thine is the light, the tide and woes of war."

In silence he remained on the floor until the sun had vanished beyond the horizon. Finally, he stood, looked to the cloud covered mountains, and returned to his horse. As he mounted, he heard the distant bleating of a few mountain goats.

"Might I be so lucky?" Kildanor whispered as he drew his sword and led his mount toward the Shadowpeaks.

CHAPTER 17

It was well past midnight when Kildanor found the expertly concealed fire in a cave some distance away from Shadow Pass. A slight smirk played around the Chosen's lips as he crawled closer. Whoever this traveler was, he had enough sense to camp off the usual hunters' trails, and a casual observer might have missed the flicker of flames shining through a dense thornleaf. But Kildanor was no casual observer.

He hoped this was Nerran's doing, although he wouldn't mind finding a handful of Jathain's assassins.

There was no sign of a horse, although the stable boys had assured him the aging warrior had taken his favorite gelding with him when he left a week ago. Nerran must have left it at a secure meadow. He inched closer, intent on the campfire. Now he heard the crackling of flames; the scent of burnt wood was heavy.

He reached the thornleaf without a sound. Preparing to stand up, he caught sight of two men stepping into the light. Neither of them was hooded, but the crest of Dunthiochagh was boldly on their tabards. He sank back to the ground in one smooth motion, dagger drawn. Unsheathing a sword soundlessly in such confines was nigh impossible.

A heavy hand on his shoulder startled him. Kildanor whirled around only to have his mouth covered by another hand.

"Stop squirming like a newlywed maiden, lad," a harsh voice grated into his ear.

The hand left his mouth. "Nerran, you bastard!" Kildanor hissed.

"My mother never denied having a dalliance with our

steward." The aging warrior sounded exhausted.

"Good to see you alive enough to spread your wit."

"Better my wit than my guts," Nerran grumbled. He motioned to the cave. "The curs have been following me for a day."

"Only two?" Kildanor scoffed.

"Only two left."

The Chosen nodded. "Let's finish this then."

"Leave one alive, I want to find out who sent the Demonspawn."

"No need," Kildanor said. He was on his feet and down the slope to the cave before Nerran heaved himself through the thornleaf, cursing and sputtering.

The old man's ruckus sufficiently alerted the two assassins who turned to face Nerran, realizing too late that the real threat came from him. Before they could correct their error, the Chosen's dagger already stuck from one man's neck. The traitor went down in a gurgle, spending his life's last few breaths drowning in his own blood.

Kildanor whirled around and unsheathed his sword. As he approached the warrior, Nerran slammed into the man from the left, his sword leading the way. The blade punctured the breadth of the would-be-killer, and Nerran's rush smashed both of them onto the floor.

"What a mess," Kildanor remarked.

Nerran straightened himself and tried to wipe his leather tunic clear of blood. "You should see the other eight."

"Don't tell me you defeated them all with your sword?"

"Stones are a nice thing, and available in abundance in a mountain range, lad," Nerran said and was about to continue their banter when Kildanor straightened.

"Something wrong?"

The Chosen's frown twisted into a mask of fury. "Demonology!"

"Did you prepare the circle?" the leader of the hooded men asked as he returned to the clearing.

"Yes."

"Good. To your positions, lay low, wait for him. We need him alive."

The four, cloaked figures acknowledged and vanished into the darkness. "We won't fail," he muttered and hurried off into the slowly rising dusk, away from the circle.

"Damn those nightmares," Drangar growled and rubbed a hand across his face. Stifling a yawn, he rode deeper into Shadow Valley. He had broken camp too early and left the cave without restocking its supplies. Now, the only choice for him was to continue through the night, braving the gorge that split the Shadow Peak Mountains ever since the Phoenix Wizards had fought their last battle of the Heir War from the highest mountaintops. Their pace was maddeningly slow, and with the little light the moon shone into the cleft even this seemed dangerous.

Sometimes he appreciated the lessons he had received as a boy. How naive had he been, thinking he could be a hero, a brave knight who rode into battle with his lady waiting for him.

"Look, what I've become, Hiljarr," he said; the horse's reply was a snort. "I know, I'm just a run-down mercenary turned shepherd who killed the woman he loved... and they say I'm blessed by Lesganagh." He guided the charger's steps between two large boulders that seemed to guard this stretch of the Valley. "Cursed is more like it."

Dog barked. *Ambush!* The word was as clear in his mind as any he had heard the nights and days before.

Drangar whirled around in his saddle, reaching for his sword. Too late he remembered he had thrown it away. Thoughts racing, he searched for options, reviving skills that had long lain dormant. He had learned to survive, even ambushes like this one.

It was almost dark; they could not get a good shot at him, he had to provide them with a small target.

Letting go of Hiljarr's reins, Drangar slid off the saddle and dashed into the shadow of the rocks. Hiljarr, his own senses still attuned to the dangers of combat, reared once, and trotted back the way they had come, Dog at his side.

In this instant a light flared up in the dark, illuminating the Valley, revealing the running mercenary.

Duck! He couldn't tell if it was the voice or himself giving the commands.

He threw himself to the ground as an arrow whistled over his head, hitting the rock in front of him.

Get up! Move!

Rolling to his left, he found his footing and zigzagged over the rubble, more arrows hitting the gravel behind.

The light vanished, leaving behind a glaring residue. Drangar blinked, tried to get his bearings.

The sky went bright and blinded him again. Instinctively he dove to the right, praying for shelter. An arrow dug into his thigh. Suppressing a yell, Drangar limped on.

Another arrow pierced his shoulder. This time he screamed, in frustration rather than pain.

His moves were slower now. His legs leaden, he turned his head to the right, slowly, as if drunk.

Poison!

Then all went dark.

"Are you certain?" Nerran frowned at him.

Kildanor scoffed, his eyes cold. "Aye. You forget that I fought in the Demon War. This is a sacrifice!"

"It could be other magic," Baron Duasonh's advisor tried to reason.

"I fought Danachamain's forces! I fought Demonologists! Don't presume I don't know how this vile sorcery feels."

Nerran raised his hands to ward off the Chosen's anger. "Easy, lad, I trust your judgment."

Kildanor began to reply when the mountains east of them lit up in a glaring light. When the illumination vanished, the Chosen was already sprinting toward the gorge. Whatever had happened there, he would not suffer a Demonologist to live. Never again would the likes of Danachamain seek to destroy mankind. Nerran's hissed warning fell on deaf ears; he could not help Ethain and Ganaedor, but he would do all in his power to save anyone the Demonologists tried to kill.

He hesitated. Something felt different, but there was no time to contemplate. When another blaze illuminated Shadow Valley, Kildanor hurried on.

He reached the rocky lip of an outcrop overlooking the gorge that magic had ripped into the Shadowpeaks, and caught sight of a single man valiantly dodging arrows shot by hidden archers. A few heartbeats later the man was hit. Another arrow found him. A howling scream pierced the air, and the man staggered on, his movements sluggish.

The man went down.

Instead of disappearing, the light remained strong over the valley, revealing several black robed figures coming out of their hiding-places to charge the stricken man. One of them drew a sword and stabbed the fallen, piercing his back. The other four picked him up and hurried off.

Dreading what would happen if the Demonologists finished their sacrifice, Kildanor hurried down the mountain, avoiding the few pits that dotted his path. Finally, after a long jog down the peak, he came to the valley floor, searching for traces of the attackers.

Nothing.

He could sense, stronger than before, the vile magic that Danachamain had released on the world. Throwing all caution aside he dashed toward its source, not bothering to wait on Nerran. A man was to be sacrificed to summon a demon. This gave Kildanor all the speed he needed. Like Death himself he smashed into the warlocks, hacking left and right, ignoring the painful sting of the enchantments the wizards had lain out in a circle. Before they realized they were under attack, the first dropped dead. Before his body hit the ground, flames burst forth, engulfing the carcass. The other four put up more resistance.

Kildanor whirled around, facing two of them. The other two were to his left and right.

At first, they attacked in unison, forcing the Chosen to defend himself, just barely. He blocked and dodged, using his opponents' weapons against them. To no avail.

The men were also trained as warriors, he realized,

hard-pressed to parry one attack while anticipating three more. Just in time he brought up his sword and blocked. Steel rang on steel. From the rim of his vision, he saw the one to the left relaxing his guard to bring down a vicious two-handed swing. Using this opening to his advantage, Kildanor released the hidden spring blade in his left boot and kicked at the assailant, hitting him in the throat. The man keeled over, blood gushing from his neck. He, too, went up in flames.

The other three, seeing their leader go down, did something unexpected. Instead of running away, they charged. Kildanor ducked one blow, brought up his blade, and impaled his opponent. At the same instant the blade hit home, the Chosen dropped to the floor and kicked away the legs of another attacker. He jumped up, shoving the man's now burning body off his blade. "Surrender or die!" he wheezed and faced the last two Demonologists.

They looked at each other, shook their heads, and slashed at their still breathing victim. Disgusted, Kildanor finished them off, not waiting for them to go up in flames.

The next instant he was at the stranger's side. The man was still breathing. Raggedly, but breathing nonetheless. Resilient. He bent over the man as his eyes fluttered open. Having experienced the demise of hundreds of comrades, he was familiar with the look of death in a man's eyes but this one actually looked peaceful. Through the bloody mask of his face, he looked up, drew a ragged breath, coughed blood, and stared at the symbol that hung from Kildanor's neck.

"Lesganagh," he whispered then smiled. "Hesmera, I'm coming."

"Damn!" Kildanor let go of his sword and looked from the burnt remains of the man's attackers to their victim's corpse. "Is this what...?"

Nerran who came up behind him, breathing as heavily as an aging warhorse, interrupted him. The older warrior eyed the scene before him and cast a frowning glance in his direction.

"Who in the blazes is that?" He pointed at the disemboweled man Kildanor knelt next to. "And what are those?" He nodded toward the piles of ashes.

"Victim of Demonologists," Kildanor spat. "His killers."

"Demonologists?"

"Aye."

Nerran looked at the corpse's face. "I'll be damned."

"What?" Kildanor was surprised at Nerran's astonishment.

"That's Drangar Ralgon."

"Who?"

CHAPTER 18

Eleventh of Chill, 1475 K.C.

She gazed down into the pool of water and saw herself reflected in its glimmering surface. Even now, after all the endless years, she looked young.

"Who am I?"

There were at least a dozen answers that sprang to her mind, each of them dissatisfying. She had been so many things through the ages and none of them caught all of her. Her deeds were apparent throughout the world, much like those of the gods but she was no deity, and neither did she want to be counted among them. Human or elf, either of them would describe her as a being of shining beauty, bright as the sun, and they would be closer to the truth than they could ever realize.

She interrupted her musings when she felt the spirit descend to her cave, and pulled up her cowl.

"Greetings, child of Lliania," she said.

"And greetings to you, Lightbringer." The spirit's countenance resembled the woman it had been before her death. One of the few that had grasped the hand she had offered.

"Am I truly a child of Lliania?" the spirit asked

"Always the same dance," Lightbringer sighed.

"And if so, why does my goddess not want me at her side?" Lightbringer said, her voice suddenly that of the ghost. "Are the gods real? This would be your next question. You always ask, although you do know my reply, child." She smirked at the luminescent, translucent being that floated before her.

"You claim they are," the spirit retorted with a clear, feminine voice.

"The task the Lawmaker entrusted you with upon the child's birth isn't yet finished, daughter of Lliania." The ghostly woman sighed and bowed her head in acknowledgement. "But don't worry, Cat, your time is almost over."

"Has it been this long already? Is the time nigh?" Dread seeped into the apparition's voice.

"No, he still has time, and that is why we need to start. This isn't Chiath where one opponent waits for the other to make his move. I am afraid keeping you whole and walking amongst the living has drained much of my focus, but no more. You know what must be done."

"Aye, Lightbringer."

"Lightbringer," she scoffed as she looked at the being hovering before her. "Don't call me that. Warbringer, now that's a more appropriate name."

"But you are the Lightbringer of legend," her opposite insisted.

"I've been called many names."

"What will happen?"

The Warbringer sighed. "How should I know? I stopped guessing the future long before your kind's blood first wetted the earth."

"But you had a plan... back then."

"Aye."

"So, you must know what is going to happen?"

"You riddle me with questions I can't answer, child. Questions I stopped asking myself a long time ago." She stood and looked around the cave. "I saw the first drops of water that carved the stone to create this cavern. I was there when the dragons erected the Veil of Fire to shut mortals out of their world." She faced the floating ghost again. "If I knew the future I might have never done what I have done, but I don't, Cat! I always hoped and hoped... and hoped again." She sank down onto her worn down blanket and sighed.

"But I want to know if he will be all right."

"Even a feline, although caring for the litter she birthed,

knows there will be a time for her offspring to be on their own. There is little you can do to ensure his well-being."

"I just wish there was more I could do."

"There isn't, now off with you. And remember, the child must not fade."

"How can I forget?" the spirit replied as it drifted off. Cat's outline flickered and vanished.

"Watch over him, little one," Warbringer said as the illumination left in the ghost's wake vanished. "The events set in motion so long ago are finally coming to an end."

She looked around the room that had been her home for time beyond human, or even elven, reckoning. There wasn't much to see, unlike the home she had had when she, and the world, had been young. Holding her clawed hands before her eyes, she wiggled her fingers.

"Now do you remember all you have learned?" she mumbled in the song-like voice of her kind. The words alone left a trace of power hanging in the air, power that craved blood, like it always did.

She had never been able to use the magic she had taught. Even after all this time she relied on life itself to fuel her magic. She shook her head.

There was no way around what was to come, and she regretted it like she had always done. Not even Cat knew of the price her power demanded.

Warbringer drew a knife and slit her wrist.

For his people Bright-Eyes was the wisest and best searcher. He knew his way around the forest and the spooky ruins of the city of the nice people. The nice people had disappeared long ago, though, and now only tales, recounted from one generation to the next, was all the tree-people had left to remember. Well, that was not quite true. There was Bright-Eyes who told tales of the niceness of the nice people. He remembered them, for Bright-Eyes was old. Some of the oldest could remember Bright-Eyes being old when they were young. He always remembered the hiding-place of the stocks, so that no one had to worry about starving but the Oldest, as some of the older people called him, also ventured into the spooky city every once in a while.

Today, Bright-Eyes led a group of bolder young ones there, knowing of some trees that bore the tastiest food.

The group skittered over long deserted paths, instinctively using the undergrowth on the ancient stone-paths as cover. Every young one felt uneasy about venturing into the spooky city. They had heard about the things that haunted the stone-place, but the promise of tasty food made them overcome their fears.

Bright-Eyes led them deeper and deeper into the spooky city. He knew his way around, following a straight path. Never looking back, he headed to the city's center.

Suddenly the young ones stopped.

Bright-Eyes felt the chill breeze, too, but he remained calm. The others, though, couldn't stand the sudden dread that surged up in them and they sped toward the safe forest. The Oldest shook his head, a habit he had acquired long ago. Something was amiss. It was a presence he last felt before the elves had left Honas Graigh, before the great trouble the burly humans had caused but it was also different.

After the elves had left the city, Bright-Eyes had stayed with his people, to help in any way possible.

He darted to an alcove and mounted the stones.

The feeling was wrong indeed. The magic the elves had released to fight human wizards had been different. He had acquired a feel for mystical energies long ago, and this power was... wrong, far worse than anything he had encountered before.

The breeze faltered and then stopped. Bright-Eyes looked around, trying to locate the source of the power. It had almost vanished, but he could detect a residue of energy, a lingering taint, just like the smell of rotten fruit. Or worse, flesh.

He hopped down the stones again and followed its scent. It was definitely elven, though it also carried the strange smell of humans. It reminded Bright-Eyes of the smell that the ugly wizards had carried after they'd magicked up some really bad things. He shuddered. Those things had been really nasty. Burly men had defeated ugly, burly wizards and the stench had disappeared. Now it had returned, though it vanished quickly.

He had to find its source.

Moving slowly across the cobblestone, Bright-Eyes traced the disappearing smell. It reminded him of events that had happened many seasons ago, and it reeked of bad stuff. He still remembered how the streets went. Long ago he had walked them among the elves, running errands for his master, his friend. Those days had ended when the humans had begun fighting and had destroyed the beautiful city. The elves had gone off and had won over those humans, but afterward they had left their dwellings. Bright-Eyes understood them; he didn't want to live in a ruined tree, either.

The smell led him into a part of the city he hadn't visited often. A quiet place then, but it had grown even quieter. He was certain the stink came from here. Standing on his hind-legs, he twisted his head from left to right and looked around, sniffing the air.

Then he scuttled to the left and followed an overgrown path toward the source. His nose led him; the stench so strong it nearly choked him. It was magic, something he had been trained to smell from half a forest away, but it was twisted. His companions, the young ones, couldn't have smelled it, but the wrongness, the tainted feel of the air, had scared them away. Bright-Eyes was glad; he didn't want to endanger them.

He reached a building that, strangely enough, was still intact. Among all those ruined homes, this single house was not. Bright-Eyes sniffed the air. Powerful magic surrounded the dwelling, protected it. The stench that covered the house was overshadowed by the wrong within.

He circled the house and looked for a way in. Every home had to have a way in, be it window or door, big or bigger hole. He knew the difference between them, but had never bothered, for his friend and master had given him the power to pass through walls, but this time the magic prevented him from doing so. He had to find an entrance.

Finally, he discovered a way in, a tiny hole in the ground. He crinkled his nose. Rats! The critters were everywhere. They didn't respect the work of the elves. They were so like the burly men, always scavenging, always digging holes, and eating away everything other people needed. They not only ate people's food, they also killed for it. Bright-Eyes shook his head in disgust. Rats! Still, if this hole was a way in, he had to take it and find out where the smell came from.

He blinked twice, making a quick gesture, and then edged toward the entrance, carefully listening for rattish sounds.

Thanks to his master's magic he had no problem seeing the dark passage beyond the hole. The path was smooth, worn by many seasons of use, and he hobbled down quickly and quietly, as was the way of his people. Fortunately, the rats had left some seasons ago; he didn't smell a single live one.

After a while he reached the exit and stood on a ledge, overlooking a nasty-smelling room.

Bright-Eyes had seen many rooms in the city, before and after the elves had left. Before, they had been nice and clean, too clean for his liking; he had missed moss and leaves. Afterward, the rooms had become covered with moss and other plants, which he liked more, but since the elves weren't there he didn't like the rooms that much. The feel of the elves had left with them.

This room was different.

Not only did it smell wrong, but it felt gloomy. As if even the mere thought of the sun's warmth spared this room. It wasn't cold, yet it made him shiver.

He wanted to discover why this place reeked.

Slowly, carefully, he looked around, and when he found it safe he leaped down and hobbled across the floor.

Flicks of ashes were strewn all over the room. They did not only smell burnt, as dead animals do when men sometimes put them onto flames, but it also stung in Bright-Eyes' mind. They were bad, evil. The ashes were everywhere, save the middle. There was a free space, many strides wide and even more strides long. Its shape was rectangular.

He crept closer, but not too near; his instincts took over, made him abandon his way, and before he knew it, he was cowering in a far corner, his body shaking. The center was wrong, more so than the rest of the room.

What happened now, confused Bright-Eyes even more: out of nowhere a breeze came and brushed over the ashes, gathering them, collecting them. The wind closed in on the middle, piling up the ashes. Then it vanished, leaving the room quiet once more. Bright-Eyes knew something was afoot.

Warbringer let her spiritform soar. She saw the world beneath, and felt her way through the myriad of souls that dotted the landscape like beacons. There were easier ways of doing what had to be done, but easy was the way and the sin of her people, and she was not willing to sacrifice others if all it took was a few drops of her own blood.

Her attention was drawn to the northwest, and she followed the pull of power. It wasn't easy to discern patterns in the muddle of what had once been Honas Graigh, home to the elves of Gathran before their exodus. The flow of old magic was strong here, not as powerful as it once had been, but still stronger than most other sites, with the exception of the Shadowpeaks further north.

Not only was there a general magical aura about the place, but as she drifted closer she felt an uncomfortably familiar malevolent presence near Honas Graigh's center.

A mindstorm.

The souls guarding this place should have been pure. Elves had voluntarily sacrificed their lives and bound their spirits to the Aerant C'lain to prevent their greatest achievement and failure from being repeated. Yes, over the ages some would have been corrupted, but this was worse than even she expected. Whatever had brought about the dissolution of the soulward, it must have been potent. Slowly the spirits that remained pure were driven mad by those that were not. She remembered the ritual, truly not one of the elves' greater achievements, but not one of the sacrifices had given his or her life without knowing the danger. A memory nagged her. Now that she thought about it, she had been here only recently, drawn to Honas Graigh by the scream of innocents. Back then she had not been ready. Warbringer shook her head, saddened by her inability to protect those who lost their lives, but she knew she could not yet challenge whoever was at the center of the mindstorm. Then, as she prepared to follow the second, albeit weaker, soul north, she discerned the tiny bright soul the mind storm had almost overshadowed.

"Would you look at that," she whispered, "a familiar."

The presence of the storm prevented her from contacting the squirrel directly, but she was certainly able to draw the creature away from the whirlpool of madness that surrounded the Aerant C'lain.

Bright-Eyes was scared. More so than ever before in his life, and he ran. *Away!* That was the only thought in his mind. The Oldest ran; blind panic overruling senses and reason, as he hurried through the rat-tunnel out into the sunlit plaza. Still he ran, even when the feeling of immediate danger was long gone he followed the urge to flee, an urge he could not quite explain. He willed himself to stop, but it was as if his legs and paws did not even hear his mind's command. There was someone else here, in his body, he now realized, but before he could summon his strength to repel the invader, he heard her voice.

"Don't worry, little one. Only a little longer and we can talk," she who was in his body said.

The mindlink had another effect on Bright-Eyes as well. He remembered speech, and more focused thoughts and ideas. Words that were not chirps and rustles, the language of elves, returned in a rush that would have stopped his run had his body not been under the control of the speaker.

With it also returned what Lloreanthoran had called his attitude. "I have a name, you know. And if you don't mind, please tell me why you are taking my body for a ride around the forest."

His unseen passenger chuckled. "You're a feisty little fellow, aren't you?"

"And you have not answered my question."

"In a moment," she said with such a certainty that Bright-Eyes could only nod, mentally.

A moment it was. His limbs stopped moving right after he had reached the outskirts of Honas Graigh, and Bright-Eyes felt the female presence leave his mind.

"So?" he asked.

"Do you know what place you have just left?"

"If that's an answer to my question, it's a very strange one, indeed," he replied as he sat on his hind legs.

The spirit let out a sigh, and said, "I could not talk to you inside the Aerant C'lain. The mind storm would have sensed my presence and that I can't risk, yet."

"But you could take me out for a ride?"

He heard a chortle. "Gods, you are a piece of work, aren't you?"

"You try living a century with a bunch of squirrels!"

"But they are your kind."

"Yes and no. Do you have any idea how tiresome it is to be the only one of your kind that actually knows there is a world beyond the forests? And when all of my senses slowly reverted to the instincts of my people, to actually be aware of your mind atrophying?" He hadn't even been truly aware of those feelings until he spoke them out loud. How could he have been, his mind had turned into that of a mere squirrel, mostly. How could a squirrel be aware of its own limitations?

He put his forepaws against his waist and looked up into the sky. "So, who are you, and what do you want?"

"A name for a name," was the reply. "You may call me Firebringer."

He nodded his head. "I'm Bright-Eyes."

"Bright mind as well," Firebringer said.

"Yup."

"And as to what I want. Let me put it this way, there are Veils which I better not pass. You, however, can do what I shouldn't. If not bodily, then with the link your master and you still share."

"If he's still alive," Bright-Eyes replied.

"If he is still alive, yes."

"And what shall I tell him?" He was getting annoyed with the voice's riddles. Could wizards not speak clearly?

"You know the place you just fled from?"

"The Aerant C'lain."

"You know what goes on there? What has been going on for

several years now?"

How could he? He had just become aware of the greater world around again, and this spirit asked him such nonsense. Now that he thought of it, Bright-Eyes could at least connect some of the pieces of what he knew to what he had seen. "The shield's failing ..."

"Not failing, being corrupted. It has been suffering for a while now," the voice interrupted.

"Whatever," he grumbled and then went on. "Some stuff that had been stored there for ages is gone. I don't know what was hidden in that tomb, but from the feel of it, it couldn't be any good."

It seemed as if the unseen speaker nodded in approval. "Inside this place the elves had stored the vilest magic ever created since the olden days. The shield that was supposed to hold the knowledge safe has been corrupted and its guardian spirits are now twisted by madness."

"And that has what to do with the wizard who left me behind?" he made his annoyance plain to hear.

"Someone has to start righting what has been wronged. The elves need to take responsibility for their mistakes. Tell your master that the door that has been locked for ages is about to be blown away. Tell him that the masters of old will soon reclaim what once was theirs, if we don't act fast."

Bright-Eyes remained silent for a moment. "You mean the demons?" he finally asked.

"The firstborn, yes."

"But didn't the humans beat them back years ago?"

"They managed to lock the small window Danachamain had opened. If the elves don't act, there won't be anything left to be locked."

He was about to ask another question, when he felt the spirit's presence leave. There was only one thing he could do, and Bright-Eyes was both reluctant and excited to do something he hadn't done in almost one hundred years. He hobbled back toward Honas Graigh, skirted the ruins to the south, and finally came to a building that seemed more than most to be apart from the way elves had built their homes.

Although the ruin blended well enough with the encroaching woods, it lacked the pristine white of other buildings that could still be seen through the underbrush. Bushes, ivy, and low hanging branches now covered this drab building. Seen from afar one could almost mistake it for another plant, if it could be seen at all.

Not much of the happiness Bright-Eyes fondly remembered could be felt in the overgrown garden; its small pond was choked by grass and scum, and the mosaic pattern of stepping stones and flowerbeds hidden by a tangle of bushes, vines, and layer upon layer of leaves. This used to be his home, but it certainly didn't feel like home anymore.

Still, it was the place where he would find what he needed to get in touch with his friend.

CHAPTER 19

Twelfth of Chill, 1475 K.C.

She felt her power and blood waning, as it had done so many times before. Her lifeblood was not enough to feed the magic needed to force into motion events that had been brewing for centuries. With the little red-brownish fellow, Bright-Eyes, she would, hopefully, stir up enough trouble with the elves that the creatures would send some of theirs to take care of some very old mistakes.

Lightbringer's consciousness slipped back into her body, and with a few uttered words she claimed the last remnant of magic to heal the cut on her wrist.

She needed more. Blood was power, and she wished that she could apply magic the way elves and humans did. Although the way was well known to her, channeling magic, instead of forcing it, was something she had never been able to accomplish; too deep was the way of her people ingrained into her body and mind. There was nothing else she could do, and so she sent out the call.

With this final sacrifice she had gathered enough power to set her plans in motion. The lives of a few were taken to ensure the safety of many.

How she hated herself. How she hated her heritage. Part of her was glad that her kind had left eons ago, another part regretted being unable to kill them all when she had been powerful enough. Magic was life, and vice versa, but her people had taken that literally. To work grand spells, lives had to be taken. A grim price for power.

"They should have called me Deathbringer," the woman known as Lightbringer to some and Warbringer to others muttered, as she closed the eyes of the last innocent child.

Gently Lightbringer placed the young girl's bloodless corpse next to those of the others. "I pray you understand, little ones. Please forgive me."

With a wave of her hand she summoned flames to burn away the bodies. "May the gods guide you home," she whispered, bowing her head.

When the fire had burned its way and nothing was left of the dozen corpses, she shed her cloak and lowered herself into the shallow pool of the children's lifeblood in the stone bowl in the middle of her cave. A wave of disgust mixed with the tingling pleasure of power coursed through her, but she was unable to hide her revulsion and grief.

"It had to be done!" she wailed.

As she immersed herself in the blood her last words emerged as her mouth filled. "Time to move some pieces."

Colors pounded in on her. Magic, the world's lifeblood, surrounded her and she stretched out her senses to find those who had the strength and the determination to do what had to be done.

Years and years ago she had watched from afar when the Phoenix Wizards had annihilated each other. She had done nothing, had seen that this cropping was necessary for humanity to learn their fallibility in and respect for the use of magic. The price of their arrogance had been high, but it had been a necessary sacrifice, just like the children whose blood now surrounded her body.

If mankind was to use magic responsibly they had to learn wisdom, trust, and humility. Lightbringer's own people had been unable to ascend beyond their own pride and the elves had followed the path their slavers had walked before.

It was time to find those who did care.

In the north, beyond the old elven kingdom, she again sensed the small well of will and power. The person was asleep, had been asleep well beyond her lifetime. Lightbringer pushed into the sleeping conscious and hesitated, surprised.

This was not what she had expected.

Her tentative first probe was repelled, and as she pushed harder, she could feel the blood surrounding her body feeding her magic. A quick mental gesture, a few thought words, and she had slipped past the barriers the Phoenix Wizardess had erected around her dormant mind.

"Curious," she whispered, blood filling her mouth.

In her lifetime she had been inside many a human's mind and this, albeit sleeping, soul posed no great obstacle to her. In a heartbeat she knew who this woman was and what had gone wrong. Waking her would be easy...

A gasp, followed by a cough, was the first sound to fill the dark room. She could taste dust on her tongue. Her eyes flickered open, and shut immediately as dust trickled in. Muscles that hadn't moved for a while responded slowly.

Something hadn't worked as it should have.

She felt the tears welling up, pushing dirt out of her eyes. Even her nose clogged with dust the moment she inhaled. The sneeze that followed wracked her entire body. Her eyes flew open.

Instinctively her hands moved through the motions of a minor spell and when the last gesture was done she felt a soft breeze freeing her of the dust. Blinking, she looked around.

Slowly her memory returned.

"This test you have to take, Ealisaid. When you wake after two weeks you will have gone beyond merely being a pupil. You will be one of us."

Her surroundings didn't look like she had only been asleep for a mere two weeks. Dust covered her bed, desk, everything!

The windowpanes were closed, quite unlike the way she had left them. She liked to rise with the sun.

Something had definitely gone wrong.

She tried to stand, but her muscles, weakened from lack of use, gave in the moment she pushed against the floor.

How long had she been in hibernation?

Her throat felt parched and she couldn't tell whether saliva remained within her. She went through the motions of another minor spell; its casting ended with a flask of water appearing in her hand. At first, she sipped carefully, but in a few moments, she began to gulp with more intensity, draining the flask.

A cursory glance showed the state her dress was in. Another spell renewed its bleached-out colors, washed her skin and hair, applied perfume, and painted her nails. Now, feeling more secure and comfortable about her body, she relaxed, and began tentatively to move her legs to shake off the numb feeling. After several long moments of bending and stretching, she thought it safe to rise. When she reached the window, Ealisaid already felt blood pumping strongly through her veins. Another moment later, her rising dizziness faded.

With deft, determined hands she opened the window, then leant forward, unlatched the shutters and pushed. The wood didn't move. She pushed, again. Nothing. Frustrated, she gave the shutters a heavy shove. Wood creaked, but didn't give.

She growled in anger.

How long had it been?

Her anger fueled her muscles where her will had been insufficient. She rushed out her bedroom to the adjacent living room and to one of its windows.

The shutters here remained closed as well. In a fit of anger Ealisaid summoned magical force and sent it smashing into the wooden barricade. At once the shields sped away, torn from their metal holdings. They smashed into a nearby wall. She gasped, utterly confused.

"That's my garden," she whispered, her voice hoarse from lack of use.

She leaned out, and stared at a dim, littered alley. Opposite her house stood a stout, quarry-stone building and it must have been there for quite some time. The weathered surface looked like the foundation of her parents' house back in Thionnaig, and her great-grandparents had built that.

Up and down the alley she saw other structures that showed the same marks of wear. The unbearable stench that assaulted her senses made her gag, and she recoiled from the window; a flick of her hand closed it.

"What is going on here?" she shrieked, slamming door after door behind her, as she rushed through her house.

When she reached her laboratory, the tantrum-flung door caused several jars and beakers to jump on their shelves. Ealisaid ignored the ringing sound and headed straight for the small chest that held her talking-crystal. Someone in Phoenix Citadel better explain this prank. Despite being in familiar surroundings, with countless scents filling the air, she saw dust had settled here also. She detected the faint stink of garbage mingling with the familiar aroma of spices and herbs.

A new fit of rage gripped her and without thinking, she cast a spell to thrust open both window and shutters. Wooden frames, glass, and shields tore through the air, ripped free of their hinges.

The flight of the missiles lasted a few heartbeats before they smashed through a window across a street Ealisaid could not remember being there. She heard frightened screams from the house's inhabitants.

"Masterful illusion!" she hissed, rushed over to her workbench and flung away the lid of the box that shielded the talking-crystal.

In an instant the crystal's smooth surface illuminated from within. Ealisaid pulled over a stool and sat, staring intently at the crystal.

"Phoenix Citadel," she said with a quavering voice.

For several heartbeats the crystal's illumination wavered, then dimmed and finally vanished, leaving a darkness that enveloped the gem's smooth surface. Ealisaid leaned forward and gazed into the trinket, fear rising. Usually when she contacted her order in the Shadowpeaks, one of her fellow students would immediately be available to fetch a master. Now the space where the other wizard's face usually appeared remained black.

"Can anyone hear me?" she said, her voice quavering with dread and anticipation.

There was no reply.

"Anyone?" she pleaded, her hands cupping the stone.

"Please, talk to me," Ealisaid whispered as she brought the stone closer to her face. "I need to speak to master..." her voice trailed off. She couldn't remember the name of the illusion instructor.

She tried again, this time her fear was evident. "Ealisaid Brandagh wishing to speak with the High Master." Tears ran down her cheeks. "I need to talk to him. I need to talk to High Master Kalaith." She bowed her head, touching the crystal to her forehead. "Is there anyone? Please, please, hear me."

"Lady, are you all right?"

At the sound of the voice her head snapped up and she once more gazed into the stone.

It remained as it had been: dark, uncaring.

Ealisaid whirled around to face the window. A young lass, no older than twelve summers, looked at her through the shattered opening, a curious frown creased her freckled face. Behind the girl Ealisaid could see other children gawking at her. She realized there was quite a crowd gathering in the alley behind her house.

Where her garden would have been.

"Lady?"

She glared at the girl. "What kind of jest is this?"

"Jest, madam?" The lass looked confused.

"Oh, this is a good illusion," Ealisaid snarled, as she jumped to her feet. "Be gone! You are not real!"

The girl-image appeared frightened and confused just as she felt herself. "This is the most lifelike mirage I've ever beheld. Now stop this nonsense, at once!"

To support her demand, Ealisaid called on the powers of magic directly, something her instructors had always chided her for, although it bore the most remarkable effects.

The force she summoned tore out of her outstretched fingers, demolished her laboratory's wall, and blasted into the childlike illusions and through the images of the walls opposite her house, bringing the entire structure down. The effect was all Ealisaid had hoped for, and more. What she hadn't expected were the tormented screams of children and adults mixed with the bursting and shattering of stones.

"No more games!" she hollered, leaving her house through

the newly created exit into the alley. "Damned illusionist pranks! Stop it this instant!"

Despite the rising noise around her, she refused to believe the buildings surrounding her were real. This was a mirage. It had to be. Again, she called forth a destructive wave of force that tore down another building.

The screams of pain and alarm doubled. Somewhere off to her left a horn was bleating, and she heard armored footsteps approaching.

Maybe this was no illusion.

CHAPTER 20

"Please tell me again why you brought this corpse here?" Cumaill Duasonh's frown deepened as his look wandered from the man's mutilated body to the Chosen and Nerran.

Kildanor had expected his friend and lord to be angry, especially in the aftermath of Jathain's rebellion, but this was something both he and Nerran had been willing to accept. He took a deep breath, readying his reply, when Nerran cut in.

"This chap deserves a warrior's burial, Cumaill."

"And why? He looks like any other corpse, maybe worse."

"He's a follower of Lesganagh," Nerran said, counting down on his fingers. "He was one of the best men I've ever seen on any one battlefield. And he was said to be blessed by Lesganagh himself."

Kildanor nodded. "If this is true, he deserves all the proper rites. To refuse him this honor would be to refuse Lesganagh himself, and with the Chanastardhians loose in our territory we can't afford angering the Lord of Sun and War." He regarded the mutilated corpse. "They slaughtered him, Cumaill. No man deserves such a death."

"What happened?"

Kildanor let Nerran do the talking while he began the ritual prayer that started the weeklong mourning period prior to the Lesganaghist burial ceremony. It was all too familiar to him. The words came out in the same raspy song priests had used ever since elves had shown men the ways of the gods.

While he intoned words so ancient that even the elves couldn't say who had written them, he retrieved a cloth and a bowl, filled it with water, and began to clean Drangar Ralgon's wounds. Each swipe of the cloth was accompanied by a nuanced word or phrase that depended on the length of the patch of body the now blood-soaked piece of cotton touched.

The original composers had given detailed instructions regarding which body part had to be cleaned with a specific line of the hymn. And there were many lines to sing.

The door slammed open.

"What blasphemy is this?"

Kildanor continued the rite, unwilling to let Braigh's outrage disturb the ceremony. He moved the cloth to Ralgon's left arm and cleaned the man's fingers.

"Cumaill!" the priest hissed. "Why do you allow this heretic ritual?"

Kildanor sang on, although he paid attention to what went on around him. The man's left hand was as callused as his right, witnesses to a life of hard work.

"He is giving this man the proper burial," Duasonh replied. "A warrior deserves this honor."

"These songs were banned, and it doesn't matter that this one is for blessing and mourning the dead."

Nerran chuckled. "I'm surprised, Caretaker."

Kildanor heard Braigh's sharp intake of breath. "And what is it that astonishes you?" he stuttered.

"That you're familiar with this hymn, it last was sung before you were born."

The Chosen dipped the cloth into the water and continued with the lower arm. Several scars crisscrossed Ralgon's skin. Most of them were fairly old; sword cuts most likely. Two recent ones—twin straight lines across the wrist—piqued his curiosity, for they were more recent.

"I ... I," Braigh stuttered.

"You what?" Nerran snapped.

"When my grandmother was buried I was to sing this hymn at her burial."

Hearing this, Kildanor almost stopped the song. He regained his focus and went on. There were more scars, all over the body. The man reminded him of the soil left ravaged in wake of the Heir War.

"You actually performed the Rite of Light?" Nerran sounded very astonished.

"Yes."

"Splendid," Cumaill Duasonh intervened.

Kildanor rinsed the cloth again and resumed cleaning.

"Why is that, lord?" All of a sudden Braigh sounded both curious and suspicious.

"Alas, I need Kildanor up and about with Nerran, salvaging whatever we can of our fortresses," Duasonh said. "And since you apparently know hymn and ritual, you will finish what he started."

"But, milord," Braigh pleaded, consternation plain in his voice. "I must not do this. It's blasphemy!"

"You are aware that your church and any other in this city are here at my sufferance, are you not?"

"Aye, sir."

"It's settled then, I command, you obey," Duasonh said. "Now get to work."

Kildanor sang on, waiting for the moment Braigh joined in. After a few moments the Caretaker's deep voice added to his, and the two sang the next few phrases in unison, while Kildanor kept cleaning the fingers. Braigh moved to his side, put fingers alongside his on the bloodied cloth.

It astonished Kildanor that Braigh, a man he had always perceived as an enemy of his beliefs, was so familiar with the ritual. Maybe later, when the time availed itself, he would have a long talk with the priest.

When Braigh's motions matched his own, he let go of the cloth and joined Cumaill Duasonh. The Baron looked as surprised as he felt, but a heartbeat later that expression changed to the determined frown he had worn the past few days.

"Shall we?" the Baron asked as he turned toward the door.

Wordlessly, Kildanor followed his friends as they left the small chamber. They headed for the audience hall; it was again time for supplicants to beg for attention. Kildanor thought it unfortunate that despite Duasonh's generous and just nature far too few villeins and freeborn came to ask for the Baron's help. Always the same faces, always the same shouts and demands.

When they neared the audience hall a profound sigh escaped Duasonh's lips. "They never give up, even with the bloodshed." Nerran snorted. "This is the only thing most of them can do. They never think for themselves." Kildanor found he agreed with him.

"Those who do aren't here," Duasonh added with a nod.

The clatter of running booted feet made the men halt and turn around. A city watchman ran headlong toward the audience chamber. In the dimly lit corridor the man seemed unable to discern the three men, and only in the last instant was he able to avoid them. He came to a skidding halt before his liege and bowed, gasping for breath.

"Lord Baron," the guard panted. "Lord Baron."

"Catch your breath, son, and then talk."

Kildanor was always happy to hear Cumaill talk to his subordinates more like a father than a lord. Yet another thing that made him a better man than the King.

Before the man was able to give his report, another guardsman rushed toward them. This one bowed and despite being out of breath, reported without pause. "Lord Baron, some witch has just destroyed Malhain's Carpentry on Beggar's Alley!"

"Boughaighr's Alley," Kildanor corrected, being well familiar with the population's nickname for the street that ran west from the Palace toward the old city wall and the more recent additions to Dunthiochagh.

Duasonh had apparently overheard the disrespectful name. "A witch?"

"Aye, sir," said the other guardsman. "Red hair. Blazing eyes. Just like in them stories."

A third and a fourth guardsman hurried toward the small group. Duasonh turned to Kildanor, his face grim. "Take these men with you and investigate this witch. I don't want the whole city watch meeting here." His words were followed by a thunderous crash. "And be quick about it!"

Kildanor ran toward the inner bailey even before Duasonh' second sentence was finished. His senses tingled; attuned to magical forces ever since the Heir War, the sensation surprised him. This was not demonology, it didn't feel as vile, but there was a tint of the same brute strength in the air that had always surrounded the demons after Danachamain had opened the Scales-cursed gates.

He raced down Boughaighr's Alley when another explosion shook the city. It sounded almost as if siege weapons attacked Dunthiochagh, but the noise was fiercer. Again, an ill sense assaulted him.

He dodged an abandoned cart and saw the destruction. A woman amidst the chaos raged, screaming at empty air while throwing spells left and right. Not only the carpenter's shop had surrendered to the onslaught of magic, but also the adjourning two merchant houses and the house of folklore known as the witch's hut, despite it being quite a stately building.

The motions the woman went through reminded Kildanor of those the Phoenix Wizards had used. He had to act fast before she caused even more damage. There was no time for an elaborate prayer, so he did the only thing he could think of. He raced toward the sorceress, hoping she wouldn't discover him and treat him the same way she did the houses. In an instant he was upon her, but before his fist connected with her chin the woman collapsed.

She looked starved, but that didn't hinder Kildanor from ensuring the witch stayed down. As he caught her in his arms, the Chosen delivered a blow to her temple, a method they had applied often to subdue wizards during the Heir War. He then picked her up, tossed her over his shoulder and headed back to the Palace.

Lightbringer felt Cat's approach long before the spirit arrived. A quick incantation masked the pool of blood that still formed the center of her cavern; then with a second spell she made herself appear wrapped in the cloak Cat had always seen her in.

The spirit-woman slid through the sediment into the chamber and hovered before her. "They killed him!" Her voice caught between whimper and scream. "They killed him!"

Her sigh should have been enough of an indicator that she had just about enough of the spirit's whining. "You have to trust me," Lightbringer said with as much restraint as she could muster. She needed the ghost.

"They killed him!" Cat hollered.

The woman of many names stood straight and let some of her power flow into her appearance. It had the desired effect. Cat shrank back and cowered against the far wall.

"Do you trust me?" Lightbringer knew her voice was akin to a thunderstorm's roar, but the spirit tested her patience. "You have your part and I have mine, and I won't suffer your childish wailing. You know your duty, Cat! Do it! Guard him! Now go!"

Had ghosts been able to weep, Cat would have done so, but she couldn't and merely stared at her. Then, with an almost defiant nod, the spirit vanished from the cave, leaving Lightbringer alone. She glared at empty air and then dissolved the illusion covering her and the pool.

As she settled into the cooling blood, Lightbringer felt the Phoenix Wizardess accessing magic in the old way, the wrong way. For a moment she was of a mind to teach the woman a lesson, but decided against it. There would be others to teach, and she had to use the children's sacrifice in a more constructive matter.

First, she had to make sure that the squirrel's message had been heard.

CHAPTER 21

Unlike the Veil of Fire, the Veil of Dreams was a spiritual barrier. Set beyond what the Phoenix Wizards had called the Border of Thought, the Veil of Dreams had been created by the elves of Gathran centuries ago. The realm beyond used to be their haven, a refuge for when the world became too cumbersome. After the Heir War, as mankind called it, the Realm of Quiet had become a permanent home for them. They preferred to remain unseen and invisible to the troubled world.

An advantage had been their ability to shape the Realm to their own liking, not bothering with insignificant details such as moving earth or wood around. In this realm of peace, beyond the world, lived the former rulers of Honas Graigh. For them it was an easy living, free from all the troubles of lesser beings, especially man. Here they enjoyed their existence, their continuing feuds and backstabbing, their magical experiments. They were long-lived, and had since forgotten the fear of death. They were patient. Intrigues spawned into being and took longer than a human's lifespan to unfold; experiments were forgotten over the opportunity to torture a spy.

Lloreanthoran was a respected member of the Council of Mages, who was rare for his kind, preferring his laboratory to an elf's execution. At one of these occasions Lloreanthoran was disturbed in a discussion with one of his colleagues.

The intruder was no other than his assistant, Kyrreandros. Although young in age, by elven standards, the lithe elf showed no respect to his elders as he pushed his way through the cheering and yelling audience. They demanded a slow execution for the hapless, foolish assassin, nothing unusual;

Lloreanthoran realized his people hadn't changed, for they still enjoyed seeing fools suffer for their mistakes. No one cared about the man's employer, all knew his identity anyway, and since the execution was part of the annual routine, a game, it was pure, unblemished entertainment.

Lloreanthoran attended these events only because protocol demanded his presence; thus, he was quite relieved to see his apprentice, even though the worried scowl on the young elf's face troubled him. He watched as the apprentice shoved his way through the crowd that willingly parted before him, recognizing his trusted assistant. Sometimes Lloreanthoran wondered if this young man would ever achieve the status of full-fledged mage, for the youth still lacked the discipline of harnessing the mighty powers of the arcane. For the moment the worried look that seemed to grow more anxious from moment to moment was his prime concern.

Finally, Kyrreandros stood before him, trying to drag in some air. "Master," he panted.

"There, there my friend, calm down and take your time to breathe before you speak," the elder elf said and looked at the horde of cheering kinsfolk as the hapless assassin was flayed alive, his irritation growing.

After a while the apprentice pulled his master's robe. "It's important!"

Grateful for the diversion, Lloreanthoran ushered his apprentice out the Hall of Judgment. After they had left the building behind, he looked at the young elf. "What is it?"

"Something happened," Kyrreandros answered.

"That much I gathered," the mage said. "What did happen?"

"You must come to the study… it's there." The apprentice was confused and Lloreanthoran wondered what had upset the young man. Indeed, he was born to this place and had never ventured into the world beyond, but being familiar with magic to some degree at least, he should have been used to strange events. He shrugged and walked to his house, a small building outside the city of Graigh D'nar.

He had lived here from the beginning, but Lloreanthoran still didn't feel comfortable with the sunless, starless sky that surrounded this elf-created realm. Birds sang in trees and a breeze whispered through leaves and grass, but the lack of the sun, sign of Lesganagh, Lord of the Gods, bothered him. Day and night were always the same, as was the afternoon rain and even a little snow every few months. He had participated in creating this new world, but had to admit he would rather perish in the real world than continue life under this monotonous sky. On rare occasions he tried to use his divining-crystal to look on his old homeland, but his attempts mostly failed. He had studied with and taught the now extinct Phoenix Wizards, traveled bodily through the Veil of Fire. He craved knowledge, but now was bound to this plane, not by spell, but by word.

He looked at the shimmering buildings, created by him and other elven mages to reflect their destroyed home, Honas Graigh. The houses were faultless, like the spells that had created them, but to Lloreanthoran this flawlessness was what bothered more and more people with every passing year. They were too perfect. In Honas Graigh all the smaller houses had been built by elven labor, not a twist of hand and a syllable uttered. He had built his own home back then, of course he had added some magic afterwards, but it was his house, a house he still loved. Many elves felt the same way and grew bored with their self-created land, calling it prison. Boredom birthed trouble and trouble spawned more intrigues, his people's favorite game. It was escalating. In the past, time had worked in their favor; now it worked against them.

They reached his house. When he created it, he hadn't attempted to copy his home in Honas Graigh, yet it was neither as symmetrical nor as perfect as other buildings. There were nooks and crannies, Lloreanthoran had even convinced the perfect growth of the plants to change their ways. His home was magical, like all the other buildings in this elf-wrought prison, but unlike these houses, his actually seemed alive.

The two entered, heading straight for the study, not bothering, as they usually did, to stop in the kitchen for tea. Despite the lack of straight lines, the interior was comfortable. Other buildings might have their insides altered by magic. Their size on the outside not reflecting the space within, which magic had turned into realms of their own; but still this oddity among magical perfection accommodated a huge library and rooms to suit the inhabitants' every need.

When they had reached the large worktable, littered with notes, books and ingredients, they halted. "I ask again, Kyrreandros. What is it?"

Instead of answering, the apprentice walked to a cabinet and retrieved a small mirror. Lloreanthoran hadn't seen the artifact in quite a while and wondered why his student chose this object. The counterpart of the looking glass was somewhere in Honas Graigh's vicinity, probably lost in the woods, abandoned. Then he saw that the mirror's flickering surface and looked closer. Symbols were forming on its frame, writings that appeared when the counterpart was active.

The wizard surprised his apprentice when he grabbed the artifact, traced its frame with thin fingers, and whispered words that were unknown to the youth. He could see his pupil frowning as the mirror's surface changed and the image of a squirrel appeared. The young elf's frown deepened when he began to talk. "Bright-Eyes! It has been a long time, old friend, hasn't it?"

The squirrel replied, "You left me behind, so watch whom you call friend! Who's the whelp?"

As Lloreanthoran replied, he realized how much he had missed his familiar. Yet another thing he regretted to have left behind. "This is Kyrreandros, my apprentice."

The squirrel leaned his head to the right. "Looks very apprentice-like to me. You trust him?"

The wizard arched a brow. "He wouldn't be my apprentice if it were otherwise."

"You, apprentice!" the squirrel said. "Bugger off!"

The older elf cast an irritated glance at the mirror, looked over his shoulder to see Kyrreandros's consternation and nodded. "Fix supper if you please." He then turned back to the mirror. "You need to control your tongue, Bright-Eyes."

"Oh, yes, it wasn't you who was left out in the world with not even half a brain to function at more than the basic level, and if that isn't reason enough to be righteously angry, that war with all them nasties should do the trick." Bright-Eyes raised his paw and pointed at Lloreanthoran. "You and your stupid people took all the baggage with you and left, but your sewage you left behind!"

"What are you talking about?" the wizard asked, but feared he knew what Bright-Eyes meant.

"Let me put it this way, you ran like scared squirrels when your precious city was hit, but you forgot something that made the human wizards' war look like child's play."

"The Aerant C'lain," he said without thinking.

Bright-Eyes nodded. "Indeed, and now trouble is brewing. The soulward has been corrupted, creating a mindstorm. Whatever is going on there, it's bad, so you better get your ass here and help!"

The connection was severed, and Lloreanthoran stood in his study, looking at the hand mirror until Kyrreandros's arrival broke his reverie.

"Who was that?" the younger elf asked as he set down a tray with glasses and a pot of tea.

"That was Bright-Eyes," he said, his eyes still on the mirror. "He was my familiar."

"From back in the days before the Veil?" The apprentice poured him a glass.

"Indeed." Lloreanthoran took the beverage and shook his head. "It's been almost a century since I've seen him. I thought he'd die once I passed the Veil."

"He didn't," Kyrreandros said, stating the obvious.

"I need to think. Return to your studies," he said, sitting down on one of the comfortable chairs.

CHAPTER 22

It was dark and cold.

The gloom surrounding Drangar was not what he had expected. Somehow, he thought that the Bailey Majestic was just that, a gigantic open area where the souls of the dead gathered before they were called forth to face Lliania, Lady Justice, and be judged by her ever-truthful Scales. He had certainly never heard a priest speak about the Bailey Majestic as being a vast emptiness.

"I felt those bastards shoot and stab me," Drangar said. "I'm dead."

Of course, there was no reply, nor did he expect one.

It was cold and dark.

"Maybe even the gods don't want me," he muttered, his voice fearful. "Don't I feel splendid now?"

He felt adrift, floating on a boat down some river. Sometimes it was as if he could hear surf slapping against a wooden hull, but neither did he sit on a bench, nor was he surrounded by wood.

Someone touched his arm; he shrank away from the gentle caress, all too aware of the nightmares that haunted his sleep. Would he need to sleep here?

The touch lingered; escape was futile. Now he thought he felt it more distinct, a rub, as if someone scrubbed him.

Drangar moved to take hold of the unseen cloth, but, as expected, couldn't grab it. Nor could he touch his own arm. If this was death, it was far more unpleasant than any being ever imagined.

"All just lonely souls drifting away in nothingness. None

of us able to reach out to the others, none of us being heard," he muttered. "We came from nothing and leave for nothing. It's pointless. Life is meaningless. There is no Round Hall, no grand feasting chamber, and no glorious celebration. Nothing!"

He wanted to smash something, pound his fists into walls, but could only chuckle bitterly at the futility of it all. There was nothing to break. Nothing left but regrets, guilt, and despair.

"What's the point trying to rid yourself of something you can never get rid of?" he muttered, somehow dreading that Hesmera's spirit would rise before him just like she had in his nightmares.

He remained alone. Aside from the feeling of cloth on his body. Now his left hand was meticulously cleaned.

"If I was to take a bath I'd appreciate some warm water and a few lasses to care for me," he grumbled. "Not that anyone can hear me."

If this was the Bailey Majestic one of Lliania's Lawlords, her heralds, would have already hailed him. Even in his hut he had had Dog and Hiljarr to talk to and keep him company. He missed the two. Not that they were talkative—Drangar felt like weeping at the thought—but at least they were good listeners.

"Have I been a good listener?" he wondered aloud. "I think I was. Of course, there were times when I cared little about what others had to say, but I think in general I was a good listener." He chuckled sadly. "Attentive some might say."

"Not that anyone ever did. Not that anyone now has the chance to tell me. Why is it so gods-be-damned dark?" he shouted.

Silence. Dark and cold silence.

"And I didn't even kill myself," he whispered.

The ghostly cloth wandered up his arm, and for a brief moment he thought he heard the melody of a song. Drangar strained to focus on the tune, words sung in whisper.

The Lamentation of the Sun.

He remembered. How could he ever forget? This song had been on his mind, his lips, and his heart all the way from Dunthiochagh to Carlgh.

These fingers held a weapon high
Now this soul runs free
These fingers held a shining light
For all the world to see
Though darkness falls and your light fades
The Hall of Gods, for you it waits
Don't fear suffering, don't fear pain
Lesganagh will shine on you again
Still wars are lost and wars are won
Your fate lies always with the sun
Lesganagh guide this fading soul
Into your shining Halls

"No one takes my hand. And no one grieves my death," Drangar said with bitter finality.

It was dark.

It was cold.

Bright-Eyes was furious. Now that he had regained his wits, it was difficult not to be angry. Lloreanthoran had abandoned him during the exodus of Honas Graigh. He remembered the slow decay of his wits; he could explain and understand why it had happened, but that knowledge was a weak balm. He knew he should have been more patient with his creator, and hoped his message had been understood. He knew how slow elves could be when it was time to decide something, knew they might share his lack of seeing the danger until the spirit-woman had informed him. The memory of how slow elves could be and how panicked they could become if things took a different turn was enough to bring forth all the bitter feelings he harbored against the wizard who had abandoned him. He also knew that he should activate the mirror once more and explain in full. Still, he was too proud to do just that.

"Have you told him?" the voice rang inside his head.

"I told him," he replied, though he knew the being could probably see the half-truth shining in his mind.

"I understand," was her reply. "I'll convince him." With

those words, Bright-Eyes was, once more, alone.

"Might as well do something useful while the spirit talks to him," he muttered and stashed the mirror away. The squirrel hopped down the ruined wall and headed back to Honas Graigh, unsure of what it was he wanted to do, yet still determined to prove, more to himself than anyone else, his anger was not all that was left of him.

CHAPTER 23

The Veil of Dreams she knew. After all it had been her kin who had studied all aspects of magic for millennia, until the elves had, with her help, risen against their masters. She had broken so many laws over the years that the sanctity of the elven realm beyond this Veil mattered little to her.

There were many Veils in the world, some physical, like the Veil of Fire, some, like the Veil of Dreams, spiritual. To pass through either was an effort that took raw magical power.

Lightbringer felt the blood around her sizzle away, consumed by the forces she fed into opening the corridor between realities. Her people had never understood that magic, like reality, was what you made of it: malleable, yet omniscient. One needn't force it into any shape; it knew shapes before anyone else had ever conceived them.

The elves had learned mage-craft from her, had learned from the mistakes she could not unlearn, so ingrained were her people's teachings. Under the elven people magic flourished. Instead of forcing magic and reality into the shapes they wanted by using life force, the elves guided magic into forms and shapes that magic had known all along. Magic needed a nudge, a word or ten, and maybe a gesture, much like shooing crows. They had learned much from the mistakes of their enslavers, but ultimately, they chose a similar path.

Lightbringer tore away the Veil of Dreams like gossamer silk. Blood evaporated around her like boiling water as she opened a gateway to the elven realm.

Her spiritform floated into a land of beautifully shaped

buildings lined by steeloaks and beeches. The walls, roofs, and even doors were gilded with gems that positively reeked of enchantments. Her heightened senses suffered none of the limitations that hampered man and elf, and she could tell that these jewels were the foci that maintained this dream world. She took in the vista, floated up to gain a higher vantage and was surprised to discover that the realm was flat. A hill here and there, but no curving of the plain, only a straight line from horizon to horizon.

One sight, however, caught her attention: a small building, overgrown with clingferns and ivy. A steeloak of incredible size pierced it and in parts replaced the roof. In this controlled environment the small house was a marvel of nature's chaos. Like a sore it stood apart from the others.

Lightbringer had seen the glorious spires of Honas Graigh, old Gathran's capital, and had traveled in those cities the elves had built after their enslavers had fled. The architecture here was reminiscent of those structures yet differed so much that Lightbringer wondered how similar the elves had become to their enslavers.

The sky was devoid of any celestial body, only waning illumination heralded the coming of dusk. It came as a shock when, in the matter of a few heartbeats, the gloom of artificial twilight changed to complete darkness. Without lights in the countless houses she would have thought herself inside the Veil of Gloom.

She began her search in the wild-walled house, feeling that the familiar's master lived there. It was no use looking for someone malleable; she needed someone who would do out of necessity what she needed them to do.

Lloreanthoran pushed the tome he was reading aside, irritated. Bright-Eyes. Long before he had seen the squirrel's face in the mirror, he had already thought of home, of Gathran, of Honas Graigh, and although the memory made him also relive the pain, he felt more certain every day that leaving the world and living beyond the Veil of Dreams was wrong. Now, Bright-Eyes had reminded him of the hidden shame of his people

A war worse than the Heir War?

What had happened to the Aerant C'lain and the secrets stored within? A mindstorm. He had read about such phenomena long ago. What could have corrupted the souls?

Back when they had abandoned Honas Graigh, none had thought of recovering the books hidden within this tomb of knowledge. He knew what had been buried, despite the tomb having been around for centuries before his birth. If there was truth in what Bright-Eyes had said, he needed to bring this news to the Council of Mages.

Maybe something would change.

Maybe facing this danger was the first step in taking the elves of Gathran back into the world. Why couldn't his people see that this wasn't life but an imitation, a fake? A glorious picture one could hang on a wall and marvel at, unreal like every dream. Were they living a dream, or reliving a nightmare? Sometimes it was a bit of both.

The elven wizard leaned back in his chair, took a sip from his mug of tea, and called his apprentice. "Tell me, Kyrreandros, what is life for one such as you? Born and raised here in this world," he asked when the younger elf entered.

The wizard-in-training looked at his teacher, shrugged, and said, "It's home."

It was maddening. How could the young, his hope for change, be so lethargic? The longer he lived here, the more he thirsted for a real sky, real rain, not this summoned water that sprinkled down from this blue canopy at the predetermined time.

"Don't you long to see the land of your ancestors?"

"Why bother, it's all overrun by humans, anyway."

This remark made Lloreanthoran sit straight. He wasn't certain he had heard the lad correctly. "Pardon?"

"The humans drove us away," Kyrreandros explained patiently. "They started their petty war to drive us off and claim our lands for themselves."

"They did?" He fought against raising his voice. How much manure did parents feed their children?

"The slaves rose against us and won."

"No."

"Master, how can you deny history?"

"History!" Lloreanthoran spat. "You weren't even born when human wizards fought each other!"

"They wanted us..."

"They didn't care for us!" he snapped. "Bystanders. We were innocent bystanders, nothing more, nothing less."

"But they were our slaves," protested the young elf.

"They hadn't been slaves of ours for a long time, and there was no rebellion, no uprising. They just grew up and we helped them along the way."

"And the destruction of Honas Graigh?"

"An accident."

"How can the destruction of a city be an accident?"

Lloreanthoran sighed, he had asked the same question over and over when Aureenal and Lilanthias had died, but had made his peace with those events shortly after the creation of the realm of elves.

This abomination of an elven realm.

"The human wizards fought, spell by spell, and, when none of them could win supremacy over their kin, they summoned dragons..."

"They pierced the Veil of Fire?"

"Aye. And so, dragon fought dragon in the skies while wizard battled wizard on the ground. It was humans and us who put an end to it. We could abide their fighting no more; too many lives had already been lost. Most were human not elven.

"But," he leaned forward, "isn't this something you should have been told by your parents?"

"They told me the slaves revolted and forced us back. Others claim the same things you do, but they are of minor families and have no position."

"So only those of power tell the truth?"

Kyrreandros frowned. "I don't know," he finally said.

"When you do know your studies will continue, until then you are relieved." With a wave of his hand he dismissed both student and tea-mug.

The young elf stood and sulked out.

"Damn them all!" the wizard cursed. "Lies and deception, it seems my race is only capable of such."

"And intrigue," a voice added.

Lloreanthoran jumped up and whirled around, scanning the room for intruders. His right hand blazed, ready with a spell of destruction. He saw no one. "Who are you? Show yourself!"

"Dismiss the magic, I come in peace," the unseen intruder said with a raspy voice.

A mental command sent the summoned force away.

"Splendid." The shadows cast by the flickering mage-candles coalesced into a grey-tinted, female spiritform.

For a moment Lloreanthoran frowned, fighting the urge to throw himself to the ground and supplicate the being. It passed. Instead, he felt a slight trickle down his legs as his bladder emptied itself.

What was this creature, he wondered as he tried to hide his consternation and embarrassment.

Another part of his mind was reeling in terror, begging for forgiveness of his mistress. "I am no slave!" he finally snarled.

"Aye, you are not," the spirit confirmed.

Despite the being's reassurance he felt weak, his urge to kneel unbroken. "What foul sorcery is this?"

"I can't undo what my people did."

"You are one of the masters?" Lloreanthoran caught himself as he started to whimper like an ailing dog.

"That and more, and I need your help." The spirit sounded tired.

"Who are you?"

"I go by many names," she smiled sadly. "Some called me Deceiving Whore. Your people called me Lainthraght."

"The Lightbringer!" Now Lloreanthoran fell to his knees.

"Gods, I thought I had taken care of this supplication nonsense!" she howled in frustration. "Breeding between those whom I helped and the ones that your people freed didn't suffice. No matter. Stand up! I need someone of action, not a yapping dog!"

Confused, he rose and looked at the translucent figure standing before him. "What do you wish me to do?"

"I need your help," the female stated.

"Doing what?"

"To correct a mistake your people and I made."

His confusion only increased. "The Aerant C'lain?"

"Aye, but hurry, time is running short. Seek me out in the world beyond."

Then she was gone, whisked away by whatever magic she had used to enter the realm of elves. Irritated, Lloreanthoran formed a spell to clean the urine off the floor and his garments. The minor spell, the slight touch of magic returned his focus.

The Lightbringer. She had spoken to him. He remembered the legends, how she had gifted his people with freedom and taught them magic. Now she needed his help. For what, he could only guess.

He sent his consciousness to the one person he knew would surely help him receive the permission to leave: Julathaen.

He felt the brief resistance of the mage's wards before they admitted him. The ancient mage sensed his presence immediately and turned to greet him.

"Welcome, old friend," Julathaen smiled warmly. "What brings you here at this late hour?"

He could hardly contain his excitement. In brief sentences he told the council leader what had transpired. The ancient elf's smile faded to a grim line of his lips. "So, she has come again," Julathaen said.

"Again? She came to us after our fight for freedom?"

"Twice." The council leader scratched his chin.

"Why haven't I ever heard of this?"

Julathaen's reply came fast, without a hint of the infamous elven deliberation. "We didn't deem it wise. The second time she came during our greatest peril since the rebellion. It was she who closed what wasn't meant to ever be opened again."

At this Lloreanthoran frowned. "She closed the gate?"

"Indeed."

He thought he knew all about the greatest failure of his people, but this fact upset his entire view on their faults. "You couldn't have done it without her?"

"We hardly knew what we had done," replied Julathaen.

"Our lore seekers deciphered some formulae carved into an ancient temple wall we had found, and being curious they followed the instructions. Much blood flowed that day."

"You were there?"

"Aye."

Lloreanthoran had always known the council leader to be old, but he, until now, had not known how old Julathaen really was. "I would like to hear more about this, later," he said. "There are more pressing matters at hand."

"Such as?"

"The Lightbringer wants me to return to the world we left behind. There I am to find out more."

"Has the old witch found a new pawn then?" Julathaen shook his head, a slight smirk distorting his features.

"Pawn?"

"Indeed, but no matter, you know that we need a good reason for the others to allow you to leave. To them the Lightbringer is a fiery tale. You need a more plausible reason, something the fools will accept."

He would have taken a step back, hearing his mentor and superior talk about their peers like this. "But, sir..." he began, only to be interrupted by Julathaen.

"Ah, don't give me that nonsense. You know as well as I do that the petty feuds our houses enjoyed while in a real world have increased tenfold since we built our little paradise. They spread lies and dissent whenever they can. And don't look as if you don't know what I'm talking about! You have seen it yourself. Yes, yes, I may have agreed to create this realm, I may have devised the spells that keep it standing, but do I like it? Horse manure!"

Lloreanthoran was glad that his spiritform couldn't show his excitement. Never before had he heard Julathaen swear.

"You were there; what choice did we have? We who think it the epitome of silliness to run and hide from the world. We need a plan, a hook to dangle before the Council members who prefer our isolation. Even the dwarves in their mountains are more in touch with the world than we are!"

"The Tomes of Darkness inside the Aerant C'lain,"

Lloreanthoran said after a moment of thought.

"You want to reclaim the books?" Despite his age, the old elf began to pace. "Good, good."

"Aye, but there is more: a mindstorm surrounds the tomb, Bright-Eyes told me."

"Mindstorm?" Julathaen frowned. "What could've possibly disturbed the tomb?"

"I know not. Bright-Eyes also told me about a war that supposedly made the Wizard War look like child's play."

At that, Julathaen stopped pacing. "By the gods," he whispered, eyes wide. "Idiot humans! That changes things! I convene the Council, immediately."

CHAPTER 24

Thirteenth of Chill, 1475 K.C.

Kildanor wandered through the sleeping city. Nerran had left Dunthiochagh immediately upon learning the depth of Jathain's betrayal, and the Chosen had been anxious since Nerran's departure. He had seen the older warrior and his Riders off even before the corpse of Drangar Ralgon had been taken to the small shrine Kildanor maintained inside the Palace. The young spy, Jesgar, rode with Nerran, as it was Duasonh's hope the younger man could learn from the older.

"I hope the geezer knows what he's doing," he muttered as he approached North Gate. Night had already taken the city in its icy hold and, to his surprise, the sturdy steeloak portals usually closed at dusk stood open, guardsmen milling about the entryway.

He quickened his pace and arrived when the sentinels admitted a white, rider-less yet fully saddled horse. A moment later he saw the mutt that held the steed's reins firmly in its mouth. At this Kildanor arched an eyebrow. The mount didn't seem to mind being led by the canine, but shied away from a guard seeking to take hold of the bridle. The dog followed suit and growled at the offending man, while keeping the rein in its jaws.

The warden of the guard saw his approach and saluted. "Sir," he said.

Kildanor nodded. "Report."

"Sir, we spotted horse and dog a few moments ago."

The Chosen glanced at the animals and frowned. "Where

did they come from?"

"The Shadowswamp by the look of it." Both had dried mud on their legs.

He left the warden behind and walked over to the two warriors who tried to calm the beasts. The pair had little success. The white horse eyed the guardsmen warily, while the mutt bared his teeth, growling at them. Aside from the other warriors who shifted their attention between the land beyond the city walls and the two curious animals, the commotion had attracted a score of onlookers.

At the warden's signal, two more guards left the gatehouse and held the gathering crowd back. Kildanor approved the man's order with a brief nod, and then turned his attention to the animals. When the dog looked at him with thoughtful eyes, he took a step back.

Take me to him.

He heard the voice clearly, but it was apparent that no one else had. It seemed as if the dog had spoken. He shook his head. "Impossible."

The mutt didn't take her eyes off of him.

I must see him! The dog barked.

Kildanor turned to the warriors who stood at the ready, awaiting the warden's command. He was known to the city's military but held no official rank. Theoretically, any Pike or Sword or Bow outranked him. Thus, it was natural for the guardsmen to look to their superior for guidance. To his surprise the warden turned to him.

"Sir, what'll we do?"

"Close the gate, do your duty. I take care of them." He nodded toward the two animals.

"Make it so," the man ordered.

The Chosen walked over to the curious pair and, following a sudden inspiration, held out his hand. The dog trotted toward him; a slight tug at the rein caused the horse to follow. When the two animals reached him, the canine let go of the rein. Kildanor caught it, shaking his head in astonishment. A moment later he walked back to the Palace, horse and dog followed him obediently.

"You can't allow this mutt into the chapel." Braigh's voice was firm.

He hadn't expected anything else. Not that he necessarily disagreed with the Caretaker. So far, none of the servants had been able to restrain the animal, he was reluctant to use brute force on it, but after all, this was a shrine dedicated to his god, not Braigh's.

"It won't leave," he stated, pointing first at the growling mutt, then at the corpse. "He probably was its master. His presence here isn't proper, but what harm can it do?"

The dog watched the exchange with an intensity that Kildanor had never seen in an animal. He turned his attention back to Braigh, brows raised. "My guess is it won't leave this spot until we allow her access."

At this the mutt whimpered, drawing both men's looks.

"The second rite is about to begin" Braigh sounded weary.

Kildanor shrugged and shook his head. "I don't see the danger of having a dog near him." He nodded to the corpse lying on a table. "And I doubt it'll gnaw on him, either."

The dog growled.

"It isn't right."

"You sound like a priest of Lesganagh I once knew." He chuckled, then realized how embarrassed Braigh had to feel and regained a measure of composure.

"You think this is all a joke, don't you? I celebrate this nonsense because Cumaill asked me to."

The Chosen began to respond but was halted by the priest.

"Are you aware that merely guiding this corpse through the ritual has caused me to fall out of favor with my superiors? And you stand there and mock me!" spat the Caretaker. "You might as well start laughing into Duasonh's face!"

"I was unfair, please forgive me." Kildanor surprised himself with these words. He genuinely had come to respect Braigh, but he was all too aware of how old habits are very hard to kill. Still, this halted Braigh's tirade and left the Caretaker gaping.

"Very well," the priest relented. "The mutt can enter when

the second rite is done."

"Thank you," Kildanor said, and meant it.

He paid the ritualistic homage to the dead, as custom demanded. Lesganagh's faith might be banned, but Braigh, who was now a crucial part of a rite given to the world by Lesganagh ages ago, didn't mind. Nor did Kildanor expect him to report this or anything else to his superiors. A part of him felt for the Caretaker; after all he knew what it was like to be persecuted. He began to like the man.

As he bowed to the naked corpse a second time, he halted, bent closer, and inspected the cut that had laid bare Drangar Ralgon's innards. Squinting, he tried to clear away the sleepiness that already threatened to overwhelm him. Were his eyes deceiving him or was the dim light playing tricks?

"Did anyone else touch the body?" Kildanor asked, looking up at Braigh.

The priest frowned at him, while he rinsed the bloodied cloth he had used to clean the corpse. "No one."

"Odd," the Chosen muttered.

"What is it?"

Kildanor straightened and scratched his scalp. "Must be the light."

"What is it?" insisted Braigh, stepping closer to the bier.

"I'm not sure, but I think this wound was wider when we brought him in." He pointed at the large gash that split the corpse's midsection wide open.

"I'll be damned," Braigh muttered and began to pace around the table. "I think you're right."

Turning to the priest, Kildanor said, "You and me both."

The Caretaker shook his head, obviously as confused as the Chosen felt. Braigh stopped and looked from Ralgon to him and back again. "It's unfortunate we can't ask any priests of Lesganagh about this," he said. "Maybe Lord Duasonh, Cumaill, has something in his library."

"Did I hear a trace of regret there?"

The priest's smile was weak, but he nodded.

"Maybe I'll find something," the Chosen said. "I think we should halt the ceremony for the time being."

"Not like he will leave anytime soon," said the Caretaker with a smirk.

At that Kildanor broke out in quiet laughter. "Aye." Still chuckling, he left the chapel.

It was dark and cold.

Voices drifted toward him. Or so Drangar thought. After the years in his hut he knew loneliness, but he had chosen that life. At least he had chosen life. He had been weak, frightened, and alone; and there had been no one to soothe the pain.

The one who could have held him was gone.

Now he stood or floated in blackness, hearing voices again. The voices were faint, unlike those he had heard after Dunthiochagh. He couldn't discern the words, but they were around him. Much like this void, intangible and uncaring.

Drangar had never bothered with timekeeping, those were things for farmers, and in this blackness, he had nothing to judge its passage anyway. It could've been days or weeks, although it hardly mattered. He was dead.

"Maybe there are no gods at all." He had lost count of the times he'd said this sentence. It didn't matter.

Even if they were around, what could he expect from any of them? The last time he had truly prayed had been in Dunthiochagh. Anything that had meant something in his life had found its end in that city. In a way, he had died there as well. He should have died there. Now it was too late for any regrets, Lliania's Scales would not judge him.

Maybe his life, his soul was too heavy even for her.

CHAPTER 25

Jesgar was both excited and confused. Why would the Baron send him on a mission when he was not yet ready to perform as a courtier? He enjoyed that Duasonh trusted him, but he was anxious all the same.

"Don't worry, lad," Lord Nerran had said with a bright smile, "you'll learn something."

So far, the only thing he had learned was that he knew nothing about horses. He was sore, his back ached, and his legs felt as if the skin was in tatters.

At noon the Riders arrived at Falcon's Creek, the first of four garrisons maintained by Baron Duasonh along the Harail road was still a mile or so away, but stood clear against the blue horizon. Nerran stretched his back and winked at Jesgar. "Ever been this far out?"

"No, milord," he said, feeling slightly ashamed. "The farthest away from home was the Shadowswamp."

"Which is almost at our doorstep nowadays," grumbled the older man. "My da used to tell me of the times when there was no swamp, and you had to go around the Shadowpeaks. When I was a wee lad there still was some snow on some of the highest summits. Now there are just those abysmal clouds and the endless rain." He spat. "Bloody wizards." Lord Nerran looked at the fortress and frowned. "See anything amiss here, lads?"

Despite being addressed as part of the group, Jesgar knew the question was directed at him. He looked at the crenellated walls, the massive towers and gatehouse, and then to the flag of House Duasonh whipping in the autumn breeze. Nothing seemed amiss, no obvious damage to the structure, and he made out a handful of guards, mere smudges against the merlons, but moving nonetheless.

"No smoke, the colors are flying, and the place is guarded," he finally said.

"Aye," Lord Nerran agreed, "but I want to be sure. You four," he pointed at a few Riders, "circle the place and report anything unusual." After the horsemen had given their affirmative, he turned to Jesgar. "You'll get over there and take a closer look."

"At once, milord," he replied and dismounted. The first thing he did when his feet touched the ground was to stretch his legs to loosen cramped muscles. Then he was off, sprinting toward the fortress. Moving unnoticed through a city at nighttime was nothing like approaching a fortified position unobserved while several sentinels were holding watch. It was a challenge, and Jesgar was willing to rise to the occasion. He rushed along a bank of thornleaves that lined a hilltop, and then used a stone outcrop of another tor to cover his further advance. A bird, probably a hawk, called from behind, and another replied from up front.

He was near to the fort now and saw Lord Nerran and his twenty Riders had closed the distance and were chatting animatedly with the guards.

"And? Can you see me lad?" the older man shouted up to the warriors manning the gatehouse.

"No, milord," came the reply. A few moments later the man added, "The chaps on the towers don't see him either."

"He either got lost, or he is really of some use as a scout, sir," said another voice.

Bastards, Jesgar thought.

This was a test, nothing more, the hawk calls had probably been a prearranged signal, and Nerran already knew all was in order.

"We'll wait until the boy Garinad shows up," Lord Nerran announced. "I want to speak with the warleader. And some wine for me lads." This last statement brought forth a small cheer from the Riders. Jesgar observed them as they dismounted and tied their horses to a few lances driven into the ground.

"I'll show them," he whispered and crawled on as the

warriors settled on the ground, waiting for their wine. When the garrison's warleader and a page carrying skins of wine arrived, he slowly made his way toward the north side of the castle. He might know little about scouting and the outdoors, but he knew shadows, and how to look out for people watching over places. To his frustration there were few enough spots where one could close in on the battlement, but finally he discovered a slight ravine that brought him within two paces of the earth-and-stone wall. So far, none of the guards were aware of his approach. Jesgar was proud of this achievement. Still, there were those last two paces. He huddled at the end of the gully and watched the sentries. There was a moment when the guards' attention lay... now!

He jumped up and hurried as silently as possible to the wall. Stealth on uneven, grassy ground was so different from the alleys of Dunthiochagh that for a moment he feared the guards heard his dash. No alarm was raised. He didn't quite know what to do next, but guessed the Riders would almost be done with their wine and Lord Nerran's conversation with the warleader was also drawing to a close. Then he had an idea, and crept along the wall, always making sure he stayed out of sight of the sentinels.

When he reached the northeastern corner of the stronghold Jesgar noticed something odd about the masonry. It was more uneven than the rest of the castle's foundation. The rest of the wall, so far, was smooth to prevent an easy escalade, but here it seemed as if this spot was meant to be climbed. He looked up, and saw this spot could only be seen by the northwestern tower, and in all likelihood the shadows cast by the rising sun wouldn't betray this crude ladder to any observer. Casual inspection wouldn't discover it either, and he had yet to meet the guardsman who, after a day of endless routine, would still pay attention to something he had always seen and perceived as normal.

His toothy grin preceded him, as he climbed the makeshift ladder. When he reached the top and swung over the parapet, the sole guard jumped back in astonishment. "You may raise the alarm now," the spy-in-training panted. "Lord Nerran and your warleader want to see this." Then, with a calm he did not really feel, Jesgar grabbed the woman's water-skin and drank.

"Well, lad, you proved one thing," the Paladin said when they were back in the saddle. Jesgar looked at the man and frowned. "You're as sneaky outside a city as you are inside."

Their stay at Falcon's Creek had been longer, because of his discovery of the hidden ladder. Lord Nerran had insisted that the craftsmen amongst the warriors start immediately on the repair of the wall. So, by late afternoon, accompanied by the sounds of hammers and chisels, they rode to Silver Meadows.

"You didn't really need me, did you, milord?" Jesgar wanted his suspicion confirmed, not that he minded, but still. Some things are better out in the open, and he reckoned this was one of those.

Lord Nerran looked at him and shook his head. "Not really, lad, but I am glad you're with us now. Justified your being here already. The Baron thought it wise to give you some time away from the city."

"So, I could learn?"

"That, but he wants me to teach you some heraldry." Jesgar's confusion must have shown, because the old warrior chuckled and shook his head. "Stuff about coats-of-arms, lad. Who is who and what is what, that sort of hogwash. Baron Duasonh wants you well-versed in this stuff so you can tell by a little stitching on one's tunic which House and which country he hails from."

He groaned. "More to learn!"

"Listen, lad, you'll always learn new things anyway, every day. And your discovery of that little stair shows me you have a decent mind, why not use it? If you don't want to use it..." He looked at his men. "We won't stop you if you want to bugger off like a pansy-assed coward."

His shock must have shown as well, for Lord Nerran and his score of Riders laughed. "No, I am no deserter."

Lord Nerran cleared his throat, guided his horse to Jesgar's and patted him on the back. "Lad, you wanted to become part of this, best get used to learning lots."

He nodded, and rode on in silence. There was so much he

did not know, and although the task was daunting, he wanted to learn. Riding with these hardened veterans, being in their company, and feeling accepted as an equal, was worth it.

CHAPTER 26

Ealisaid awoke with a splitting headache. Her mouth and throat were parched, her tongue felt like a lump of meat. Also, her arms were tied behind her back, and her fingers seemed encased in solid iron. As she tried to move her arms the slightest fraction of an inch, she discovered that the pain in her head was nothing compared to that of her shoulders. The chains that bound her arms were attached to some hoops in the wall and she had basically spent however long it had been since the alley on her knees with her body held in place by chains and arms. Struggle was useless, and most of her magic needed gestures.

From what little she could tell, there was also a strange taste on her tongue. Not only taste but feeling as well. She could breathe; moving her tongue, if only to probe her teeth, was impossible. If she strained her eyes, she was able to see the black wires that lay on her cheeks and penetrated her mouth. She could guess what those were for, and it also explained the metallic taste. Whoever her captors were, they had effectively crippled her, magically and physically.

The dim illumination of her cell was amplified by the glow of a flame that came closer; she heard footsteps. The hallway distorted the echoing sounds, but she guessed two people were coming her way.

Then, as the torchlight flickered bright, Ealisaid could discern a pair of shapes in its glare. "She's awake," one of them, the taller one, said. Her eyes adjusted to the light, and she saw the two men more clearly. One was built well, muscular, with short-cropped hair, and a look in his eyes that was honest, and hostile. The other man, slightly smaller than his companion, had broad shoulders, graying black hair, and his midsection proof of the well-fed life he led. Their attire was similar: dark, earthen colors. Yet the bigger man also had House Duasonh's falcon embroidered on his lapel.

"So she is," the younger man said.

"Any suggestions?" the other replied.

"Aside from the usual? No. And I'm quite sure had you wanted that, she'd already be dead."

So, the pair was not contemplating her death, but they might have done so before, and the idea that common men had thought about killing a Phoenix Wizardess was plain insulting.

"How dare you!" she wanted to shout, but her tied tongue only let mad ramblings past her lips.

"Well, Lord Baron," the younger man said, his voice edged with menacing humor, "we could tell her what happened."

The other man nodded, "You're right." He faced her. "You are in the Palace of Dunthiochagh; I am Cumaill of House Duasonh, Baron of Boughaighr, and Higher Cherkont. I don't know how you got here; I don't care who you are; I don't care what you have been doing here, aside from killing fifteen people and doing a whole lot of damage to quite a few buildings. Know this, woman; you will remain here until I judge you. If you're hoping for a rescue, know you are the last of your kind."

Ealisaid stared at the man claiming to be Baron Duasonh. She could see some resemblance to the Baron who ruled over Dunthiochagh, but this man could surely not be him. The Baron was a young man, in his early thirties; this man had seen more than forty summers at the least. The last of her kind? The man wanted to unsettle her, break her. She could not be the last of the Phoenix Wizards. Even if she had been unable to contact anyone in the enclave, there had to be others like her.

As she contemplated this, the one accompanying the impostor Baron stepped forward. "Know this, wench, I am Kildanor, Chosen of Lesganagh, and what Lord Duasonh told you is true. The Wizards are no more; I killed the last of them in the Shadowpeaks. How you managed to escape the War is beyond me, but I don't care. You will stand trial for the people you killed and for the property you destroyed. For that you need to be alive." He smiled as he said, "Your choice, gagged and starving, unable to use your magic, or you give us your word of honor—Baron Duasonh thinks it means something. I know better, but it is his decision—to refrain using magic and eat. What say you? Nod if you agree to the terms, or remain as you are. If you break your word I will hunt you down and kill you without a trial." She gave a slight, hesitant nod.

Kildanor gave the impostor Duasonh a skeptical look, and, after the man grunted his approval, opened the cell door. With deft moves he unhooked the contraption binding her tongue and mouth, then, almost gently, he held a mug to her lips and began to pour. She gulped greedily. Water, cold and clear, and although she could feel it soaking the front of her dress she closed her eyes, enjoying the relief it brought.

When Ealisaid had sated her thirst, she again looked up at the two men and tried to speak. Nothing but a sore croak escaped her lips.

As if he could read her thoughts the impostor Duasonh said, "Your speech will return, the physicians assured me. The tongue-bond dried up your mouth and throat. So, until you can utter more than this, know that you won't be harmed..."

"...yet," Kildanor interrupted.

She saw a flicker of annoyance on the impostor's face. "Yet," he concurred. "You have murdered, and destroyed homes; even if this wasn't a time of war, those crimes are punishable by death. You will stand trial, and I assure you it will be fair, although the outcome will be the same."

All she could do was listen and nod, play along with the game. This had to be a prank played on her by the other apprentices. The Phoenix Wizards could not be dead. Even if everything about the situation was unusual. The state of her home, the lack of communication with her superiors, seemed to indicate that something was amiss, but she refused to believe that her order was destroyed.

"You'll be fed," Kildanor said.

"And several guards will be close by, should you decide to ignore the terms," the other man added.

Then, after they had locked the cell door again, both left her alone with her thoughts.

Her bonds merely encased her hands and arms, allowing her to stand and move, even though sleeping in any position other than upright would likely prove impossible. Dizziness claimed her, as she rose to look out the small, barred window inside the door, and it took several deep breaths before she managed to stay on her feet. For a moment she wondered how long she had already been inside this cell, but glancing at her gown she realized it could not have been that long. Hunger and exhaustion ruled Ealisaid's body and mind, but finally she managed to hobble to the door and look out.

There wasn't much to see. A similar door across from her, and stout walls, interrupted by more doors, up and down the long corridor. She heard the water dripping down the ceiling into puddles. This truly was a prison, not some illusion, she decided, and with that realization the tiniest flicker of doubt crept into her mind. Could the man be Baron Duasonh? Could the men, women and children she had flung away like ragdolls have been real? This doubt was quickly overshadowed by the rising dread that she was alone, in a world where the Phoenix Wizards were no more. If the Wizards were gone, how long had she been in hibernation? Was there anyone left who would still remember her? What had happened to her parents and siblings?

The prospect of a quick death, so strange, surreal, just mere heartbeats ago, seemed almost welcoming. What could be left for her in a world where her family, friends, and her fellow Wizards were no more? If the man she thought an impostor was truly who he claimed to be, then the man she knew as Baron Duasonh must have been dead for a while. Was he his son? Then the hibernation had lasted, instead of the supposed fourteen days, more than fifty years! If this man was the grandson... she refused to follow this thought to its conclusion. Although wizardry had set her apart from her family, she had still belonged. Now she was alone.

CHAPTER 27

"What the bleeding Scales do you think you are doing?" Kildanor barked at Cumaill Duasonh. He was furious at the younger man. Wizards had brought more harm than good to the lands, here or elsewhere. The Shadowpeaks had been the main stronghold of the Phoenix Wizards, but not the only one. Even now, a century later, merchants and minstrels who passed through town told of battles that had been fought in places he had never seen or heard of before. Whenever he heard some of the tales, he felt small, insignificant. As a young man he had never ventured far, and in the aftermath of the Heir War there hadn't been the chance to see more of the world. No matter where the storytellers hailed from, no matter how dreadful the tales of woe were, one look at the shattered mountains north of Dunthiochagh was enough to prove that the fighting here had probably been the worst.

Now Cumaill let the sorceress live.

The Baron shook his head. "We have just gotten our hands on a potent weapon, my friend."

Kildanor held up his hand. He had feared Duasonh would think along those lines. "True, an army out there that has already taken much of the realm, but to think you could control this wizard, or any other for that matter, is madness."

The room they were in was a small study, set aside for clandestine meetings, conversations none of the servants or courtiers could be privy to. He sat down on one of the chairs and buried his face in his hands. "You have no idea what she is capable of."

"Oh, but I do," the Baron replied happily. "I've lived in sight of the Shadowpeaks all my life, and I know that the gorge rent through the mountains is unnatural. I've also seen the damage this woman alone has done to my people and their houses. But think of the possibilities!"

Kildanor's head snapped up. "A wizard on a battlefield is a sight I would not wish upon my worst enemy. Only the oldest controlled the fury they unleashed. This child, she can barely control what she has summoned. We should be grateful what she called wasn't a firewraith or a dragon. With her lack of experience either beast would have laid this city to waste! Scales, she collapsed after what should have been easy work to her. Trust in catapults and the skill in arms, not in sorcery. Flesh and blood and steel win battles. Wizards can't be controlled, Cumaill."

"I will use whatever is available to me, and if this woman can take some of the Chanastardhians with her when her magic kills her, so much the better."

Kildanor understood his friend's desire to use whatever means necessary to fight the invaders, but to bring sorcery to the battlefield was not the same as recruiting a new band of bows or swords. "Magic is more powerful, yes," he said as he traced the seam of his tunic, "but you will have the guilds and all captains against you." He paused for a moment before he spoke again. "Not only them, but think of the victims' families, of the churches. Damn, do you think Braigh will tolerate your actions? Or the Lawspeakers?"

"I'll do what I have to," Duasonh said. His voice had taken on the same steely quality the Chosen knew well when his friend was determined to pursue a path. "The people will fall in line."

"We are better prepared than Harail." He knew it was a weak argument, especially with Jathain's failed rebellion only a few days past.

"We don't have any confirmed numbers regarding the enemy's strength," the Baron said as he began to pace the length of the room. "We don't know what kind of hidden doorways my cousin left behind for the Chanastardhians. And who is to say there aren't more of his accomplices left within the city?"

"Anything we could retrieve from the rubble of his room?" Kildanor asked although he already knew the answer. Aside from the list of contacts Jesgar Garinad had stolen from the smuggler's hideout, there was not so much as a scrap of paper left whole in Jathain's study or chambers.

"My cousin was thorough," Duasonh grumbled. "Think the Wizardess could help?"

The thought had crossed Kildanor's mind, but he'd dismissed it on the grounds that the woman had collapsed after just the bit of magic she had used to blast her path through two buildings.

"She might," he finally said. The Chosen wanted to say more, when he felt the Calling. His brothers had need of him. "Ask her," he said, stood, and added, "But first you need to convince the others that this is a risk worth taking."

Before Cumaill could speak again, he left the study. He needed solitude and sunlight to focus on the message. The sun was setting, so the appropriate place to be was one of the towers on the western side of the Palace's battlements. Servants, clerks, warriors, and courtiers passed as he hurried through the hallways, down the stairs and onto the inner bailey. He ignored the greetings some of them muttered, ignored the salutes a few of the men and women he had fought to free the Palace, his mind racing.

A Calling. Such a thing hadn't happened in years, and the last time was well before his banishment from Harail.

Despite being Second of the Chosen, his status wasn't as valued as Orkeanas'. He was just second of a score and two, not the leader. Nothing in the past decades had demanded his attention. So why now? Why call him now when Chanastardh had invaded... he stopped abruptly.

Could it be that ...? No, he dismissed the thought immediately. Who would dare?

There had to be another reason. When he reached the western rampart, he ascended one of the towers and looked to the west. "I'm listening," Kildanor whispered. And listen he did.

CHAPTER 28

"We'll reach Dragoncrest Castle tomorrow," Lord Nerran said as he dismounted.

Until this moment Jesgar had thought the weapon training with Baron Duasonh's men had been very harsh, but now he knew better. He was no horseman, barely knew how to ride such a beast, and yet he had sat in a saddle for almost an entire day. His back, rear, and legs felt like one big bruise, and when he tried to lift himself off the horse, he fell like a sack of grain. "I'll just remain here," he grunted, the ground felt safe and comforting.

The Riders laughed and began to set up camp. Jesgar watched as they, albeit stiffly, moved about their business much like he and his brother had done after a hard day at the forge. Riding a horse seemed casual with them, but would they feel like he did were they to stand a day in a smithy? That thought gave him the focus to sit up, if they could still walk and talk, so could he.

"That's the spirit, lad," Lord Nerran grinned and held out a hand to pull him up to his legs. "You need to keep moving; otherwise you'll be of no use to us tomorrow."

Today they had inspected the strongholds of Silver Meadows and Rainbow Ford, and after his discovery of the hidden steps that led up the wall of the castle at Falcon's Creek all of the men knew what to look for. The traitor Jathain had tampered with all of the fortresses' walls, but Jesgar agreed with Lord Nerran that finding and destroying the ladders was more important than searching for the man responsible. Jathain would almost be in Harail by now, and if the handholds were removed at least part of the traitor's plan was thwarted. There had been some desertions, but it seemed that not one man loyal to Jathain was left in the castles.

Jesgar stood and winced as he tried to stretch his back. "Bloody horses," he grumbled.

"Nothing wrong with the horses, lad," the older man said with a chuckle. "You just ain't used to them." The warrior looked at him and shook his head. "You need to straighten up." And without a word of warning he drew Jesgar into a hug, wound his arms around his lower back, and pulled. He howled in pain as he felt his spine pop into place. "See?" the warrior released him, grinning widely. "That's better, eh?"

"I'll tell you when my ears stop ringing," Jesgar grunted, but already he felt the pain lessening. "How can you stand being in the saddle for so long?"

"Ah, lad, when you've spent as much time riding as I have, you can even sleep while your horse just walks on."

He didn't want to consider that idea. There was something oddly comforting about the thought of sleeping on a cold stone floor, compared to resting on the back of a horse. "I'll never get used to that," he muttered.

One of the other riders, a man named Briog, came up to them. "Mate, you better get used to it."

Jesgar looked at the tall, blond, older looking man and frowned. "Why's that? I'm no horseman."

Briog looked to the leader and shrugged. "You want to tell him?"

"Nah, lad, you do it. I'll set up the guards, and pick a cook for supper." The old warrior turned and walked toward the camp where Riders had begun tethering the horses and starting a fire.

"Don't let Gavyn anywhere near the pots!" Briog called.

"Never! Not even if my life depended on it!" Lord Nerran's reply was equally loud, and Gavyn, the youngest of them, muttered something unintelligible, much to the amusement of the others.

Jesgar chuckled along with the rest of the party, and immediately felt the pain in his back returning. He hissed and was rewarded with an amused snort from Briog.

"It gets better," the warrior said. Then he added, "After a while that is." He looked at Jesgar and chuckled. "First time outside the city-walls?"

The spy nodded. "All the other times I could still see the walls. That doesn't count, does it?"

"No, not really." Briog walked to Jesgar's horse and began to remove the saddle. "I'll do this for you, tonight. By tomorrow you have to take care of your horse yourself, understood?" The warrior hit the mare on her rump when she started to inch away. "Hold the reins, will you?"

Jesgar complied. "How long have you been riding with Lord Nerran?" he asked. He was curious about the old, fatherly, yet distant warrior.

"A couple of years," Briog replied, hoisting saddle and blanket off the horse's back.

Silent, he waited for the man to continue. Instead of talking, Briog opened one of the saddlebags and retrieved something that looked like a small, bent poker. "Ever scraped a horse's hooves clean?" the rider asked, taking hold of the reins.

Even though he had worked in a smithy for most of his life, he had never done such. Ben had always taken care of the horses, so the only thing he knew about them was how to beat the iron into horseshoes. Jesgar shook his head.

"A day you learn something new is a day well spent," Briog said and handed him the scraper. "Just stand next to her, facing her rear end. Then gently grab her lower leg, she'll do the rest. When her hoof is up, just scratch out the dirt and you're done."

He followed the instructions, and indeed it was easy, aside from his legs and back still protesting whenever he moved. The mare seemed used to the procedure, and within a few moments all four hooves were clean. "Done," he said.

"Next time, just remember not to move around the horse's back," Briog said with a hoot. "Some aren't as docile as our girl here. Some do kick. My brother got one in the head once, and he couldn't see straight for a few days."

Jesgar blanched. "I'll remember that."

"Now you rub her down. Get that piece of cloth from your

kit when you return the scraper, make sure the bugger is free of dirt, mind you."

He replaced the tool in the saddlebag and pulled out a two-foot square of blanket, there wasn't much else in the bag. "And now?"

"Now you rub her down, top to bottom."

"What for?" he wondered aloud.

"We didn't do any galloping today, but after a day of hard riding, horses, like men, get wet. They sweat like us, you see. If they don't get a chance to get rid of that sweat they'll catch a cold, sometimes."

He realized Briog hadn't really answered his question, yet, and while he began to rub down the mare, he repeated his query. "So how long have you been in Lord Nerran's warband?"

The warrior stroked the horse's muzzle and looked at Jesgar. "He usually doesn't like people calling him Lord Nerran. To us he's just Nerran. One of the lads, you know? I've been riding with him for the better part of twenty years, I think."

"Always for Dunthiochagh?" Jesgar kneeled to wipe down the mare's front leg.

"Nah, Nerran was always busy doing this and that for one lord or another."

"He's not from Dunthiochagh?" he stood and wiped along his steed's back.

"Top to bottom, mate," Briog said. Jesgar complied. "Oh, he is from the city, sure enough, but he ain't the sort to get caught up in all those politics."

"So, what did he do?" the spy asked.

"He, and most of us for that matter, were traveling, looking for trouble, that sort of thing, you know?"

It seemed as if Briog avoided the heart of the matter. Jesgar decided to be diplomatic; after all, he did have experience with learning what he wanted to from people reluctant to talk. "So, what did you mean with me getting used to long rides?" he changed the topic.

"Well," the warrior said and scratched his chin. "It's like this; Dragoncrest is furthest away from the city, and closest to Harail. If I were the Chanastardhian general I'd get my troops moving to Dunthiochagh as soon as possible before winter comes. That general probably still believes Jathain is with us and that he'll open the gates." Briog paused and scratched his chin again. "See, you don't want to lay siege to a city in winter."

"He won't bother with the castles?" Jesgar said, more to himself than to the warrior.

"Not if he can take the city before the snows come. But that's just it, to claim the city before it starts snowing, he has to move fast. Gods know it's already getting crisp and cold."

He moved around the horse's front to the other side and began to move the cloth up and down the mare's left flank.

"Ah, you're catching on," Briog said.

"So, you think the enemy is already on the move?" Jesgar concluded the other man's thought.

"Aye. He'd be stupid not to get his troops moving. And if we see their vanguard it'll probably be too late for us. Dragoncrest will have scouts out so if we're lucky, we get a warning and can make for Dunthiochagh at a decent speed. If not, it will be slightly quicker, with no rest."

Jesgar groaned, partly because of his aching back, partly because of the thought of spending more time than he already had in the saddle.

"You'll get used to it," Briog said, winking.

"So, what did you do when traveling with Nerran?" He hoped to get an answer. The warrior appeared to have let his guard down.

"Why, in Lesganagh's name, do you want to know?" the rider growled. "Pretty nosey for one so young, aren't you?"

"I just..."

"You just want to know, eh? Tell you what, mate. We all know who and what you are. Nerran told us. Duasonh trusts Nerran, Nerran trusts us. You should trust the Baron's judgment, after all he made you." Briog spat and thrust the reins back into Jesgar's hand. "Once you've proven your mettle, ask again, and any of us will answer, until then, shut your trap and learn. Understood?"

Dumbfounded, all he could do was nod and watch the warrior walk away. Getting information from a drunk in a tavern was easier than getting anything out of Briog, and he feared that the others might not be as gentle as this one in their dismissal. He only wanted to know what the bond was between the Riders; it wasn't that he didn't trust Nerran. He liked the old warrior. He just wanted to get to know him, learn from him.

Yeah, he was on his way to become the Baron's spy, and it startled him that Nerran had told his companions, but Cumaill Duasonh had not ordered him to spy on Nerran. He was just curious. The hurt and disappointment made him forget the pain his joints still felt, and when he walked to tether his mare with the other horses, he was certain the others were observing and talking about him.

"Don't fret, lad." Nerran's voice brought him out of his brooding, and Jesgar looked up at the old warrior. "We won't eat you, it's just that..." He paused and looked at him. "The lads and I have been together for a long time, we need to trust you." Jesgar was about to reply, but Nerran's raised hand cut him short. "No, lad, we do know you are on the Baron's side, so no worries there. We just need to know, for sure, if you're also on ours."

What the Scales was the man talking about?

"Aren't we all on the same side?" Jesgar hissed.

"In the fight to keep our homes the way they are, yes."

"But..." he protested.

"We mean you no harm, lad," Nerran interrupted. "Leave it at that, all right?" The older man pointed at the campfire, surrounded by his riders. "Fynbar did the cooking, and you better get some food before they've gobbled it all up."

Defeated, Jesgar could only nod and acknowledge his rumbling stomach. If they wanted to let him in on their secret, he was certain he'd be the first to know. He sat down, his legs and back again screaming in protest, and accepted a bowl handed to him by Briog.

"Thanks," he muttered and began to eat.

As Nerran had promised, the food was excellent.

CHAPTER 29

Fourteenth of Chill, 1475 K.C.

Julathaen had called the Council of Mages to assemble. It had been a while since the last meeting, and if past events were an indicator for what would soon happen, Lloreanthoran dreaded sitting in the House of Sorcery. Many wizards had perused the tomes in the huge marble library, but he avoided the place. Yes, it was bigger and more thorough than his own meager collection, a fact that Kyrreandros stated every other week, but he avoided the company of his fellow mages whenever he could.

Unlike most houses belonging to wizards, the House of Sorcery was plain, no fancy sigils or gems disturbed the pillars and walls, and since the elves also controlled the weather there was no roof.

Lloreanthoran knew it was customary to teleport to the meeting-chamber. His peers frowned upon walking, and to break with tradition once again, he opted to walk. The curious glances children and adults threw his way certainly would keep the rumor-mill running, but he didn't care. If all went as planned he would soon be out of this prison.

Despite his annoyance with this artificial world, the sight of the House's central pillar took his breath away when he turned a corner and walked up the path leading to the building. He had helped create the massive column. Even from this distance the magical construct made him feel insignificant. Without the pillar Graigh D'nar could not be; the world would simply collapse without it, much like a keystone in any arch.

As he came closer, Lloreanthoran's entire horizon seemed

to be occupied by the column, even the House appeared to huddle at its base. From one moment to the next, the light pulsing out from the top of the realm's foundation dimmed. Then it was gone. Night, as prescribed, replaced day. By now the rest of the Council was surely assembled, and the gossip and backstabbing would be in full swing. It was time for him to join his... colleagues.

He entered and spotted Julathaen, who looked much older than the image he had seen in spiritform earlier. Even by his race's standards, the wizards' leader was ancient. Rumors were that he had been around when Honas Graigh was founded and that his magical power was the only reason he still lived. Despite his age, or maybe because of it, the old wizard had held the position of chairman for over a thousand years, and because of this experience Lloreanthoran doubted there were many things that could still surprise him. The Lightbringer's appearance and the apparent threat that seemed to stem from the Tomes of Darkness, however, were among those things.

"Brother Lloreanthoran brought something to my attention that should have been noticed long before now," Julathaen said, his voice booming to drown out the hushed talks all along the table.

Lloreanthoran waited, etiquette demanded that he sit next to his peers, but he was in no mood for the gossip and intrigue that surely was taking place. He ignored the looks other wizards cast his way, and focused on the chairman.

"I have broken through the Veil of Dreams," Julathaen stated and spoke on before the protests grew too loud. "Into the past and present I looked, and what I saw was shocking." He paused for a moment and stood. "We have made a mistake, my friends." Lloreanthoran could hear a slight hesitation before the wizard said "friends" and caught a mischievous wink from the old elf that was certainly meant for him. "Who knows why the Aerant C'lain had been built so many centuries ago, and what its purpose was?" The younger wizard noticed how the other used the past tense in his question, and wondered if the others were keen enough to notice it as well.

Haqualonar, one of the older wizards, stood. "It was meant

to store the Tomes of Darkness, and the Stone of Blood."

Julathaen nodded, more to himself than to the wizard. "Indeed, that was one of its purposes."

"One of its purposes?" echoed another mage. Lloreanthoran was too astonished by this revelation to bother looking for the elf in question.

"Indeed," Julathaen said.

"What is the other purpose?" Haqualonar asked.

"To prevent the knowledge stored inside from ever being discovered and used again," the Council leader said. "There is more: I found out that the Aerant C'lain is surrounded by a field of terrible power, a mindstorm, and no scrying can discern whether its contents are still there. The soulward surrounding it is failing, and soon the power contained within the Tomes and the Stone can be used once more." He held up his hands to silence the muttering of the other mages. Lloreanthoran gasped, it was worse than he had suspected. Julathaen paused. It seemed as if the old wizard waited for the others to come to the conclusion themselves.

"What powers do the Tomes bear?" Rutharion, one of the younger wizards, asked.

"They teach anyone how to open a gateway to the realm of the First Ones beyond the Veil of Gloom," Julathaen replied. "And they have already been used once." Lloreanthoran added his voice to the communal gasp. "A human, one Danachamain, set out to plunder our old home. He and some of those who followed him were enticed by the power promised by the Tomes."

"How can mere words of magic promise power?" Rutharion asked, a trace of doubt in his voice.

"The writings we found on the walls of an ancient building," the chairman said, "told of immense power that would be gained by opening the door." He paused to sip some water. "An error in translation, I fear. The meaning of words the First Ones used changed over the millennia, and so we misinterpreted the inscriptions.

"What it really said was that power would be released again should the door be opened! The Lightbringer helped us bar the door once more. At great cost."

"And why is this our problem?" Rutharion asked.

Did these fools understand so little, Lloreanthoran wondered. He stepped toward the table and said, "Because we did not take the precautions necessary to prevent the knowledge being used again! Because the creators of the Aerant C'lain never foresaw the possibility of us abandoning Gathran and Honas Graigh!"

"How was it possible that the Tomes of Darkness were left behind in the first place?" an elf asked.

The assembly's response was silence.

Julathaen glared at his fellow wizards, challenging them. He dared them to raise their voices against him. "Well?"

"We all know that we forgot the Tomes and the Stone during the flight from our beloved city," Haqualonar said.

"I know that," Julathaen snapped. "But at that time, we didn't bother with the question of why they were left behind. Now the situation has changed. We need to recover both the Tomes and Stone!"

"And why should we all take the blame for this mishap?" Rutharion asked.

"Because we all are responsible!" the Council leader replied. "Because none of us remembered the Aerant C'lain, and now we have to deal with our unwanted legacy to the world. The tomb of knowledge is our responsibility! Also, the soulward is being corrupted and once it fails, the Tomes will be usable on a grander scale."

Clearing his throat, Rutharion said, "Why should I care? I didn't forget the tomb. Let the one responsible go to Honas Graigh and deal with the problem!"

"If that is so," Julathaen replied, anger seeping into his voice, "we will lead an inquiry until the culprit is found. I want to know who was responsible!"

The noise started to rise as the elves began to bicker. Lloreanthoran eyed the assembly, silently cursing the petty fights that always accompanied Council-Meetings. Of course, someone was responsible for the disaster and it was important to find this one person. In his experience the process of trying this wizard might well take over two years, a lot of time to waste. Time they might not have.

He walked over to Julathaen and talked in hushed tones, while the other elves bickered and continued their feuds in the hallowed halls of sorcery. The chairman made a small gesture and a shimmering globe of silence appeared around them, effectively cutting out the chatter of the other mages and allowing the two elder wizards to talk in private.

"You want to go on with this?" Julathaen asked.

Lloreanthoran looked down the table. The fighting ceased as the assembled elves looked at the two, wondering what they were talking about. "What other choice do we have? If you go, the fools will tear out their throats." Julathaen nodded. "If you send anyone else, the gods only know what he might do. Also," he continued, "the Lightbringer has spoken to me; she wants me to help."

"Are you ready to take the blame for this?" the older wizard frowned. "This could mean exile."

"You said we needed a hook, you have given us more than that," said Lloreanthoran, pointing at the assembly. "They have swallowed the bait. They don't care who is responsible, they all just want to see someone hang, preferably not themselves." He glanced at the wizardly mob as it started talking again.

"But it's time for us to take some responsibility for our actions," Lloreanthoran said. "We need to get our people out of this place."

"The poor children," Julathaen muttered absentmindedly.

"What?"

"The guardians of the Aerant C'lain."

"I don't understand," Lloreanthoran said.

"And I pray you never will."

He nodded, "I understand."

"No, you don't. Be glad of that."

He nodded again, gazing at the other wizards. They were probably throwing insults at each other, losing their tempers in a way that only elves could. Even though humans viewed elves as the most patient of all, save dragons and gods of course, once amongst themselves they were quite capable of behaving like spoiled children. When they bickered, they did so patiently.

Shaking his head, he looked at Julathaen who also watched the unfolding spectacle. Patience was an elven virtue, but this was weighed out by their jealousy. Only once in a while two beings of equal status actually resolved a problem together, leaving cooperative magic a thing of dreams. The only time they had actually worked in unison was during the Heir War and when they created their new realm. Ever since, they stuck to their ways of living, not bothering to contemplate the outside world.

He and Julathaen belonged to those who had tried to work against their race's weakness but were too few to succeed, for the elves had grown so accustomed to their ways that the voices that were raised from time to time were ignored. They were raised again and again in the hope that someday people would pay attention.

"Listen," Lloreanthoran said, "you must work to undo this magic here beyond the Veil! I will find out what is happening with the Aerant C'lain; you will prepare our people's return."

Finally, the globe was lowered and Julathaen's voice thundered through the room. "Silence!"

He didn't have to say it twice; all elves looked at the two in anticipation. "The one responsible for the grave mistake of leaving the Tomes of Darkness behind has been identified. It is Lloreanthoran."

There was a gasp as all heads turned his way. "He has admitted that he was so busy maintaining the bridge into this realm that he forgot to retrieve the artifacts. Thus, I have decreed that he is to fetch the Tomes now. Further, he is to discover where the Stone of Blood is and destroy it."

Julathaen's voice shook as he added, "All his possessions will be taken from him, save the bare necessities, until he finishes this task."

The muttering started anew, everyone asked questions, either directed at he who answered them with silence, or at each other, about how foolish they could have been to allow one such as him to walk amongst them. They all knew this was a ruse, that he had never had the obligation to retrieve the books and that he was doing this to prevent any further harm, but jealousy overwhelmed reasoning.

Lloreanthoran stood and all fell silent. His face a grim mask, he addressed the assembly. "I'll retrieve all I need and leave for Honas Graigh at once."

"So it shall be done," replied Julathaen, nodding gravely. The old elf rose. "This session is over."

Few preparations were necessary. He gathered several items he thought useful. He sent for Kyrreandros, instructed him to take care of the house, and reassured the young elf that he would return.

He had just finished packing, when Julathaen's spiritform appeared. "Nice barriers you've got here," the old wizard remarked. "Took some time to pass them."

Smiling at the senior elf, Lloreanthoran shrugged his shoulders. "I never doubted you could circumvent them, especially since I left a backdoor for you, so to speak."

"Two who trust each other, quite rare." He hesitated. "You didn't have to take the blame, you know?"

"I do, and I bet those overeager magelings are already wetting their pants to get into my house. Apart from fighting over spoils not yet won that is." He sighed, "I didn't do this to prevent the infighting. You know it can't be stopped." The other elf nodded. "I wanted to prevent several years of discussion."

"Not to mention the chance to escape this prison of ours," the old wizard added with a chuckle. "I appreciate the sacrifice."

"If I die it will be under a real sky, in the real world, closer to our real home," Lloreanthoran shook his head. "Prison indeed."

"Back then we thought it best to leave, and you know I regret this decision also."

"We can't change the past, but we can try to correct errors. Maybe those fools will understand this someday."

"Maybe, my friend. Give my regards to that squirrel of yours and good luck to both of you."

With a nod and a gesture, Julathaen had gone.

"They failed?" he already knew the answer, but he asked anyway. The tedious rules of protocol had to be obeyed.

"Yes. We have received no word, and assume they're dead, Priest High." The robed warrior bowed.

In silence the old man regarded his opposite. Thoughtfully he scratched his beard and gazed out the window, taking in the scenery. So many things were on his mind, so many things he wanted to say to his cohorts. He knew he could not. They wouldn't understand, would demand the threat be eliminated. "But they initiated the ritual."

"Yes, sir. We all felt the circle's power."

The Priest High withdrew the old drawing from its resting place and hesitated. He knew it was too late, that the younger man had already seen what he was doing. "It's a link," he explained, more to himself than to the frowning warrior. He concentrated for a moment and felt the bond's pull to the north and west. "He's in Dunthiochagh. The ritual must be completed or all will be lost."

Some choices were easy, some harder. And some choices, he knew too well, one would regret for the rest of one's life. If all other options were exhausted, those one didn't dare consider were the only options left. "Send for Dalgor." The man swallowed.

"But, sir, is that wise?"

He knew full well that sending Dalgor was not the wisest choice of action. The boy was too full of himself, proud to a degree he hadn't seen in a long time. Pride, however, was not the only flaw of Dalgor's; his fanaticism frightened many. "I refuse to send out more men to die," he said. "I want this business finished!"

"Yes." The subordinate bowed and left.

The Priest High looked down on the drawing. Was this regret? He wasn't sure. Given the chance he might change his past mistakes, but life never gave one the option to alter history. He still remembered the young boy who had drawn this picture, the lad who had sat in a corner of this very room, eyes pinched in concentration, his tongue poking out of his mouth. The child had been so fascinated with tales of the gods. He remembered telling him stories, how he had felt drawn to the lad, and his revulsion.

Still, he wondered if things could have been different. Not that it mattered now. The time was drawing near and it was his duty, his entire order's duty, to eliminate the threat Drangar Ralchanh was. No matter how he might have decided in the past, the outcome would have been the same.

Something about the caverns was different. He saw that the entire complex had been added to a shallow outer grotto. Somebody had carved out these winding tunnels and rooms. Creeping forward, he strained his hearing for the shuffling of feet, the mutter of guards, anything that could pose a threat. The only sound he could discern was a chant.

He shook his head, dismissed the scene. Remembering how all this had begun would not undo it, it would not prevent what had to be done. Far too often had he tried to search the past for answers, always reaching the same conclusion. There was no other way. He replaced the picture, closed the drawer, and stood. Dalgor would have to be briefed.

CHAPTER 30

Dragoncrest Castle was unlike any stronghold along the road to Harail. That much Jesgar could tell even from a distance. The deep gorge southeast of the Castle had given it its name. Legend had it that before man or elf walked the world the gods had fought each other, creating the realms in the process. It was said that Dragon's Crest, as the gorge was called, had been created when Lesganagh, God of War and Sun, and Eanaigh, Goddess of Health and Fertility, had battled an unspeakable foe. Jesgar knew the tales surrounding the Dragon's Crest, but seeing the gorge he wondered who in his right mind would call the ravine a crest.

The legend was different now; the Priests of Eanaigh claimed their goddess had won by herself, and the few remaining followers of Lesganagh knew better than to shout out their knowledge.

"Why is it called Dragon's Crest?" he wondered aloud.

Fynbar, another of the Riders, laughed.

Briog said, "He's starting to think."

"Give him some credit, lads. He is trying," Nerran said. His deep voice shut the others up. "Well, Fynbar, why is it called Dragon's Crest?" Now the other Riders made fun of the confused look on Fynbar's face. "Come, lad, it isn't that hard." Jesgar heard Nerran add in a mutter, "If you can think that is."

When the younger rider did not reply, Briog cut in. "There's an old elven tale that dragons once used this place as a graveyard." Jesgar cast him a disbelieving look. "It's true, mate. Well, the tale is anyway, whether dragons really came to rest here, no one knows. Some went down there to look for bones, but all they found was gravel and more rocks."

"Aye, lad," Nerran added, "there's nothing down there but rocks and more rocks." He nodded to Jesgar. "Besides, there's a fortress to inspect."

The third day in the saddle was not as bad as Jesgar had feared, mainly because he hardly felt anything from his lower back down, aside from his legs still being there and following his commands. That was about it. Once, shortly before noon, he had wanted to relieve himself, and when he pulled down his breeches he discovered the insides of his thighs were raw, pus-oozing meat. The riders had mocked his embarrassment and pain, and it was Briog who had handed him an ointment that was supposed to close the wounds. The occasional sting on his thighs and his crotch indicated that the salve was doing something.

Now he looked at Dragoncrest Castle. It was barely noon and aside from the imposing walls that towered above the gorge, he saw several banners flapping in the wind. At first sight he thought everything was in order, but when he took a closer look, he saw that the main flagpole did not hold the colors of Boughaighr and Higher Cherkont, but the royal sword and stallion. Baron Duasonh's flag was flying beneath it, and there were other banners upon the other towers as well.

Nerran must have seen it as well, since the old warrior muttered, "Scales, what's this?"

Fynbar, whose eyesight was even better than Jesgar's, said, "There're other ornaments on the battlements as well." He fell silent and stared at the castle. "Damn," he added, "they hung a bunch of corpses to rot."

"And here I thought they'd put their laundry out to dry," Gavyn remarked. The others snorted in amusement.

Briog guided his horse next to Jesgar's. "Legs feeling any better?" he asked, eyes remaining on Dragoncrest.

"A little; still hurts though." Jesgar wasn't sure what else to say. He couldn't complain, didn't want to complain. They were toughened by years on the road, and he feared the journey back.

"You need to get rid of those pants," Briog said, nodding at his cramped legs. "The shit will never heal if the seam keeps digging into your legs." He must have seen Jesgar's despair, and added, "They'll have something in the castle, don't fret."

"Garinad!" Nerran's booming voice halted their conversation. Jesgar looked up, his eyes wandered along the path the older man was pointing. "What do you make of this?"

At first Jesgar was uncertain what Nerran meant, but then he discerned a feature unlike any he had seen on the castles so far. Part of the outer wall, which in itself was breathtaking with its massive slabs of stone lined along to form a perfect square, seemed almost liquid. Here the rock had been fused together by... something. He stared at the section. Nothing, not even the hottest forge fire, could melt stone. As they came closer, Jesgar grew more confused. The wall itself was taller than even Dunthiochagh's, but unlike any wall he'd ever seen, this one was not made of many cubes of stone. The slabs were huge. From what he could tell no part of the curtain walls, aside from the gatehouse, was built in the usual fashion. It looked as if giants had placed immense blocks of stone next to each other and then cut away ramparts, battlements, towers.

"Shut your mouth or a bird'll nest there," Fynbar said to the amusement of everyone else. Jesgar did as he was told, his eyes still lingering on the towering fortress.

"Don't ask who built this," Nerran finally said.

Jesgar blinked and looked at the warrior. "What happened there?" He pointed at the glass.

"The weakest part of the bugger, if you can call five yards of solid stone with another foot or so of glass weak," Nerran muttered. "Dragons did that," he added, "during the Heir War. No clue why they wanted to burn through the wall, though. The place has been here for much longer than anyone can remember, lad. Even the elves have no idea who built it. Giants? The gods? All we know is that it took dragon fire to hurt the wall some. The Chanastardhians will smash their heads against it and won't achieve anything."

Jesgar was about to ask about siege engines when they reached the moat. Except that there was none, Dragoncrest was built on a spire of stone that sprang from the depths of the gorge.

"Damnation!" he hissed.

Nerran must have heard his oath; the warrior chuckled and said, "That's what I said when I first saw this thing."

They closed in on the chasm surrounding Dragoncrest when a voice challenged them. "Who are you? And what do you want?" a woman shouted from the gatehouse.

Now Jesgar saw the corpses clearly, hanging from the battlements. From this distance—it wasn't that far, maybe twenty yards—it was apparent that they'd been dead for at least a few days. The stone was free from excrements, so none of them had been alive when they were draped alongside the barricade. He was so busy staring at the bodies; he almost missed Nerran's reply.

"The name is Nerran, friend and advisor to Baron Cumaill Duasonh. You best lower that bloody bridge now, lass!"

The older man sounded angry, and when Jesgar chanced a quick look, he saw Nerran's eyes pinch and his jaw muscles spasm. He couldn't see a Chanastardhian banner, and nothing about the place indicated the enemy had taken the citadel, but, he reminded himself, he wasn't truly experienced in anything regarding war.

"One can enter, the rest stays outside!" the voice from the gatehouse shouted.

At this Nerran barked a harsh laughter and replied, "You really think any of us is that bloody stupid? Let me talk to warleader Loarne Dowell at once!"

"Warleader Dowell isn't in command any longer, sir!" Nerran's features darkened, and Jesgar could only guess at what went on in the man's head.

Something caught his attention, and while he continued listening to the shouted exchange Jesgar stared at one of the corpses. He thought he remembered the features. Of course, he couldn't be certain; the last time he had seen the man it had been at a distance, but it was possible.

"And who replaced him?" Nerran shouted.

"General Kerral of the Royal Army, sir," the warrior stated. Then she added a moment later, "A Caretaker Kieran wants to send you his regards."

"Ah, they made it," Briog said.

"So, what's keeping you, lass? Fetch your general."

"That's Jathain," Jesgar muttered; now he was sure.

"Say what?" Nerran asked, as he turned to look at him. Jesgar pointed at the corpse. "That's Jathain, sir." He saw Nerran's gaze following his finger. The older man scowled, squeezed his eyes almost shut; then he frowned. "You sure?"

"I think so, sir." He didn't know what else to say, from this distance matching the horrid, eyeless features of the corpse to the Jathain Duasonh he knew was difficult. He had always prided himself with a good memory for faces, could even tell if two people were related by merely looking at them, but those feats had always been performed from a few feet away. This was ten times that distance.

"Are you certain?" Nerran asked again.

"As certain as can be from here, given the circumstances that the man dangling there is dead, milord," he replied. He wanted to say more, but a shout from Dragoncrest interrupted their little conversation.

"The general wants to know your business!"

Nerran snorted derisively and replied, "I want to ascertain that Dragoncrest has not fallen to the enemy! Deny me entrance, I will assume you are traitors even with the King's colors and the banners of House Duasonh flying above you."

"If they were traitors, Kieran and the others would hardly be alive," Briog remarked.

"They might have interrogated then executed them," one of the female Riders, Diorbail, said.

"And we might end up being here for them to practice their archery," Edmonh, another Rider, said.

"Don't give them ideas," Gavyn added.

Their banter was interrupted when the massive oaken drawbridge creaked down. Nerran dismounted, but motioned them to remain in their saddles. "No need for all of us to be shot down, eh lads?" he said drily and walked toward the place where the massive wooden beams would rest on the soil.

The drawbridge came lower and Jesgar saw a lone figure standing its foot. Once the man might have been dressed in fine armor and surcoat, but now it seemed the man had seen more than his share of fighting and forced marches. General Kerral, he guessed judging by the royal crest on the fastener of his cloak, was a tall man with short blond hair. As the bridge touched ground, the general walked halfway and waited.

"If you want to talk, come," General Kerral said, his voice and eyes alert despite his apparent weariness.

Nerran complied and moved across the other half of the bridge toward the warrior. None of them could discern a word that was said, and before long Jesgar focused again on the body he suspected to be Jathain's. Prolonged examination from a distance yielded little extra insight. There was only a small trace of blood on each, and that could have either come from birds pecking at the flesh or from a cut to something beyond Jesgar's line of sight. He couldn't tell, and neither could any of the Riders. With the walls being well over twenty yards high, the bodies, even with the rope they hung from, were still ten yards above them.

"I hope I get some rest," Jesgar muttered, closing his eyes. "I can't go on."

As if on cue he heard the others' horses moving. He opened his eyes and saw the Riders crossing the bridge. Briog turned and said, "Come on, you can sleep inside!"

Glad and relieved, he nudged his horse onward. He had barely reached the middle of the drawbridge when his head began to feel as if wrapped in wool. The clatter of horseshoes, the flapping of the banners, everything except his breath sounded muffled, and the world felt far away. Inside the fortress, Jesgar dismounted, teeth clenched against the reemerging pain, and stood next to the others for a brief moment. He wobbled, felt his balance and conscience fading, and was barely aware of being carried somewhere. "I guess your ointment isn't really helping," he heard someone say. Then everything went black.

Bright-Eyes wasn't sure what he could accomplish on his own. At first the idea had seemed like a perfect plan, but now, after scurrying through the ruins of Honas Graigh for the better part of two days, he scolded himself. He could have gone back to the

Aerant C'lain, but the memory of feeling helpless and terrorized was strong. There wasn't anyone to help him make up his mind and as he scampered through the city he regretted severing the connection with Lloreanthoran. Sure, there were reasons for being angry at the elf, but—and he wasn't really sure about it—Bright-Eyes had not been left behind on purpose. So many things had been abandoned during the exodus, most of it looted by humans. Had Lloreanthoran also forgotten about him? The more he thought about it as he wandered through the ruins, the more he came to the conclusion this was the case.

Lloreanthoran had lost so much during the Wizard War. Aureenal and Lilanthias, mate and offspring, both had died a few years before the exodus, so now that he thought about it, it was likely Lloreanthoran had been so preoccupied with their deaths and his duty to the city he had forgotten his familiar. The thought did not calm Bright-Eyes' anger, but it tempered his feelings. He also considered the haste with which the elves had left.

"I should contact the old geezer," the squirrel said aloud, scratching his nose. "He'll need my help."

Bright-Eyes hurried back to the mirror across the once white-marbled baths that were now overgrown with ferns, the stones' seams cracked by roots and shrubs and trees. When an overanxious fox tried to make a meal of him, Bright-Eyes released some of the pent-up anger and frustration in a blur of motion and violence, much to the canine's yelping surprise. He let the predator live, and the beast scampered away, tail between legs, howling pitifully.

"That'll teach him," he grumbled and resumed his trek. The trip across Honas Graigh was faster than traveling along its outskirts, but his small legs could only carry him as fast as an elf or human on a slow stroll. By nightfall he reached the ruins of Lloreanthoran's home.

He retrieved the mirror and quickly went through the motions to activate its magic. A few moments passed then the elven wizard's face shimmered into being. "Greetings, again, old friend."

"Listen," Bright-Eyes began. He felt uncomfortable with the

words he was about to say. "I'm not good with apologies, you know that, and I'm still pretty angry about the entire affair, but let bygones be bygones, all right?"

Lloreanthoran sniggered. "Aye, you aren't... good with apologies that is. But I appreciate the sentiment. Where shall we meet?"

He thought for a moment, and when he couldn't find the answer he said, "I don't know where your blasted bridge began, so I've no idea where you'll be."

"I'm already in the woods," the wizard said. "Quite a way to Honas Graigh still, but if memory serves I think I'm about a day's march from the old steeloak."

"We'll meet there then," he replied. "In a day."

"Very well."

The connection was severed, and Bright-Eyes stowed the mirror away. He was of half a mind to carry the artifact with him, but the looking glass was too bulky. In the end he put it in a hollow that had once served Lloreanthoran and his family as wine storage. Then he was off, heading for the steeloak.

CHAPTER 31

Fifteenth of Chill, 1475 K.C.

Urgraith Mireynh, High General of the armies of Chanastardh, looked up as the door to his office opened and a black-and-red-clad man entered. "What is it?"

"The Chosen have ambushed another warband, sir," the youth said.

"Thank you, Caluan." The High General nodded, "Dismissed."

After the door had closed, Mireynh returned to the maps spread on his table. All went as planned; even the resistance of the Chosen had he foreseen. He would deal with them soon enough.

They only counted a score or so, and even though reputedly the best warriors known, they had weaknesses and they could be killed; the torturer had proved that.

He despised such crude methods, although he admitted it sometimes was necessary to use them. The torture and succeeding death of the three fighters had been to no avail, other than the surrender of Danastaer's pitiful king. The traitors had done their job well.

The enemy's army was in such disarray that the conquest had been faster than he had anticipated. Remnants of the Danastaerian army were still afoot, but even those would surrender in time.

Having a large number of foes still roaming the countryside disturbed him a little. Their tactics were surprising, and their leader was as lucky as he was ingenious. This Danastaerian general had already caused enough trouble to force battle plans to be changed. At one point he even saw some of his own tactics used against him, effectively, and that bothered him more than the losses. Maybe his adversary had learned the art of war from him. He wasn't worried, though. The enemy was all but routed, and there remained now only Boughaighr and Higher Cherkont, which could take longer, for Cumaill Duasonh had a reputation for being rather independent.

He looked at a map, calculating the time it took the main body of his troops to reach Dunthiochagh. Ten days, if all went well, but before they could lay siege to the city, they still had to deal with the garrisons. More wasted time. They needed to make haste, for winter was approaching fast.

The traitor in Duasonh's staff might be true to his word and deliver Dunthiochagh's garrisons, he thought, anger rising.

He hated traitors. When King Drammoch had informed him about the sources at the Danastaerian court and in Duasonh's staff, he had wanted to quit, not that he could. Traitors were without honor, and so he had received the permission to deal with them as soon as the conquest was over, arguing that a traitor could betray his new master. The king had agreed. Nevertheless, he hated using them.

He consulted the maps for a short while, then stood and walked to the door. The chamber had been some Danastaerian King's office, and Mireynh had to admit that even though the current king was a sick fool, someone must have had some taste for furniture. Maybe one of the king's ancestors had ordered this chamber to be furnished.

He passed his armor, hung on an oaken rack. Casually his fingers traced the ornamentation that decorated the breastplate. He had owned this armor for half his life, a trophy of his first successful campaign some thirty years ago. Back then he had led his mercenaries from victory to victory, from hoardes of riches to even greater wealth. The High General smiled, remembering his past.

The armor was a piece of art. Sturdy as any plate-armor ever made, it was covered with symbols and knots of ancient making. Flowers were entwined with swords, while those again were knotted into fine lines that spun the metal from left to right, back to front. It wasn't dwarven; he had paid a horrendous sum to find that out. It was merely finely crafted steel he still had to carry to the blacksmith and pay even more money to get it fixed. Now? He carried it around unwilling to part with it, unable to wear it any longer. He felt lazy and fat. A typical warlord who let others do the work. He missed fighting but now it wasn't merely his growing belly that prevented him wearing armor, but also his back.

At first, he had thought it just another injury to mend and be done with. The healers had told him after endless visits his was the disease of old age, a hindrance many elder people suffered. Many elder people...

Grimly he shook his head. His back had also betrayed him. "Dammit," he cursed, opening the door.

His two black-clad guards snapped to attention, eyes forward. They accompanied him without a hint of emotion. So far none of them had deemed it necessary to interfere in his decisions, but he was certain they would act if any of his orders went against their masters' wishes. Yes, he knew what they were. Bodyguards acted differently. These men and women were watchdogs, they reported all his dealings to Herascor, and should he ignore an order they would slay him, but only after showing him his wife and children one last time.

Mireynh grunted. He had made war before these two lasses were a glint in their parents' eyes; he knew what he was doing. Why this veiled threat?

It didn't matter, he decided. As long as he did as ordered, it would be all right. At least they had the decency to leave his chambers when he went to bed.

Ignoring the two women, he headed down the long corridor straight toward the castle's main-hall; time for another meeting. The guards stepped into place behind him and followed at an appropriate distance.

Left, right, left. Thankfully he could still walk without a cane.

As he approached the huge double-doors the two warriors guarding it opened the portal, saluted and stood at attention again. The General grimaced. Chanastardhians knew etiquette if nothing else.

The army was powerful, but lacked the discipline he was used to. There were no deserters, only muggers and rapists and their warleaders weren't much better. These nobles were as dedicated as mastiffs, and just as fierce when it came to tearing out each other's throats. How he enjoyed this. Inbred incompetence and infighting were hallmarks of Chanastardh's aristocracy; he had higher hopes for this army, his army. With that warrior woman from one of the lesser Houses that King Drammoch had ordered to join his army, a woman that truly knew warfare, he'd soon have at least one true warrior at his side.

At least the backstabbing idiots he had to deal with until she arrived obeyed his orders.

Now they rose from their chairs, showing as much initiative as a wooden crate. He nodded to the assembly as he walked to the large chair at the far end. "Good evening lords and ladies."

"Evening, sir," the warleaders said, and waited for him to sit.

There were times when he wished for a less disciplined but more creative staff, like some of the fellows who had served with him years ago. Maybe this new woman, Cirrain, sent to him from Herascor, would prove more helpful. He remembered some of the individuals he had trained or commanded. A handful of them would be worth ten score of this bunch. Forcing his face to mask his amusement, he sat down and watched as the nobles collapsed into their chairs. He saw their confused looks and let his jaw muscles relax.

Clearing his throat, he looked around the assembly. "Well, so far the campaign's proceeding as planned. Our new objectives: Higher Cherkont and Boughaighr. You know Baron Duasonh is far more independent than the other nobles; comes from the longevity of his House, I reckon. He swats aside orders as easily as he would a fly, and although we have a traitor in his midst, I fear from now on we will meet more resistance."

One of them raised his hand. "Sir, won't the freeborn and villeins resent us?"

The High General shook his head. "As our esteemed King said before me; people are like cattle, dumb and uncaring. They don't care to whom they pay their taxes. The person that could stop us is Cumaill Duasonh." He wondered why his subordinates wanted him to think for them. Some faces lit up with understanding. These people were nobles in blood, but decades of complacency had made them soft, turned their brains into peas. Urgraith Mireynh had seen commoners more noble than this group of Chanastardh's elite.

"Sir, what shall be done about the Chosen attacking our patrols?"

Mireynh looked at the warleader. The blonde woman was new, and, he noted with some pleasure, had a fiercer look in her eyes than the rest of the nobles. Was this the Cirrain woman? "They will be dealt with. However, since the Chosen are a small group, it will be nigh impossible for them to stop every single patrol we have out there. As for stopping our forces in general, I doubt that even they can accomplish that. Does this answer your question?"

She nodded.

"Good." He looked around, eyeing the bored warleaders. "I take it you have received your orders?"

"Yes, sir."

"Then you know that most of our warriors have already left for Higher Cherkont. Get your personal warbands moving. I want you to reach Duasonh's foremost outpost, Dragoncrest Castle, within two days."

Without any further comment the nobles stood and hurried out, to Mireynh's surprise. Only the fierce looking woman remained seated. He eyed her curiously. "You don't, by any chance, have any marching orders? Lady … do I know you?"

"Anneijhan of House Cirrain, sir. No, sir, I don't. I arrived here this morning, and haven't been permitted to see you until now," she answered.

Despite his backache, Mireynh stood quickly. "What?"

"Your warleaders, and guards, deemed it improper for a mere second born daughter to have a private audience with the High General, sir."

"Why, then, are you here?" he asked, inwardly cursing his watchdogs and bloated nobles' heads. Already he liked this woman, and he could guess why her peers might not want her in direct contact with him.

Anneijhan of House Cirrain smiled. "I am here by the King's order. Your captains could prevent my seeing you with a load of bureaucratic bullshit, but they couldn't deny me this. It is my right!" He saw she wanted to say more and motioned her to continue. "Permission to speak freely, sir?"

Mireynh nodded. He hadn't heard this question in a long time; none of the others had ever wanted to overstep the lines of protocol. This woman was, as he had expected, from a different breed. "Granted."

"I don't trust those buffoons, sir."

"Excuse me?" he wondered if he had heard correctly. "What was that?"

"I don't trust those warleaders of yours and the people who serve them, sir." Anne looked at the door, scowling.

Frowning, but grinning inwardly, Urgraith Mireynh said, "How dare you insult my most ... most trusted leaders?"

Seeing through his ruse, she replied, "Well, sir, I know them. Even though I hail from a lesser House I have met your trusted nobles before, and I know of their feuds." She continued, "I hail from Chirnath, sir, one of the..."

"I know where Chirnath is and what is happening there. Please spare me the details."

The woman gave a curt nod. "My family has been dealing with the barbarian intruders for decades now; we know war." He really liked this woman. "But we also know the petty feuds between our noble allies from the south. It's a small miracle they haven't already continued their vendettas here."

She looked at him as if expecting a harsh remark, but he gave her a concerned frown. "What do you mean?"

"I mean they hail from different noble houses that over the years have had more than one disagreement over taxes, cattle ... you name it, sir."

"Does the King know about this?" He scratched his beard.

"I don't think he cares, sir."

Slowly he walked the length of the table. "I thank you for the information, Lady Cirrain. As for your assignment, consider yourself a member of my personal staff. I need people with combat experience."

She straightened, "Yes, sir!"

"Dismissed!"

She saluted, turned, and strode out. Urgraith Mireynh waited and watched her until the door was locked again. Then he slammed his fists onto the table and glared at the banners of the various Chanastardhian Houses that decorated the walls. "Damn those nobles!" he cursed.

CHAPTER 32

The trip through the magical tunnel that connected Graigh D'nar with the forest of Gathran was uneventful, and thankfully short. Now that he had a destination, other than the Aerant C'lain, Lloreanthoran knew which way to go. His journey was as much a hike as it was a trip into his past. Here, now he preferred walking over magic, wanted to enjoy his old home.

The vast chaos that was nature delighted him, and even though his memory was by no means bad, he had forgotten how it felt to tread on real soil, to listen to real whispers of the wind making its way through branches and shrubs.

How foolish they had been.

Leaving nature behind had been, in his opinion, the gravest mistake the elves of Gathran had ever made. Many argued against it, saying that teaching mankind magic was worse, but seeing the power and strength that pulsed through the living forest, Lloreanthoran knew the elves had been wrong.

For the first time in many years he was at ease, and he sat down beneath a tree, dropping his meager belongings next to him on the leaf-covered ground. His senses gathered more and more fleeting impressions of his surroundings, and he was certain the elves had to return. Others of his kin still lived beneath the real sky, still enjoyed the warming rays of the sun, and shivered when winter held the land in its icy grasp. He closed his eyes and inhaled, taking in the scent of the moist earth. Distant thunder and the sounds of animals strolling through the underbrush reminded him of the life his people had so carelessly thrown away. He understood the reason to leave the shattered lands, but instead of the change he had hoped the new existence would bring, living beyond the Veil of Dreams had not changed the ways of his people.

Slowly, he drifted into sleep. The rumbling thunder, the whispering wind, and the forest animals that skittered through the underbrush sang him a lullaby.

When the last tendrils of consciousness drifted closer to restful slumber, something changed. At first his lulled senses didn't register the muted sounds. Then, with a start, he was aware of it, the air grew colder, wind and thunder had seemingly ceased to exist and it felt as if a shadow surrounded him. Lloreanthoran sat up and stared into the growing gloom. Something dark—wrong—had just passed him. Its presence was so strong that the last remnants of autumn were immediately wiped away. The few leaves that still clung to their branches were withered and dark, decayed. Patches of grass had lost their color and the cold that permeated the air was not born of night drawing close. What disturbed him most was the silence.

Lloreanthoran shuddered, searched for the direction of the shade's origin. Alarmed, the elf realized that the shade's path had come from the vicinity of Honas Graigh and his sudden urge to investigate his old hometown was suppressed immediately by the knowledge that he would go there after he met with Bright-Eyes. He and the squirrel would be more of a force than he alone. He was looking forward to have his companion at his side again.

Sleep forgotten, he retrieved his pack and continued his march to the place where he and Bright Eyes were supposed to meet, to the place where he had transformed the squirrel into his familiar.

As he moved through the forest his thoughts wandered back to the Lightbringer. What had Julathaen said? That she had found a new pawn to move about. He didn't feel like a pawn, but then, he guessed, a pawn never felt as if it was moved. Of course, he knew the legends, myths rather, regarding Lightbringer. The elves had shaken off the yoke of their oppressors with her help; some revered her almost as much as they did the gods. And who could blame them? Where the gods had stood aside and let things proceed, the Lightbringer had been the one to take matters into her own hands and free the slaves. The Lightbringer... part of him still wanted to piss himself and fall to his knees and grovel. He didn't know where this urge came from, but it was there, always lingering. Was this part of his slave heritage?

Certain she would contact him sooner or later, Lloreanthoran went on. He had barely walked a few yards when he felt the presence; he wasn't sure if this was the same shade as before. Its chill came from a direction different than the first, but it traveled, he felt, toward the same goal. Frowning, he halted, whispering a prayer to Lleeanthar, Goddess of Insight and Wisdom. As always, she remained silent.

Finally, after standing in the clearing for quite a while, he continued his walk.

The answer would present itself as soon as he truly knew how to put his question into precise words.

As he moved deeper into the woods he came across broken trees, some ruined by the ravages of time, others evidence of the Heir War. A few were rotting beneath the pale light of the moon that shone through the thinning roof of red and brown leaves, illuminating the carcasses of trees that slowly returned to the soil from which they had sprouted. Others, dead as well, were more bizarre. Strangely twisted statues of stone and soot that human magic had killed in the most horrible way. These statues were surrounded by dead soil that no amount of time could heal.

Indeed, the magic the humans had learned from the elves was terrible, but only because of the way they had twisted it to their own needs. Although mankind's magic had been to some degree more powerful than their elven counterparts, it had also been their undoing. In some places the effects of the Wizards' magic would remain a silent testimony to the war.

His walk continued for a long while, but finally Lloreanthoran halted beneath a mighty steeloak. The surroundings had changed over the centuries but the mage remembered the meeting place. Here the little squirrel had attempted to steal nuts from his pouch. Smiling at the memory, the elf turned around and gazed at the tree. It was a witness, a millennium old watcher over the forest, one of the last of the first ones. Its bark was cracked in places, and its leaves had already fallen to the ground. Still, it was a majestic sight, a god guarding his followers. Standing as high as two hundred feet, the tree loomed over the others, silently watching the forest and its inhabitants. Lloreanthoran gazed up the tree and knew he was home, and no sooner had that thought crossed his mind than Bright-Eyes popped out of one of the lower branches.

"I thought you'd never come," the mammal said.

"As endearing as ever," he replied. "Did you sleep well?"

"Who said I was sleeping? I haven't slept properly ever since you sent me into that human wizard's lair!" Bright-Eyes snapped. "I still see his eyes glaring down at me!"

"You still bear that grudge?"

"No, I don't. I just pointed out that I still can't sleep properly... After all, I defeated him" The squirrel descended the tree, jumping onto the mage's shoulder.

"No, you didn't," the wizard corrected. "I did."

"Without my help you wouldn't have! I defeated him!"

"Well, let's settle on 'we defeated him'," Lloreanthoran laughed. "Shall we rest here?" he looked to the place he had used as a camp before.

"Unless you want to walk all the way to Honas Graigh tonight. And I could do with a fire also. Awfully cold here."

That question settled, the wizard dropped his pack to the ground and summoned a comfortable bed and a fire, and soon the two companions drifted off into sleep.

By the time the sun rose over the treetops, elf and squirrel were already on their way. Again, he walked.

"Shouldn't we get there quickly?" Bright-Eyes complained.

"Next, you'll want me to run through the forest in haste," the mage said.

"Great, now you show you are truly an elf."

Lloreanthoran turned his head. "I've been away so long; I need to walk for a while. Get reacquainted with the forest."

That shut the squirrel up, but the wizard increased his pace. As he walked the two shared past anecdotes, but soon Bright-Eyes remarked how tarnished everything became in hindsight.

"Indeed," Lloreanthoran said after a few moments of silence, "we had some very great adventures back then, but..." He fell silent, gazing at the path ahead.

"But what?" the familiar looked down from a branch a couple of yards above.

"But we have some grave business to attend to, and what happens after that is as uncertain as our success." Lloreanthoran looked up at his familiar. "We go against forces that were strong when the world was young."

"You don't mean the humans, do you?" the squirrel jumped onto his shoulder and looked at him. "Those fools caused the Heir War and that other war after you were gone, but they aren't as powerful as you elves, now, are they?" He frowned. "No, no, no, no, no. Don't you even dare to tell me we have to fight demons! What I saw was scary enough."

"Listen, from what you have told me..."

"You were pretty quick to sever the connection through the mirror," Bright-Eyes interrupted.

"Me?" Lloreanthoran halted and stared at the squirrel. "You severed the connection!"

"Yeah, yeah, blame it on the furry fellow!"

"You accuse me..." Lloreanthoran began; then he laughed. "Are you enjoying yourself?"

His friend pulled a face. "Actually, I am. Besides, you can't blame a body for being upset about this entire abandonment business, can you?"

"I think I have apologized enough..."

"Nope," the squirrel interrupted him. "Some muttered words before you fell asleep hardly counts as a decent apology! I was stuck with a whole bunch of squirrels that used me to fetch their food most of the time."

"And I am stuck with a squirrel who complains far too much," Lloreanthoran countered.

"Can you blame me? I was the one who lost more wits than that apprentice in your precious new home has." Bright-Eyes stood on his shoulder, arms crossed, glaring at him.

"I am sorry, I am sorry, I am sorry!" the elf growled. "Now, are you happy?"

"Happy? No. Mollified? A little."

He shook his head, laughing. "I missed you. I hope you know that."

The feeling that always came when their minds linked arose, and Lloreanthoran knew Bright-Eyes was looking for the sincerity of his words. Satisfied, the squirrel nodded. "Don't leave home without me," he said and pointed one claw at his own chest. "You'll only get in trouble."

"So, you were at the Aerant C'lain."

"You're in my mind oaf, you already know."

He severed the link and frowned at his familiar. "Indeed, but I'd rather hear things from you. Squirrel thoughts are somewhat alien to me."

"Oh, you noticed? Me too."

"But you handle the smells and perspective much better than I do," he replied.

Bright-Eyes told him, and when he was finished Lloreanthoran was in a thoughtful mood. "So," the squirrel said, "you left the doodads in the Aerant C'lain? Good boy."

"That's not the case; we had to make a quick decision."

"The first time I ever saw you guys make a quick decision. The last one took you a couple of months and that resulted in more destruction during the Heir War."

"Have you ever tried to talk to my fellows?" When Bright-Eyes remained silent he continued, "Well, from what you told me, the Aerant C'lain has been violated."

"But you already knew that," the squirrel remarked.

"No, unfortunately we didn't."

"Oh."

"Yes. If you say the room is empty, and that you felt a vile presence surrounding and enveloping the chamber, we can assume that the Tomes of Darkness and the Stone of Blood have been stolen, but the protective magic has been corrupted nonetheless."

"Do tell."

"Cut down on the sarcasm!" the mage snapped.

"How about you tell me something that I don't already know!"

"We have to find out what's afoot."

"We aren't, that's for sure." Bright-Eyes looked down and then back into his eyes. "If we want to solve this mystery you can talk while walking." The squirrel grinned at the mage. "And I will stay quiet as long as you don't play the ambitious but innocent wizard again, right? Right!"

Lloreanthoran resumed his hike. "As I was saying, the Stone of Blood is a sacrificial instrument of sorts."

"What do you do with it? Drop it on the sacrifice?"

The mage couldn't hide his amusement. "No, it was supposed to gather the life-force of people to open a gate to... somewhere."

"But didn't the Dark Tomes already take care of that part?" Bright-Eyes inquired.

"To a degree yes, but my ancestors wanted to subjugate the Realm of Demons, and the Stone of Blood was meant to open not merely a small door but a portal similar to a castle's gate."

"I hope it only works one way..." the squirrel's voice trailed off. "No, don't tell me it works both ways."

Lloreanthoran climbed across a fallen tree and looked around, trying to get his bearings. Many things had changed over the decades. When he finally continued his march he said, "Unfortunately, yes. The doors that opened with help of the Dark Tomes were comparatively small; only individuals could cross the border." He jumped into a small ravine, carefully paying attention not to drop his friend, but the reassuring paws of the squirrel were firmly planted onto his shoulder. He remembered the treatises he had read about the vile magic his ancestors had wrought in a delusional attempt to master the forces of the unknown. To master the universe itself.

As he walked along a small brook that lead him deeper into the forest, he thought how arrogant most members of his race still were. Now with the impenetrable wall that surrounded the Realm of Elves, they thought themselves invincible, and even though they enjoyed their solitude, some bold minds—he called them delusional fools—envisioned themselves the soon to be conquerors of their ancestral home. Fortunately, the Council of Mages had disallowed any further contact with the outside world and those foolish minds were quickly silenced. The ban affected all: delusional fools and those who merely longed to live in the real world again.

"So, who opened a portal?" Bright-Eyes inquired after a few moments of silence.

"My guess: a human."

"Oh, and what, pray tell, did he do?" the squirrel began pacing Lloreanthoran's shoulders, a habit he had picked up centuries ago.

The elf remained silent.

Bright-Eyes was now standing on its hind-legs, scratching his tiny nose. "Hang on a moment," he said, his voice ringing with a mixture of dread and enthusiasm. "What if this human just handed out the key, so to speak? What if this human struck a deal with those demons?"

Lloreanthoran halted, furrowing his brow. "That's possible, but what would he have gained from that?"

A quizzical look on his face, the squirrel stared at the mage. "A question like that from an elf? You're kidding me, right? What would you demand of a being that is as powerful as a god, and as ambitious as an... elf?"

"You're right, sometimes I just try to see the world as a beautiful place," Lloreanthoran sighed.

"I don't believe that for an instant; for someone a couple centuries old you are still too optimistic. And you fought in the Heir War."

"Sometimes I just wish that the world would be without any problems." The mage stared at the ruined tree that used to be his home. Here he had lost his wife and his daughter, victims to a fiery boulder that one of the Phoenix Wizards had summoned. It had been here that his personal war with humanity had begun, a war victorious but nonetheless painful. Over the years he had forgotten the anguish he had felt when he'd first gazed at the smoldering ruin, the charred and mutilated body of Lilanthias, his daughter, clinging to the last threads of life. The girl had fought so valiantly against death. He could still see her ruined mouth silently calling him, the stump that used to be her hand reaching out. Without a second thought he had put her out of her misery, knowing she was beyond any help.

"I'm sorry," was all Bright-Eyes could say when he realized where they were. The squirrel looked at him and for the first time since they'd known each other, he saw him cry. Back when he had killed his dying daughter, he had known only hatred. Now tears ran down his face.

It took Lloreanthoran some time to regain his senses. He was lost in a haze of blood and ashes, reliving the life that had been destroyed.

After he had ended Lilanthias' suffering he had searched for Aureenal, his wife, but all that remained of her was the molten remains of the necklace he had given her when he had proposed to her. The power of the human's spell had been too much for the protection charms he had placed over the house.

He wiped the tears away and looked past the ruin. "Let's move on," he whispered.

They reached the Aerant C'lain shortly before dusk. Clouds reclaimed empty spots of heaven that the sun had wrought from their grip; the two companions were assaulted by the cold. It was unnatural, originating from the Forbidden Chamber. The silent resting place of the Stone of Blood lurked in the shadows, taunting them, testing their strength. Lloreanthoran listened to the magic, cast by long dead Elven mages who had erected the building to store their most dangerous works. It was a warning from the past, gone unheeded for centuries; when the Heir War had shattered Gathran, none of the survivors bothered to listen to a chant that had accompanied them all their lives. Now it was far too late.

"Creepy," Bright-Eyes whispered, gazing at the structure. "Even worse than last time. Any idea what's happening?"

The wizard scanned the building just as carefully as his companion, but unlike the squirrel his senses were attuned to the Aerant C'lain's magic. Only half hearing his friend's question Lloreanthoran said, "Now that's odd. I thought the remnants of the artifacts' powers would have disappeared."

His mage-sight perceived a whirlpool of blackness intermingled with white, the last remnants of the soulward. It was as if the dark was fueled by the power that the mages of old had invested into the integrity of the structure. He frowned and listened. In the days before the exodus he had come here on occasion to listen to the souls as they chanted, sang, and drew his thoughts regarding the forbidden knowledge. The songs had changed slightly, but to his accustomed ears it was obvious. Nuances were set wrong; pitches had been changed, as well as words and syllables. The guardians of old were now increasing the blackness; only a few feeble shouts against the thundering choir, their chant felt as if too few hands were casting a net meant for many. It did not matter how the change had occurred, he was interested in the source of this power and its intentions. If a human had removed both Stone of Blood and Tomes of Darkness, what perverted the enchantment now?

A couple of spells came to his mind, spells to unearth the mystery. Ignoring his familiar's questions, Lloreanthoran withdrew a few objects from his pouch. A mirror, some salt and powdered charcoal. Then he set the mirror on the ground, its surface reflecting the dim, clouded sky. Holding salt and coal, he gazed at the building, intent on capturing one of the guardians. He took a deep breath and concentrated on the spell, his gaze wandering to the mirror, where both salt and coal would imprison the magical creature.

On the looking glass's shiny surface stood Bright-Eyes. Instantly the wizard's concentration was broken and he glared down at his familiar.

"Would you please tell me what you think you're doing?" the squirrel asked.

"I want to find out who is using the guardians' power," Lloreanthoran grumbled, annoyed.

Bright-Eyes looked at the Aerant C'lain and stumbled off the mirror. Again, he looked at the wizard, concern written on his face. Years ago, his instincts had helped them survive and it was his knack for dangerous situations that had saved his life time and again.

The elf was doing something terribly wrong and stupid, Bright-Eyes was certain. Overcome with dread, the squirrel watched his friend resume his position. Hands held close together above the mirror, eyes shut in concentration, the mage started to cast his spell. Carefully he mouthed the arcane syllables, forming them into words no normal being could comprehend, forming them into words of power, of magic. Specks of salt and coal flew from his hands trailing a path down toward the glassy surface. Slowly they floated down, dancing and twirling around each other. Every word gave the steady trickle of material a new direction, a new spin.

Bright-Eyes had seen his friend cast a similar spell before but back then he had not felt such fear. Something was bound to happen and whatever that was, he knew it would be bad. His legs quavered, shook like leaves in the wind, and the squirrel retreated to a nearby wall to hide in the safety of the stone.

CHAPTER 33

Lightbringer pondered what next to do. She had enough humans to feed her magic which meant she could breach the Grand Library's defenses soon, but there was also the elven wizard to consider. By now he should have reached Honas Graigh and begun his investigation. Briefly she concentrated on the Aerant C'lain and felt that something was amiss. In his ignorance the mage had opened a rift that would destroy him. The elf's plight decided her actions, and Lightbringer thrust her spiritform toward the wizard and his familiar.

At first the spell proceeded as expected. Tendrils of smoke rose from the mirror's surface, stabbed into the air, and then reached out for the building, reaching out for the wailing voices that sang of woe and destruction, drowning out the dwindling choir of protective chants. The gray smoke drew closer and closer to the invisible barrier that surrounded the Aerant C'lain, its fine fingers probing, searching.

From his vantage point behind a tree, Bright-Eyes observed what he thought was a doomed mission, dread paralyzing him. The part of his mind still capable of clear thought, the part not overcome with terror, tried to convince his body to retreat even further. To no avail. His feet refused to budge.

He stared at the spectacle, eyes darting from the clasping tendrils of smoke to his friend, who stood transfixed over the smoke-spitting mirror, and back to the tender fingers that attempted to drag a wailing voice out of the mindstorm. He saw Lloreanthoran quiver, shake as in a fever, his hands grasping for the cloud, trying to rip it apart, to sever the connection.

The mage's eyes were filled with fear, and now even Bright-Eyes could hear the banshee-wail that surrounded the Aerant C'lain. They beckoned Lloreanthoran, taunted him, daring him to perform the last step and join the perversion of powers that his ancestors had summoned long ago. Every muscle in the squirrel's body screamed against the horrible choir that ensnared his friend.

Shaking with frustration, Bright-Eyes watched and tried to gather strength to fight the horrors, to help his friend.

Then time stopped.

The presence that had once already linked to his mind was with him again. For a moment Bright-Eyes feared the spirit would take over his body, but a gentle touch assured him this was not the case. "Don't you think you should do something other than watch, little squirrel?" she whispered, her voice stern despite the gentle words. "You have to help."

Renewed strength, hope, and love surged through Bright-Eyes. He felt the being giving him an encouraging nod; his fear changed to determination, washing away all traces of horror and causing his heart to hammer in his chest, but instead of the staccato-like pulse it grew steady.

"Where would the old fool be without me?" Bright-Eyes grumbled, stepped into the open, and hefted a stone twice his size. As he turned toward his friend the spirit's presence vanished. His courage remained.

With all the strength his little arms could muster, Bright-Eyes smashed the mirror, its glass shattering, giving way to the stone he wielded like a battering ram. Hundreds of splinters flew through the air, propelled by the force that had already been imprisoned by magic, cutting his fur and skin, piercing his flesh.

The evil choir was muted immediately; silence reclaimed the night. Weakened, the squirrel collapsed onto the stone he had wielded so valiantly. A pained smile on his face, he looked up at his friend. "Guess you should have listened…"

The smoke rose toward the Aerant C'lain and as the voices reached for him, Lloreanthoran knew something was wrong, but his will was ebbing. He felt the cacophonic cries of the twisted guardians drawing his spirit closer, promising him a life he had stopped dreaming about. They guaranteed power to turn back time, the reunion with wife and daughter, the strength to thwart the Heir War, thus giving Turuuk all the strength himself.

It was tempting.

He saw Lilanthias and Aureenal rising up from a sea of blood that was his doing, but he reveled in the havoc he caused, the pain he wreaked onto humanity, eliminating it before it could ever become the nuisance it now was. He felt hatred within, swallowing him, and making him part of the evil that was the Aerant C'lain.

Forgotten were his goals. Drowned out was his soul. Now the anguish, hate, and pain that had lain dormant for so long within the recesses of his mind came to life, surging out, transforming him.

Then the voices were gone.

With one final scream Lloreanthoran freed himself of the spirits that had tried to meld his soul to the Aerant C'lain. The struggle left him shivering and shaking, staring at the black wall of hatred that was now visible to him. Swirling around the old building was a dark mass of shadows that moaned and howled like whipped slaves, but with a viciousness that revealed their true nature. The tendrils of white that still floated amidst the blackness were fading and the battles that occurred between the forces were always won by the dark, swallowing whatever tendril rose against the evil surrounding the tomb of Tomes.

Then a flash of pain burst into his mind. Lloreanthoran wheeled, screamed again, this time from grief over the loss of his companion. When he had left for the new realm, he had felt the squirrel's presence dim to the point where almost nothing remained. Now the link was broken, ripped apart by forces he did not wish to explain, destroyed by his mistakes, and killed by his magic. Angry at his foolishness, Lloreanthoran slammed his fists onto the ground beside the shattered mirror and Bight-Eyes' corpse.

"No!" he screamed, tears running down his cheeks. "No!"

His arrogance had killed the squirrel, and in his moment of grief, understanding overwhelmed him. Bright-Eyes had given his life to save him! He had given his life to free him of the shroud of souls surrounding the Aerant C'lain. This realization doubled his pain and grief. Yet another friend lost. Yet another part of his life gone to ashes, vanished in the mist of death and decay, and nothing would bring Bright-Eyes back. The familiar was gone, like Lilanthias and Aureenal. Dead, because he had failed to protect them.

"No!" he wailed again, wishing his voice could push death away from the friend, hoping he could undo his mistake. Like his wife and daughter, death was all that remained. His lament changed nothing.

Finally, after he could cry no more, the pain subsided and was replaced by an emptiness he hadn't felt since the Heir War. He was miserable, but reminded himself of the familiar's sacrifice. A sacrifice that had saved his life so he could continue. Lloreanthoran looked at the Aerant C'lain and then back at the squirrel's corpse.

"Thank you, dear friend," he whispered as he picked up the squirrel. "Thank you for saving my life. Thank you for giving me the chance to do what must be done."

Again, tears welled up but he forced them back, blinking fiercely. Many of his fellow elves would scorn him for such a display of affection, wouldn't understand his love for the dead animal. Then again, his race had declined in such a way that he despised them in return. Bright-Eyes had been there for him when he had grieved for his family. They had fought alongside each other, defeating the horrors of the Heir War, relying on the other's strength, and repressing the other's weaknesses. Now, his last real friend was gone, killed by his inability to see beyond the mindstorm's perversions.

A last time he gazed at the lifeless body. "Farewell, old and dear friend," he muttered. "Farewell." With those last words he muttered a quick incantation and the squirrel's corpse rose into the air. At first the flicker of flames that danced over the tiny body was almost imperceptible; a light red-yellow hue trailed the red fur. It looked like the last heartbeat before the sun made its way over a fog-shrouded horizon, glimmering softly. Then the flames engulfed the tiny body, roaring toward the heavens for a brief moment, and then vanished, leaving nothing behind. Determined, the wizard then confronted the Aerant C'lain. Wrapping himself in the most powerful protection-spells mortals had ever created, using every ward he could think of, he started for the chamber's low-lying entrance to end the terror.

As he entered, Lloreanthoran felt the onrush of dark souls trying to penetrate his wards, but they held. Now, after his fatal error outside, he was ready. Prepared to strike back and fight off any hostile power that might threaten to destroy his spirit. Slight flickers of light danced around him, showing where the shades of the Chamber tried to penetrate his shields, but the souls were held at bay.

"I should have set these wards earlier," he growled, the words as much scorn for his own lack of thoughtfulness as a reminder that he was the only being alive in the Aerant C'lain. The lights continued to flicker around him, but the onslaught lessened with every step he took down the stairs.

When he reached the end of the stairwell the ghastly attackers disappeared. He was alone, standing in a darkness that even his heightened elven sight could not penetrate. With a flick of his wrist he summoned a mage-light, which immediately rose to the ceiling.

The room was empty.

Lloreanthoran frowned, anger, and despair boiling up. "Damn!" he cursed, and fell silent. From the corner of his eye he detected movement. A trickle of dust slithered across the floor, making its way to the abandoned spot where years ago the Stone of Blood, the portal to the Realm of Demons, had stood. The mage tracked the flow of the dust with his eyes. He observed the motes of whirling, slithering ashes—he now realized what it was—meander toward the abandoned spot. More rivulets of ashes were crawling in the same direction.

They were everywhere.

"What is this?" he whispered, his shock of finding the Chamber empty, although expected, was replaced by curious dread.

More and more tiny streams joined the others, piling themselves up in the Stone's empty resting-spot. A silent whisper arose from the walls, chanting something he could not at first identify.

The more ashes gathered in the middle, the louder the voices became. Some whispered, "Rise!" others joined them, urging with another word "Danachamain!" The sounds grew compelling, forcing him to join in the chant. Ashes trickled in from every opening, crawling like a horde of maddened ants toward the center.

"Rise, Danachamain!"

Desperately, Lloreanthoran fought to keep his senses together, struggled against the urge to join the ghastly choir. More ashes made their way to the pile that grew constantly.

"Rise, Danachamain! Rise!"

He felt magic being wrenched from his surroundings. This made him find new focus. Keeping his barriers and wards erect, supporting them with magical energy he channeled from pools only the most powerful wizards could access.

"Rise, Danachamain! Rise!"

His every sense reeled against the onslaught of voices and perverted magical energy that penetrated the Aerant C'lain. Trembling, Lloreanthoran fell to his knees, staring wide-eyed at the trails of ashes that slowly ebbed away. It was as if the gathering came to an end.

"Rise!"

The ash-motes circled around each other, spiraling, dancing, and performing an eerie ballet of things past, joining each other in a dance of death. Lloreanthoran gasped, trying to discern a pattern, as he sensed yet another increase in power.

"Danachamain!"

While ashes danced with and circled around each other, motes of light, as dark as any the elf had ever seen before appeared, and joined the shuffle. Now the chanting voices were supported by a low hum that rose from the depths of the darkness. Lloreanthoran cringed in fear; despair threatened to overwhelm him.

"Rise!"

Out of the chaos rose a figure, and with every turn of ashes and light it gained more substance: a human.

"Danachamain!"

"Arise!"

CHAPTER 34

Sixteenth of Chill, 1475 K.C.

Now was the time. Kildanor refused to say his goodbyes. Cumaill was busy arranging new warbands, Nerran was still out inspecting the fortresses, and even though he had seen a lot of Braigh during the past few days, he didn't yet consider the Caretaker that much of a friend to warrant a farewell.

Of course, he intended to return, but what the Chosen planned to do was slightly more dangerous than a trip to The Shadowpeaks. Besides, he was certain Cumaill would balk at their goal. Yet it had to be done.

At the ring of the evening gong, he rode Dawntreader to the western gate. By horse the journey from Dunthiochagh to Harail took five days, but Kildanor made it in moments. When the last rays of Lesganagh's glowing orb crossed the horizon, he guided his mount onto the light of his deity and reached the glade north of the capital in a few heartbeats. He hadn't been this close to Harail in years, and neither had he been in much contact with his fellow Chosen. Now, as his horse departed the beam of light, he saw the grim and determined faces of his brethren.

There were no enthusiastic smiles, no warm welcomes. Everyone knew Chanastardh's invasion posed more of a danger than just the loss of land. They all felt it. Someone in Chanastardh wanted to get to Dragoncrest and aside from the Chosen, only the king knew where to find the exact place.

"Has he spoken?" he came right to the heart of the matter.

Orkeanas shook his head. "No."

"So, we can still prevent him being interrogated."

"Aye."

"Let's get to it then," Kildanor growled.

They waited until nightfall, twenty-two silent figures lurking in the shade of nearby trees. Kildanor didn't miss the conversation; ever since he had been exiled from the capital he had barely spoken to the others. There was no need. He had been the one to speak out against Lerainh's brutal pleasures, had intervened when he couldn't stand the monarch's perversions any longer. Had he killed the king, he would have done so with a smile.

Kildanor glanced at his companions, twenty-one as they had been ever since the Demon War. Many of them hadn't even been born when Danachamain had led that fatal expedition to Honas Graigh. Of the first Chosen, only Orkeanas and he were left.

Ethain. Ganaedor. The names flashed through his mind like the strike of a whip. Traitors, both of them. They had been with Danachamain when he discovered the means to release the demons onto the world. "Bloody fools," he muttered.

In a way he was glad to have been banished from Harail, seeing his fellow Chosen always reminded him of the two who made their order incomplete. Lesganagh had made twenty-four champions and guardians, and any one would be replaced upon death.

Ethain and Ganaedor were still alive, if one could call their existence living.

"Memories?" Orkeanas's voice broke his reverie.

"Aye."

"Too many bad ones," the First of the Chosen said.

"They always are," Kildanor replied.

"We never considered the consequences when we accepted The Call."

"Aye."

"Sometimes it seems unbearable, but what can we do? We are Chosen. For good or bad, we are the guardians."

"The dead are the lucky ones; they have no more burdens to bear." Kildanor glanced at the rising moon and lowered his head in silent reverence.

"We all have a choice," Orkeanas said, his voice barely a whisper. "We are the choices we make." When Kildanor remained silent, he went on. "The two that are missing made their choice as well. You can't blame yourself still."

"Why not? I promised to look out for them."

"Danachamain asked you to stay behind; he wanted to make sure King Halmond was safe."

"Danachamain." Kildanor's voice was dripping with venom.

"We don't know what happened in Honas Graigh; he may have been a victim as well. But that is in the past, and now we must keep to our duty."

Kildanor smirked, as he drew his sword and stroked the blade with his gloved hand. "I could've spared us all this inconvenience years ago."

Orkeanas rose angrily. "What do you want to hear? You know there is no heir!"

Kildanor stood as well, just as furious as his companion. "Since when is politics something we are meant to dabble in? Our mandate is the safe-keeping of the Hold!" he said acidly.

"And that can best be…"

"…accomplished by backing a monarch," finished Kildanor, the sentence all too well known to him. "Spare me the platitudes. It was in our power to avoid all this by ridding the throne of one unworthy of living! Lerainh brought this nonsense about us all."

"By being weak?"

"By surrounding himself with idiots who danced to his tune!"

"What are you saying?" Orkeanas snarled.

By now the other twenty Chosen paid attention to the two oldest of their group arguing.

"You damn well know what I am saying! You!" he glared at them. "All of you! Have failed to act, have become as guilty of the Chanastardhian invasion as the warlords who indulged themselves in whatever nonsense instead of listening to what every single bird sang from the trees by this summer!"

"We aren't rulers," Orkeanas snapped.

"No, but guardians should have some authority over the area they are protecting."

"Damn you, Kildanor, we all agreed that this was the way to go! We did not want to rule this country."

"That was when Halmond was king. His grandson should never have ascended the throne, being the monster that he is! Now, we run around and try to gather the pieces of the mess we created. In the future, choose your paths more wisely!"

"Is that all?" Orkeanas hissed.

"I have nothing more to say, let's get this done. I am needed back in Dunthiochagh." He stood and headed for the passageway he knew existed in the dark of the woods.

"You are needed here!" barked Orkeanas.

Kildanor whirled around. "I do my duty, better than any one of you, so don't tell me where I am needed. With Cumaill Duasonh the Hold is safer than it was with Lerainh!"

Orkeanas shook his head and looked to the ground. "What has become of us, old friend?"

"People with a mission," Kildanor growled and turned toward the entrance. "Let's finish this."

Anne Cirrain looked about her quarters and was unsure what to think. This was certainly not what she had expected life in the Chanastardhian army to be. Yes, there were routines, drills for the forces still gathered in Harail, but she wasn't part of anything. Even though High General Mireynh had attached her to his staff, she had nothing to do. It felt as if Mireynh wanted her to stay away from any planning. Which in itself was odd, for Anne felt that the general appreciated what little advice she had been able to give. Still, she was on her own most of the time, and she was bored.

The sound of a gong signaled the warleaders who still remained in the royal palace that supper was being served, and she decided that even the company of the southern noblemen lowlifes was preferable to another evening of solitude. As she headed out of her room, Anne thought briefly about changing from her leathers into something more suitable. Then she reminded herself that her father's stable boys would be suitably attired for the company of nobles she was to sup with. "Double-tongued, inbred bastards," she muttered and walked down the stairs toward the great hall that served as the mess hall.

When she entered, she was surprised to see the room almost empty. Still more troops had left Harail, and of the few noblemen that remained Anne knew none. "Good evening," she said, walking toward the table.

"Ah, the Lady Cirrain graces us with her presence," High General Mireynh, whom she had not noticed, said.

"Milord," she replied with a curt nod. "Lords," she said to the others, who mumbled their greetings and resumed their conversations.

"I've good news, Cirrain," Mireynh waved her to his side.

She sat and looked at the general. "Yes?"

"You're to remain with my staff," he said, and leaned toward her, continuing in a whisper, "you know more of warfare than most of these buffoons, and you can also enlighten me regarding the qualities of the various nobles." He raised his mug, and a servant rushed forward to fill it. "I take it you prefer ale to wine also?" he asked loudly.

"I do," Anne replied, and ignored the hushed talk that arose because of her statement. "Wine is quicker to dim one's senses, and you never know when wits come in handy," she added with a smirk.

Her statement was greeted with angry silence from her peers, but Mireynh burst out in howling laughter. "Indeed, indeed," he said, guffawing.

The servant filled her mug and retreated. "And a few more people regard me with scorn," she muttered into her ale before she drank deeply.

"Say," a noble sneered down the table at her, "Lady Cirrain. Isn't it true that you people from up north are more alike the beasts you are supposed to fight?"

Anne put down her mug, wiped the foam from her lips, and smiled. "If more alike them means that we can fight, yes, I guess we are similar," she said, as she put food on her plate.

"What do you mean by that?" the man continued, his sneer gone. "Do you mean that you fight better than us from the south?"

"Why do you bother asking questions you already have the answers for?" Anne cut a chunk off a haunch of beef.

"Do you insult me and mine?" the man continued.

If Mireynh was paying attention, she couldn't tell, he was engrossed in a conversation with another noble. Not that his opinion mattered in regard to her family's honor. She weighed her options. Either insults would continue to fly about the table until one of them, she was certain it would not be her, had enough, and challenged the other to a duel, or the insults would fly until the idiot tried to strangle her in her sleep. Or she could just let it rest and spare herself the trouble. She opted for the latter, and began eating.

"Do you insult me and mine?" clearly the man refused to let the matter rest.

The advantage of having spent so much time on a battlefield was that one could ignore most noise and focus on a given task. So, Anne focused on her food, but the nobleman, whom she still did not know by name, refused to be ignored.

"Do you insult me and mine?" he shouted across the table, silencing all other conversations.

Thoroughly fed up with this oaf's attitude, Anne looked up from her plate and smiled. "Lord… what was your name again?" He began to reply, but Anne went on, "Not that it matters. As to your question, my guess is that yours were exactly the same words your father said to your mother when he saw what she had given birth to."

"You whore!" the man shouted. "You will pay for this!"

"The challenge is accepted," Mireynh said, his voice cutting through the colorful insults the man continued to throw at Anne. He turned toward the nobleman. "Callan of House Farlin, you have the choice of weapons, as you are the one being challenged."

"Weapons?" Callan Farlin sputtered.

"Aye," Mireynh said. "You accepted the duel and have therefore the choice of weapons. What be it, milord? Swords, clubs, axes? You choose."

"I… I… apologize, Lord Mireynh," Callan of House Farlin

stuttered.

"Don't apologize to me!" the general roared. "Apologize to her!" He pointed at Anne. When the man remained quiet, Mireynh looked at her and then the silent nobleman. "You have accepted the challenge, yet you refuse to make a choice of weapons or decide how this duel will end. As you won't do so, Anne of House Cirrain will determine the weapons."

She nodded, unsure of what the High General's intention was, but she knew which weapon she had preferred ever since she'd wielded one for the first time in a battle against the northmen. She had lost her sword, and the only thing within reach had been a heavy, two-handed hammer. Even though it was not knightly, she liked the raw power of the ungainly weapons. "Mauls," she said, and could tell by the astonished gasps that none of the attendants had expected this choice.

"Mauls it is then," Mireynh said. The High General looked at Callan Farlin. "You can still apologize, milord." Anne knew Mireynh was giving him a last way out, but the man remained silent. "Until first blood then," he said with a chuckle.

First blood. She knew what it meant with regard to her choice of weapon. Mauls did not cut a foe, they shattered them, and as such Mireynh might have ordered a fight to the death. She knew House Farlin, and she knew Callan's father to be a cruel, selfish man who scorned physical weakness. She didn't know if the young man could fight, but what she did know was that fighting and killing an inferior opponent in a duel was not honorable. Her decision to spare the young noble's life came quickly, but she would slap him around a few times before accepting his surrender.

"Prepare," Mireynh said. "I want this over with before we move out tomorrow."

"We'll fight tonight?" Callan of House Farlin asked, his voice tinted with dread.

"Aye, so you best get your armor." The High General turned to her, "The same goes for you, Cirrain."

She stood and left without another word. What the other nobles would say behind her back mattered little; already they saw her as an outcast, and her choice of weapons merely confirmed this. The sword or the lance was a noble's weapon, but a maul! In all likelihood they had never encountered one in battle. In the right hands it could be a devastating weapon.

In her chamber Anne slipped into her chain shirt and fastened beaten steel plates to her legs. As she was finishing with the last clasp, someone knocked at her door.

"Enter!" she barked as she righted herself.

In came a young woman with a mane of curly, unruly red hair. She wore the colors of House Farlin, and Anne surmised that she was a servant to the lord she was about to fight. Then she noted the girl was out of breath.

"What do you want?"

"Lady Cirrain, I came to warn you," she panted.

"About what?" Anne asked as she slipped into her surcoat and wound her belt around her waist.

"The bastard's going to try and poison you, madam."

Cocking an eyebrow, Anne inspected her visitor. There still were traces of a recent beating on her face, and the way the young woman stood showed she favored one leg.

Another bruise, Anne guessed. "Did he do this to you?"

"Aye, said a squire should behave differently." The girl smiled shyly and winced; the motion seemed to cause pain.

"Squire? What's your name?" Red hair certainly was not uncommon among the nobility, and if she wanted to owe some nobleman's daughter a favor she wanted to be certain this girl was noble in blood and in spirit, something quite uncommon in Chanastardh's nobility.

"Gwennaith of House Keelan," she replied with a curt nod.

House Keelan, a family with its own share of scorn from the nobles in Herascor. But whereas Anne's family fought the northmen in the mountains, House Keelan had the duty of protecting the coast without the benefit of its own ships. The impoverished Keelans were bound by debt to serve a merchant family. Poor girl, only the gods knew what her parents had to do to get her a position as squire.

Gwennaith stiffened under Anne's scrutiny. "Watch out for his dagger, madam," she said and left, slightly dragging her left leg.

"More honor there than in most of the palace," Anne muttered. At least she owed her life to someone who wanted nothing in return.

CHAPTER 35

Lightbringer tore through the protective wards of the Great Library when she felt Cat's presence next to her body. She thrust her spirit back into her prone, blood covered form. Her eyes opened and beheld her companion's ghostly form.

Cat floated next to the hollow and stared at her blood bath, revulsion plain on her face. "What is this?" she snapped. "What are you doing? Where did the blood come from?"

Lightbringer took a rag and cleaned caked blood from her lips. "I do what is necessary."

"With blood?" Cat shrieked.

"There is no other way for me," she replied, lowering her head. It made no sense to explain the necessities to the ghost. She would not understand.

Cat glowered at her, then after a few heartbeats she said, "The fools killed him."

Her head snapped up and she focused on the apparition before her. "What?"

"The boy is dead."

"Who killed him?"

"I know not. He was ambushed in the Shadowpeaks, and his body is now in Dunthiochagh." Cat trembled with fury and disgust; Lightbringer saw the spirit's emotions plain on her face.

"This was the reason I didn't want you here," she whispered.

Now it was Cat's turn to stare at her in confusion. "What?"

"The blood, my way of working magic. I was afraid you'd hate me for what I do."

"Help me save him."

She hadn't seen this coming. A big part of her wanted to

help Cat, but she dared not. The boy's soul probably drifted in the one place she dared not go. Given the circumstances, it was likely his spirit had not gone to the Bailey Majestic. Should he cross the Veil not much would change; there would be another pawn, another life to destroy. That she could not allow.

"I can't help you directly."

"Why not?" Cat snapped.

"I can't tell. Believe me, please."

"Can he be returned to life?"

"He isn't truly dead. Still, there is danger."

"I am willing to face any danger for him, for Lliania's, Darlontor's, his and my sake!" Cat shrieked. "I endured too much to let my revenge die."

"Your revenge is insignificant," Lightbringer stated.

"How can you say that?" Cat growled.

"I open my mouth and use speech."

"Don't mock me, witch!"

Lightbringer sighed. How could she explain what had taken her more than a century to understand? "I can help you. I can take you to the boy, but be warned: if you do, you will fade!"

"So be it, if this grants me revenge!"

She shook her head and looked at Cat. "Nothing is written in stone. His survival isn't certain. Your sacrifice might be in vain." Ashamed, she cast her eyes down, staring at the pool of blood. "Besides, I would miss your company."

"Just help me."

"When you do this, you will die!"

"I am already dead," the spirit replied.

Something powerful had entered Castle Duasonh, Ealisaid was certain of it. She felt the swell in magical energy much like a farmer feels a change in weather. The surge came from inside the Palace, and it seemed as if it did not spread but focused on a specific place, maybe a specific being. She was unsure. Without proper examination she could not be certain, and any divination would break her oath to the Baron. There was something odd about the magic, it did not feel right to her, but neither did it feel wrong. It was akin to her inner strength, but it was far more potent, and yet it seemed also strangely soothing.

"Guard!" Ealisaid shouted as she rattled on her cell's door. "Guard!" She shook the bars again. "Hello?"

From down the corridor came a grunt, the turn of a key, and then, with the creaking of the door, light spilled into the hallway. The sound of footsteps approached fast, and within a few heartbeats a man wearing the colors of House Duasonh above his leather tunic and chainmail came into sight. He carried a torch and his expression betrayed his sleepiness.

"Wha'd'ya want, witch?" he yawned. The smell of ale penetrated even the rank stench of the straw inside her cell.

"I need to speak with the Baron," she replied, forcing down her nausea. "It's urgent."

"Ain't it always," the man mumbled. "The Baron ain't at call from the likes of you, witch."

"It's important!" she repeated. Even now Ealisaid felt the power surging within the Palace, and was unsure what it meant. It did not feel hostile, but magic never felt hostile, only those wielding it did. If one was prepared and knew what to look for.

"So you say," the man snarled. Obviously, he did not want to alert either his liege or anyone else for fear of his drunkenness being discovered.

"Get your warden here!" Ealisaid turned the shout that had almost left her mouth into a hiss. "Now, warrior!"

The man must have seen the determination on her face, but merely shrugged. "Stay quiet, woman. Baron'll come when he wants to. Food'll come at sundown." He turned and walked back down the corridor.

She stared at the space abandoned by the guard as the torchlight faded away. Even without the Baron's permission she had to discover the source of this power. This investigation was against Duasonh's strict order, but to her anything felt better than to remain in this cell and dwell on all the people and things time had taken away. She had to do something to keep from losing herself in the past and grief. Anything, any action, was better than this.

Ealisaid sat back and considered her options. She could blast out of this cage at any time, which meant certain death;

Duasonh had been quite clear on that. She had promised not to cast any spells, but to discover the source of and reason behind this surge of energy she would have to cast spells. Unless...

Spiritform was no spell, but a state of being, and nothing done while in it affected the world. How could it? No one would notice her if she walked the Palace as a ghost, and this other state of being might aid her in discerning what kind of magic was at play here. She would not break any oath, technically, and the information gathered could help her when she went to trial.

A smile crept onto her face as she considered this option. Sure, it could be construed against her, but in the end anything she did or didn't do would be used against her. Spiritform was no spell, this fact made up her mind.

She leaned against the wall next to the door, in a spot where only direct light would actually show her face, and closed her eyes. To any observer it'd look as if she was asleep, a common mistake made by the untrained. It was almost like going into hibernation, but instead of drifting into the dreamless sleep, she would be mobile and could return to her body at a moment's notice.

Her mind slipped out of her body and she drifted into the corridor, the pulse of magic her beacon. Ealisaid felt too uncomfortable to merely walk through walls and ceilings, even though these barriers were just smoke-filled mirages of their real-world counterparts. As she floated along the hallway she could almost make out shouts coming from the center of power. This was odd in itself, because in spiritform one should be unable to hear anything at all. By the time she reached the door at the end of the corridor the Wizardess could discern voices, but what they said was blurred. She also felt silly because of her fear of not walking through walls and ceilings. She did not need to know the path back to her cell: one thought and she would return to her body. This realization made following the magic much easier.

Walls, ceilings, and floors were left behind as she floated toward the now brightly shining, magical whirlpool. Despite knowing that she could move more speedily, the Phoenix Wizardess refused to hurry. She was still new to this method of travel.

When she entered the room's echo in which the magical vortex pulsed, Ealisaid was glad she had decided against faster movement. Within this chapel she saw a body that appeared very much solid in this world of shadows and smoke, and next to it was something she could not truly describe, even to herself. The thing that even now laid its hands—paws—onto the body, howled... screamed at something she could not see. The woman-dog bared its fangs, scowled,pleaded, and whined. She felt another presence, but it was too weak to make out, and the little she felt made her want to cower in fear. The woman-dog screamed, her voice a howl that was almost discernible. Then the howl became a whimper, a shield, to Ealisaid as solid as the body, interposed between the woman-dog and the man, and the faint nightmare presence.

"Honor the bargain," a voice thundered, and before the last remnant of sound—how was sound possible in the realm of spirits?—faded away, the malevolent presence vanished. The feeling left by the faltering shield was one of resignation.

Ealisaid looked at the man who, while the woman-dog looked less solid with every passing heartbeat, seemed as firm in this spirit realm as he was in the real world. Whatever or whoever this man was, he was anchored in two worlds, and yet there was no visible presence that consciousness existed.

The magic faded, and was gone, but the body remained. A frown creased her forehead when Ealisaid closed in on the still man. She had to know if he was truly an island of solidity in the spiritworld. If her hand passed through his, he was merely another mirage, more focused than the walls around her but still just an image, if not...

The man's fingers closed around hers and held on. She screamed and this yell, pushed through her own mouth, slammed her into her body, and still she screamed. The feeling of being held fast remained with her until she heard the guards' door being unlocked and opened.

"What the bloody Scales is goin' on?" the warden of the watch shouted.

Ealisaid tried to answer but her sore throat made speech impossible, a wheeze the only sound escaping her lips.

"What are you screaming about?" the warden asked, as he poked a torch through the bars to get a better look.

They both heard another pair of footsteps approaching, and the warrior turned away from her and looked at the new arrival. Ale-Breath, Ealisaid realized as the guardsman's stench wafted toward her.

"Witch said she wannet t'see de Baron, sir." Judging from the smell, Ale-Breath had resumed his duties with another bottle to join however many had gone before.

"I told you, pea-brain, that if I caught you with more than a pint of bitter during duty I'll have you lashed, and now you're not only going to get one score but two score caresses o'the cat!" the warden barked. "One of 'em is for you drinking yourself piss-silly on duty, and the other is for you not telling me at once about her request to speak to the Baron!" The man leaned closer to the drunk, but Ealisaid still heard what was being said in a harsh whisper. "You're also gonna be sent to a new post—Dragoncrest!"

The guardsman sniveled and stumbled away, as the warden turned toward her and gave a quick nod. "I'll speak to the Baron, but don't get your hopes up too high; he's a busy man, what with the invasion and all."

Invasion? What was going on in this new world? She still couldn't cope with the apparent fact that her order, her family, her friends were all dead and gone. Now that her thoughts touched the subject of her prolonged hibernation again, she felt like screaming, wailing yet again. Ealisaid fought back her tears and glared at the warden watching her.

"You all right now?" he asked. She nodded. "I'll talk to the Baron." His voice seemed almost gentle, but when she looked into his eyes she saw the barely suppressed rage that was in almost everyone's eyes whenever speaking to her. Not that she could blame them.

A century had passed; she had thought the buildings her magic had blasted mirages. She had killed a dozen or more people, and with the new knowledge of an invasion, she understood the bitterness of the guards. More townsfolk would die in the fight to keep the invaders at bay. Starvation would come, as it always did in the winter, but now it would be more thorough with people from the countryside fleeing to Dunthiochagh. Thank the gods, she had never been in a war, or a siege, but what she knew about both was enough to make her shudder. People would die, and her anger and confusion had already killed some.

Ealisaid sat with her back to the cold stone wall, hugged her thighs against her body, and rested her face on her knees. One hundred years. Did it matter if it were only three score or four score years instead? The people she knew would still be dead. She couldn't hold back any longer; tears ran down her cheeks and soaked her already filthy dress. The man in between worlds, him she envied. At least he did not know what had happened to his loved ones, and he would never feel her guilt, because there was nothing left of him to feel anything. Trapped between worlds, she felt the same. But while the stranger's body and soul rested in both places and neither, hers was in a Now she couldn't understand, and she longed to be in a Past that was no more, destroyed by people she had called colleagues and friends.

One hundred years. This world was without magic, or so Kildanor had told her, and yet there was the vortex she had seen above the trapped man. No, not without magic, she realized since she could cast spells, but without teachers. Was it only here in Janagast... Danastaer that wizards were no more? What about the rest of the world? They couldn't all be gone, could they? She couldn't be the only wizard left. She was still a novice, even with her hibernation finished, a century later than intended, what did she really know about magecraft? Again, Ealisaid felt tears running onto her dress; she drew a shuddering breath and tried to banish the fear, the uncertainty, and the grief. What was there to hold on to? Who was there to hold on to? The only thing she had left was magic, and that was an unreliable friend at the best, and an uncontrollable killer at the worst.

She remembered the day her parents, filled with pride, had sent her away to learn with the Phoenix Wizards. The promises she had made that day, to visit them and help them with the farm, all made void by her sleep. The thought of her mother and father brought on the vision of what might have happened to them during this Heir War. She could see the farmstead burning, the fields torn apart by the same magic she had used when fighting her "illusions." She didn't remember killing anyone, but the houses she'd destroyed had been real, people had lived there.

Guilt, despair, fear; these were her companions as she huddled on her cell's floor, waiting for Baron Duasonh. She had to do something, anything, to keep those maddening thoughts away. Without it, she knew, her fate would be worse than the man caught between two worlds.

Ealisaid woke when someone shook her shoulder. Her back ached, and when she straightened her neck she felt the popping of her spine. A shadow, highlighted by a blinding glare, leaned over her, but the Wizardess could not tell who it was. She blinked away the grit in her eyes, and then wiped her hand over her lids.

The glare was still there, but now she was able to discern the warden who had gone to relay her message to Baron Duasonh. "You awake?" he asked as he withdrew his hand.

She nodded.

"The Baron will see you now," the man said and turned to leave her cell. Ealisaid tried to stand, but the moment her legs left the awkward angle they had been, they cramped. Stifling a whimper, she clutched the doorframe and leaned against the cell wall. She couldn't remember ever having rested in such a weird position, and now knew why people did not sleep this way. It was hardly worth it. But the agony helped keep her mind off her misery.

"You coming?" the warden said. He had already reached the door to the guardroom, and she bit back the vicious retort forming in her mind. Teeth clenched, she nodded and hobbled toward the portal, hugging the right wall as she went. The more she walked, the more she moved her legs, the lesser the pain became. When she stood next to the warden at last, panting as if the twenty-yard walk had instead been a climb up the Shadowpeaks, the Wizardess felt better.

"Where are you taking me?"

The warden took a quick look at her, and then walked into the room. She held back a comment about chivalry regarding a lady when she realized he saw her as nothing more than a prisoner, and a murderer. The same moment she heard the thump of something heavy hit the ground, and when she entered the room, she saw Ale-Breath sprawled on the floor. Underneath the disgusting man lay the remnants of a chair, and next to him were splinters of what must have been a mug.

"Did I not order you to be lashed?" the warden shouted.

Ale-Breath shook his head and looked at his superior, his eyes glazed from drink. "Huh?" was all he said.

"I'm sick of you!" The warden grabbed the guard by the collar and pulled him up as far as he could before his muscles surrendered to the watchman's bulk. "Forty lashes and a night and a day out in the open with only your fat carcass and breeches to keep you warm!"

Instead of leading Ealisaid on, the warden hollered for the next pair of sentries. When the two arrived, he pointed at Ale-Breath. "Get this piece of shit out into the courtyard. You," he pointed at the taller of the two, "administer the lashes. Forty. Then you are to hogtie him as he is, breeches only, and leave him there for everyone to see. The Baron does not suffer drunkards in his guard; make that clear to all who'll be watching this."

After the two warriors had dragged Ale-Breath out, the warden turned back to her. "Procedure," he said, as if that word explained it all. The man turned and walked out the chamber into a larger corridor. Ealisaid followed.

CHAPTER 36

Something moved in front of him. Drangar frowned and looked on, trying to decide whether his imagination still played tricks on him, even in death. No, the blackness before him pulsed, deepened. It looked as if someone was trying to push through a layer of heavy fabric.

Now he could discern dim light shining through the darkness. It heaved and strained against the barrier holding it back. Pinpoints of luminescence pierced the dark, leaving him staring at the spectacle.

A few moments later more light broke through and Drangar saw the faint outline of a person. It was vaguely feline. Its features seemed strained, torn, as if the darkness's mere presence snapped and clawed at it. Drangar watched, curiosity winning over confusion.

"What are you?" he asked.

The being looked his way, and despite its attempt to look compassionate Drangar recoiled at the sheer malevolence the entity's face held. A large part of him despaired at the sight, but a small fraction of his conscience, the part of his soul that had always lashed out when he had been drinking too much, the part that fed his furor, reveled in the creature's presence.

Here in this dark void he had more control over his mind than ever before. His daily rituals, the meditation, even his baths had given him the mastery needed to suppress the piece of his soul he hated most.

The creature's sneer was replaced by a mask of frustration and anger, as it pounded against the fine netting of darkness that held it back. In the formless space Drangar occupied, he couldn't feel any of it; but he saw the strain on the feline beast's face. Yet despite all the attention this monstrosity put into breaking through this veil, he felt its eyes burning into him.

Fear like nothing he'd known welled up inside; he struggled to move legs that weren't there, desperate to get away. His will seeped away and he stared at the fiend in frightened horror.

"What do you want from me?" he howled.

The creature didn't answer; instead it clawed at the seemingly indestructible netting that held it back. Then, when Drangar thought the monster would give up, it smashed into the barrier again, howling. Its voice was inhuman, worse than anything he had ever heard. It was the scream of the dying mixed with so much hate, anger, and frustration all muddled into a bone-chilling wail.

Terror renewed in his heart and Drangar desperately tried to turn and flee. "Who are you?" he roared, trying to banish his own fear.

"Your future," said the demon—it had to be a demon—its voice a growl that would have frozen anyone's blood. Even in death Drangar felt the vile power emanating from the being.

Then a soothing presence enveloped him.

Dog was the only living being to witness Drangar's corpse thrashing and twisting on its bier. She closed her eyes, took a deep breath, and hopped onto the table. The moment her paws touched wood, the frantically whipping body ceased its movement. The canine stepped forward, paws touching the cleaned, marred stomach. Immediately, Dog collapsed and lay still, breathing shallowly.

"You need to help me!" Cat repeated, ghostly eyes glaring at Lightbringer. "Now!"

"Very well," the ancient witch said. "I can bring you to his side, but from the moment you enter the Veil you will be on your own."

Lightbringer thrust her clawed hand through Cat's spiritform and began a low, humming chant. Mere heartbeats later the spiritform was gone.

"Stay away from him, creature!" snarled a female voice.

The black netting holding the demon grew more solid, forcing the struggling fiend back. Drangar tried to discern the origin of the female speaker, but aside from the feeling of comfort surrounding him there was nothing.

"Harlot, you can't change what is predestined," snapped the demon, teeth flashing against the black of the veil.

"The time has not come!"

Drangar's confused look wandered from the comfortable darkness around him to the demon. The net pulsed as the creature tore at it with renewed vigor.

"Yet! Damn you, shrew, don't interfere!"

"No," the formless shadow around Drangar said with calm conviction.

Suddenly, a wisp of light escaped from the veil, lanced toward and pierced him and the surrounding shade. Drangar screamed like he had never screamed before. Agony, pure white pain roared through him.

Mindless, senseless, he writhed in anguish.

This was his soul the demon tortured! A small part of his conscious woke, despite the torment. He grew aware of the shadow's howl echoing his own inhuman scream. How was this possible? Detached, the tiny sliver of his mind that remained unaffected by the pain observed and analyzed his tormentor. He was a spirit, and spirits shouldn't be able to touch one another.

He hadn't even been able to touch his own arm, and this being of light could cause indescribable pain. Even the sword that had gutted him had not caused so much agony. The female's scream was cut off, and he felt alone again, the presence that had enveloped him was gone.

Drangar expected the pain to vanish, but it remained. Stronger than before. That portion of the attack the shadow had shielded him from thrust into him as well. It consumed the last shred of reason, and he screamed, louder than before.

The Chosen of Lesganagh entered Harail through a hidden passageway. Halmond, Lerainh's grandfather, had it constructed back when Harail had been a small village. Halmond had wanted this to be the Chosen's way into the royal palace, and had never passed the secret on to his son.

"I doubt the High General had regicide in mind for us when he had this place built," Kildanor whispered, using Halmond's Chanastardhian rank.

"He'd turn and thrash in his grave if he knew what his grandson has done to strengthen the realm," Orkeanas replied.

"I said it then and I say it again, I should have drowned the brat like a sick puppy when I had the chance," Kildanor growled, fury distorting his voice. He didn't know whom he was angrier at, himself or his brethren who had prevented him from killing Lerainh forty years ago.

"Enough of that," the First ordered.

They had reached the end of the tunnel and the flickering, hissing torches cast their shadows against a seamless wall. Engraved into the wall was the sun and sword symbol of Lesganagh. There were few people who remembered this sigil; even Kildanor hadn't seen it in a long time. He resented being back in Harail. He resented being back among the ranks of the Chosen. Despite Orkeanas, despite everyone else, he felt he did not belong with them. New faces, most of them, and from the sidelong glances they gave him, he felt that they resented him too. They didn't say as much, but their looks told enough. He was the outcast, the prodigal son. Twenty-four had started out at the eve of the Heir War, following the mandates of Lesganagh. Twenty-two had fought off the demons, again according to Lesganagh's wishes. Then there had come nothing but endless routine, guarding the land, the realm's protector, Halmond and his scions. He had not sat by idly to wait for things to unfold; he wanted the Chosen to intervene, to change who ruled. They had banished him when he had told them Lerainh was endangering everything. He was an outcast, and now, despite all their misgivings, all their differences, he stood here to pass judgment on the man he, Kildanor, had already found wanting so long ago.

"Where'll he be?" Galen asked.

Galen was one of the oldest, chosen during the Demon War.

Kildanor turned and beamed at the older-looking man. There was a resolution in Galen's eyes he had not noticed before. Of all the Chosen, he had expected Galen to be on his side when he had wanted to put Cumaill Duasonh on the throne. Galen had been the last to voice his concerns about the regicide, and only after Orkeanas's prompting.

"They won't keep him in the dungeons," Kildanor said. "There are rules, remember," he added. "A king must not be touched; the same goes for nobles."

"We saw some pompous asses dangling on Gallows' Hill, mate," Galen replied. "Guess they barely resisted."

"They'd also put Caddoc and Vailin to the sword there," Sellic, one of the youngest Chosen, said.

"You hang people that refuse to surrender," Galen said. "At least that's what I'd do if I was in their place."

Much had changed, Kildanor thought. He felt it. There was dissent in the ranks. He looked at Galen and inched over to him. "Come to regret past mistakes?" he whispered.

"I understood the need for unity, but the last few weeks have been proof enough you were right," the other replied. "I'm sorry."

"What's done is done, friend, just make sure he won't make any more mistakes like that. You're the voice of reason, now that I'm gone." He had always liked the man, more so now.

"Reasonable? You?" Galen chuckled well humoredly. "You're the most cold-blooded of us. Straight and searing, like His rays. Orkeanas is too proud to admit his mistake. You know that. Yet, the sun can't rule alone, he must be tempered by the cold of the moon. Lesganagh, Eanaigh, two sides of the same coin. There's no one here to temper a rule of Chosen."

He shook his head. Galen was right, of course, but he felt certain the invasion and what came at the heels of the Chanastardhians could have been avoided if Lerainh had been killed decades ago. He was about to say as much, when blinding sunlight outshone every torch in the tunnel. The surge of illumination glared for a mere heartbeat, and was followed by a slight grating of stone on stone and a soft breeze that carried with it the stench of rotting straw, urine, and shit. The way was clear.

A hush went through the line of Chosen, and Kildanor followed Orkeanas's lead as they rushed through the dungeons. The First sent two of their number ahead to clear the way, and a few long and anxious breaths later, two muffled thuds signaled the score of remaining men and women that the path was free. A few passed him, people he did not know, replacements for the dead.

Elara, who had joined their ranks shortly before he had left the court, halted before him. She looked dangerous, green eyes flashing like emerald daggers, hair as shortly cropped as any man's. "Welcome back," she whispered and was off again.

Apparently, Galen wasn't the only one who had come to their senses. He glanced at his brethren. The older-looking Chosen put a firm hand on his shoulder. Then all but the two of them were through.

More out of habit than necessity, Kildanor and Galen formed the rearguard, and when they entered the small watch-room the others had already surged ahead. He noticed the same cruel efficiency he had used against the insurgents inside Dunthiochagh only a few days ago. Then they were on the stairs and headed up, fast on their brethren's heels.

The pair passed more corpses, but so far, no alarm had been raised. Everything was quiet. It had been a long time since he had been inside the royal palace, but his memory of the place was good enough. After this set of stairs, behind a heavy steeloak door lay the great entrance hall. They had to cross the thirty yards or so to reach the main stairway that led to the second floor, which had long hallways leading east and west to the respective wings. Lerainh's quarters were in the eastern wing, and Kildanor suspected the monstrous king was being held there.

They stormed through the entrance hall. A dozen bloodied corpses lay on the floor, and four Chosen remained to cover their way back. From the look of it, Kildanor could tell some of the Chanastardhians had not gone down without a fight, and he wondered why no one had heard the struggle and acted upon it. His hand shot out to stop Galen, but the other must have thought the same thing and was standing still.

Kildanor wanted to order the other four to easily defensible points, but saw that the quartet was already in position. "What the bloody Scales is going on?" he whispered his voice barely audible.

He wasn't sure if Galen had heard him, for the other was turning slowly to inspect all entryways. When he wanted to repeat his question, Galen held up his hand, motioning to remain silent. From the banquet hall to the west came the clash of weapons and the frantic cheers of several people. "Duel?" Galen asked quietly.

Kildanor strained his hearing, concentrated on the din of voices and weapons. Someone was certainly taking a beating. He nodded his confirmation, and then continued up the stairs, motioning the rearguard to pay attention to the doors leading to the great hall.

When they reached the second floor, they saw another set of dead guards, and another pair when they made their way toward the eastern wing. The two hurried down the corridor. Next to every other door stood one of their number, and when they reached the king's quarters, a place Kildanor had guarded so many times in the last century, they found Orkeanas.

The First of the Chosen of Lesganagh kneeled before the gilded door, deep in prayer. The pair slowed, and when they stood next to their leader, Orkeanas opened his eyes and looked up. A first, quick glance at Galen, then he took his time to inspect Kildanor.

Kildanor had never seen the man so sad. He knew pride and devotion burned deep inside Orkeanas's eyes, but now they were replaced by grief.

"You were right, old friend," the First finally said. "We should have listened to you. I was wrong. We should have made Duasonh king. We have to save what we can." He looked at Galen, whispering, "Wise choice, Lord."

Fire returned to the leader's eyes, but instead of the bright, flickering flame of purpose he had always associated with Orkeanas, he now saw sadness, guilt, and determination. Then, straightening his shoulders, the First stood and touched the door.

His fingertips caressed the wood, and in a heartbeat, flames leapt up from the gate. There was no protest from the material, no popping, no tearing; the fire came and went far too quickly for that. No sooner had the searing begun than it was over, and the trio saw the bloated form of Lerainh, King of Danastaer, sitting on his bed, quilted covers held up to his mouth, gaping in horror at the slowly whirling ashes of his doors.

Then, seeing the intruders were his Chosen, he leapt up and rushed toward them. It was then that Kildanor showed his face, gave Lerainh one of his grim smiles, and a mocking salute. "Your *Highness*," he spat.

"You've come to rescue me!" the king pleaded as he stepped back from the blistering heat of the door.

"Lerainh, third King of Danastaer," Orkeanas began, as he seemingly grew taller. Kildanor had seen this display of divine power before, but it surprised him how much disdain and loathing were in his leader's voice and posture. "Lerainh, Lord Protector of the realm, first guardian of the Hold, you have been found wanting." Kildanor thought this pomp wasted on the King, would have preferred to kill Lerainh and be done with it. He had never been a friend of ceremony, yet this was Orkeanas's task, to judge the monarch and follow Lesganagh's orders. "You have failed in your duties, Highness, and must be tried."

Lerainh whimpered, like so many children probably had when they had been called to the King's chambers. When Kildanor thought of all the bodies that must have been carried out of these chambers by willing servants, week after week, his fury toward the ruler rose once again. Now, the King was on his knees, pleading for mercy, but Kildanor did not hear him, would not hear him, all he saw was a man who deserved worse than death. "Guilty," he managed to growl, and had his sword almost out of its sheath before he felt Galen's restraining hand on his.

"Guilty," Galen said.

"Guilty." Orkeanas's voice so full of bitterness and venom that for a moment he was uncertain whether it had been the First saying the word. "Lerainh, King of Danastaer, you have been tried by Lesganagh's Chosen, and have been found guilty of treason. The penalty for traitors to Lesganagh, traitors to the cause of protecting the Hold, is death." Orkeanas stepped toward the monarch who edged away, whimpering.

Kildanor pushed Galen aside and strode across the room. He grabbed Lerainh by the collar and picked him up.

"Bastard, look at me!" he shouted. When the King didn't acknowledge him, he slapped the man. "Look at me!"

He wanted to strangle the life out of him, wanted him to at least slightly feel what all those children had felt when they were murdered by his royal hands.

"Bastard! You gods-damned bastard! Look at me!" This time he punched, and shattered the King's nose. "Open your eyes, murderer! Traitor!" Again, he smashed his fist into the King's face. "Look at me!" He didn't care if Orkeanas or Galen saw him. All the years of pent up anger and rage released themselves as he held Lerainh in his hands. "Murderer, look at me!" he shouted, his fist shattering the King's jaw. Kildanor felt Orkeanas's hand on his arm, the one holding the King, and he turned to face his fellow Chosen.

"You want to give this animal the benefit of being burned quickly?" he roared. "Look me in the eye and say he deserves mercy!" His stare held Orkeanas's. "Come on, give me your sermons about how we are not supposed to interfere! Tell me how there is no heir to the throne! Tell me we need to honor Halmond's legacy!" He wanted to spit into the First's face. "Tell me!"

Instead he punched Lerainh again. "Tell me we mustn't interfere! And tell the poor souls who suffered at this monster's hands there was nothing we could have done to save them!" His fist smashed into the King's jaw a second time, driving bone splinters through chin and lips. "Tell me he deserves a merciful death!" This time his fist drove into the king's left temple. By now Lerainh's head was a bloody pulp. "Tell me!"

Orkeanas bowed his head. "I can't," he whispered. "Damn you, Kildanor, I can't. You were right, and I have failed. The pig should have died decades ago."

Startled, he looked at the First, saw him turn his back and

heard him say, "Do with him as you wish, we'll wait."

They didn't have to wait long, for Kildanor had barely enough time to punch Lerainh once more when shouts of alarm and the sound of steel on steel reached the royal chambers. Their entry had been discovered.

CHAPTER 37

The center of the Great Hall of Harail's palace was empty. Tables and chairs had been moved aside to make way for the coming duel. Anne tested her maul's weight as she looked across the room to her opponent. Callan of House Farlin regarded her with a mixture of fear and disdain. Disdain she knew and could live with. The dread that crept into the nobleman's ash-grey face was new to her. Her gaze wandered up and down the man as he tried to gain a feel for the massive weapon in his hands. She had to admit, she liked this feeling of power. To have a southern noble trembling before her was almost as good as the thought of giving Callan Farlin a good thrashing. To draw first blood would be quite a feat, but she thought she could accomplish that without shattering too many bones. Her feelings of superiority were quelled some when she thought of Gwennaith's remark.

"Pay attention to his poisoned dagger," she muttered absentmindedly as she looked for a dirk on her opponent. Nothing out of the ordinary; hauberk, half helm, plate gauntlets. The gauntlets would hinder the man more than aid him. She knew that from experience. Farlin would certainly wear leather underneath his chain. His legs were protected by plate, another mistake if he didn't know how to move properly. Anne remembered how long it had taken her to get used to the interlocking plates. She had trained in plate in her father's great hall for weeks, but in the cold mountains no sane warrior would wear it. The things were too prone to freezing up in the snow and if one wasn't properly trained, its superior protection did not make up for the lack of mobility, even against a maul.

There! Callan Farlin's right boot seemed a little thicker at the ankle than his left. The squire was right. Given the chance, the noble would try to stab her. "Then he won't have that chance," Anne muttered. She lifted her maul one final time, and let its heft slam onto the marble floor. "Ready!" She gave Mireynh a nod.

"And you, Callan of House Farlin?" the High General asked. It seemed to Anne he could barely hide a smirk.

"Ready." But he didn't sound it at all, and she wasn't the only one to notice. A few catcalls echoed from one side to the other, but were silenced when Urgraith Mireynh stood.

"Any rule breaking will result in summary execution. Fight fairly, 'til first blood. Begin!" No sooner had the last word left Mireynh's lips when Callan Farlin attacked. He came at her with raised hammer as if he wanted to drive her into the ground. Anne saw the man had a little training with plate, but that wasn't enough. He was too slow.

She sidestepped his swing, let the head of the maul slip down, and thrust the long handle between her opponent's legs when he moved past her. Farlin's momentum carried him forward, the maul pulled him sideways, and her quick thrust stopped both motions so that the noble hit the floor quickly, much to the amusement of the men and women who had toasted, only recently, to his health. Instead of using her advantage and bringing the maul down upon the prone Farlin, Anne stepped away. She wanted this humiliation to last longer than a few heartbeats.

The nobleman stood and glared at her. A quick glance confirmed the dagger was still in his boot. His next approach was more cautious, but Anne could tell her opponent was still getting used to the ungainliness of the maul. This time his attack came horizontally. She stepped back to watch Callan Farlin pirouette around until he faced her again. The audience's laughter was much louder this time.

Farlin's scowl gave her enough of a warning before the nobleman charged her. Instead of a retreat, Anne thrust her maul's head straight for the onrushing opponent's face, and she had to give the young man credit for his reflexes as he bent low to avoid her attack. Still, she stood in his path and merely let her maul drop, so that it hammered down onto his spine. Again, the noble was flung to the ground.

"Can we start the fight soon, or is this a dance?" Anne taunted as she stepped away. "In which case I think I need to get my dress." Now the audience cheered for her.

She watched her opponent get up, dagger still in the boot. At least he was trying to win fairly.

"Is this all you can do, whore? Dodge and mock?"

Anne cocked an eyebrow. "You want more? Fine with me," she said. She hefted her maul as she would a quarterstaff, like her teachers had taught her, and advanced. A quick thrust with its head, a teasing poke with the haft. Callan Farlin parried one but was too slow for the other. He still held his maul more like an axe, forgetting one of the most basic teachings that any weapons-master would offer: a weapon is. Any part of a melee-weapon can be used to injure. Her maul's haft connected with his helm and sent the nobleman stumbling.

She gave him no time to recover. Leading with the handle, she stepped toward him. She blocked his weak counterthrust with the maul's wood, swept into the man's range, and smashed the haft into his groin.

The men in the audience groaned alongside Callan Farlin but she wasn't finished. With the noble's guard down, she gave his shoulder a resounding blow with the maul's steel head. The noble lost hold of his weapon and stumbled to his right, his face a grimace of pain.

Anne let her maul's heavy top drop to the floor and leaned casually against its shaft. "Do you yield?"

"No!" Farlin hissed through clenched teeth.

"Retrieve your weapon then," she said and took her hammer into both hands again.

The nobleman walked over to the spot where his weapon had hit the ground and bent over to retrieve it. He swayed for a moment, and then brought his hands to the floor to steady himself. To any of the spectators it was quite a normal reaction, considering the punishment he had already taken. But when he stood, Anne saw that the bulge in his boot was gone. She focused on the man's stance and how he held his weapon. There were only two hands in which he could hold the dagger, but he also had to maintain the illusion that he was going to keep on fighting with his maul.

There was only one way to find out. Again, she led the attack with the shaft. She thrust the staff forward, and watched how well Farlin parried. He countered her attack with the shaft as well, although she detected a hint of clumsiness. The noble's right hand held the top end firmly, which meant the dagger was in his left.

Anne retreated a few steps and considered her options. Callan Farlin did not follow; he obviously waited for her to present him with an opening. She turned her grip on the maul so that the weapon's head now hung under her left hand. Then she advanced, her right hand sliding down the shaft to rest next to her left. Using the shaft much like one used a sword in high guard, she attacked.

Farlin looked confused as he parried her slashes on his maul's wooden handle. She thrust to his right again and again, forcing her opponent to parry with the head of his weapon, and she noticed how insecure his left hand's grip was. As he countered her thrusts, Callan Farlin retreated, his eyes darting left and right, searching for an opening. Anne denied him his chance and feinted her next thrust to which Farlin expectantly raised the shaft, but instead of pushing her improvised blade all the way forward, she reversed the momentum and smashed her maul's head into the hand holding both shaft and dagger.

Not only was there the telltale crunch of bones breaking under the assault, but also the clatter of a blade dropping to the floor. She heard the word "Foul!" echoing through the room, looked over to the High General and waited.

Urgraith Mireynh stood and the noble mob quieted down. Disdain and anger were plain on his face; Anne almost expected him to finish Callan of House Farlin himself, but the general did not move. He looked at the treacherous aristocrat and then at her. "Finish it," he said.

"By your leave," she replied and looked at the wounded nobleman. "Now, can you fight for your life?"

From the corner of her eye she saw a few other nobles leave

the hall. They probably did not want to witness the slaughter of one of their own, one who, in all likelihood was as much a coward as they were.

Callan Farlin rose to his feet, maul clutched in both hands, the weapon's head straight before his face, despite his apparent pain. She couldn't help but give him credit for facing death standing tall, and honored his gesture with a salute of her own. Briefly she tipped her hammer's shaft to her forehead before whirling it around so her hold on it was again with both hands a decent space apart.

Then Anneijhan of House Cirrain attacked in earnest. Jab followed by a smash; both were deflected by her opponent. Sheer desperation seemed to drive the man, but it was more luck than skill that kept her from hitting him. Thrust, parry—the bastard was fighting back!—counterthrust. Suddenly the one-sided contest straightened itself. In Farlin's eyes Anne saw his fear replaced by determination, and it was she that retreated from a vicious swing. She parried the next thrust and used her opponent's momentum to whirl her around. Her maul's heavy shaft smashed into the nobleman's shoulder; again, she heard bones snapping.

Dizzy, she stepped back, weapon held before her to block any possible attack, and tried to regain her sense of direction. Callan Farlin was beaten, and from the look on his face he knew it. Her world stopped spinning and she raised her maul to finish what now became an execution when she and everyone else in the room heard the ring of steel on steel accompanied by shouts.

The castle's defenses had been penetrated.

Drangar felt the fury emanating from the luminous being that tried to push through the shadows.

"I know your plan, Lawpisser!" the male voice snarled.

"Your kind never knew to watch your tongue."

"You can't interfere!"

"Says who? Which law states I can't defend me and mine?" the voice surrounding Drangar held a cold determination.

"He never was yours, Lawspitter!"

"You are bound by your word, sunargh!" Her voice boomed.

Drangar felt as if a powerful gale passed him and shoved the light back. Then darkness engulfed him once more, and he was alone. Again.

"Could have stayed to chat," he muttered.

After the exchange the silence became even more unbearable, even though he didn't quite understand what the argument had been about. The demon wanted his future, or so it claimed. And who was the other being that had protected him? He had called her Lawspitter. Could it be... His thoughts halted; he was unwilling even to contemplate such a thing. Had everyone forsaken him?

How could a demon want his future? He was dead, beyond the grasp of man and god, adrift in this black nothing. How could anyone want his future if he didn't want it himself, and wouldn't want it even if he'd still been alive?

Dunthiochagh.

Hesmera.

He tried to recall her easy laughter, her mischievous grin; she had always managed to make him feel good about himself. Instead he saw the smears that had been her body on the floor, glassy, dead eyes looking at nothing. Hatred took Drangar again, multiplied, and burned inside him. He hated himself.

How could anyone want such a future, a life so filled with self-loathing that he could hardly stand it? The scars from his unsuccessful attempts to take his life felt real, even in this world of gloom.

Hate and fear. He remembered the force with which he had cut his wrists, and he also remembered his fear of being stranded in the vast nothingness reserved for those the gods deemed unworthy. Somehow, he had bandaged himself and the cuts had mended, despite their depth.

Was there anything left, he wondered. After all, to the world he had left behind, he was dead and the gods didn't want him; otherwise he would not be stranded here. He could hardly blame them. He deserved to be adrift in this nothingness. The demon? What did it want with him? Why would a demon have an interest in a soul adrift?

He should have died with Hesmera. Now he would never

have a chance to tell her how sorry he was. The past years hadn't washed away his pain. Indeed, they had dulled it to the point where almost everything he saw was plain and pointless. The bandages that healed his cuts had done nothing to heal his heart. No bandage would ever heal the wounds Hesmera's death had left behind. He recalled his face, the reflection cast by any shiny surface, and growled, "I hate you! I don't want you! Get lost!"

He did not. All that was left to him was himself. He felt a hand touching his cheek. A ghostly, fluttering caress that left a tad of warmth where there had been only cold, dark emptiness. Then it was gone, but it left behind something he had not felt since Dunthiochagh: the feeling of being loved.

"You shall not fade. I'll be with you," the female voice from before whispered. Or at least he thought he heard something. In this darkness, nothing and everything seemed possible. Why would anybody love him? How could anybody love him when he didn't love himself?

CHAPTER 38

"Kildanor! We must go!" He heard the anxiety in Galen's voice, and all he felt was disappointment. He had imagined Lerainh's execution differently. More slowly, at least. Now with the Chanastardhians alerted to their intrusion there was no time. The Second of the Chosen shook his head, hoping against hope that it wasn't true. Galen's voice shattered that hope, "Kildanor, we have to get out!"

He grunted in disappointment as he grabbed Lerainh's head with both hands. "This should have been slower, bastard," he hissed and twisted. The King's neck snapped, but although he felt the royal monster shudder and die, he kept turning the head until Lerainh's sightless eyes looked down his back.

Kildanor stood and headed for the corridor; Galen and Orkeanas had already left to join the battle. As he left the king's chamber he had an idea. The other Chosen were too honorable to consider spying; they were warriors of Lesganagh and their main duty was to fight. In the time he had spent with Cumaill Duasonh he had learned that knowing was the better part of fighting any war. His brethren usually just reacted. Instead of merely killing the King they should have also searched the palace for clues, orders, anything that would explain why Chanastardh was suddenly so interested in a country it could have owned a century ago. What reason did King Drammoch have to send troops south now?

Torn between two options, helping his fellow Chosen or using the time they were buying to find out what he could, Kildanor stood in the hallway, sword in hand but undecided. He wondered what Cumaill would do in his stead. Cumaill

Duasonh the leader, the crafty bastard who gathered enough information to make his opponents nervous before he let loose the dogs. Once convinced, Cumaill had provoked Jathain into action, hoping his cousin would not be prepared. Well, he actually had gambled with the traitor's unpreparedness but had judged Jathain's situation well enough. Maybe the others would buy him time to search for the enemy general's quarters. He recalled the palace's structure, its rooms and hallways, possible guard-posts and likely staff-rooms.

"If I was a Chanastardhian general, which place would I pick? A room already furnished for paperwork."

There were at least a dozen of those in the royal palace. It had to be one with easy access to vital areas and the mustering ground to the north. There were only two rooms suitable for that. One was Halmond's office and the other belonged to the chief tax collector. "Halmond's," Kildanor whispered and hurried away from the sounds of battle that came from the grand staircase.

There were two ways through the palace to get to Halmond's study, and both required going through guarded passages. At least they had been guarded during his time here, but any watch-captain worth his pay would post sentries where Danastaerian sentinels had stood before. He didn't know how long the others would be able to hold the enemy back, didn't even know how they planned to escape, and this left only one option. Head to the room directly above the study, through the window, down into the office and pray his hunch was correct.

Kildanor turned left at a corner; just a few more steps and he had reached the chamber. He opened the first door on his left and knew the moment he caught sight of the room's interior it was the wrong one. He had spent so much time not thinking about Harail and the palace that he had forgotten some of its features. The suite he was looking for had windows on two walls, north and west, this one's were just to the west. Kildanor poked his head out onto the hallway and looked down both directions, still focused on the sounds of battle. The corridor was free of guards, at least for now, and he ran to the north, the way he had originally been going.

The next two doors he dismissed, for there were at least another pair of doors, judging from the frame of one to the west, and a second entry facing north. He tried the first one.

It opened into a small chamber, which was occupied by a young woman with flame-red hair. She wore chainmail and held a sword with both hands. "I don't have time for this," he muttered and pulled the door shut again with such a force that it splintered and cracked as it wedged into the frame. It had to be the other one; he wasted no time checking to see if the lock was in place and slammed his body into the portal. The wood gave way after creaking under the onslaught, then he was through. Halmond's study was directly underneath.

Kildanor paused, looked about the room, and found what he needed. On the east and south wall, a hideous tapestry still mutilated the plaster. It told the tale of the Demon War. Halmond had had it commissioned right after the costly victory, and when the piece had been finished the King had decided to let it grace the diplomat quarters.

It was truly a particular piece of utter tastelessness, but had the length he needed. Sounds of guards were coming his way from the east, if his ears served him right, making the descent more hurried than planned. He grabbed the tapestry's end near the door and pulled. The cloth felt heavy in his hands, and the nails holding the monster up offered enough resistance for his plan to work. He pulled away more of the wall hanging as he walked toward the window that should be directly above the one in the study. It would be a close call, the cloth might not be long enough, but the time was up. The sound of the sentries was closer, and the woman imprisoned in her own room was cutting her way through the door. It had to be now.

Kildanor sprinted to the window, tapestry on his shoulder, eyes buried by his left arm. He jumped, felt the splintering glass shred his cloak and surcoat, cutting his face and scalp. Then, for a short moment, the cloth snapped taut and then gave way. The chill night air briefly caressed his bleeding face, before he slammed into the wall. The impact drove the air from his lungs. His boots scraped along the glass of the window below, and just as he began to wonder how he could get into the room, the tapestry ripped out more nails and his descent began again. Plaster rushed past him; he heard shouts from up above, his nose scraped against the upper stone of the window frame, and then his feet touched the sill.

Despite the commotion upstairs, Kildanor heard the din of battle raging in the castle. He looked up and saw a woman looking down. The head withdrew and shouted something unintelligible into the room. As he kicked in the window, its lacquered wood splintering, he saw the guards upstairs heaving out a heavy cabinet. He let his body follow the thrust of his leg and tumbled into the room. A wooden cross that held some piece of armor slowed his fall, and all came crashing down onto the floor.

"Bruised but still in the fight," Kildanor muttered as he stood, groaning. "That's what I call breaking and entering," he chuckled. The moment of mirth passed, and the Chosen looked about the room.

It was Halmond's study; his guess had been correct. On the steeloak desk were several maps atop each other and next to them a low pile of weighed-down parchments. There was no time to sift through the letters. He grabbed everything and turned to face the door as it was thrust open.

Two black clad women rushed in, swords drawn. Kildanor shoved paper into his tunic and unsheathed his blade. The light from the corridor illuminated enough of the room to reveal the limited space available. But the pair knew what they were doing. One moved to the left while her partner remained to block the doorway. By now there would be warriors coming down to join the black clad women, and possibly even some marshalling on the ground.

From the sound of it the fight was still going strong, but as he assessed his options, he felt the first Chosen dying. In Dunthiochagh he wouldn't have felt anything; distance was relevant to the bond. Here only a few score yards away, the loss of life, the release of Lesganagh's Call, the searching soul, all was felt. It wasn't a new sensation, far from it. During the Heir War the first Chosen had died, but they had been the first to die in line, and their Call, their spirit, hadn't been so filled with knowledge and memories as the ones who came after them. Now, the death of one of his brethren felt like a shout uttered by a choir.

Kildanor recovered his senses quickly enough to parry the advancing woman's blow. He hadn't felt the death of another Chosen in three decades, was not used to the death-wail anymore. From the sound of battle, he knew the others were unhindered by the pain of a Chosen's death.

He parried another slash, and another, and fell back, trying to think. There were two options, rejoin the others, or flee into the night. Neither was easy, but his chances were best if he stayed with his brethren. A lone fugitive in the streets would be caught much easier than a score of Chosen.

The woman came at him again. This time he drove her blade to his left with a two-handed slash of his own. For a moment the warrior looked confused, gave him the chance of surveying the room. He stood near the scattered armor. He beamed a smile at the Chanastardhian, went to his knees, switched his sword into his left hand, and grabbed the breastplate with his right. His opponent was still on guard, eyes on him. The study's table was between her, her companion, and the armor; he guessed neither had seen him take the plate. They probably suspected him to throw a knife, but he did not give them the anticipated attack.

Instead, Kildanor pulled his right arm back, and then let the breastplate fly toward the face of the unsuspecting second woman. His throw was rewarded by an unhealthy crunch as steel bit deep into her face. The same moment the piece of armor cruashed into one woman, the Chosen jumped toward the other, his sword still in his left hand. His blade blocked the enemy's slash, then his fist connected with her jaw.

He was out of the study in a heartbeat and rushed toward the ongoing melee. Another Chosen fell, the Wail unbalancing him for a few steps; then he stumbled into the great hallway.

The Chanastardhians had their backs to him. The stairs were littered with the dead and dying, and his fellow Chosen were slowly pressing forward. These were the warriors of Lesganagh, and as such they fought. Unyielding, merciless, like the sun itself. Galen and Orkeanas formed the center; he had to stand with them.

Kildanor used his chance to wreak havoc among the defenders. In battle the only rule that mattered was winning. And if the wars and battles he had fought had taught him one thing, it was how to win. He slammed into the defenders, barreled one man to the ground as his sword lashed out left and right into the throats of two more. Before the enemy had time to react to this new threat, another man went down in a gurgle of blood. The sun didn't care whom it burned, and neither did he.

Galen saw the opening and shouted something to the Chosen standing to his left. They wheeled about, their swords driving the defenders back. Kildanor cut down three more and then closed the line.

"We need to get out!" he panted.

"Do tell," Ultan, the Chosen next to him, replied as he thrust his blade into an enemy.

Another Chanastardhian attacked. He parried, turned the blade to his left, and punched the woman in the face. Before he could finish her off, he had to bring his sword up to parry an overhead swing from a man coming from behind her. He blocked the two-handed sword, chanced a quick kick into his downed foe's stomach, and then focused on the man wielding the greatsword.

There was a commotion to his right, and he felt more than saw his brethren wheel about. He followed, retreating to the right, back to the stairwell; the Chanastardhians seized the advantage and pressed on. He stumbled across a corpse, regained his footing just long enough to deflect the greatsword again. Still their line retreated. A puddle of blood made him slip; his next parry was clumsier than the last, the Chanastardhian knew how to use the weapon and had the strength to deliver arm-numbing attacks. He chanced a quick glance over his shoulder.

By now the line of Chosen had turned into a **V**, with Orkeanas as the center. The main door that led out of the palace was next to him, and now Kildanor knew and felt what was about to happen. Despite his opponent's attacks he wept, parrying blow after blow with tears running down his cheeks.

CHAPTER 39

Callan Farlin fit Anne Cirrain's assessment perfectly. The nobleman indeed resorted to betrayal at the first opportune moment. Urgraith Mireynh saw the man draw a dagger from his boot, and would have interfered immediately had he not caught a glimpse of the Cirrain woman's apparent notice of Farlin's action. So far, she had shown skill and intuition, and her change of posture assured him she was indeed prepared for the man's hidden weapon. He would let the battle play itself out, for now. If House Farlin's scion was as inept in the use of the dagger as he was with the maul, there was no real danger for Cirrain.

As he watched the woman fight, Mireynh considered the missive he had received just before supper. The letter was still tucked into his tunic, and its contents disturbed him. Of all the nobles in his army Cirrain was the only one who behaved like a warrior. She knew how to handle weapons, without a doubt. Wielding a maul with skill was hard enough, and if this knowledge was any indicator there would be few weapons she was unfamiliar with. She had an eye for detail, as evidenced by her noticing the concealed dagger, and she had a cool, rational head on her shoulders. Had things been different he would have made her a warleader.

Things had changed, though. House Cirrain had broken with Herascor and allied itself with the northmen. The High General had no idea why, but that hardly mattered. His orders were to keep House Cirrain's warriors under close observation, use them in fatal missions, and keep any news and messengers away from them. Cirrain was to be kept from her men at all costs, and should the need arise, she was to be arrested and transported back to Herascor where she'd most likely be used as a hostage against House Cirrain's rebellion.

He scowled. There was nothing he could do. Should he disobey, his wife and children were doomed. There was no option; the High Advisor had been very clear on this. Obey or suffer the consequences.

At first, the position of High General had been nothing more than that of any other leader. His duties were like the ones he had had before: see to the training and drill warleaders. Army stuff. He had been able to talk with King Drammoch, had enjoyed having the monarch's confidence, but things had changed, and he still had no idea what had really happened. Not that he was or had been in any position to influence things. Now, it mattered little; the King had assured his obedience by taking his family hostage. Obey or suffer the consequences.

It would be the same with House Cirrain.

How the woman could fight! Now Farlin's dagger clattered to the ground, his left hand shattered by a hammer blow. Now that his treachery had been revealed, protocol demanded that Callan of House Farlin die.

"Finish it," Mireynh said. He saw several nobles get up and leave the Great Hall, most likely friends or supporters of the foolish man who was about to meet the gods and be judged by Lliania's Scales.

Although his attention was still on the battle, he glanced at those who were leaving and tried to commit their faces to memory. With so many Houses, he had a hard time remembering all of them. So many details. Which House was of importance, which wasn't, who was allied with whom and why. A dozen other things he had to pay attention to when assigning duties and warbands.

Back in his mercenary days, things had been so much easier. Feuds had always been short-lived, usually ending with a brawl or the head of one aggressor mounted on a pike as an example to others not overstep their bounds. With all these nobles' alliances, it was difficult even to get the army mustered without having fights break out between two rivals. How Drammoch kept the peace, Mireynh did not want to consider.

Cirrain was about to finish off her opponent when the door the nobles had left through was flung open again. One of them, Duncan of House Argram, rushed back in, sword in hand. Mireynh rose and was about to shout a challenge to the nobleman when he saw a battle was being fought in the hall and stairway beyond.

"The castle's under attack!" Duncan Argram shouted, then turned around and rushed back into the melee.

"To arms!" Mireynh barked as he rose. His right hand wandered to his belt only to discover that he had not brought his sword.

All about the Great Hall nobles and squires jumped up, drew their blades, and made for the hallway. Some hurried, the High General noted, others dawdled. He saw Anneijhan Cirrain halt her final assault on Callan Farlin and rush in the opposite direction. His first impulse was to send his watchdogs after her, but he knew they would not leave his side. Then the woman turned to face him, gave him a brief nod, and rushed on through the servant's entrance. She was running to get reinforcements, Mireynh realized.

He walked over to the injured scion of House Farlin. "You should be dead, boy." The noble looked up at him, dread in the young man's eyes. "Prove yourself now and you may live, be a coward and I'll let Cirrain finish you." The aristocrat nodded his head and stood.

With his injuries the man would not be able to fight, one shoulder and one hand shattered, so the best he could do was to direct part of the defense, and Mireynh saw understanding in Farlin's eyes as the noble moved toward the fight.

"Damn those cowards," the High General grumbled and picked up the discarded maul. The weapon felt good in his hands; he could smash a foe to pieces with it, provided his back played along. For a moment he considered joining the melee, but dismissed the idea. As much as he hated admitting it, he was too old for this. There were younger, more enthusiastic people fighting and dying in the hallway. What they lacked in experience they made up in numbers, but whoever had infiltrated the castle was good. Mireynh looked at his two guards, pointed toward one of the tables, and was surprised when the two men turned to fetch it. A few moments later the pair had put the table into position.

From his heightened vantage, the High General could observe the chaos unfolding before him. Already he could tell many Houses would mourn the death of their children. Despite inferior numbers, the enemy held his warriors at bay. The nobles were armed, but few of them were in armor, whereas their opponents were ready for battle. In the mass of flailing weapons and bodies, he could make out the Danastaerian royal colors on a few of the blood-splattered surcoats. But there was something wrong with the symbols; it seemed as if part of the seal had been torn off.

Another two men rushed down the stairs to join the fray, and he recognized one of them. The Chosen were attacking the palace! One of them was a match for a dozen warriors, and without their armor his nobles hardly stood a chance.

"Hold them!" he shouted. "Don't attack!"

For a score of nobles, it was already too late, but those who lived seemed made of sterner stuff. They had already formed a vague line, but at his order the last of them joined the group. One of the few who wore armor was Duncan Argram. Mireynh saw blood on the man's tunic as well, but from the way the nobleman moved he guessed that none of it was his. Also, unlike his peers, Argram wielded a massive greatsword and knew how to use it. The blade was red with blood. If the man made it through the night, the High General would keep an eye on him. Apparently Cirrain was not the only one with experience, and House Argram was loyal to the throne.

The door behind him was thrown open. A quick glance confirmed Cirrain had returned. A steady patter of marching feet filled the hall, but his attention had already returned to the skirmish in the hallway. Two score of warriors passed his table and assembled in front of him.

"Wait for it," he heard Cirrain shout. Another forty warriors joined those already standing between him and the door. He saw the noblewoman walk past the troops toward the tattered line of men and women holding the Chosen at bay. She reached the rearmost rank, leaned over to a taller man, and spoke with him. The man nodded and she walked back to the warriors. Mireynh saw the noble pass whatever message Cirrain had given him along the lines.

A few moments passed. Duncan Argram cast a look of grudging respect toward Anne Cirrain, nodded his head briefly, and then held his sword up in high guard. "Now!" he screamed.

As one the warriors charged while the assembled nobles closed ranks, stepping away from the door to allow the armored men and women into the breach. Mireynh couldn't help but admire the woman who stood behind the warriors and directed them. There was something about her that spoke of unyielding determination and authority. If her father was like that, no wonder Drammoch feared the man.

Not only did she direct the advance, she also found time to pull nobles back into the safety behind the armored line. Callan Farlin was next to her, directing the wounded to the healers assembled in the room.

The High General saw more guards pouring into the killing field from the west. He saw Duncan Argram cleave a Chosen in two, advance again, and engage another one. Judging from where he was standing, Lerainh's bodyguard could not last much longer. Still, the price his troops paid for every yard they gained on the Chosen was steep. Already he saw the lines thinning, but reinforcements streamed into the Great Hall.

There came a slight commotion from the west. Mireynh saw a blood drenched man charge in, skewering warriors left and right as he joined the line of Chosen. For a moment the defenders wavered. Then their attack resumed.

The High General was surprised by the maneuver the Chosen executed now. The left line folded back toward the stairs! Not only that, but the right flank mirrored the move, and as one the double column shifted toward the exit. He glimpsed the center of the line; a man covered almost head to toe in blood, wielding his sword in both hands. The man remained standing, pivoting so that his back remained to the others. As the column slowly made their way to the grand double doors the single Chosen stepped with them, his sword lashed out, each strike a deadly hit.

Then he could only see the one Chosen. In that moment, the man scythed his blade in a half circle before him, forcing the defenders to retreat. The warrior raised his sword high above his head and spoke.

Suddenly flames surrounded the man. The next moment the flames spread out, toward the Chanastardhian warriors. Anne Cirrain sprinted his way, jumped up the table, and dragged him down. Then the ground shook, glass shattered, and like leaves in a hurricane, doors and warriors were torn into the room.

Both Mireynh and the noblewoman were thrown across the room; a fiery gust of wind set everything aflame. Mireynh felt his lungs ignite. Desperately suppressing the urge to breathe, he limped to a ruined window, fresh air the only thought on his mind. He heard Cirrain moaning behind him and glanced over his shoulder, saw the woman following.

White specks already danced before his eyes, when he reached the shattered window and leaned out, not caring about splinters still protruding from the wooden frame. The cold night air was tainted by fire, but it was colder than the boiling atmosphere of the Great Hall. Gratefully he sucked in air, lungs rattling. Cirrain stood next to him, her breathing as desperate as his.

The sight of the large room stunned him. Beautiful tapestries and banners were all ashes, as were the remains of most warriors and guards, who could only be identified by their armor and the charred remains of their weaponry. The nobles had escaped the worst of the flames.

All wood in the room was burning, but what caused his senses to reel was a skeletal being that kneeled on the floor, clad in the charred remains of a chain mail suit of armor. The being clasped the hilt of its sword, the weapon firmly embedded in the stones of the hallway. Its skull shuddered as it turned its stare toward him. He screamed in terror as the being stood, focusing its empty eyes on him.

With ease it pulled out the sword and headed toward them, bones and armor creaking with every single step. The survivors came to their senses, and Mireynh saw in their eyes the same battle that raged within him, fear and instinct fighting to take over. He raised his maul. "Stay back!" Mireynh shrieked, heart pounding in terror.

It continued to move toward him.

Then, after a few more steps it came to a halt. "Know this!" Its voice was loud and hollow. "You have entered a war you can't win!" Its eye sockets blazed as the skeleton transformed into something frightening, divine. "You have begun a path that will lead to your destruction. You have chosen the worst enemy of all."

The High General gasped. Anne Cirrain stood in stunned silence.

"You have overstepped boundaries set by the gods! You will fail, and the Chosen will be your doom!" The being raised its sword and collapsed, leaving shivering Chanastardhians behind.

CHAPTER 40

In Baron Duasonh's presence Ealisaid felt shabby. Her dress was rags held together with a sackcloth belt, and her stockings weren't much better. Prisoners were denied fresh clothing, she knew that, but knowing and experiencing something were completely different.

Despite the lateness of her audience, Duasonh was still awake, the rings under his eyes a silent testament to his lack of sleep. He looked up at her, waved her forward, and smiled. "If you've come to complain about the food, I'm afraid there's nothing to be done about it." His smile was genuine, and she felt he was not mocking her. "What is it you want?"

"My lord Baron," she began, still wondering how she could tell him about her stroll in spiritform.

Duasonh must have sensed her hesitation; he lowered the parchment he had been studying and looked at her. "Well? You roused the guards, so whatever you've to say must be important. I suggest you start talking."

This man was so unlike any of her instructors. Ealisaid didn't feel quite comfortable being treated so politely; she was, after all, a prisoner. That didn't seem to matter to the Baron. "Before I begin, you have to understand that there are things a wizard can do which might seem like magic but aren't."

Duasonh nodded and motioned her to continue. "There are ways, for those who know how, to leave their bodies and walk the spiritworld." She saw his irritation, understanding, and anger, and hurried on. "I have kept my word, milord. I did not cast any spell! One can't perform magic while in spiritform!"

The Baron relaxed a little. "Go on."

If she were to reveal what had transpired in the small chapel, she had to be honest with him. "Frankly said, I was bored. After all, you can count the stones in your prison only so many times." She snorted in wry amusement. "I explored the Palace." Quickly she held up her hand to prevent an outburst. "Not to spy on you! I was bored!"

"And you are telling me this because...?" the Baron hissed, fury obvious.

"Something odd is going on in the Palace," she said.

"Aside from having a woman from an extinguished people as a prisoner, you mean?" Duasonh's clenched fists reinforced the threat in his voice.

"There is a man in the chapel in the west wing, is there not?" She had to speak fast in order to prevent the Baron from calling the guards and ordering her gagged, or worse beat her unconscious.

A stunned look crossed Duasonh's face. "Aye," he said.

"Who is he?"

"Some corpse."

She could hardly blame him for being annoyed. Instead of getting the explanation he deserved from her, the Baron was the one answering questions. "When I was in spiritform I felt, rather than saw, a strong force of energy surrounding this man. I went to investigate and found that the man is trapped in the spiritworld as well as in ours. What's odd is that he isn't there, neither here nor there."

"He's dead," Duasonh stated.

"I believe you, but his body should only be in this world, not the next."

"Are you trying to tell me this same corpse is floating in... you know, the other world?" The Baron's brow furrowed as he stood.

"That I am, milord," she said, glad that Duasonh believed her.

"There's been something damned odd about the bloke ever since Kildanor dragged him back from the Shadowpeaks," Duasonh said as he walked for the door. "Come with me." He left the room, looked at the two guards, gave them a brief nod, and walked toward the chapel; the two men followed silently. She hurried to keep up, as he forced his way through guards and servants too slow to move out of the way. For a man of such proportions, Cumaill Duasonh was fleet of foot. At one point, he halted for a moment and spoke a few words with one of Eanaigh's Caretakers.

"You're coming with us, Braigh, there's something wrong with your corpse. Don't give me that look, man. You're the one who did the Rite of Passing, so you should explain some stuff, not me!"

They arrived at the small room moments later. Inside a dog was barking fiercely at empty air, while the corpse shook on the bier as if pulled by unseen hands. For a moment it seemed as if the body would be rent in twain, its legs stretching in one direction, its arms and torso in another direction. Then both the convulsions and the dog's barking stopped. Corpse and canine were still.

"What in the gods' name was that?" Ealisaid asked, aware of the curious onlookers gathered in the hallway.

"I... I... I have... I don't know," Caretaker Braigh stuttered, obviously flabbergasted.

Duasonh pushed his way through the assembled gawkers. "Move aside!" he snapped.

Servants, courtiers, and guardsmen obeyed quickly, bowing as they stepped back. The two guards remained at Duasonh's side, and both followed him into the chamber.

"Braigh," the Baron said, "what the bloody Scales is going on?"

"I don't know, Cumaill."

"You are a Caretaker of Eanaigh, man. You're supposed to know things about that," Duasonh barked, motioned at the corpse, glaring.

"Healing the wounded, yes. Not the dead!"

Ealisaid walked around the bier, and tried to ignore the argument. This most certainly was the man she had seen. A thought occurred to her: Maybe she could shift part of her conscience into spiritform and look around. Then she saw the trembling paw. She kneeled on the floor and took a closer look at the dog. It looked as if no one had fed it in ages; there was only skin and bones to it. She looked up, wanted to interrupt the heated conversation, and saw one of the two guardsmen frowning in what could only be disbelief. The man stared at the corpse.

The next instant the guard hurried closer to the bier. Duasonh and the Caretaker fell silent, as surprised as she. The lone warrior stared at the corpse. "I don't believe it."

There was movement. The dog, despite her desolate condition, stood, placed a paw on the corpse's shoulder. Then it sat at attention next to the body, eyes wide but apparently unaware of its surroundings. Before she had the opportunity to study the mutt any further the guard spoke again.

"It can't be," the man whispered. "By the gods, Drang."

He knew the dead. Ealisaid took in the guardsman's appearance. He was a warden. The bronze ribbon showed as much, if ranks hadn't changed in a century. This meant he had spent at least five years as a city watchman, and had moved through the ranks until he became part of the palace guard.

"You know him," she stated.

"Was he part of the city's watch?" Duasonh asked, having apparently reached the same conclusion.

"Aye, milord," the sword replied. "He vanished two years ago, after... Milord, do you remember the slaughter in Cherkont Street?"

"Of course," Duasonh said. "We never found the killer."

"Aye, my lord." The man nodded toward the corpse. "Drang... Drangar Ralgon is his name. He was betrothed to the victim."

She saw Duasonh glance toward Braigh, who nodded and closed the door. The Baron didn't want an audience.

"What are you saying?" Duasonh looked at the guardsman.

"He vanished. I mean, Drang wasn't found when we discovered what was left of Hesmera, the woman."

"Did you work with him?" The Baron began to pace to room.

"He was my superior in the watch, sir. We all assumed he had gone to hunt the murderer."

"What's your name, son?" Braigh said.

"Glaithan, Lord Braigh. Glaithan Millerson."

Duasonh nodded thanks to his friend and resumed the conversation. He paced across the chapel, halted in the middle of the room, and regarded the warden. "You assumed, but was there further investigation?"

"Aye, lord Baron," Glaithan said. "We searched the house and found Drang's belongings were gone. That's when we began to suspect he had done the deed, but that's impossible, sir."

"Why?" Ealisaid asked, her gaze wandering between warrior and dog.

"He loved her dearly. He'd given up the mercenary life to grow old with her. He wanted a normal life. But why do you ask, sir? Everything is in the reports we gave Lord Jathain."

"The watch was Jathain's responsibility," Braigh muttered.

She didn't know who this Jathain was, but from the straightening of Duasonh's back and his glare at the Caretaker, she figured this person was not popular in Dunthiochagh.

"Millerson, I want everything on this murder on my table first thing tomorrow morning. You have the permission to go through what's left of Jathain's office to obtain these reports."

The warden saluted. "Very well, milord." He turned on his heel and left, closing the door behind him.

Duasonh shook his head, and then looked at Braigh again. "What the bloody Scales is going on?"

The Caretaker shrugged. "I have no idea, Cumaill, this is unnatural," Braigh said. The priest stood at the bier and inspected Ralgon more closely.

"What is it now?" Duasonh took a deep breath, as he walked to stand next to Braigh.

"His last injury is mending as well."

"You can't be..." The Baron's voice trailed off, as he looked at Ralgon's body.

Ealisaid watched as the remains of the man's stomach wound closed. Never before had she seen anything like that, not even the priests' ointments had such power, especially over the dead. Was Drangar Ralgon truly dead? There was no breath. But why was the body healing itself? And who healed Ralgon?

"A miracle," whispered Braigh.

"Aye," Duasonh agreed.

The Caretaker frowned and moved to stand next to the corpse's head. He placed his left hand on Ralgon's chest. "No heartbeat."

"Maybe it was the woman?" Ealisaid suggested.

Duasonh and Braigh turned to look at her. "What woman?" the Caretaker said a moment before the Baron.

"That's what I wanted to tell you in the first place, Lord Baron," she replied. "I saw the commotion." She paused briefly to gather her thoughts. "The body moving, I didn't see that, but I saw the dog barking, a woman screaming. I don't really know how to explain, milord."

"Try," Caretaker Braigh ordered.

"The dog was standing on its hind legs, paws on the corpse. It's hard to understand, sirs, the spiritworld does not distinguish between matter, only souls, spirits. A body is seen, but through a haze, and there isn't much shape to it." She pointed at Ralgon. "With him it was different. He was both here and there, his body, not his spirit. There was no spirit I could detect. Instead I saw the dog, as a haze in the spiritworld, and above it..." she trailed off, unsure of how to explain what she had seen.

"Yes?" This time it was Duasonh who spoke up.

She had an idea. "My lords, you know how a drawing can be altered, so to speak, when one places a sheet of translucent parchment above it, and then draws something upon it?" Both men looked at each other, at her, and then nodded reluctantly. "The dog was the painting, and on top of it, its haze in the spirit world, there was a woman. She screamed at empty air while the dog barked. That's what I wanted to tell you, but there is more going on here."

Braigh looked at the body. Her eyes followed his gaze, and she saw the wound fully closed.

"No corpse heals like that, sirs. But you know this." The dog whined and laid one of its paws on the corpse's chest. For a moment Ealisaid was under the impression that the skin twitched under the touch, but when she blinked and looked again, the corpse was as still as before. "What happened to him?"

"He was gutted," Duasonh said. "Some sort of demonology ritual."

She frowned. "Are you certain?"

"My source is very reliable."

"Why did you bring him here?" She wanted to understand what had transpired, and needed all the information she could get. Maybe through the telling of the tale she could uncover what was going on. Demonology was nothing but a theory, not one wizard had ever managed to prove there was a world where unworldly beings dwelled. There had never been any successful attempt to conjure a nether being, and people had lost interest in the topic fairly quick.

"He's a follower of Lesganagh," Braigh spat. "The Chosen who dragged him in wanted the ritual Lesganaghists are so fond of performed: The Rite of Light..." Underneath all the scorn, Ealisaid detected something else in the Caretaker's voice. She couldn't tell what was wrong with the statement, but this was neither the time nor the place to question the priest.

"You performed most of the bloody ritual, Braigh, so don't you dare blame Kildanor for this," the Baron said.

The priest looked crestfallen and turned his back to them. Ealisaid understood his dilemma. Duasonh's scorn was difficult to ignore, and there was yet something else troubling Caretaker Braigh.

"So why are the wounds closed?" she said.

"A miracle?" Braigh's voice sounded doubtful, yet somewhat resigned. The Caretaker took a deep breath and looked over his shoulder at the body. "Lesganagh wants him to live?"

"And here I thought you denied his existence," Duasonh said with a snigger. "I wish Kildanor was here to hear that."

"Damn you, Cumaill, I have enough problems as it is. Do you think my superiors are happy that I performed the Rite?" Before either the Baron or Ealisaid could reply, the Caretaker went on. "Yes, your servants talk; they are like everybody else. Gossip is part of their duty, it seems, and you damn well know you can't stop it." He whirled around and pointed at Ralgon's corpse. "Don't you see what this means? Everything the Church of Eanaigh has preached for decades is undone by this... miracle." He took another deep breath and made one step toward the bier. "How can a god be evil when he heals the wounds of a dead man? How can Lesganagh heal at all when that has always been Eanaigh's domain?"

She understood the predicament, to a degree. What she couldn't fathom was the disdain Braigh showed toward Lesganagh. The Lord of Sun and War was not evil, he just *was*. He had made the world, gave it light and life, his spear had pierced the veil of the heavens to create the stars. Why would the priests of his wife consider him evil?

She was about to ask the Caretaker, when Baron Duasonh said, "I have no patience for this. Argue religion on your own time!" He wanted to say more, when the dog barked. They froze and turned, staring at the canine.

One moment he floated in darkness, the next Drangar plunged down. He felt more than saw that he was falling. Still everything around him was purest black.

The dog jumped up onto Ralgon's corpse, and barked into his face.

"Wake up! Damn you! Wake up, child!" The voice echoed from all around him. He had heard it before, whenever there was doubt in his heart, whenever he looked at Dog. It carried the same timbre as the one that had defended him against the bright light.

Now the dog snarled into Ralgon's face, her paws appeared to pound his chest in a fit of rage. Ealisaid shifted part of her consciousness into the spirit world. She wasn't sure this would work, but she had to try and see what happened. Again, the dog was overlaid by the female spiritform, this time the woman pounded Ralgon's chest. Duasonh moved to free the corpse, and Braigh followed suit, but she hurried to block their path. Whatever went on in both worlds, she felt that interference would be wrong. She didn't know who or what the spirit was; her spiritsight again showed her the golden bowl hovering above the body. She couldn't tell for sure which of Lesganagh's children worked its power here, but one of them was intervening.

"Wake up!" The voice sounded more insistent, desperate. Now Drangar felt as if a rope he was tied to dragged him down.

A slight tremor coursed through the body. Ealisaid's gaze wandered from the fiercely barking dog to the two men, her own astonishment reflected in their eyes.

"What the bloody Scales?" Duasonh hissed.

Neither Ealisaid nor Braigh spoke. The Wizardess glanced at the priest and found her own confusion mirrored on the man's face. A heartbeat later she felt as if a tremendous force was ripping her insides apart. It was as if her brain was aflame, her soul screamed while her mouth could not. The agony that coursed through her mind and soul found its bodily echo in Ealisaid's throat and arms, and then reached out to tear at her entire body.

Drangar fell. Faster and faster he plummeted through the darkness.

"What do you want from me?" he screamed.

Fear, unlike any he had felt before, rose in him. He relived his nightmares. The haunted feeling of losing his mind made him claw at the unseen walls that had to surround him.

They had been in his dreams, those walls, but now his fingers grasped nothing.

Now the body thrashed on the bier, but Ealisaid stared on, unable to move or talk. And unable to hear. She saw Duasonh step into her view, blocking Braigh's face. The Baron's mouth opened and closed in rapid succession, but nothing reached her ears.

She wanted to tell him what she felt, that everything in here happened for a reason. Of this she was certain. There was no malice in the pain, in the presence that surrounded them. She had seen the same recognition in Braigh's eyes: a god was interfering! Directly!

Duasonh took hold of Braigh's body and shook the priest.

When the Caretaker didn't react, the Baron walked over to her and did the same to her. Compared to the soul-wrenching pain that flared through her, the shaking was nothing. Again, Duasonh said something, then, shook his head at the futility of his actions.

Ealisaid's spiritsight vanished, and all her senses slammed back into the real world. She saw Ralgon's hands twist into claws, as if trying to hold onto something. Even the body's mouth moved; lifeless lips went through the motion of words, baring teeth in a twisted snarl.

Then, with a suddenness that caught her unprepared, the divine pressure was gone. Without the support of strained muscles, Ealisaid simply fell to the floor. Braigh struggled only a moment longer, before his staff slipped and he dropped as well.

Try as she might, the Wizardess could move no limb, and so she only saw the outline of Ralgon's body, as the corpse shook as if someone dealt it a mighty blow. He sat up on his bier, screaming at the top of his voice. "What do you want from me?"

Then the body collapsed.

CHAPTER 41

Seventeenth of Chill, 1475 K.C.

Kildanor wasn't sure how he felt. Part of him was happy, almost excited, about their escape from Harail. Another part wanted to wallow in misery. Orkeanas was dead, had sacrificed himself to buy them time to flee.

He had succeeded. The flamewave Orkeanas had summoned was the last resort, everybody knew that, and Kildanor wondered why the First had gone down this path. Summoning the wrath of Lesganagh killed the summoner; it was a price most deemed too high, especially since the Phoenix Wizards had summoned more devastating forces without being burned away.

"We're no wizards," Kildanor reminded himself.

The Chosen were extensions of the Lord of Sun and War, and what was fire if not self-consuming? Their duty was to guard the Hold so that no one would ever free what was buried beneath. This vigil was eternal, and they were not meant to interfere in the affairs of men. A silly notion; there was no way to avoid man's business. The only way to guard the Hold was to support a strong leader. Lerainh was anything but; he should have died years ago. Maybe that failure, Orkeanas seeing his errors for what they were and what they had led to, was the cause of the First's decision. At least he would be remembered for his sacrifice.

Was there anything the others would remember him by when his time came? Kildanor didn't really care, there was too much ahead to fret about such nonsense.

The fifteen Chosen had retreated in orderly fashion, and

with the Chanastardhians too shocked to worry about the small band of warriors, they had left Harail almost unchallenged. The warriors guarding the northern gate had decided to halt their passing; the ensuing battle had been brief. The Chosen focused their anger at Orkeanas's death on the dozen warriors manning the gatehouse.

Now they hurried for their horses.

Kildanor looked at Galen who led the others with a firm yet relaxed hand. By seniority the new leader should have been Kildanor, but he was quite happy to leave the command to Galen. Only fifteen had made it out of Harail. Soon, there would be seven new Chosen among them, one of them to replace Orkeanas.

"You're coming with us?"

For a moment, Kildanor thought Galen's voice sounded pleading, but as he glanced at the other he saw the man's faraway look. Galen was already calculating how many would be available to do what was necessary. "No, I'll be heading back to Dunthiochagh," he replied. He saw his comrade's face sag with disappointment and added, "The Chanastardhians will first try to claim the city before they turn their attention to the Hold; everything else is suicide." There wasn't much to add, and he knew anything he could say would be just empty words, except, "If Dunthiochagh falls, I'll be there, one way or another."

Galen swallowed. "I wonder who'll be coming in Orkeanas's stead." Then, after a brief pause, he added, "You should have been First. With you it might have gone differently."

He said it with so much conviction that Kildanor was unsure how to reply. Leading the Chosen... the idea was something he didn't want to consider. "I am not, and never will be. Besides," he said, "I'm far too pig-headed to bully you lot around."

Galen remained silent, and none of the others said a word. Most of them were still in shock over the loss of their leader. Unlike Kildanor, the others had never been separated from one another since the Choosing. The community they belonged to wasn't his, and yet he felt the hole Orkeanas's death had left. "He did what he thought was right," he said, unsure whether he was comforting Galen and the others or himself.

Shortly before dawn the Chosen reached their horses. They had zigzagged across the fields and meadows surrounding Harail, and so far, no pursuit had been spotted. Kildanor looked around, saw the same sadness he felt reflected in the others' eyes, and almost decided to join his brethren. He felt the connection his departure had severed four decades ago mending, but he could neither forget the reasons for his exile, nor forgive these people their determination not to interfere with politics. They all shared a bond—that much was true—but his path was different from theirs. He wanted to exchange Cumaill Duasonh for Lerainh, and with the old monarch dead, it was time to repel the invaders and groom Cumaill for the throne. However, there was one thing he could do.

Kildanor rummaged in his saddlebags while the others prepared for their departure. When he found what he was looking for, he sat down and began to write. "Galen!" he called out, barely looking up from the parchment.

"Aye," the Chosen said.

He handed the letter over. "This will help you with the commanding warleader at the Hold," he said as he stood. "It will prevent any confusion."

"They don't know?" Galen asked, casting a quick glance on the missive.

"No one knows, and it will remain that way," he replied. "This should be accepted. If not, send for me."

Galen nodded. "Thanks, I guess." He held out his hand and Kildanor clasped it, and then hugged the man fiercely.

"I'll see you, one way or another," he muttered. Parting now didn't feel like it had forty years before. Back then, him leaving had drawn only the barest attention from his brethren. Now they surrounded the two oldest of their group, and clapped Kildanor on the back. It was a fond farewell, and he knew the battle inside Harail was the start of a healing of rifts that had grown over the years. The only thing he regretted was that so few of the original Chosen were there. "Galen?"

"Aye?"

"Do you remember... my... my brothers?" he forced the

last two words out, almost as if he was vomiting. "Ethain. Ganaedor." He felt the others' resentment when the words left his mouth. The two Fallen, the two traitors.

"Part of me remembers being killed by them," Galen said.

A few others said the same; he should have never broached the subject. Kildanor felt awash with emotion. "Should the Hold be attacked there will be twenty-four again." He wasn't sure if he could keep that promise, and he never was one for big promises, but here, among men and women who understood him, he felt certain he could fulfill it. Although he didn't know how.

Galen patted him on the shoulder and frowned. "You know what I know, and if you think you can do better than those who went after the pair during the Demon War, then try. If you succeed, none of us will complain. If you fail, we'll know after a while. But first," he added.

Kildanor inclined his head. "First the Chanastardhians, then we worry about the rest. Fare thee well, my friend."

Galen nodded, and to Kildanor's surprise the other Chosen followed his example, called him friend, and wished him farewell.

"Fare thee well, my friends," he replied, mounted his charger, and when the first rays of Lesganagh's glowing orb touched the ground he directed the horse onto one beam.

Lightbringer looked at the hazy figure floating before her. Cat was but a sliver of her former self; the fight in the spiritworld had cost her, not as much as expected, but still. The spirit was almost gone. Yet Cat's presence seemed strangely powerful. Some other magic was keeping her soul in the world now.

"Your words were true, Lightbringer," the spirit said.

"They usually are." What was Cat hinting at?

"What you did to me was wrong. What you did to my soul was wrong. But you already know that, don't you?"

This was not the same woman she had bound so many years ago. There was a certainty underlying Cat's voice she had not possessed in decades. Gone was the almost docile spirit she had rescued. "I do what is necessary," Lightbringer said.

"I understand," Cat simply said.

"You understand? I doubt that."

"I understand more than you told me, and I see now you were right to do what you did, wrong though it may be." Cat hovered above her.

She blinked at the apparition. A Servant? It seemed impossible, but the spirit had a confidence about her Lightbringer couldn't deny. "Tell me what happened," she demanded, unsure if she still had power over the woman.

"I couldn't shield the boy for long. Just like you said my presence faded."

"Yet you remain."

"Aye, but not for long. My task isn't yet complete."

"Your task?" She had a suspicion, but it seemed impossible. The Lawgiver had never interfered directly, only through her priests. And Servants? Again, the word came to mind, and now she thought she understood.

"There are gods, and they watch over us. Even you, princess," Cat said.

Lightbringer straightened. Nobody had used this title in millennia. Nobody knew. "What did you call me?"

"I called you by your title, milady. I'm here to tell you that your deeds never go unnoticed, and the gods approve. Not necessarily of your methods, but approve they do."

"What of the things I've done?"

"They approve, sunargh. Now I will go. My time is short." The apparition vanished.

Lightbringer blinked, shook her head, and tried to comprehend what she had just been told. Of course there were gods; she knew that. She did what was necessary, what was right. The gods knew, and approved! A smile crept onto her lips. Cat was in Lliania's care now; she, on the other hand, had other things to tend to.

CHAPTER 42

His journey back to Dunthiochagh took moments, and as Dawntreader left the bridge of sunlight, Kildanor urged the charger into a canter. They passed South Gate without incident, and the Chosen was pleasantly surprised to see the city's battlement alive with warriors.

A quick tug at the reins and the stallion halted. Up on the wall he discerned wardens barking at their charges. Several scores of archers assisted by many city youths distributed baskets of arrows along the merlons up and down the wall. Things were changing for the better, and he was glad about having used young Garinad as bait. A passing woman-at-arms recognized him and gave a warrior's fist-on-chest salute. He returned the greeting, squeezed Dawntreader with his thighs, and they were off again.

Despite the morning chill, Trade Road was already abuzz with activity other than that of warriors. Servants, cooks, craftsmen, all hurried one way or another, some carrying baskets to fill or to empty, others merely trying to blink away the bright sunlight. This morning brought a crisp cold. He passed a group of youths who chipped away at the ice that had formed in the second arm of the new canal, and for a moment Kildanor worried the chill might affect the Dunth as well.

His worry increased as he passed the first arm, three score yards off the river. Several children were testing the strength of the sheet of ice that covered the channel. The last time the river had frozen was before the magic of Shadow Academy had transformed the entire eastern reach of the Shadowpeaks into a temperate zone. Sure, further west and north the mountaintops still were covered with snow and ice, but down here things were different.

Seeing a constable of the watch, the Chosen reined Dawntreader to a halt. After a brief exchange of salutes, he asked, "What's with the ice?"

The guard scratched his mustache. "The water ain't flowing right, Lord Kildanor."

"What do you mean by that?"

"Ah, sir, you can't smell it now, but for the past two weeks or so, whenever the air got a wee bit warmer, there was this smell. Real 'orrible.

"No one complained?"

"Sure we did, sir, and Lord Jathain assured us it would be taken care of," again the man scratched his mustache.

"All right, fetch a few children with keen eyes. The channels are blocked somewhere. They are to find the blocked spots. Order whatever people can be spared to help get rid of the stuff. You know the drill, don't you?"

"Aye, milord," the watchman said and headed off.

Jathain had been gone for a while, and he was certain Cumaill had ordered the sweeping of the canals and moat. If the dirt had not been removed here in the new canal, was it possible that more of Duasonh's orders had been ignored? That would mean the traitor still had men loyal to him in the city.

"Constable?" he asked before the man was too far away.

"Yes, sir?" The watchman halted and turned to face him.

"Did you go through the usual channels?"

Again, he scratched his mustache. "Certainly, sir. 'Tis right an' proper."

"Who's your warden?"

"Bren Glaiden, sir."

"Thank you, constable. Carry on," he said, urged Dawntreader into a canter, and quickly reached Dunth Street. So Jathain still had people inside the city. They had expected as much, and had time allowed there would have been thorough examinations but things had been rather shaky since the revolt.

He crossed Old Bridge. Thankfully, his perch on the charger's back was high enough to spy over the roofs of ramshackle stalls and makeshift booths to see that the Dunth was still flowing strongly. The river would keep their rears free for a while, until that Chanastardhian general either forded the bloody thing, sent a warband through the Shadowpeaks, or west down Dunth Street to the next bridge, some sixty miles away. Merthain was vassal to Herascor, so the army might cross the Dunth there. The bridge could still be destroyed; after all, the enemy general would be a fool to leave the four castles at his back unguarded.

When he reached the northern shore of the river, Kildanor saw that the city walls were not the only place where warriors were busy. If the Chanastardhians managed to penetrate the southern part of Dunthiochagh, they would still have to cross the waterway, which would take a while; the banks would be bristling with defenses. But seeing sharp-eyed pairs of warriors patrolling the outer curtain wall, with clusters of guards at vital spots posted all along the battlement, was a vast improvement over what had been before.

The drawbridge was down as was the custom during the day, but the massive steeloak gate that blocked the entrance to the Palace grounds was lowered, blocking his path. A precaution that had, until about a week earlier, seemed unnecessary.

A sentry's head poked out of a third-floor arrow slit to his right. The woman, Kildanor couldn't discern who it was, recognized him and shouted, "The portcullis'll be up in a moment, Lord Kildanor!" To whoever was inside, she barked, "Get the gate up, you louts!"

The pulley creaked and groaned under the gate's weight, but moved up quickly. He urged Dawntreader forward and across. As horse and rider halted inside the gatehouse in front of the seldom-used inner gate, the woman gave the command to lower the portcullis once more. From the left tower Kildanor heard a man ordering his crew to raise the inner gateway. Then he was in the outer bailey.

Here, things had also changed. Warriors drilled with bow and arrow, sparred against one another with sword and shield or pike, while smiths hammered away at new weapons and armor, and fletchers went about producing arrows by the bushel. Kildanor saw some warriors lounging by the open entryway to the inner bailey. They looked exhausted. Most likely the two women and two men had been practicing until just a little while ago. Their swords were stacked against the wall, with each balancing wooden practice weapons on their knees, a jack of wine changing hands occasionally.

As he neared, the four moved to stand at attention, but he waved them away. "As you were, save your strength for things that matter."

"The Chanastardhians, milord?" asked the lithe blonde of the group.

"Know anyone else who deserves a poking, sword?"

"The swine Jathain," she replied, green eyes glimmering with barely contained anger. Her companions hollered their agreement.

Their sincerity gave the Chosen an idea. "I want you four to report to me in a short while. I'll send for you."

"Yes, sir!" the warriors replied.

He rode into the inner bailey, gave Dawntreader's rein to a stable hand, and hurried into the keep. As he made his way up the grand stairs, he passed a pair of Caretakers. The two women, both apparently part of the conservative Lesganagh-hating faction, didn't even return his cordial nod. They cast icy stares his way and put their heads together. The only words he heard one of them say as he passed were "no miracle. Blasphemy, that's what it is," then he was out of earshot. He had no idea what the two were talking of, but right now he had more important things to worry about.

Braigh was leaving Cumaill's office just as he arrived. The priest stopped and glared at him. "What sort of sick joke did you play on me, Chosen?" he snarled.

Taken aback, Kildanor could only gape at the priest.

"You tricked me into doing this! You had it all planned from the beginning!"

"I have no idea what you are talking about, man. Make sense or get out of my way, I have more important things to do than being pointlessly accused!"

Braigh looked at him, blinked, then frowned. "You don't know?"

"Know what?"

"I... the ritual..."

"Stop babbling," Kildanor snapped, then calmer, "Take a deep breath, and then explain yourself."

"The ritual I performed," Braigh demanded. "Has it ever returned a man from the dead?"

"The Rite of Light?"

The Caretaker nodded. "Aye." After a brief pause, he continued, "The wounds were closing, as you remember. Well, by the time you were off to Harail, the man was fully healed. There was no heartbeat, he still had his deathly pallor, but the wounds, all of them, had vanished."

A miracle, Kildanor thought. A sign sent by Lesganagh, it could be nothing else. "And then?"

"You brought the dog, and well, she barked, the body shook, and the Lady Ealisaid saw that a woman was standing in the same place the dog was, yelling at something."

"She used magic?" he asked, concern growing.

"No, she just slipped into spiritform, whatever that may be," Braigh replied. "Then the body came back to life. He's been in the dungeon ever since, mumbling nonsense, like some madman."

A thought crossed his mind. "Your church isn't too happy with you?"

Braigh's face turned stony. "I'll be lucky if they just renounce my title."

So, the idiot fanatics were turning against their own now. Kildanor pitied Braigh, but the man was better served by old habits than condolences. "I hear there's always a need for gardeners, or midwives," he said, trying to keep a straight face. "You know, Health and Fertility and all that."

A glimmer of resentment shone in the priest's eyes, faded quickly, followed by a mere sad shake of his head. "We'll see what my superiors will do to me," Braigh said, then changed the topic back to its original course. "So, the ritual does not bring the dead back?"

"No, it's just one of those things people used to do for the departed. More stylish than the endless drones of Jainagath's Deathmasks, and far more appropriate for one who worshiped the Lord of Sun and War."

"This kind of resurrection has not happened before?"

He thought for a moment, then declined, "Not to my knowledge. This is a sign, man, a sign. A dead warrior of renown coming back. He returns to life here when we have great need of heroes."

"You forget one thing," said Braigh. "He is a murderer, and must be tried, resurrection or not. If our guilt vanished with death, Lliania's Scales would be useless."

"Murderer?" he echoed

"Aye, he was the only suspect in a killing that happened two years ago."

"That hardly matters, man. Can't you see? It's a sign!"

"A Lawspeaker will decide his fate."

The Caretaker couldn't see the big picture. More than Kildanor himself, Drangar Ralgon was a symbol, a hero. With him standing on the wall, the other warriors would be inspired to fight much more fiercely.

"We'll see," he said. "He may be a murderer, but when the time comes, he could also be the standard to rally our troops around."

Braigh was about to answer when someone hailed him from the stairs. "High Priest Morgan Danaissan requests your presence, please come with us."

The priest paled. "Excuse me," he muttered, sketched a quick bow and headed for the group of priests standing at the bottom of the staircase.

For a moment Kildanor was tempted to halt the procedure, but held back. His interference would make matters worse. Instead, he watched the group of Eanaighists—some of them armed with heavy cudgels—escort Braigh out of the keep.

Heavyhearted, he finally entered Duasonh's office. Cumaill sat behind his desk, studying various papers, which he quickly put down when he looked up and saw Kildanor.

"Good morning," the Baron said. "Everything taken care of in Harail?"

He closed the door. "Orkeanas is dead."

"I'm sorry, old friend."

Kildanor pulled a chair away from the wall and sat, stretching his legs. "I'm the last of the first Chosen now. It doesn't make me happier, either."

"What of Lerainh?" Duasonh asked.

"Dead by my hand," he replied. "Should have killed the bastard decades ago." His hands balled into fists as if they had a life of their own.

For a moment, Cumaill was speechless. Then he said, "You never told me what happened, but I guess it's better that way. Judging from the rumors, though, he deserved it."

"It was too quick a death if you ask me."

"Who'll succeed him?"

"You, if we kick the Chanastardhians out and provided you want the crown."

Again, Cumaill sat there quiet, thoughtful. "We'll see," he finally said.

"Aye. I have something for you," Kildanor said, as he dug into his tunic and retrieved the documents he had stolen from the office. "I took them from their general's office. And before you ask, I have no idea what they're about." Duasonh took the bundle, barely looking at him.

Kildanor thought it best to leave the man to his studies. Heading for the door, he briefly looked back and said, "I heard about the miracle, and what role the Wizardess had in it."

"When the Chanastardhians come we'll use her," Duasonh replied. "I made that clear to Lliania's priests, the Caretakers, and to the families of those killed." Kildanor wanted to reply, but didn't when the Baron held up his hands. "None of us is happy, but we are at war. She's the best weapon available, old friend. She'll remain in the dungeon until I have her word she won't harm us. Besides," he added, "she has already been helpful with Ralgon. And he is a killer. That murder in Cherkont Street was his doing."

"I heard. I've read the same reports as you," the Chosen said. "Still, there is something damned odd about this man."

"You should talk to Braigh."

"His High Priest has him in custody," he replied.

"Damn fool Danaissan!" Cumaill growled.

"Nothing you can do, mate."

"I know. Church matters are church matters."

"I'll get Braigh out; he can help me find out more about Ralgon."

"Leave Braigh out of this," Duasonh ordered. "We have enough trouble as it is. The Eanaighists police their own, let them. Helping Braigh would stir up a whole load of trouble. What shall we do should they decide not to heal our wounded? We have to let them proceed."

He had feared something like this would come up. "Maybe we just have to wait until Nerran shows up again."

"You think it's time for that?" Cumaill asked, alarmed.

Kildanor shrugged. "This nonsense has to stop somewhere first and the Riders have waited long enough."

"What do you mean? More deaths even before the Chanastardhians start their siege?" Duasonh stood and began pacing through the room.

"You damn well know, same as I do, that there are enough progressives out there. The fools are gathered here; Kalduuhn, Merthain, and even Chanastardh still have temples dedicated to Lesganagh, and nobody bothers the priests there either. The gods disapprove of this idiocy, but they let mankind take care of its own business."

"And so, we'll have more bloodshed before the walls are actually escalated?"

"What do you want me to say?" Kildanor snapped.

"I don't know... something positive for a change." Duasonh halted in the middle of the room and ran his hands through his hair. "Braigh might be tortured."

"Great, you don't want me to get involved with the Caretakers, and yet you tell me they'll poke some needles and other shit into him?" The next words came haltingly across his lips, "I like the man, Cumaill; he has done nothing wrong."

"I know that, but don't forget a noble's word means nothing where church matters are concerned." Duasonh headed back to his chair and sat. He leafed through the pages, halted once, frowned, shook his head, and resumed the scanning of the texts. Whenever Cumaill behaved like this, it was certain the conversation was at an end.

"If you won't help a friend of yours, I will," he said as he left. Any of Nerran's riders would not hesitate to help Braigh, and neither would he.

The door had barely closed behind him when it was flung open again, and Baron Duasonh bellowed, "Get your foolish ass back in here, Chosen Kildanor!"

His turnabout was drill-perfect. "Sir!" he said as he snapped to attention. He returned to the office, face straight, still he noticed the astonishment on the sentinels' faces. The door shut behind him.

"I won't have you start another Dawnslaughter at the eve of a siege that might very well be our end!" Duasonh snarled. "We need the healing. You're not amongst your fellow Chosen, Kildanor. I appreciate your loyalty, but use your senses, man! There is far more at stake here than one life."

He stood rigid, listening.

"Braigh, as much as it pains me, will remain with his brethren; if you free him they'll blame Lesganagh again, but also point an accusing finger at me because I call you my friend. The entire thing will spiral out of control!"

"And what about the miracle that is Drangar Ralgon?"

Duasonh sat down again, and again grasped the wrinkled letters. "I don't know. See if you can make heads and tails of this... don't call it miracle, mate, please."

"Why not?"

"Because I don't need every freeborn and villein harping about this so-called blessed man, blessed by Lesganagh no less, returning from the dead. It will be even more water on the mills of Danaissan and his ilk. As I said, I don't want another Dawnslaughter."

There was a knock. "Enter," the Baron called.

Kildanor stepped aside as the door opened and Gail Caslin entered. He was glad to see the Rider recovered. She bowed to Duasonh and gave a brief salute to the Chosen. "Greetings, my Lord Baron. And to you, Sunsword."

"Good morning, Caretaker," Cumaill replied.

Eyes wide with astonishment, Kildanor stared at the woman.

She was a Caretaker? And yet she called him by his formal title.

"You seem surprised, Sunsword," Caslin said, humor twinkling in her blue eyes.

"I thought you a follower of Lesganagh," he stammered. Indeed, he knew there were Eanaighists among Nerran's Riders, but no one, except a member of Lesganagh's church, used his formal title.

"Those who follow the wife, don't they have to revere the husband as well?" she replied. "After all, where would she be without him?" To Cumaill she said, "I'll attend to the chapel in Caretaker Braigh's absence, milord."

Duasonh arched an eyebrow. "Are you certain that's wise?"

She shrugged. "I belong to Her church in Kalduuhn; your High Priest has no authority over me, Lord Baron."

"You can appoint her," Kildanor suggested.

Duasonh's face brightened. "Splendid, consider yourself the Palace's Caretaker."

"Great!" Gail whispered, almost too quietly for him to hear, and the way the Baron turned his attention back to the letters he had not heard her exclamation. The Riders had never made their allegiance public, and he doubted Morgan Danaissan, or any other member except Braigh, knew much about them. Nonetheless, this situation might provoke just such a spiral Cumaill was so worried about. He would keep an eye on Caretaker Gail. "By your leave," she said, and headed for the door.

"Don't do anything to antagonize the High Priest," Duasonh said, barely looking up from the letters.

"Certainly not, milord," came her reply, and then she was gone.

"So, you don't like the smell of this either?" Kildanor asked when the door had shut.

"The Riders have worked for the return of Lesganagh's Church since the Dawnslaughter, mate," Cumaill replied. "Their goals haven't changed, and though I don't doubt Nerran's loyalty, I fear that should Danaissan find out what their objective is, we'll have trouble brewing anew. Luckily, with her I can claim ignorance." He winked at the Chosen.

"One more thing," Kildanor said. "I almost forgot. Jathain's influence isn't gone yet, it seems." He told Duasonh about the incident with the canal freezing, and his measures to have the blockage removed.

"I'll see to it," Cumaill said. "Thanks," he muttered and returned to studying the letters.

This time the dismissal was obvious. Kildanor left.

CHAPTER 43

A determined knock woke Kildanor. "Yes?" he shouted, rubbing sleep from his eyes.

The door opened, revealing a servant. "Your pardon, sir, but you asked to be awakened shortly after the noon gong."

It felt as if he had slept for only a few moments. As he pushed himself up from the bed, a yawn crept up and caught him unable to cover his mouth. The servant couldn't hide his amusement.

"It was a long night," he mumbled. A weak apology, but he didn't care what the servant thought. "I'm no courtier. Fetch me some tea and fruit from the kitchen." The servant bowed, and he added, "Please." At the man's surprise he said, "Can't go wrong with courtesy, eh?"

After a brief, grateful bow, the Chosen was alone once more. He stretched, pulled on his boots, and then washed his face. The cold water cleared his mind. He fastened his sword belt when the servant returned, tray in both hands. "Thanks," he said, as the man placed food and drink before him.

"Certainly, sir."

Kildanor sampled the tea. It needed honey. "Now, I need you to find warden Kaltairr. Bring her and her three friends to me."

"Of course, sir," the servant replied and was off again.

He added some honey to the tea, took a sip, and was satisfied. Then he began to wolf down an apple. Gods, he hadn't realized how hungry he was. Down went another apple. Between bites, a few mouthfuls of tea.

By the time the warden and her companions arrived, he had

begun an assault on a bowl of plums. Janed Kaltairr saluted, and the four stood at attention. The plums were good, a bit on the sweet side for his taste, but good nonetheless. He spat out another stone, and then turned to face the warriors.

"Door."

One of the brothers Bolrain closed the entrance.

"Well," he began. "Judging from your desire for killing Lord Jathain, I assume you're not overly fond of him."

Now that they were here, they were more formal than in the courtyard this morning. "Yes, sir," the warden replied.

This formality wouldn't do, he needed co-conspirators. "Listen lads and lasses, leave the 'yes sirs' and 'no sirs' for your superiors. I'm not one of them."

"Yes, s..." His glare altered Janed Kaltairr's reply. "As you wish."

"Well now, I need you to do some things for me, and Dunthiochagh," Kildanor said.

"And what would that be?" Noela Odrain asked.

"Spread the word that you are going to destroy the Merthain Bridge, sixty miles to the west."

"We are?" the younger looking of the brothers said.

He smirked. "Yes. But first I need two of you outside the city; you are to look out for anyone leaving the place and heading either west or south."

"You assume whatever spies Jathain has left in the city will be off to warn him or prevent us from destroying the bridge," the warden said.

"Smart girl," he remarked. "Exactly. Two of you will be spreading the word that I've ordered the destruction of the bridge, and the other two will slip out of the city and intercept anyone trying to leave."

"No one is to leave, sir," young Bolrain said, and received a smack to the head, administered by his brother. "Oh, now I get it!" he exclaimed a moment later.

"The brothers will be outside the city," Janed Kaltairr decided. "We girls will spread the word."

"I'll draw up the order, and get you two," he pointed at the men, "out of the city."

"When?" old Bolrain asked.

"Now. You'll get horses and will observe both roads. When you see anyone, notify the other. Are there more folks you can trust?"

"Aye," Odrain said.

"Good, gather them. There need be more outside to pursue the traitors."

"Aye, sir."

"Now get going. The order will be with you shortly," Kildanor said as he withdrew parchment, ink, and quill from a drawer. He was already busy writing when the door had barely closed behind them.

It was shortly afterwards that he again stood before warden Kaltairr. He handed her the missive, and was off again. The woman was capable enough, and Nerran had recruited her. This made him even more confident of the mission's success. Cumaill might not like the way he handled business, but if it produced results there would hardly be any argument against it.

Satisfied, he headed for the dungeon. Maybe he could discern what Drangar Ralgon's purpose was.

When the evening gong rang across the city, Kildanor headed back up the stairs into the Palace's main corridor. All his attempts to reach out to Ralgon had led to nothing. The man kept banging his head against the wall, muttering nonsense. He was at his wits' end, nothing he said or did mattered to the man.

The witch didn't help, either. All through the afternoon she had tried to advise him in the matter, from four cells away. Wizards should be dead, were all dead until this woman had blasted onto the scene. Cumaill wanted to use her as a weapon! Had it been his decision, he would have ended the Wizardess' life with a quick slash through the throat.

Maybe Caretaker Gail could help. After all she was much more progressive than Braigh. Also, with the younger man gone, he had no other choice. He rather relied on some firebrand Kalduuhnean priestess of Eanaigh than on any of the others. Then again, what choice did he have? Fullon of Trannagh's church was no healer. The Chosen scoffed at the notion of a priest of the God of Trade and Politics trying to heal anything but his own pockets or a bad deal. The Upholders of Lliania were in Justice, not the Healing business. The Deathmasks... aside from burying the deceased, no one knew what their duty was.

Gail it was then.

As he walked toward the chapel the Caretaker now occupied, he wondered how to find out what the plan was, once Nerran and the other Riders returned. He wasn't sure asking her was such a wise idea. Maybe it was best to let things play out. Then again, maybe the priestess was worried about how the local Eanaighists would react to her being the replacement of Braigh. Maybe it was better to keep her occupied with the mystery that was Drangar Ralgon. From what Nerran had said the man was renowned, and the guardsmen had told him he was a formidable fighter. Or had been a formidable fighter, rather.

There was also the hideous murder to consider. During the time spent observing Ralgon, he was now filled with doubt about his initial assumption Ralgon was a herald of Lesganagh. Why would the Lord of Sun and War send such a wreck to do his bidding? From the look of him, Ralgon had tried to kill himself. Some scars looked fresher than the others his body bore, and so he guessed Ralgon had slit his wrists at least once after the deed.

While down in the dungeon, Kildanor had taken the time to review the Cherkont Street slaughter. It was strange that the notes and reports and the men's recollections did not match entirely. The watchmen who had been friends with Ralgon claimed he never drank alcohol, yet there had been two glasses and an empty, shattered wine bottle at the scene of the crime. Also, it seemed Ralgon had fled his house seeming in full capacity of his senses. He had committed the crime, and yet had tried to kill himself. It didn't make sense.

Further, he had come back from the dead, his wounds healed, and Braigh was certain some divine presence had shielded Ralgon from something. The Wizardess Ealisaid had confirmed this. There was more to this story than he or anyone else could discern and what was this demonology business in the Shadowpeaks? Why had five men, who had so conveniently burst into flame, tried to sacrifice Ralgon?

Kildanor was still pondering this problem when he rounded a corner and saw Caretaker Gail talking to a servant. He halted and overheard the last sentence the priestess said, "You will tell them once I give the word, understood?" The man nodded, held his hand out, and received a coin. Then he turned and hurried off.

Pretending to have just arrived, he headed toward her. "Just the Caretaker I'm looking for."

Gail Caslin turned and greeted him with a quick bob of the head. "Sunsword, a fair evening to you."

"And to you as well," he replied.

"What can I do for you?" she asked, taking hold of his left arm and steering him into the chapel.

He matched her pace and when they stood before the small shrine dedicated to Eanaigh triumphant, he stopped. "I assume you heard about the new prisoner?"

"The resurrected mercenary?"

Her statement surprised him. "Mercenary?"

"You're talking about Drangar Ralgon, I assume."

"Aye," he replied. "You know of him?"

"You obviously don't frequent the dives my comrades and I go to, Sunsword," Caslin stated. She winked at him. "Good for you. As to your question, yes, I know of him. Was pretty much a bastard on the battlefield. Talk was he favored a decent slaughter."

He arched an eyebrow. "What?"

The priestess shook her head. "Let me put it this way, I never talked to anyone who fought directly against him."

That did not match what Ralgon's former friends had said. According to them, he was a quiet, gentle, yet determined man. Her statement was far more in line with the Cherkont murder. "Did he ever leave anyone piecemeal?" he wondered.

Caslin frowned. "Not that I know of, why?"

He retold the events of one week ago, and concluded with,

"Have you ever seen our new prisoner?"

The Caretaker declined, and he continued, "His wounds are fully closed, he refuses to eat. And ..." He paused.

"And what, Sunsword?"

"You best see for yourself," Kildanor replied. This time it was his turn to lead her.

The two walked down the stairs and into the guardroom. "Have you ever cured madmen?" he finally asked.

"Sometimes," she replied, but she sensed his doubt.

"Good," he said as he unlocked the heavy door and grabbed a lantern.

They walked down the corridor and stopped before the cell holding Drangar Ralgon.

Kildanor was by now used to the smell emanating from the confined place; the Caretaker clearly wasn't. She crinkled her nose. Then she saw the man sitting on his bunk. Ralgon's eyes were open but he seemed not to see his surroundings. Every few moments he slammed his head against the wall, and muttered something.

She looked at him in askance. "What is he saying?"

He shrugged. "I don't know, I listened to him for quite a while but never actually heard what the words were."

"He says 'What do you want from me?' and 'Leave me alone'," a voice from another cell further down the corridor supplied. The Wizardess!

Before he could stop her, Caretaker Gail walked to the bars that held back the witch Ealisaid. Away from the stench of Ralgon's cell, she took a deep breath before she addressed the woman. "Is there anything else?"

The sorceress replied, "I've listened to it for almost an entire day, but most of the time he just screams."

"Anything else you can tell us?" Caslin asked.

Kildanor walked to the priestess. "This prisoner, milady, is dangerous."

"Oh, really now?" the Caretaker said.

"She killed a score of people."

Gail scrutinized the witch. "Had to be very fragile people."

"She is a Wizardess. Her kind can't be trusted!" Kildanor

snapped. Was it only he who understood the danger?

"Funny, Chosen, my brethren in your local temple say the same about you," she replied with wink. "Now, if you want my help, you will have to let me do it my way, understood?"

For a moment, he just stared at her. She was definitely from a different stock than Braigh. Her argument was flawless and left him only one thing to say, "Proceed."

"Thank you," the Caretaker beamed at him. Then, turning to Ealisaid, she asked, "Now, what else can you tell me?"

"I've seen madmen before, but this man's lunacy is different," the Wizardess said.

"How so?"

"Well," she began, "I've looked at him twice in spiritform. The first time, before he came back to life, he was present in both worlds. Dead in both, but his body grabbed me when I approached his... spiritform, if that is the right word for it. Whatever shielded him then isn't protecting him now. That much I can tell you."

She must have sensed Kildanor's resentment, because her next words were addressed directly to him, "Yes, I walked about in spiritform again, to see what is wrong with him. He's still there in both worlds, but he is bound to the spirit realm. I can only see that something is holding him, not what."

He scrutinized the Wizardess and wondered whether this woman had also lost her mind. His knowledge of magic and spirits was lacking; a Chosen had better things to do than worry about spells. Next to him, Gail's brow was creased in deep thought. He wondered what the priestess was pondering. There was enough in the Caretaker's life to occupy her mind, but it seemed as if Ealisaid's words had triggered something. "What do you think?" he finally asked.

Her eyes lost their faraway look and focused on him. "Maybe we can follow the lady Ealisaid into the spiritworld."

Kildanor cocked an eyebrow. "You're serious?"

"Aye," she said. "I've read about spiritform, and it is possible for a traveler to take along... passengers, for lack of a better term."

"To what end?" He didn't like this idea of following a

Phoenix Wizard, of all people, on a journey to the realm of spirits. During the best of times, trust came hard to him, and to put his faith into a woman who belonged to an old enemy was something that caused severe apprehension.

"You could see what I see, for one," Ealisaid answered in Caslin's stead. Obviously, her line of reasoning went the same as the Caretaker's.

"Aye," Gail added. "And we might be able to free the poor soul from whatever is holding his mind prisoner."

"Why should we do that?" He was skeptical. "The man is, in all likelihood, a murderer."

Now it was Caslin's turn to arch an eyebrow. "It was you who wanted the Lesganaghists' rituals performed, if I remember correctly. Had you known what the man was, would you have denied him this last honor?"

Astonished Kildanor looked at her. He thought for a moment, considered the facts, and then nodded. "I don't think so, aye. He's a follower of Lesganagh."

Mischief twinkled in the priestess's eyes. "And isn't it possible that this Drangar Ralgon was sent back for some purpose?"

Now she was proposing the same idea he had already toyed with. Maybe Lesganagh had healed him. "Possibly so, but I don't trust her." He pointed at the Wizardess.

"How many times must I tell you that I destroyed the buildings by accident?" Ealisaid snapped. "I thought your world was a prank! I've done all you asked of me!"

"You are a Phoenix Wizard!" The statement alone should have won the argument.

Caretaker Gail intervened. "And you're the Chosen of a banned deity; you two have something in common. Besides, if that bag of bones over there was sent back for a reason, don't you think you should do all in your power to help?"

Kildanor raised his hands in defeat. Gods, how he hated being outthought. "Damn you, woman! Must you fling logic back at me?"

"The sun burns and nourishes, does it not?" Caslin asked, blowing him a kiss.

"Aye," he grudgingly acknowledged.

Ealisaid cleared her throat, and he turned from Gail's enticing face to look at her. "You are forgetting one thing," she stated. "First, I still have to agree. And second, I have heard of such things as you," she pointed at Gail, "mentioned. But I have no idea how to perform such a thing."

"Then," Kildanor said, "you should start thinking about it. Even if Ralgon serves no greater purpose, having a lucid murderer in court is better than one who shits and pisses himself during trial."

CHAPTER 44

Ealisaid didn't know what to do. Her teachings had never gone as far as taking others with her into the spiritworld. The Chosen and the Caretaker had given her a task, and figuring out that problem was better than sitting in a cell hearing the ramblings of a madman and the thumping of his head against the wall.

Where should she begin? How should she begin? In the past—again the mere reminder made her fight back despair—she would have asked one of her teachers. Now she was master and had to teach herself.

She began with the facts, with what she knew of the spiritworld. Using this knowledge as a starting point, she considered movement and the connection between spiritform and body. Transportation spells were more complex, but they should be based on the same principle, since one teleported with one's clothes. The spiritform usually was also dressed, which implied that taking along clothes was, essentially, a subconscious act. Now the only thing to do was test her theory, turn conscious thought to the matter of taking additional items along into the spiritworld.

"It has to be something that I'm not really attached to," Ealisaid said aloud to convince herself of the idea. Back during her schooling her peers had sniggered at her mumblings until she had forced herself not to speak her thoughts out loud. Here in the dungeon, with the exception of Drangar Ralgon who didn't mind one way or another, she was alone.

She looked along the two yards of wall on each side of her and saw a cup she must have forgotten after one of her meals.

"This should do."

She retrieved the mug, sat on the straw and concentrated to enter the spiritworld. With the container. What seemed easy in theory was more difficult in execution. It felt as if she was pulled into every direction at once. Now that she focused on what to take with her, she became aware of everything on her body. The action of taking along the cup forced her to think of every piece of clothing she wore; Ealisaid realized that forcing her subconscious thoughts into conscious action was not the way to proceed.

"I don't think about walking, I just walk," she muttered, deep in thought. "I picture the destination and I just walk there. I don't worry about lifting first one and then the other foot." She stood, raking both hands through her hair. "I don't think about breathing, I just breathe."

Maybe she approached the problem wrong. If walking and breathing, and the gods knew what else, was second nature to man or beast, then each creature should know how to do it. The spiritform, as she had reminded the Baron Duasonh so aptly, wasn't magic. Anyone could do it! Provided they received training. To take Kildanor and Caretaker Gail along they would have to learn the basics. She had to teach them. She called for the guard and asked for both.

She didn't have to wait long. The Baron accompanied the pair. In the dungeon's gloom she found this Duasonh's likeness to his ancestor even more remarkable. Every time she saw him the resemblance reminded her how much she had lost, but there was also a tinge of relief. She was glad not to have been part of the war, which had destroyed her world.

Duasonh briefly halted at Ralgon's cell, took in the miserable sight, shook his head in disgust, and then moved on.

"What nonsense is this?" the Baron asked when he stood next to the others.

"No nonsense, Lord Baron," she replied. "Chosen Kildanor and the priestess Caslin want to investigate what has happened to Ralgon. I assume they told you of my discovery."

"That they did," Duasonh said. "It seems these two have set their mind to it. Not that there aren't more important things than figuring out what ails a madman."

"Have you found a way to take us along?" Kildanor cut in.

"In a way."

The Caretaker frowned. "What do you mean 'in a way'?"

"I can help you follow me, anything else is as of now beyond me," she replied. She was annoyed at her own limitations, but there was nothing she could do.

"No magic?" Duasonh asked.

"No magic, milord," Ealisaid said. "I explained, or rather tried to explain it before. This isn't magic, unless you say dreams are magic also." The look she gave the nobleman would have been condescending in different surroundings; here in this cell she guessed it was rather silly.

"Very well. Proceed." He looked at the Chosen and the Caretaker. "This is your hobby horse, don't take it too far, there's much that needs be discussed." Duasonh turned away and hurried down the corridor, muttering to himself.

"Poor chap," Kildanor laughed. "The letters have all his attention. He called some lore men to make sense of them."

"Lore men? What letters?" the priestess asked.

"I procured several letters from the Chanastardhians. Turns out some of the stuff is gibberish. He thinks it's code."

"A cipher?" Caslin sounded astonished.

"Aye! I suggested he get some scribes and maybe a priest of Traghnalach."

"Lore men?" The priestess smirked.

"Aye, lore men."

"I can guide you, but it is you who have to do the work here," Ealisaid interrupted the pair's banter. "I tried, but to perform what you want of me I need more time, a commodity we don't have."

"What do you need of us?" Caslin asked.

"You know how to meditate, I assume?" Everything hinged upon how the answer would be. If one of them knew, she could take that person with her, she hoped. If neither knew the attempt was doomed to fail.

"Certainly," the Caretaker said.

Both Ealisaid and the priestess turned to look at Kildanor.

The Chosen seemed hesitant. "I'm not sure," he finally said.

"What do you mean, you're not sure?" Caslin asked.

"You heard me," Kildanor snapped.

"There is more to this than you are letting on, man."

"If meditating is like prayer, then I know it."

"It's close enough," Ealisaid said. If Kildanor didn't want to reveal what troubled him, it certainly wasn't her business to find out.

"Sit down." The two obeyed. "When you pray, I assume you close your eyes, am I correct?" Their response was an affirmative. "Well, then close your eyes." She thought how to explain the next part of what she wanted them to do. "Breathe deeply, in and out. Focus on my voice and your breathing, nothing else." For her the process was, by now, second nature. She had traveled the Palace in spiritform several times and knew what she was doing. "Picture in your mind the corridor. Yourself. And yourself looking down on you." She thrust into the spiritworld briefly, like she had done in the chapel, and looked around; she was alone in the hallway. Her conscience slipped back into her body. "Think of nothing but the corridor, and looking down on you." Again, her body slipped away.

This time she saw a flicker. No, two flickers where Kildanor and the Caretaker should be. Ealisaid tried to touch the two shadows. She felt her hands brush against their flecks of spiritform, grabbed, and pulled. Both stood before her, confused and disoriented. She maintained her hold on them and drifted to Drangar Ralgon's cell.

This was the most uncomfortable Kildanor had ever been. The sorceress had said to look down at himself and he did. Or rather he tried to. He felt as if dreaming, drifting from wakefulness to sleep, in the heartbeat moment before one lost conscience to restful slumber. Part of him wanted to sleep. If this was the spiritworld, ghosts had to be sleepy all the time. Still, he couldn't really see his body sitting on the floor. He couldn't even see the floor, or anything other than murky twilight. Someone grabbed his hand and yanked. From one moment to the next he floated in the corridor.

He saw Gail; the priestess's face a mask of mild confusion. Holding them both was the Wizardess. Instinctively he tried to take a deep breath, but there was nothing. Ghosts didn't need air, and in all likelihood neither did he.

Kildanor looked around. Below him he saw his body, slumped alongside Caslin's against the cell door. It seemed real, and yet everything around him, even the others, felt as if there was no true weight behind them. Almost like mist, or smoke. Nothing he did here would have any impact on the world; he couldn't even speak. There was no sound, no substance, only light, smoke, and darkness. The spiritworld was a dream, a nightmare, a reflection in which nothing was real.

Yet how was he able to feel the witch's touch? Her grip on his arm was strong. Now she pulled them along, through the cell walls, into Ralgon's room. She halted their flight before the man's body, and what he saw turned his initial understanding about the spiritworld upside down.

Ralgon sat in his cell, above him floated his... what? This was no spiritform. Kildanor looked from Gail to Ealisaid; both of them were the shape they had in life, but, like everything, they were translucent. Ralgon was as solid here as he was outside the spiritworld.

The Chosen scrutinized the body floating spread-eagled before him. It looked almost as if... as if he was crucified. His arms were tense, as if struggling against some bonds. The legs seemed coiled, ready to jump. Occasionally his chest heaved, his muscles twitched and his back arched as if in terrible pain. Kildanor looked to Ealisaid and nodded and pointed toward Ralgon's form. The Wizardess understood, and the three glided forward.

Now, as they floated closer to this solidity amidst a world of smoke, Kildanor saw something odd. Had he not been in the spiritworld he would have thought it a trick of the light, but here that was impossible. A thin line protruded from Ralgon's chest, right above the heart. He leaned closer and saw the line was smooth, like a wire, its length not merely a few feet; it appeared to reach into the mist-like ceiling and beyond. Following a sudden insight, Kildanor reached out and touched the wire.

CHAPTER 45

Eighteenth of Chill, 1475 K.C.

His eyes fluttered open and he saw Cumaill Duasonh standing next to his bed. Not even during Jathain's treacherous attack had Kildanor seen his friend look so concerned. He wanted to speak, but before the first word formed on his lips a memory flashed through his mind.

He saw rivers overflowing with blood. In them beings of unspeakable grace lounged. Their heads, the only part of their bodies completely visible above the surface, bore the hard curves and features only seen on cats.

Unable to turn away, he looked on, his position rising. He saw that the rivers weren't natural, but built channels and holes, similar to a bathing house. And above the blood-covered felines, mighty energies were woven into a blinding tapestry.

Unseen hands guided his sight toward the higher levels of the blood-bathing house. There, beyond countless elevations, bodies hung from the ceiling, their wrists and throats slit, their blood first gushing, then slowly dribbling into basins, which in turn fed the pools through blood-channels.

"Demons!" Kildanor whispered. He remembered the gruesome rituals the Demonologists went through during the Demon War, but never before had he seen the beings that had taken possession of so many and killed even more.

He blinked and the vision was gone. Instead he saw Duasonh frowning at him.

"What happened?" the Chosen asked, his voice raspy.

"Caretaker Gail called me. It seems that during your little

excursion you did something rather foolish."

"I... I touched something... a straight wire... out of Ralgon's body," Kildanor whispered.

"The Wizardess Ealisaid said something like that. She also said your spiritform began to fade. Then she thrust all of you back into your bodies. Caslin summoned the guards and brought you here. Then she called me." Duasonh scratched his chin. "What the bloody Scales were you thinking?"

"I... I... it felt the right thing to do," he replied. "How long was I out?"

Duasonh shrugged. "It's past sunrise now."

"An entire night? That long?"

"Caslin said you'd be out for much longer," said Cumaill.

"What of..."

"Ralgon?" Duasonh shook his head. "Same as before."

"I need to..." What? He wasn't sure what needed to be done, but he knew speed was important.

"What?"

His head ached, but he had to get up, had to get to the Wizardess, had to sever the spear. Kildanor didn't know how he knew the line was a spear, he just knew. "I need to get back to the dungeon!"

"What?" Duasonh barked. "You can't be serious."

"You heard me, old man," snapped Kildanor.

"Whatever for? You look like shit, mate."

Kildanor smirked at his friend, "I still look younger than you." His humor faded quickly when the headache reminded him of his ordeal, and for a moment he was lost for words. How could he explain what had happened when he himself wasn't certain?

"I wouldn't be so sure right now," Duasonh replied.

"I have no time to explain, I need to do something, now!" he said and righted himself. His head felt as if some giant had mistaken it for an anvil. For a moment he felt consciousness slipping, but he pushed the pain aside. "Get the Caretaker, will you, Cumaill?"

Duasonh nodded. "Certainly."

When the Baron had left, Kildanor forced himself to focus

on what lay ahead. How he would sever the spear he didn't know, but there was no doubt in his mind that the demonic link to the world had to be cut. Slowly he rose from his bed. There was a moment when he felt faint. He took a deep breath, gathered his resolve, pushed away the dizziness once again, and straightened his legs and back.

For a moment the room spun around him. Kildanor closed his eyes. He would not give any ground to the demons!

His eyes flicked open again, and although he could now see unhindered by loss of balance, a small sense of vertigo remained. The door opened and Gail strode in. "What the Scales do you think you're doing?" the priestess asked. "You are in no condition to strut about. Get back to bed!"

"I need to clear my head," he replied.

"Sleep some more."

"There's no time, Caretaker," he hissed. "The connection between the demons and Ralgon is getting stronger. We must save him!"

Duasonh entered and stood next to Caslin. "You can barely stand, mate. How do you want to fight this thing?"

"I don't intend to fight it, Cumaill."

Priestess and nobleman looked at each other and then at him. After a moment Gail said, "You need rest."

Kildanor breathed deeply and took a shaky step toward them. "This is why everyone was afraid of the Church of Lesganagh. It chose to do something while every other faith sat on their asses and discussed what needed to be done against the demons! If there's no time to contemplate, you act! We need to get in there and cut this link."

He didn't care whether the others were offended by his words; there wasn't a thing he could do about it. Being diplomatic was for diplomats, not Chosen. "Gail," he continued before either one could speak, "you have your goddess's favor?" The priestess nodded. "Then give me something to clear my head!"

"You need to lie down."

"Fuck that! I've seen what Caretakers can do with herbs!"

"Are you sure this is the right way?" Duasonh asked.

"Damned if I know. You'll never know until you do it; all the preparation is worthless if your enemy does something unexpected. Then you adapt."

"This is no war!" Duasonh snapped.

"Wrong!" he replied. "Those men in the Shadowpeaks wanted to use Ralgon as a sacrifice to the demons. They failed. But only in part. There is a link between the demon realm and this poor sod in the dungeon. I don't know if Drangar Ralgon is blessed by anyone, but he is important to the Demonologists. Neither of you were alive when Danachamain let the fiends loose on the world. I was, and I will do whatever is necessary to prevent their return."

The Caretaker thrust a mug into his hand. "Drink this.

He obeyed, gulping down the concoction of water and leaves. "And now?"

"We wait."

Whatever Gail had given him, it worked. Kildanor felt better, and before Cumaill could argue with him, he strode out of his room and headed for the dungeon.

CHAPTER 46

Where was the bloody dog? It was already past noon, the witch was waiting, and still Kildanor hadn't found Ralgon's mutt. Some people recalled seeing the beast somewhere: the inner bailey, the outer bailey, the pantry of all places. It seemed as if the animal had vanished. A cook told him of sausages he had left for the dog, just yesterday in fact. Where? Outside the kitchen. That really wasn't much help, and time was slipping away.

A stable boy finally yielded the answer. "The mutt's with that white horse you brought in about a week ago or so, sir."

He had no idea why Ealisaid wanted the beast with Ralgon, could hardly believe his ears when she insisted, but her seriousness convinced him. Upon entering the stables, he saw the massive white charger in a nearby box munching oats. He walked toward the animal and it perked up its ears. The horse turned its head to face him and whinnied in greeting. "A little late for a snack, don't you think?" he said. The reply was a snort that blew dust into the air.

"Now where is your little friend?" He looked up and down along the lines of boxes, but aside from two cats he saw nothing. A nibble on his shirt brought his attention back to the stallion. The horse looked at him and then nodded to the back of its own box.

Kildanor was surprised; he knew smart horses, but this one put them all to shame. In the box's corner sat the mutt. He opened the door, squatted on the floor and motioned for the dog to come to him. "Here boy! Come here! Damn this, I should've brought some sausages."

I'm a girl.

His mutterings stopped, and more or less surprised, he looked at the canine. This was the same voice as before, the same voice he had heard back when the dog had led the horse after him. Now the nonsense Ealisaid had been talking about didn't seem so silly after all: a woman's image overlaying the dog when Drangar Ralgon was thrashing on the bier. "What are you?" he asked.

Almost out of time, I fear.

"We need to..."

I know, take me to him.

He shook his head, laughed in confusion, and then led the way through the inner bailey to the keep and into the dungeon. Several servants and warriors ogled the two of them, but Kildanor was in no mood to reprimand them. The mismatched pair went through the lighter outer door into the guardroom and then through the heavy steeloak door into the corridor, from which the individual cells branched off left and right. The dog followed willingly, and kept his quick pace, despite her rather underfed looks. They reached a group comprised of three people: Cumaill Duasonh, Caretaker Gail, and the Phoenix Wizardess Ealisaid.

The Baron looked at the mutt and his frown deepened. "What the bloody Scales do you think you are doing?"

"Saving a soul, mate," Kildanor replied.

"With a dog?"

"Aye, now shut up!" The Chosen knew addressing Duasonh this way was wrong, but at the moment he didn't care. He was tired beyond belief, and the dull headache was returning, a reminder of the nightmarish vision. "Sorry," he muttered, then turned to the other two. "I can't explain how I'll get that spear out. Damn, I don't know for sure."

"Why the dog?" Duasonh cut in.

"Because she needs to be here."

"Why exactly is that?" the Baron persisted, looking at the Wizardess.

"Ask him," she replied

He turned to his friend and sighed. "You remember how

she," he pointed at the sorceress, "told you the dog's presence somehow calmed the turmoil around Ralgon?"

"Think I'm a dimwit?" Duasonh snapped. "Of course I do."

"No, I don't!" he grumbled. "But she also told of the image of a woman overlapping the dog in the spiritworld, aye?"

"Yes," Duasonh asked.

"Magician's babble if you ask me. But still..."

"She told you what she saw, and you believed her enough to go and check on him in the spiritworld, eh? So now you revise your attitude? How political of you!"

Kildanor wanted to reply, but Duasonh went on, ignoring him. "If my grandfather had that much lack of faith and understanding in magic I'd be lording over a pile of rubble! Do you think blood, bone, and mortar held the city together? No! Magic was used to fight magic; I want to use our lady wizard here to blast the Chanastardhians straight to the Bailey Majestic, but this dog?"

"The mutt is important, Cumaill. She told me."

"Who told you?" Duasonh glanced at Ealisaid, who in turn merely shrugged her shoulders, a confused look on her face.

"The dog."

Duasonh guffawed.

"Trust me. Now let me explain what I want to do, if you please." Kildanor was tired and annoyed.

"Go ahead," Gail said, casting a reproachful glance at the Baron.

"We go in again, into the spiritworld," he began, his voice crisp, businesslike. "Once we are with Ralgon..." all of a sudden his vague idea formed into a full-fledged plan. "Once we're with Ralgon, Gail will pray to the Mother and I to the Father. Wizardess, your duty is simple, keep us in the spiritworld." He paused to see if the two understood.

"Which prayer?" Caslin asked.

"You know the Hymn to Sun and Health?" This song had been forbidden for the past decades. It was a duet praising both Lesganagh and Eanaigh; naturally it had been banned alongside Lesganagh's priests and faith.

Caslin nodded.

"We're going to sing that little ditty."

A frown creased the priestess's face. "Little ditty? Do you have any idea how long your little ditty is?"

"I see you do know it," he grinned. "Well, I have no idea what the dog will do, but it'll be important, I'm certain."

"When should I pull us back?" the witch asked.

"When the spear is out of the body, you'll know."

"You are bloody insane," Duasonh muttered.

"Thanks for noticing." The Chosen bowed mockingly. Then, serious again, he said, "Cumaill, I know this is damned odd, but everything about him is. Yes, he most likely is the murderer of this Hesmera, but it seems Lesganagh has a higher purpose in mind for him. How else could you explain him being slaughtered and almost sacrificed to the very demons that now have pierced his heart and are filling his mind with madness?"

Duasonh gave him a look that showed he had convinced him. When the Baron was just a lad he had looked at Kildanor the same way whenever the Chosen had not only won an argument but also made the other see and understand the reasoning behind said argument.

Then he had another thought. Cumaill Duasonh was worried. The Baron hid the feeling well, but how else could his behavior be explained? He had refused to become emotionally attached to anyone, had cut himself off from the other Chosen to prevent the pain of loss he still felt over Ethain and Ganaedor. Cumaill was his friend, but he had never thought strong Baron Duasonh relied on him so much.

Kildanor pulled his friend to the side and whispered, "Don't worry, mate, I know what I'm doing."

"In all my life you have been the one constant," the Baron replied. "Teacher and friend, that's what you have been and still are," he continued.

"I'll always be your friend, until Lesganagh calls." He gave Cumaill's shoulder a reassuring pat. "You need a wife."

At that Duasonh laughed heartily. "Damnation, I think you're right."

"That Wizardess is a fine-looking woman," he mocked.

The Baron grinned, slapped the Chosen's hand off his

shoulder and left, muttering, "You take care in this spiritworld, let me worry about the womenfolk. There's a merchant or ten who'd dearly love to see their daughters share my bed."

"Not to mention your wealth," Kildanor called after him.

He turned back to the others, determined to finish the business at hand quickly. "Ladies, shall we?" He hated to rely on the Wizardess, but it seemed the only way. Maybe Cumaill and Gail were right in that he was too prejudiced.

Didn't you forget something?

The dog! He almost had. "Just a moment," he said to the others and hurried down the corridor to the guardroom. The key ring was right next to the heavy door barring entrance to the dungeon. He grabbed it and returned to Ralgon's cell. Finding the right key was more difficult than retrieving the thing. Kildanor tried one then another, and finally he found the correct one. The door creaked open and the dog slipped in.

Don't worry. I'll do my part.

"Very well," he said, locking the door and returning to the others. "Now," he took a deep breath. "Let's begin."

Entering the spiritworld this time was easier. Now that they knew at least in part what to do, their spiritform floated in the corridor with only a few instructions from Ealisaid. The sorceress took hold of their arms and they glided toward Ralgon's cell. Kildanor grew more accustomed to this world of mists and shadows, and now the dual-presence of Drangar Ralgon felt truly out of place. When this ordeal was over he decided to ask Ealisaid about it. For now, however, he had other things to worry about.

They reached the body. Kildanor saw the spear claimed more space now; it wasn't a mere needle in width anymore. Ralgon's chest was pierced by a solid finger's breadth of gold. Even though he couldn't hear Gail singing, he felt the Caretaker had begun the Hymn to Sun and Health. He was grateful for the first section being dedicated to Eanaigh. This way he could gather his thoughts and bring to mind the melody and words of the song.

His mind drifted to the last time he had sung the Hymn,

to the last harvest Lesganagh's and Eanaigh's church had celebrated together. Despite the misgivings already coursing through the Hearthwarden's church, the Hymn had brought upon all participants a warmth that none had felt since.

With the memory bright in his mind and heart he heard Gail's song as if he was standing next to her. The words burned their way into his being, and then the moment, the brief unison, the mere two words "bright world" sung together, came. He joined in and took the words on from there. Or was it the words taking him along the way? Kildanor wasn't sure, but it felt as if the Hymn had taken over; a vibrancy, light, and life filled him. Gail joined him with the final two words of his verse, and then both sang together. Strength, warmth, life, growth, death, and rebirth filled his soul, and judging from her expression also the Caretaker's.

The crescendo, the final entwining of words, spirit, and notes came, and Kildanor knew what to do. Holding the final note, as Gail did, he reached out and pulled the spear from Drangar Ralgon's chest.

CHAPTER 47

One moment Drangar saw the feline beasts stretched in their bloody baths; he didn't know why he was seeing such things, such demons. Fear, anger, sickness, all these coursed through him, and still he could not look away. He wanted to die, the pain in his chest was immense, and again and again he screamed at the monsters.

The next moment both pain and visions were gone. Air ran unhindered into his chest, no pain, no fear to stab him. The bleak, shadowy surroundings slid away and he slammed into... something. Now that he was the monsters' prisoner no more he could shut his eyes again. For a moment Drangar merely enjoyed the blackness that came when his lids closed. He felt a hand caress his cheek and opened his eyes. Looking down at him was Dog, her paw on his face.

He was in a cell. It stank of feces and urine, but that rank stench was like summer flowers to him, compared to the place he had seen. Dog touched his face again, and in a heart beat he felt himself being dragged into the air, through the cell, another cell, a wall, and through solid earth. A glowing hand traced his shoulder and he turned to look at a luminous woman. Her face, framed by long blonde curls, was calm as death, but the love emanating from her told him she was very much alive. Her smile warmed his heart and he felt at ease, trusting her immediately.

"Come," she whispered and took his hand into hers as they glided southward, leaving the courtyard behind. "There's something you need to know. Something that can't wait."

"Where are we going?" He looked down at the city as it

changed before his eyes. People walked backward, the sun set in the east only to rise in the west, and the slower their journey across the city, the faster people and sun and moon moved. Autumn turned to summer to spring to winter to autumn. Twice he saw snow cover the trees to be replaced by bright red and brown leaves turning into fresh green to little buds. They were going back in time. Two years into the past, into his past. Why would this woman show him his past, his terrible deed to the one person he loved?

"You must see the truth, boy," the woman said. "You must know the past before you can let it rest."

When they arrived over Dunthiochagh's merchant quarter it was summer. Birds sang mirthful tunes, awakening the depressed minds of many a poet that inhabited it. The buildings that dominated Dunthiochagh as they leaned into each other, that cast such a bleak pallor across streets and alleyways, seemed lighter, taller. Despite the gloom that lasted six months and was the city's foremost feature, flowers shone skyward, their colors easily discernible from the gray background of shingled houses, from the roads of paved stone and mud hardened by boots that trod them day in and day out. Seen from above it was spectacular. Foreigners reported how marvelous Dunthiochagh was, how splendid.

To Drangar it was a nightmare come true.

Groaning, he looked at the ghostly woman. "Why here? Haven't I suffered enough?"

Without replying, the luminous being moved on, continuing their way, but now time didn't change as they drifted across the bustling town.

Children's voices wafted up as Drangar gazed down at the city that he and Hesmera had made their home before that fateful summer day. He recalled several places; naturally the memory sprang to his mind. It was pain intermingled with pleasure that now invaded his soul. Drangar recalled the friends he had made in the city watch, and apart from the decent pay it was the wonderful nature of those he had worked with that had prompted him to call Dunthiochagh home. The first home he had had since leaving the Eye. He saw the building that housed the watch of the merchant quarter, the building he had been assigned to. It was noon, the midday gong rang across the city, and he heard merry laughter welling up from the house.

Noontime. How he had enjoyed spending that time of day with his comrades. Glaithan, the ever sarcastic but gentle swordsman, whose mouth was as mean as a mallet and whose heart as big as the ocean, always willing to shock people with his rudeness before holding them so they could release their grief. Rob, the stern and serious man from Harail who had come to Dunthiochagh to begin a better life; he always claimed to be a former guardsman of Danastaer's king and the anecdotes he told when he was drunk credited his stories. There were more. Drangar had forgotten their names, but the memory was vivid and as they descended toward the house, he heard his booming laughter.

"What?" he looked at the woman again.

"Just watch, listen, and learn," her gentle voice pierced his confusion. "You will see the past as it really was."

They drifted closer, until they floated well within the house and observed the events unfolding within. It was the first time that Drangar actually saw himself. Not a reflection but a living and breathing human being who had no idea that tragedy was going to strike.

Drangar slammed his hands onto the table, laughter welling up his throat again. "And then, you're not gonna believe this, and then the merchant said, while his wife was watching him from a safe distance," he grinned at the assembled watchmen, "and I swear to Lesganagh this is true, he was buck-naked and this woman was right beside him… he said he was investigating a rather serious matter of his trade-partner's swindling. At this moment his wife sped out from her hiding place and screamed at him, wondering aloud who was swindling who?"

"Well, maybe the woman was his trade-partner," Rob suggested, causing the men and women to laugh even harder.

"And what happened then?" Jasseira, a woman whose life had taken almost the same path as Drangar's, asked with a chuckle.

"Drangar gave her his dagger and said that *he* could

not kill him or mutilate him, otherwise he'd be locked up,"
Glaithan answered. "And the woman thought he had given her
permission to unman her husband. She jumped straight for him
and only Drang's arm prevented her from doing the obvious."

The ghostly Drangar heard his nickname, and smiled
despite the circumstances. He looked at his younger self and
saw his eyes gleaming with pride and mirth. "Well, we helped
that good woman getting rid of her cheating husband legally,
why watch her dismember him?"

That comment caused his companions to roar and applaud,
and the mercenary turned guardsman stood up and did a very
passable imitation of an actor's bow. "My duty for today is over,
ladies and gentlemen, and now I will head back to my lovely
wife-to-be and take away all daggers." He winked at them.
"Just in case..."

He chuckled and left the building, whistling a merry tune as
he walked down sunny Trann Street. Despite its rough exterior,
Dunthiochagh was a peaceful place and the mercenary enjoyed
it more than he would ever admit. West onto Trade Road and
then north across Old Bridge. Unbeknownst to him a pair of
ghostly observers and two not so spiritual beings followed him
closely.

Drangar looked at his guide. "Who are those two shady
folk that trail him... uh, me?" Seeing things from above made
observations easier and he had discovered the pair almost
immediately. Their clothing was common for Dunthiochagh
where every citizen dressed according to the rules he set for
himself, until a certain point of decency was reached; beyond
that only the brothels were terrain where one could get away
with less.

It was their demeanor that set them apart, haughty yet
cautious the two men followed Drangar, every few paces they
exchanged glances and watched their surroundings. Now and
then they examined one of the booths lining the bridge, but the
happy watchman didn't pay attention to what was going on
behind his back.

A couple of children dashed out of a dock street and
slammed into Drangar, who stumbled and went down, a

surprised six-year-old girl gaping at him as he tried to regain
the wooden sword that had found its way to the ground. Her
companions regained their senses a little quicker and taunted
the child as the lass stood up and reached out for her sword.
Drangar wiped the dirt off his clothes and eyed the would-be
warriors with a gleam in his eyes. "Attention!" he yelled.

The surprised children jumped back, staring at him. "He
must have been a warrior," muttered one of them.

Any comment on that remark was silenced by Drangar's
vicious glare. "Did I permit you rabble to speak freely?" he
asked winking at the youngsters and they understood. In the
shadow of the Palace's battlement he began to play a role he had
known for almost half his life.

One after the other the children assumed an erect standing
position and one of them yelled. "Warband assembled and
arranged, warleader-lord sir!"

Even the observing Drangar grinned hearing the boy yelling
nonsense at his "superior".

Trying to hide his mirth, Drangar looked his warriors up
and down and then yelled in his best warleader's voice, "Turn
left!" which some of the kids immediately did while others had
trouble finding out which side left was and it took a couple of
shoves and pokes by their fellow "warriors" to actually get all
children in line. By that time, Drangar couldn't hold back his
laughter.

"Listen up, lasses, lads!" he yelled, and the equally amused
children looked at him. "If you want to be warriors you have
to know where left and right is. A good warrior always pays
attention to his surroundings and is careful not to bump into
anything or anyone. A good warrior has discipline! Got that?"

"Yes, warleader-lord sir!" the enthused children cried
in unison, still standing in a somewhat straight line. By now
the act had caught the attention of several passersby and the
warriors on the battlement. Some people halted and observed
him and his "troop", while the guards hollered down good-
natured advice.

Again, both Drangars grinned. "Good, now head home
and learn about directions and how to be disciplined. Dinner

is waiting for you. Dismissed!" The ghostly Drangar was mouthing the same words as his corporeal counterpart. Their faces now stern and serious, the children attempted to become disciplined warriors for about twenty heartbeats, then the stumbling of one caused the line to break and the good-natured yelling, screaming, and shoving continued.

"So much for discipline!" a guardswoman shouted. The younger Drangar turned around, gave the warriors a merry wave and continued his way back home, the two pairs of observers following shortly afterwards.

"Have you noticed the two following you?" the woman asked Drangar as his younger counterpart walked into Beggar's Alley, politely greeting people he recognized.

"I have," he answered, frowning. "What about them?"

"You'll see," the woman answered like an oracle, and Drangar knew complaining wouldn't help.

The watchman made his way through Beggar's Alley, drinking in the vibrant activity of the place as many others would have enjoyed a rare wine or dish, but Drangar had never known such peace before. Rigorous schooling and learning had marked his childhood and when he had been old enough, he had carved himself a position in a world that was still torn asunder by war. He looked at two women in front of a goldsmith's shop who eyed him curiously, and then blushed as he bowed to them, the imitation of a courtier. Hesmera was used to his antics, and even though it bothered her that many women adored her handsome man, she knew well that he did everything for her. She was sure of his love, as he was of hers.

As he passed the Drunken Unicorn, a tavern that hosted bards from across the world, or so its proprietor claimed, he wondered how the owner could have chosen such a silly name for his business. Then again, the name was far better than others he had seen during his travels. The Drunken Unicorn was a far better name than The Thoughtful Wolf or The Drowned Mermaid, but where did people get ideas for such names? He shrugged and continued on his way, a broad grin on his face. Even little things amused him nowadays.

Finally, after turning into a quiet street that was just

off Old Wall Street, the constant mutter and tumult that had
accompanied grew silent, and even though he somewhat
missed the liveliness around him, he enjoyed both the growing
calm and the closeness to home.

Home, the word rang well in his heart, and he truly felt
it. This was his home, Hesmera's and his home. It was not the
temple-like fortress he had grown up in, a fact he was grateful
for.

As the younger Drangar walked up to his house, his older
self and the ghostly apparition remained aloof, staying atop a
house that formed the corner of Old Wall's and Cherkont Street,
watching as the guardsman approached the door.

"Aren't we going to follow him... me?" the older Drangar
asked, looking at his companion.

"No, we will wait here and then take a different path. You
have to see the truth," the ghost said.

Shortly afterward, the two spies reached the corner and
stopped, observing the guardsman as he was greeted by his
beautiful lover. They watched as they embraced each other, the
woman's voice ringing with laughter that could be heard all the
way up to their position.

Drangar sighed, wished he could still hear that laughter,
wished he could still feel Hesmera's arms wrapped around him.

"The past is the past, let it rest, dear," the ghostly figure said,
sadness plain on her face.

Hearing the familiar words, Drangar tore himself away
from the scene and he stared at his guide. "Who are you?"

"Nothing but a memory," she muttered. "But I can't rest,
yet." She pointed at the two men below, "Listen closely."

The shepherd turned his attention to the pair that lurked
behind a barrel, placed at the corner to gather rainwater from
the house's shingled roof.

"Here the bastard lives," exclaimed the smaller of the
two men, his voice dripping with disgust and contempt as he
observed his apparent target.

"And he has the woman with him, too," the other supplied.

"Now is our chance." The first speaker's right hand
wandered to the hilt of the dagger he wore at his belt.

"Patience!" the other hissed, placing a calming hand on his companion's. "That's not what I have in mind."

"Oh, and what do you have in mind?"

"We shall break him; make him lose his will to fight! Then, we shall do the deed!"

Drangar frowned. Make him lose his will to fight? Bastard? Who were those men and what had he done to them?

"We'll meet the others," the second said. "Let's go!"

Both of them turned and meandered through the throng of people that still crowded the streets; the two spirits followed them slowly.

More than once Drangar turned to look longingly at the street where they used to live. "Gods, I still love her," he whispered.

"The past is what it is. Learn from it."

CHAPTER 48

A while later the two men reached a hut huddled against the western city wall. This was the rough part of town, he remembered. The watch rarely came here. Killings were commonplace, and gangs that controlled the various parts of the slum meted out justice. The building barely deserved the name hut, even for a place like the West Gate slums it seemed almost too decrepit, a perfect hiding place. Signaling a beggar who loitered in the shade of a nearby tree, the pair made for the door.

Of course, they had lookouts, Drangar thought. If they had operated in a larger group from a fixed base, they would have been stupid not to have any.

His attention now attuned, it didn't take him long to discover several other sentries dispersed about the street at strategically important places.

Well-guarded, indeed. How had they managed to gain a foothold here? His answer came in the form of a pair of toughs who began to kick the beggar-outlook. Before they could assault the man in earnest, the vagabond lashed out with his walking stick. Even to Drangar's still somewhat experienced eye the man was fast: one quick jab and one man covered his left eye with blood spurting out from under his hands. The other ruffian didn't wait for a second strike which would most certainly have been aimed at him; he dragged his whimpering companion away, and both hurried off.

"What is the point of all of this?" he asked his guide. "Why do you show me all this? I know there have been various attempts on my life, the last in the Shadow Peaks."

"You need to learn the truth." Again, the ghostly figure

replied with a simple sentence.

He knew the truth. He had butchered Hesmera with his sword. Why revisit the past? Why did she remind him of his deed?

"You will learn soon enough," she said.

To them the roof was like air, and they glided into the building and settled in what once could have been the hovel's rafters, above a group gathered in a dug-out space between the ramshackle walls. The two newcomers bowed to a black-clad man, apparently their leader.

"We found him, sir," the second said, plainly. "I already have a plan." The last words he added with a smirk that did not go unnoticed.

"A plan? From a lousy acolyte such as you? Amazing!" the leader replied with a sneer. "So, tell us."

"He's still with that raven-haired bitch he met four years ago," the bold acolyte started his speech.

"So?"

"We know he loves her, if his kind can truly love."

His kind?

"Yes?" apart from the leader's, several pairs of eyes now looked at the speaker and he seemed elated to be the center of attention.

"What if we take this woman away from him?" the acolyte beamed into the round of his accomplices.

"Um… did it occur to you that this cause of action might bring the bastard after us directly? He would go after the killers of his beloved!" the leader remarked coldly.

The other attendees sniggered.

"Not if he's the one who kills her," the acolyte replied, his eyes gleaming in triumph as the assembly fell silent.

Looking from one man to the other, Drangar tried to make sense of their words. "What's the meaning of this? Why…" He fell silent when the acolyte continued.

The former mercenary tried to discern more of the assassins, their faces, notable features. Until now the only thing he had seen were vague images of men in rags.

The leader had a hawk-like face. His black hair stood in

contrast with his blue eyes, and the mustache that crowned his upper lip gave him an older appearance. His voice slurred a little, but that seemed to be a way of gathering everyone's attention, for in his outburst he had snarled and spoken without the slight touch in his speech.

She noticed Drangar's intense stare. "Don't bother," she said. "They have failed and died."

Frowning he looked up at her. "What?"

"You heard me. They are dead; they don't matter."

"They failed? Failed at what?"

"To kill you, boy. They weren't meant to kill her, they were ordered to kill you, and only you. But watch and listen."

"Ordered?" He frowned.

"Hush! Listen!"

Another of the group nodded. "We do know he loves this woman, so if he kills her, his resolve will shatter."

The leader scowled. "What do you propose?"

"Easy. We prepare a potion. One that influences the mind, and then we let him see what we want him to see."

With a suddenness that startled Drangar the two rushed through the hut's ceiling and away from the building.

"Wait!" he yelled, confused at the turn of events. "Why do we leave now? Why now? They just started talking about the important part."

"We need to see more and I don't have time or strength to keep us in one place longer than necessary; the important parts were said," she explained, and without further comment they flew across Dunthiochagh.

Trees and houses streaked past. They flew over a few public wells and the one park that hadn't fallen victim to more houses. Drangar tried to follow their path, but at this speed he could hardly discern the features of a city he had lived in for only a couple of months. He tried to locate landmarks to know where they were, but couldn't. When they finally halted above a mansion, he looked at his companion and, apart from seeing her face more clearly now, he also realized it was nighttime.

"Where are we?"

"Unimportant, come and see and listen," she said roughly

and they sank into the building, passing walls and servants, crossing through various rooms, both sparely and lushly decorated. Some noble or rich merchant owned this place, Drangar figured, judging from the pictures and carpets he saw. Elven work was paired with some Samaarian maps, which certainly did not come from this part of the world. When he saw the decorated and jeweled breast plate, adorned with tusks of various beasts, he knew the owner was very rich—this armor was of elven make, no human had created this. Not many people alive had ever seen such armor, and even fewer could afford it.

They entered a small room. Its walls were covered with wood, several furs were spread on the floor, and a small but warm-looking fireplace crackled in the corner. In the center of the room, loaded to its limit with delicacies, stood a small table. Around it were gathered four women dressed in long gowns with their hair loose. The loose hair was somewhat curious. He remembered that at the time he had lived in Dunthiochagh, braids had been the one thing that dominated women's fashion, and the only woman who had refused to tame her hair with silk had been Hesmera. He frowned and then blanched when hearing her voice. In a mixture of giggle and laughter her beautiful voice rose above the others.

"And he really said, 'May I court you, milady?'"

The other women howled with laughter.

Hesmera grinned, wiping tears from her eyes. "Can you imagine, in the middle of nowhere, on a battlefield, this man comes up, covered in blood, the fiercest fighter of the entire warband, a man as mad as they get, and asks if he may court me! I mean, I had wanted him in my bed before, because he looks real good," she beamed saying that, stroking the amulet that hung from a chain around her neck. "But, he comes up to me, after he rescued me from several attackers who had broken through our wall, beheading one and gutting the others, one of the bodies still twitching on his sword, and asks me in the most knightly manner 'May I court you?'"

One of the other women, a lithe blonde, looked at Hesmera, her cheeks still red. "He never had a woman before?"

She snorted. "Sure he had, but he had never fallen in love."

Gently she stroked the fine curves of the pendant.

"Had you?" asked another woman, older judging by the crow's feet at the corners of her eyes.

"Yes, I had men before, what better thing is there than to fuck after a boring day, or when you are wracked by the pain of losing a friend?" the raven-haired woman leered at the others, who gasped at her crude language.

"But... but, isn't making love sacred? Shouldn't you save yourself for your husband?" the blonde asked, a little subdued.

"Well, making love is sacred, yes, but fucking? Besides, it's way more fun if you know what you are doing," Hesmera said. "I mean, you don't go full gallop on a horse before you learn how to ride, do you?"

The other two women bobbed their heads in agreement.

"How long has it been since he asked you?" the blonde asked dreamily.

"Tomorrow it will be four years," Hesmera replied. "How about you, Neena, are you in love with someone?" As an afterthought she added, "And don't tell me it's Drangar!"

For a while Neena said nothing, blushing silently.

"No, you don't!" Hesmera snapped.

"He is handsome," said the woman who had, until now, been silent. "And you're damn lucky he's yours, Hesmera. For the younger women he represents almost everything they ever dreamed of. He is a hero. For us with a few more winters, well," she smiled, "let's say I wouldn't send him packing." Hesmera snorted. "He's mysterious." The warrior-woman's mirth vanished. "And Neena is perfectly right, he is handsome."

"But there are other good-looking men in Dunthiochagh, too, Kara," said the second older woman. "Neena just hasn't seen them, right, child?"

"Mum!" Neena moaned.

"Is she trying to find a suitable husband for you?" Hesmera asked, laughing.

After the young woman had nodded her affirmative, Hesmera grinned at the mother. "Maybe she should take to the field, grab a sword, and fight her way through life for a while. Then, after she has grown up, she will find a suitable husband.

If she survives that is. What do you think, Leonore? Isn't that a good idea?"

Neena looked at Kara and both shared a knowing glance, and Drangar knew from the sound of Hesmera's voice she was joking at the expense of the older woman, who almost fainted at the suggestion.

"She will stay here!" Leonore all but shouted.

The other three women burst out in laughter. "Of course I will, mother," Neena said. "I would never do that to you."

"Besides, she is too old for holding a sword; most people learn to fight at an early age. I picked up a sword when I was ten, I think. Drangar when he was four or so." Seeing their astonished faces, Hesmera added hastily, "He didn't learn to fight at that age, but he picked it up. He was strong even then."

"So, what will you do for your anniversary tomorrow?" Leonore asked.

Now it was Hesmera's turn to blush. "I think I will buy one of those fabled love potions and see how things unfold."

"And that she means rather literally," Kara said, causing all four of the women to burst out in laughter again.

Drangar smiled, despite himself. Hearing her voice again was blessing and curse. Although it dawned upon him what the ghost intended him to see, he could not quite discern the truth, yet.

Again, they rushed out of the building and crossed both city and night, and when they arrived over Old Bridge it was noon of the next day, their anniversary.

Drangar shuddered. This was the day she had died.

The bridge market was busy. To Drangar it felt almost like the one in Carlgh, only bigger. Next to the vendors' booths stood bards singing tales of woe and love, of passion and warfare. Jugglers entertained squeaking children and fortune-tellers, pretending to use crystal balls made by long forgotten Phoenix Wizards, telling lovers and loners their future. People hailing from many countries offered wares from all over the world.

In the middle of that ruckus, Neena and Hesmera made their way through the pushing and shoving crowd. Both wore their hair loose; it appeared as if Neena tried to mimic the older woman's attire and behavior. She wore a dress similar to the warrior's, only that hers was blue while Hesmera wore green. Around her wrists were several bracelets, each finger bore a ring. Hesmera only wore the amulet, one bracelet and one ring, presents given by Drangar when he had asked her to marry him. Personally, he thought Neena was overdoing it, but saw the looks men gave her. Or was it Hesmera at whom they were looking? He wasn't sure.

The women were enjoying themselves. Stopping at booths and even halting at one of the fortunetellers and waiting in line for a while to see what the future held for them. When Hesmera caught the pickpocket that tried to steal hers and Neena's purses, the selfsame fortuneteller made haste to get out of the city, followed by a mob of angry townspeople who all found their moneybags missing.

Then the ghostly figure directed his attention toward a booth that sold trinkets and potions. He did not remember either the vendor or his staff, for even though he knew the booth, its owner had changed.

He hesitated. One of the vendors had observed Drangar's younger self yesterday. No! He wanted to warn his lover, his love, his everything. From the direction the two women were taking, Drangar knew they were headed for the booth, intent on setting Hesmera's plan into motion.

He rushed forward, wanted to stop her, only to be restrained by the strong grip of the spirit woman next to him. "You can't change the past, boy! You can only learn from it. Let it rest. Hesmera has been dead for more than two years!"

"But…" he struggled to find the right words. "But maybe I can help her; maybe I can undo what has been done."

"I'm sorry, you can't! The past is past and nothing can change it!" The last words held him back and steeled his mind against what would inevitably come to pass.

He watched from afar as Neena and Hesmera approached the fake vendor and, after some haggling and questioning, bought a dark vial. The merchant explained its use to Hesmera while Neena rummaged through the various trinkets, finally discovering something she liked. After debating over the price for a while longer, both women retreated from the booth, happy with their purchases.

Both made for their homes. Again, time and space rushed past and he suddenly hovered in the middle of his and Hesmera's house, overlooking a candle-lit table set with various dishes, most of them certainly not cooked by his lover; she had never been much of a cook. Drangar suspected Neena, of whom he had no idea she even existed two years ago, had somehow had her hand in this feast. Porcelain plates and two glass goblets marked their places. Next to the plates were spoons and forks and knives. At first Hesmera had not grasped the concept of civilized eating, as she called it, something he still carried on from his monastic upbringing. Having lived amongst wanderers all her life, the woman was used to knife and spoon, but a fork had been alien to her, more so the use of both, knife and fork, together. Drangar remembered her first lessons in civilized eating, a failure if ever there was one. Actually, it had been Hesmera who had asked him to teach her, and now, having seen her with the three higher-standing women, he knew why.

"The past is the past!" the ghostly woman reminded him.

He acknowledged.

Then the door opened and in came the younger Drangar, carrying his wife to be, Hesmera. "Gods, I love you," he said, as she snuggled against him, slender but muscular arms wrapped around his neck. He halted, his eyes on the set table.

"Surprise," she whispered in his ear, nibbling his earlobe. "And I love you, too."

"You didn't," Drangar stuttered. "You couldn't... you... Gods!" He held her close and brushed his lips against hers. "All this just for our anniversary?"

She nodded. "And that isn't all, just wait and see," she whispered seductively, kissing his neck.

Laughing, Drangar set her down and as soon as her feet touched the floor she twirled around him and embraced him from behind, her fingers searching for his belt-buckle, opening it. "I doubt you need this sword tonight, kind sir," she teased.

The ghostly Drangar drew in a sharp breath, knowing full well what came next.

"How about some wine, my love?" Hesmera asked, hanging his sword belt on the hook near the door. His younger self stood, perplexed.

"Um, you know I don't drink."

"But this night is special," she pouted, and he relented.

Giggling, green dress swirling around her ankles, Hesmera rushed to the small closet, taking the two goblets with her. She opened the closet's door, removed a bottle, and uncorked it. Then, carefully paying attention not to spill a drop of the vial she had retrieved from the folds of her dress, she poured its contents into one glass, mixing it with the wine she added a moment later. This glass she handed to Drangar, and then filled hers.

Turning around, her eyes sparkling, she raised her drink and smiled. "To eternal love."

"To love eternal," he replied solemnly and drank, mimicking her actions, draining the glass without setting it down. He saw good-natured mischief sparkling in her eyes, chuckled, and straightened a bit. "Nice music," he muttered.

Hesmera grinned. "Shall we dine?"

"Yes, I'm starved."

They sat down and as always, Drangar started the prayer he had learned as a child. "Lesganagh, Eanaigh, two as one you fought. To bring us light and health and food. To you we dedicate this meal and…" He fell silent, looking about in confusion.

The ghostly Drangar groaned. "Must we see this?"

"Yes, you have got to understand!" His companion's voice was relentless.

"Drangar?" Hesmera asked, her eyes wide. "What is it?"

"Hesmera?" he whispered, his eyes wide, searching, unable to see. "Hesmera? Where are you?" Stumbling, he stood and gazed around, eyes darting from left to right. "Hesmera?"

"I'm here," she said. "Right before you."

His eyes were dull white, unseeing.

Again, he turned, staring straight at and through her. "Hesmera?" Instinctively he reached for his sword, his hand grasping empty air. "Hesmera? Where are you?" Then after a moment he asked, "Where am I?"

Fear clawed its way into her eyes as she reached out to hold him. Startled he withdrew. "Who are you?" he yelled. "Show yourself!"

"It is I, Hesmera!" she replied firmly.

He tore himself free. "Stay away from me, fiend!" Again, he searched for his sword. Both Hesmera and the ghostly Drangar were stunned by what happened next. The confused warrior held out his right hand. "Sword!" he growled and by itself the weapon leaped from its sheath, jumped straight into his hand, fingers wrapped around the hilt, tightly.

"Impossible," Drangar muttered, as the scene below unfolded in cruel detail.

His younger self jumped to the left, slashing blindly at a curtain, ripping it down. "Stay away from me!" he shouted. "All of you!" He swiveled the sword from left to right, stabbing at empty air, but the Drangar who observed the unfolding horror knew what the younger man saw. His nightmares were full of the monsters.

Hesmera's face was taut with fear as she watched her beloved rave through the room. "Run," the ghostly Drangar shouted, praying she might hear his words and escape her cruel fate. "Run! Run for your life!" But of course, she didn't hear, couldn't hear.

The weapon plunged into a desk, its wood cracking, splintering beneath the onslaught. "Please run," Drangar whispered, while his young counterpart screamed her name in his mad rave, as he looked to his left and right, a haunted expression on his face.

Then, slowly, he turned to face her.

"Who are you, monster?" he shouted.

"I... I," stammered the confused warrior-woman, unable to utter more. Her eyes were wide as she looked into the pained, vacant face of her lover, the man she was going to marry. "Drangar, please! Please, it's me, Hesmera!" she finally shouted, her voice drenched with fear.

"Die cunt!" the young man growled, his voice feral. His blade neatly slid into her stomach, to the hilt. Hesmera let out a surprised gasp and dropped to her knees as her mad lover withdrew the blade.

"Drangar," she uttered, blood welling from her mouth. "I love you." Her last words were all but a whisper as the sword plunged, its steel going right through her chest.

"No!" the ghostly figure above them yelled, trying to avert his eyes from the spectacle. But he couldn't.

"Watch! You have to watch!" his spirit companion said, her usual calm voice reflecting the hurt she felt.

"Why?" Drangar screamed. "Why do I have to watch myself killing her?" he shouted, beneath them his younger self hacked Hesmera apart, the sound of splintering bone almost drowning out the former mercenary's pained voice.

Suddenly the world around them grew silent and the ghostly figure drew near, staring intently. "Don't you realize, silly boy? Can't you see it? This is only your body moving the weapon, it isn't you!"

"But..." Drangar stuttered.

"Look at the person down there!" the woman shouted.

Drangar glanced down, and saw himself driving the sword into her mutilated body. All across the room, around her lifeless form lay the already severed body-parts. He shuddered.

"Is that you?" She continued to shout. "Have you ever been able to call upon your sword and it readily jumped to your hand?"

Then he understood. "No," Drangar whispered, his mind reeling with comprehension. "No, I'm not responsible for Hesmera's death."

He looked at the spirit, and felt loved, understood, appreciated without any conditions. "Mother?" he asked, and as he spoke, the world around him began to blur and he rushed away from the cruel scene.

CHAPTER 49

The High General had assigned her to the vanguard. Anne's duty was twofold: to scout ahead, flush out enemies, and close on the army's main body which, given their slower speed, should be only a few miles ahead.

They had left Harail two days ago, after a day of burials and messages written to inform nobles of their scions' deaths. Mireynh's anger at the Chosen's infiltration had subsided but when the theft of several missives from his office had been discovered, an entire detachment of guards had been whipped bloody. Then, in the aftermath, a courier was sent north with several letters to Herascor.

When they finally left Harail, Mireynh had given precise orders: the fortresses along the road to Dunthiochagh were to be guarded only so the siege of Baron Duasonh's city could not be interfered with. She thought it unwise and had voiced her opinion. Now, with so many arrogant idiots dead, and given her performance in the battle with the Chosen, the voices raised against her were few.

Mireynh had said, "We must revise the plan. That's why we head for Dunthiochagh immediately."

Anne obeyed the High General; she didn't have to like it. Now, the vanguard reached the outlying guard posts of the army's camp, which had settled and dug in around the only spot of land from which to reach Dragoncrest Castle. Already there were siege engines in various states of assembly, but when she saw the gorge and the spire upon which the fortress stood, the futility of a siege was obvious. Nothing short of birds could come close to the keep. Even if they bombarded the place day in and day out, the walls were too massive to breach and the defenders would repel any attempt to cross the void.

She pinched her eyes against the rising sun as she looked at the fortress. To her astonishment there were three banners flying above the main gate: Duasonh's, Danastaer's, and Lesganagh golden Sun and Sword emblazoned on blood red cloth. Three Danastaerian factions held Dragoncrest? She had a suspicion what the third faction was, but given the discrimination against the Lord of Sun and War's faith in these parts she doubted the Chosen would flaunt their allegiance so carelessly.

When she saw House Cirrain's standard flying above a cluster of tents, Anne guided her horse toward them. It seemed her absence had already lasted months instead of mere days, but the idiocy of Harail, the tedious squabbling between warleaders, and the veiled insults made the time with Mireynh seem eternal. She ignored the confused questions of the other warriors in the vanguard and jumped to the ground when she spied Dubhan preparing the breakfast porridge.

The older warrior looked up when he heard her boots thumping on the ground, and his sleepy annoyance was replaced by a wide grin. He tucked his unbraided long hair behind his ears and said, "Lass, now here's a sight for me sore eyes!"

"A sight for you at least," she replied.

"Aye, but nonetheless!" he guffawed and hugged her. The show of emotion was nothing new, but after the haughtiness of Harail, the affection of one of her own held the comfort of home. "Up, lads and lasses!" Dubhan bellowed as he lowered her to the ground. Anne dwarfed most women, but the weapons master was yet another foot and a half taller.

From the tents came angry mumbles. Then, one by one, the entrance flaps were pushed aside and the warriors of House Cirrain blinked sleepily, first at Dubhan and then at Anne.

"Oh, the lady managed to get her nose out of the High General's ass," Paddy said, standing up and yawning.

"Next, I'll have my boot out of yours," she replied, playfully glowering at her cousin. What came next was as much a ritual to the two as their mutual insults.

Paddy walked toward her, his steps slow and measured, arms outstretched as if to embrace her. She held her arms forward as well, her smile widening. They clasped each other's shoulders and butted their foreheads together with enough force to send them reeling. For a moment Anne only saw bright lights; then she blinked away her tears and grinned at the man she considered more brother than cousin. "We've got to stop doing this!" she exclaimed.

"When we're old and wrinkly..."

"Maybe," she completed the sentence.

They hugged; then the others greeted her with hands on her shoulders and pats on the back. The palace, the nobles, to her none of it was home or family. These warriors, whom she had known all her life, were.

When the affectionate greeting was finished, Dubhan handed her a bowl of porridge. She smiled. "Thanks, mate, just what I needed. Listen, when you're done filling your bellies, pack up."

"We're leaving?" Paddy mumbled, with his mouth full.

"Aye," she said. She pointed at the pot containing the porridge. "You got enough for them?" She nodded to the men riding vanguard with her.

"Aye, lass," Dubhan said.

"All right, ladies," Anne said, "grab some grub!" Which the warriors did with relish.

She turned back to Paddy and Dubhan. "Who's leading? And where is she?"

"He. Some bugger called Lord Commander Noel Trileigh," Dubhan said. "Hardly knows which end is which on a sword, but he's the man who orders us around."

Before she could again ask for the Lord Commander's whereabouts old Alayn pointed to the east. "His highness lives behind the fence." The others sniggered, and when Anne turned to see the place, she noticed meager palisades surrounding a colorful tent.

"We thought about planting some flowers," Paddy said.

Anne snorted. In other circles, namely at court in Herascor, such behavior wasn't tolerated. In the grim mountains that

House Cirrain called home, people knew loyalty was a blade that cut both ways. So, although Lord Cirrain ruled, he considered himself no better than those working the land. "Hasn't anyone told him that a position like that is far too obvious?"

"Sure, some fool did, and he was whipped for questioning the Lord Commander's orders," Dubhan said.

"Trileigh rules with an iron fist, eh?"

"Aye, lass, but also with a brain of lead."

The warriors shared a healthy laugh, and then Anne was off again, the vanguard following her. On her way she ordered wardens and warleaders to start packing, which they relayed immediately. Before they had reached the Lord Commander's tent, half the camp was already busy disassembling their positions.

Anne and her small group reached the ridiculous fence just when a sleepy looking man stumbled out the tent.

"What?" he snarled at her. His clothes looked hastily assembled and unsuitable for the chill autumn air. Clearly, the man thought the world of his position, but had no true sense of what it meant to be in the field. The lace nightgown would have been more suitable in a Herascoran brothel, and the slippers that barely covered his feet would have caused them to be cold even in front of a roaring fire. The best feature of this clown's costume, Anne thought, was a lush brocade and fur cloak that might have been very fashionable in the royal palace, but was utterly out of place in an army camp.

"What?" Noel Trileigh asked again, this time his look went to the troops who stripped down and packed up the camp.

"Anneijhan Cirrain, adjutant to High General Mireynh. And the question should have been 'who' not 'what', Commander!"

Nodding briefly at her, Trileigh resumed scanning his surroundings, only to be interrupted.

"If you wonder why the army prepares to march," she said with a cooing voice. "The High General has decided to push toward Dunthiochagh, not bothering with the strongholds. They are, after all, poorly manned and no match for us on the field. Wasting our strength on them isn't necessary."

"But..." Trileigh stared at her and then back at the camp.

Everywhere warriors disassembled tents and makeshift smithies, as well as siege-workshops. "Who gave the order?" he asked.

"You must listen, Commander," she replied, barely suppressing her disdain. "High General Mireynh himself. And since you are awake now, your men can also look after your tent." To one of the now attending warleaders she said, "Select a group of no more than threescore to stay They're to prevent anyone from leaving." She pointed to a few nearby warriors who immediately set to work. "You better get your gear together, Commander." She reined her horse and sped toward the road that connected Dunthiochagh with Harail. A last look at the massive stonework that was Dragoncrest Castle reassured her Mireynh had made the right choice.

By noon the entire Chanastardhian army was on its way. Mostly they ignored the fortresses that dotted the way, leaving behind several scores of men to bar the troops holding the castle exits, and quickly finishing the various skirmishes with enemy scouting parties. Urgraith Mireynh drove his troops toward Dunthiochagh. Two days after his force had united at Dragoncrest, the army was almost a week away from Dunthiochagh, and its scouts reported contact with enemy troops.

CHAPTER 50

Jesgar was glad to see the walls of Dunthiochagh again. Even though the journey back had been by horse as well, his legs had healed nicely during the one day the riders had stayed at Dragoncrest. He still marveled at the speedy mending of his wounds, which Briog attributed to the potency of his ointment, and since his legs continued to recover despite the long days in the saddle, he could hardly voice his skepticism.

The Riders' ranks had swelled at Dragoncrest. Kyleigh Mondar, leader of the half-dozen that had chased the traitor Jathain from Dunthiochagh all through Boughaighr, gave Jesgar a good-natured salute. She never tired of telling of the hunt.

The six Riders had finally managed to reach Dragoncrest before Jathain, overtaking the refugee resting somewhere in the foothills. When the Baron's cousin had arrived at the fortress, the castle's commander had already ferreted out those loyal to Jathain. The noble's reception was rather direct; with Lliania's blessing, Kyleigh was an Upholder, and the execution had come quickly.

Half a day behind the Riders came many warriors. Nerran had immediately assigned several score to remain at the castle and ordered the others to follow him to Dunthiochagh. The army's warlord, a General Kerral, had initially protested, but after a long face to face talk with the Paladin he had relented. Jesgar had watched from a shady alcove, unnoticed by the room's occupants. It was in this meeting chamber that he had found out from which family Nerran came. House Ghonair. In Dunthiochagh's seedier taverns the name Ghonair was still whispered with reverence and awe. He hardly remembered the tales, but from what little he did recall, he knew the Ghonairs had been Paladins of Lesganagh. Whether Nerran clung to that old tradition he couldn't tell, and the black eye Fynbar had given him for being too inquisitive was a not so gentle reminder not to pry.

"Nerran'll tell you if you need to know," Gavyn had said.

Jesgar obviously didn't need to know, and when he saw Dunthiochagh's high walls the only thing he cared about was a decent bed and maybe some food that wasn't porridge. The more he thought about sleep and proper food the more his thoughts turned to home, his room, Maire, even his brother. Somehow, during the past weeks he had pushed his family to the back of his mind. He had been so busy that no stray thought had wandered to his brother and sister-in-law whom he had left without a word of goodbye. He missed them.

When the riders passed South Gate and were closing on the Trade Road/Trann Street intersection, he had come to a decision. "Lord Nerran," he said after guiding his horse next to the nobleman's.

"What is it, lad?"

Something was on the warrior's mind, Jesgar could tell by the distant look in the man's eyes. "I'd like to see my family, sir," he intended to say, but in his nervousness the words came out mumbled and half-swallowed.

"Pardon?" Nerran said. "Spit it out, lad, you know I won't skin you alive."

"Yet," Briog muttered to everyone's amusement.

Jesgar repeated his request. He didn't know if leave was allowed in time of war, but the Chanastardhians were still days away, and he could think of nothing to do for the Baron right now. Of course, Cumaill Duasonh might have different plans. Still, he hoped his performance at three of the four keeps leading to Harail had convinced Nerran of his ability and that he was loyal.

Nerran looked at him, and thought he detected mischief sparkling in the man's eyes. "Well, lad, I believe you've earned a short leave of absence." Jesgar smiled. "However, there's a hostile army strolling up yonder road." The warrior's right

thumb stabbed south. "I think I can convince the Baron you
need some rest."

"And considering where you put all that ointment," Briog
added, "stay away from the ladies!"

He knew he was blushing before the riders began to guffaw.
"I... I'll be leaving then, Lord Nerran," Jesgar stammered and
turned his horse.

"Not so fast, lad," the aging warrior snapped.

Pulling the reins, Jesgar looked back. "Sir?" he said,
wondering what the man wanted of him now.

"You should leave..."

Nerran was interrupted by the rushing approach of a band
of robed and cloaked people. There were a score of them, armed
with clubs and staffs, and to him it felt as if they were ready for
battle. Jesgar frowned.

"What's the meaning of this?" Nerran asked, his voice and
bearing no different than if he was speaking to a merchant
instead of a mob of muggers.

"The meaning of this, milord," a tall man armed with a
mace said, "is that we'll take you and your Riders into custody
for being either followers or priests of the banned one or heretic
disciples of the Lady of Health and Fertility."

Nerran barked out a laugh. "You're joking, right? Besides,
I recognize your voice. Caretaker Girec, is it?" The hooded
speaker stiffened. "Why this change of mind, Girec? You've
known me and my lads for years, why come after me now?"

"Your kind has led one of ours astray and planted within
him the seed of doubt," Girec said.

"My kind?"

"The cursed Chosen," another hooded man said.

"The Hearthwarden's High Priest Morgan Danaissan,"
Nerran sounded genuinely surprised. "Isn't this an illustrious
group of murderers?"

Jesgar realized that priests of Eanaigh surrounded them,
what he didn't understand was why.

"We are not murderers," the High Priest snapped.

"Weren't those the selfsame words you told my mother
when she let you into our house?" Nerran's voice could have cut

steel. "And you also know that I am no Chosen, if I were I'd be at Dragoncrest with the rest of them preparing to fight either the Chanastardhians or some other threat!"

"We need you all to come with us," Girec said.

"Why?" Kyleigh Mondar asked.

"And you be?" the head of Eanaigh's Church demanded.

"Upholder Kyleigh," she replied.

"You are not from Dunthiochagh, stay out of this!" Girec commanded. "These people are accused of continued heresy and fermenting rebellion among the Caretakers of the land."

"Do you, as the Hearthwarden's High Priest, agree with your disciple that justice is no business of a lawful Upholder?" Kyleigh looked at Danaissan.

"You have no rights here," the High Priest stated.

"Justice knows no boundaries," she replied.

"They are heretics and blasphemers! Those of our church who work with Paladins and Sunswords will be judged by us!"

Briog rode up to Nerran's side, hand on his sword. "Forgive me, sirs. I am a Caretaker of Eanaigh. I hail from Kalduuhn. I defend those who can't fend for themselves, and you call me a heretic? Why?"

Jesgar saw the other Riders were also resting their hands on their swords' hilts. The mystery surrounding the Riders seemed to unravel before him even though he still didn't fully understand what was going on. He hadn't known Briog to be a Caretaker; the man certainly didn't behave like any Eanaighist he knew. Nerran a follower of Lesganagh? It seemed possible, but if the High Priest of Eanaigh in Dunthiochagh knew about it why hadn't he acted upon this before?

"I see no Upholder is with you," Kyleigh said. "Neither is there a representative of Baron Duasonh's. The proper form requires you to bring along either one, so that the arrests are legal."

Jesgar waited for a reply. When none came, Nerran said, "As yon Upholder has pointed out you have come alone, I can only assume this is an illegal action. Say your purpose!"

He knew any arrest outside the church's clergy had to be sanctioned by either the local lord or a representative of Lliania.

What he didn't understand was why all this was happening. He hadn't observed any untoward acts performed by the Riders, and, so far, every action Nerran had undertaken was for the good of country and city. The Eanaighists' actions were strange. This encounter, even though he had not been born when the Purging had taken place, reminded him of the persecution of Lesganagh's clergy some thirty years ago. Nerran had even said as much.

"We are under authority of the Lady of Health and Fertility," Girec hissed.

"Then I suggest you look to your health and be fertile," Briog said to the amusement of the Riders.

"Blasphemer!" several of the priests cried and made a step forward, weapons raised. The riders flanking Nerran unsheathed their swords.

Nerran held up his hand and sighed rather dramatically, if Jesgar was to judge. "We will move on to the Palace. Please don't interfere."

"You are under arrest!" Morgan Danaissan yelled. "With the authority bestowed upon me by the Church of Eanaigh and the blessing of the Hearthwarden, I name you heretics and enemies of the faith. You will submit to our authority."

"And then?" Fynbar asked. "What then? Will we receive a fair trial? I think not. Your actions are without the Lawgiver's consent."

"Will you burn us like you have burned parents, relatives, brothers, and sisters?" Briog growled. "You claim the goddess is on your side, but elsewhere Lesganagh isn't banned, his followers weren't burned or hanged or beheaded. Eanaigh is daughter and wife to the Lord of Sun and War..."

"Heretic!" the High Priest shouted.

The priestly mob advanced another pace, upon which the riders who had merely kept their hands on their weapons drew steel as well.

"You!" Girec pointed at Briog. "You wield a sword instead of the flail or staff. Why? Why have you forsaken her holy weapons? Why have you turned your back on the Lady's edicts?"

The Rider shrugged. "Never was good with either. Besides,

her will was that we shall not spill innocent blood. Any who wield arms against a Caretaker are not innocent."

"Are you saying…?"

"Aye, you dare raise weapons against your own kind! You attacked and slaughtered priests of Lesganagh and all those that stood with them!" Briog barked. "You may be a lot of things, but innocents you are not!"

"Lawbreakers, I say," Kyleigh added.

"Stand aside!" Nerran commanded.

Fynbar turned to Jesgar. "This isn't your battle. Go, and seek your family. Tonight, blood will flow. Best not be near any temple or shrine."

He swallowed. There was nothing he could say, and although none of them gave a direct order, Jesgar felt there was more going on here than he was able to discern, he turned his horse and rode into Trann Street and the Merchant Quarter.

The street and the two groups of people were barely two dozen feet behind when he heard the roar and the clash of steel. Jesgar had never bothered with religion; or rather he had never cared for the ridiculous hatred of Eanaigh's clergy toward Lesganagh. The sun shone, wars were fought. Enough people in Danastaer worshiped the Lord of Sun and War still, although in secret, and he had yet to meet the warrior who did not pay homage to the god.

The battle on Trade wasn't his, and he was fairly certain Nerran and his Riders would win. He was proud of his accomplishments, his discovery of the hidden ladders, but the itching reminder of his unfamiliarity with horses marred the feeling. A good night's sleep in his own bed instead of the cot in the Palace or the chill ground, now that was something he really looked forward to. It felt as if he had been away for years; he had seen so much more than he had imagined he'd ever see, and when the Garinad smithy came into view, Jesgar knew he was home.

"Dalgor has reached Dunthiochagh," the Priest High said to the high-ranking members of their order. He still wasn't certain that sending the young, energetic man had been the right course of action, but there was nothing else that would have appeased the others.

"The ritual will be completed," one swordpriest said.

"It has to be finished. There isn't much time left," another added.

He knew the men were right, but even if Dalgor succeeded, the inevitable was only postponed. Again, he wondered if there was something he could have done differently. When he thought back at what he had seen, what he had done, what had been done in the cavern, helpless rage all but consumed him. There were moments of doubt.

"We'll see," he said, feeling that the more often they failed, the more his authority was questioned. The Priest High dismissed the others with a wave of his hand.

Alone, he leaned back and stared at the ceiling. Should Dalgor fail, he'd have to order his own nephew's death. All the killing, the weeding out of failures, and still their task was not accomplished. He withdrew the pictures and stared at them. "Cat, I wish you were here," he whispered. He hadn't felt so lonely in a long time.

CHAPTER 51

They had moved Drangar Ralgon into the cell opposite hers, and even though his mutterings had ceased, Ealisaid wasn't sure what she preferred, the silence or the endless babbling. Again and again, whenever he awoke, she tried to talk to the man, but when he reacted to her words it was merely by a slight turn of the head or a flicker of his eyes.

The guards had brought a lamp, and in its light she saw Ralgon staring holes into the air when he wasn't sleeping or eating. At least he was eating.

He still looked haggard, half starved, more like corpse than breathing man. The rise and fall of his chest and his eye movements were almost the only indicators that he was alive.

She had looked at him again in spiritform. The shadow he had cast into the spiritworld was gone. She was no closer to understanding what happened to bring forth such a phenomenon than before, but there wasn't anything she could do about it. Ralgon never reacted to her questions, and the only thing he said was "I didn't kill her, it wasn't my fault."

The Chosen had told her about the grisly murder this man must have committed two years back, Ralgon's woman hacked to shreds in their house. She had an idea.

"What happened to Hesmera?" Ealisaid whispered when Ralgon had fallen silent again.

At the mention of his lover's name, he looked up and, for the first time, focused on her. Finally, she had his attention! "She died," he replied.

"How?" Ealisaid wasn't certain this was the way to continue the conversation, but she was at a loss.

The laugh Ralgon gave was a mixture of sob and growl. "They made me kill her."

She had heard of such stories before, people claiming some other power had forced them to commit hideous crimes. It was easier to blame someone else than to take responsibility for one's actions. Her thoughts must have shown on her face, and before she could reply, Ralgon said, "I wouldn't believe myself either, if I were in your place." The statement didn't make sense. The man seemed lucid enough to see the idiocy of his words. "Believe me, I've heard such nonsense before as well," he continued. "Some poor bugger claiming demons made him kill his family, trading partner, the old woman next door. Sure, demons can take over one's body, but during the Demon War the slaughter was different, not just simple stabbings." He hesitated and smiled sadly, "Given how I... killed Hesmera... it could have been demons guiding my hand."

"How do you know what the demons did? You're just a..." she paused, unsure how to continue.

"Lowly mercenary?" he finished her question.

The man was certainly not a dumb brute, she could tell that much already. "Aye," she said. "I thought your kind were only good for killing, defiling women, and plundering."

He chortled. "True, you rarely find a great philosopher amongst the sell-swords." Ralgon paused, thinking. "I was born and raised in a monastery; my adopted, extended family knew a great deal of demons, because they fought them."

A smile of disbelief crept onto her lips. "Truly?" she asked, not quite able to keep the mockery out of her voice. "Your kind usually hardly knows how to read."

Drangar Ralgon glared at her. "And your kind usually pays a fine and goes back to work," he replied acidly, "not put in a cell for days if not weeks."

"I am no harlot!" How did this murderer dare insult her? She was furious.

"What then? Killer? Cheating wife? Spy? Offending courtier?"

"I'm not one of those, either!" she snapped, and felt her face flush.

"Yet you painted your nails only recently, your hair still bears the resemblance of stylish braid work, and despite the dirt you try to look respectable even in those rags you wear," he replied smugly.

"Don't judge a book by its cover!" she snapped, and knew the same instant he had goaded her. He smirked and cocked his head. "I concede your point."

"So why are you in the..." he looked around, "Palace's dungeons?"

This person, decided Ealisaid, was a definite improvement over the groaning, mumbling body she had first encountered in the cells. He was perceptive, but she was unsure whether she liked this trait. "I destroyed some property and killed a dozen people," she said. To her surprise, Drangar hooted. "What's so amusing?"

The former mercenary shook his head. "The Baron must like you, or see further use in you," he said with a chuckle. "If I were inclined to guess, I'd guess the latter."

In her deepest, most desperate thoughts she had come to the same conclusion. Duasonh didn't appear to fuss over cases like hers, even if there hadn't been a case like hers in the last century. One thought led to the next, and she found herself awash in memories and despair.

"This place is better than many a dungeon," Drangar interrupted. Her feelings must've shown on her face.

"I've never felt so alone," she whispered, and looked down at her feet.

Ealisaid expected her cellmate to answer, but the man remained silent. She looked up, through the bars across into the opposite chamber. What she saw seemed the embodiment of loneliness and despair. Ralgon stood straight, hands clutching the bars. Was this the same man whom she had heard laughing just a few moments ago? His grey-blue eyes brimmed with tears, his face a twisted mask of rage and misery. For a moment she thought he had retreated back into the head-thumping idiot, but then his eyes focused on her.

"In the end we're always alone," he said in a hoarse whisper. "Always alone..." His voice trailed off and he regarded her, his eyes wet with unshed tears. "Why am I here still when I should be dead? Why is anyone here when in the end we all die?" He snorted, snot gushed from his nose, onto his beard and shirt. "You really feel forsaken when you wake up with your bloody sword in hand and the one person you love lying before you in countless pieces."

Try as she might, Ealisaid couldn't imagine this miserable creature killing anyone. Seeing his grief helped her. Ralgon's misery put things into perspective. She had lost her family, true, but she had not slaughtered them. She hadn't been involved in the Heir War, and thus she wasn't responsible for the destruction. A sigh escaped her lips. Maybe what this man had done for her she could repay in kind. "You said you are not responsible for her death," she said.

He looked at her, wiped the snot from his beard with his left hand, and then brushed the hand clean with some straw. Then he shook his head. "No, I'm not responsible. I saw what happened."

"Someone else killed her?" Talking to him tried the patience of even a priest. He could speak plainly when he wanted to, only to revert to cryptic phrases like this one.

"No, my hand wielded the sword."

She frowned, but stopped herself from asking the obvious. Ralgon would eventually come to the meaning, she decided.

"I saw it. I saw the past..." He must have seen her frown, because he snorted again. "I've not lost my mind." His upheld hand stopped her reply. "Your look gave you away..."

"Ealisaid, I'm Ealisaid."

He shook his head. "Under different circumstances I'd say it is a pleasure to meet you, but my manners seem somewhat misplaced in Baron Duasonh's dungeon."

"Graveyard humor? Better than no humor at all, eh?" Under different circumstances the man would have been quite charming, but the bitter streak that permeated his every action made him less likeable.

"Sarcasm, when you hate the world and yourself it's hard to be truly jolly," he replied with a shrug. "How did you kill a dozen people, Ealisaid?"

The Wizardess felt the dismissal, and could hardly blame him. He alone must work through whatever he imagined he had seen. After all, he had just recently been returned to the world of the living, body and spirit. Now she was unsure whether to tell him why she was here and what she had done. Up until now she could still be a mere mass murderer, but maybe Ralgon's reaction would be like anyone else's, resentment and mistrust. Trust, however, she decided had to begin somewhere. "Magic," she said.

Ralgon cocked an eyebrow. "Really?"

Was there amusement in his voice? At least he didn't react with worry or fear, just a little... curiosity. "Really," she said.

"Next, she'll tell me she learned sorcery from a musty old tome she found in some abandoned wizard's tower," he muttered. "And to think I was mad."

Unsure if he had meant for her to hear him, she nonetheless snapped, "I learned magic in the Shadowpeaks!"

"If I believe you, will you believe me when I say I went into the past and saw myself slaughter Hesmera, that my hands and body acted without me?"

She had to admit both claims seemed mad. She knew who and what she was, and although Drangar Ralgon was at times incoherent, he was neither mad nor stupid. If her story was true, why not his? Was it possible that he had traveled into the past? Had he truly seen himself kill his lover?

"How did you go back in time?" Of all the questions, this was the one she really wanted to ask.

Ralgon chuckled. "So, you do believe me?"

"I admit that my story is as unlikely as yours," she said. "I doubt my disbelief, if that is any consolation."

He shrugged. "Better than nothing, I guess." He paused, took a deep breath, and began to speak.

The more Ealisaid heard the more convinced she became his tale was true. Certainly, it might all be a mere figment of Ralgon's imagination—it certainly had the feel of a fiery tale—but she couldn't think of any reason why madness would play such tricks. "This 'ghost', what did it look like?" she asked when he was finished.

The man shrugged. "She was never really there," he said. "I mean, unlike me, she was nothing more than a haze."

"She?" Ealisaid asked, a suspicion creeping into her mind. There had been a ghostly woman with Ralgon when he was trapped in two worlds.

CHAPTER 52

Kildanor looked at the documents he had stolen from the Chanastardhian general's office then back at the decoded messages. "Urgraith Mireynh, High General," he said.

"At least we can put a name to our foe," Duasonh replied. "The thing that bothers me, is this High Advisor who signed most orders."

The Chanastardhian court and its ministers never held special interest for him, so he waited for what Cumaill would tell. He was still exhausted from his ordeal in the spiritworld, but neither he nor Gail had been able to rest. Gail had received a missive and was back at the shrine, and Duasonh had requested him at once. Now the Baron leafed through the translations again. Kildanor's patience wore thin. His headache had lessened, but he felt his bed and sleep still beckoning. "And?" he finally asked, stifling a yawn.

"There is no such position at the court of Herascor," Duasonh said. "The kings have advisors, but none of them is above the others."

"So, they formalized Drammoch's favorite pet." He yawned again. "Who cares?"

"There's more," Duasonh said, and looked up from the papers. "Gods, man! Wake up!"

"Just..." he didn't finish the sentence. The Baron complied with his unvoiced request before he could. The sharp pain registered on his cheek before Kildanor saw him move. For a man of middling age with sufficient weight on him, his friend and pupil could move quickly, if he wanted to. The slap shook his senses awake. "Thanks," he grumbled.

"My pleasure," Cumaill replied, grinning.

"So, what is it about this High Advisor?"

"Most of the orders to Mireynh weren't signed by Drammoch but by this Zamar, whoever he may be."

He leafed through the papers. Duasonh was right; this High Advisor had signed each missive. Drammoch or somebody else authorized other orders, which apparently had not passed through this man's hands. Most regular messages were written plainly.

One document caught his attention. Kildanor scanned several others before he returned to this paper. "Have you seen this one?" he asked and held it out for Duasonh to read. Now he was wide-awake! Whatever other plans the Chanastardhians had, until this moment he had merely thought them bent on conquest. This missive changed everything.

"I studied them all while you were busy holding hands with Gail and the Wizardess."

The Chosen felt a leer creep onto his face, and he couldn't hold back. "Jealous?" he asked mockingly.

"I've more important things to do than playing Caretaker for a lunatic prisoner!" The Baron took the paper and read. "What is this Dragh-Hold?"

"Dragoncrest," Kildanor replied.

"Why would they bother with that old place? And what's with the name? Never heard that one before."

"If you want to find out about it you'd either have to go to the Great Library, or become a Chosen, or die," he said flatly. So, Dragh's Rest was what the High Advisor was after. "Don't worry about it, mate," he grumbled. "The Hold is safe for now."

"Hold? Rest? What the bleeding Scales are you talking about?"

"Chosen business, you don't need to know, right now," he replied. "My brethren are at Dragoncrest, and the enemy won't get in anytime soon." He didn't like being so cryptic, but to worry Cumaill about things he couldn't control—and frankly weren't his business—would not help Dunthiochagh. "The High General will make sure he has no enemies at his back before he can secure the Castle."

"How…"

"Would you act any different?" Kildanor interrupted. "It's the only logical choice. He will sack Dunthiochagh first. Wouldn't you if you were in his place?"

Duasonh thought for a moment, then said, "Aye."

"So, worry about defending the city. If it falls, I guess we won't worry about much else anymore." A groan escaped the Baron's lips. Kildanor knew how he felt; Ethain and Ganaedor had invoked the same helplessness in him decades ago.

"We still don't know how large this army is," Duasonh said. He was glad his friend had no difficulty focusing on a different issue in a matter of moments. "Mireynh's speed is uncanny, especially if his host is big enough to take Harail as quickly as he did."

"Considering how useless our defense was, and that Jathain was not the only traitor on Chanastardh's side, they might've only worried about safe camps and a little forage. They would've taken most supplies from the villages along the way."

There came a knock.

"Enter!" Cumaill said. Kildanor glanced over his shoulder and saw warden Kaltairr saluting. "What is it?" the Baron asked.

"My Lord Baron," Kaltairr said, "we have intercepted and apprehended a group of spies who were bound for the Merthain Bridge, milord."

Cumaill looked at him. "You know of this?"

"I do. I thought it wise to relieve our troops of people who might still be in favor of Chanastardhian rule." He quickly summarized the plan with an occasional addition of the warden.

"I also sent a detachment to the Bridge to rig it so that it will collapse," Kaltairr concluded.

This statement not only caught Cumaill by surprise, but Kildanor as well. "Bloody brilliant," Duasonh said. "Congratulations, warleader, good work." Despite her exhaustion, Kaltairr beamed at the promotion. "Your first order is to fetch the fastest riders, and drovers, and see to it that the outlying farms store their reserves in the city."

Alert, she replied, "Yes, sir."

"Get every cabbage, turnip, every bushel of feed," Cumaill continued.

"Given her initiative, I think she understands."

The woman saluted. "Consider it done, milord." Then she turned about smartly and left the office.

"Think Nerran has…"

This time it was the Baron's turn to interrupt, something Kildanor didn't mind at all. "Even if he did, better safe than sorry, or low on food in spring. Our granaries are full, but we might not be able to feed everyone who comes seeking refuge inside our walls."

There wasn't much he could add. Cumaill Duasonh had been taught well, he admitted with some pride.

An urgent knock interrupted his sleep. Kildanor had trouble waking, and only after the knocks sounded like a battering ram did he shout a reply. "I'm up!" He stood and shuffled to the door. "What is it?" he snarled at the man he faced when the door was open.

"Sorry, Lord Chosen," the guard uttered.

"This better be good," he said, realizing too late that he had spoken out loud. The spiritwalk in the dungeon had taken out more than he thought possible; it wasn't like him to say what went on in his mind.

The guard nodded, clearly preoccupied with something else. "Sorry, I was asked to fetch you, sir."

"By whom?" He had no patience for riddles this early in the—he turned and saw the sun was already beyond his western window—afternoon. Had he really slept half the day?

"The witch in the dungeons, sir."

Ealisaid? What did she want now? "Thanks," he said, closed the door and dressed. When he left his chambers, Kildanor found the guardsman still standing at attention. "What the Scales are you waiting for?"

"I'm to take you to her, sir," the man replied.

"I know the way to the bloody dungeon, man."

"The witch ain't in the dungeons no more, sir."

He halted and faced the warrior. "What?"

"Lord Duasonh has pardoned her, sir."

He couldn't remember the last time he had been speechless, but now found himself unable to utter a single word. Had Cumaill lost his mind? If he hadn't, had he consulted Lliania's church before doing so? What had he done to appease the families of the victims? Question followed question, and he had no answers.

His first impulse was to head for Cumaill's office, but whatever Ealisaid wanted, it couldn't be unimportant. So far, the woman had been able to help, in a way that might be less useful for the war, but help she did. Without her Drangar Ralgon would still be in his fugue state or worse. Kildanor had seen the beings that had held Ralgon in thrall, and he was glad to have severed the connection between man and demons.

"Very well, take me to her," he finally said.

"You should talk to him," Ealisaid said the moment he entered her chamber.

The room she had been given was better than her cell. But then again, Kildanor thought, all closets in the Palace were better than the dungeon. "Talk to whom?" he asked, irritated at her unexpected greeting.

"Ralgon."

"Why?" Maybe she was still getting used to the freedom she now enjoyed, even if there were two guards at her door. "You just asked me here to tell me I should talk to him?"

Ealisaid hesitated. "Yes," she finally said.

The nerve!

"You are of Lesganagh's faith," she continued. "You believe Ralgon is important, so does Caretaker Gail, but she is gone, and Caretaker Braigh hasn't returned either. I heard you and Caslin talking. There's something special about him. You both feel it. Ralgon isn't convinced that he is special, but he is sure about his innocence. He just can't prove his innocence."

"Braigh still hasn't returned?" This news worried him. The past days had seen many changes; suspicions against the priest had been uttered. Now Gail was gone. Had the church taken her into custody as well? If so, why was Braigh still with them? He hadn't done anything untoward. Braigh had said as much before his brethren had taken him, but his not returning to the Palace to look in on Drangar Ralgon was suspicious. He had picked up some of the rumors of Caretakers worrying about the resurgence of Lesganagh's faith, as if there had ever been any doubt the Lord of Sun and War still ruled the heavens. He needed to talk to Duasonh.

"I was told so," Ealisaid said, then shook her head. "You need to speak to Ralgon."

"Why?" he asked again.

She took a deep breath and let it out slowly. "He told me some things about the day he murdered his lover. I believe him, but I can't confirm his words without breaking my oath to the Baron, without using magic."

"And you think I can?" He arched an eyebrow.

"Aye," she answered with a shrug.

"Even if I could, what does it matter?"

"If his story is true, he is innocent."

"That's up to the Upholders to decide, not a Chosen."

"Well, then fetch a bloody Upholder and let him see if Ralgon is telling the truth," she snapped. "And don't tell me the Church of Lliania can't be involved as long as the man hasn't been formally accused of a crime. You know that's hogwash as well as I do!"

He had to admit the sorceress was right, and the conviction she spoke with convinced him. "Very well, I'll see to it when I have the time." Kildanor headed for the door.

A group of bloodied men and women halted his descent to the main hall. For a moment, Kildanor didn't know any of them. Then he discerned Nerran. The aging warrior's grim visage split into a wide grin. "Ah!" he shouted. "Just the lad I'm looking for."

"What the bloody Scales happened?" the Chosen asked, realizing too late that his phrasing opened the door for all sorts of puns.

Nerran's response, however, was sullen, "Some fools wanted to start a revival festival of the Dawnslaughter."

Now Kildanor looked closer at Nerran's companions. He recognized a few of the Riders, but one of them, held upright by an angry-looking Gail Caslin, seemed to have mainly his own blood on skin and clothes. The man's eyes were almost swollen shut, his wrists were heavily bandaged, and he stood on trembling legs. He hardly recognized him. "Braigh?"

"Aye," Nerran said. "Bastards took him, tortured him for his involvement with Lesganaghists... some business with hymns and returning people from the dead, that sort of thing. The poor lad was almost dead when we got to him. Health and Fertility my ass! If that's nurturing and growing and raising shit, I prefer war. It's not that nasty."

Kildanor remembered the Dawnslaughter, when Eanaigh's priesthood in Danastaer had ambushed the clergy of Lesganagh on their way to the dawn prayers. "Did you leave anyone alive?" he asked.

Nerran sniggered. "Lad, we're idiots, not fanatics."

Briog tapped the warrior's shoulder. "That's idealists," he said with a grin.

"Ain't that one and the same?" the Paladin asked. To Kildanor he said, "Aside from yon Braigh? Sure, turns out the fools had already bashed up some priests who disagreed with their plans for our lad Braigh, here; we saved whom we could."

"And the others?"

"They paid."

He knew what Nerran and many of his Riders had gone through in the past. Some of them had lost their families to the Dawnslaughter, having themselves survived only by chance, hidden by parents or away in Kalduuhn or elsewhere. Sons and daughters of priests and Paladins had banded together. Nerran had gathered these survivors and the followers of Eanaigh who had objected to the night of murder. "Talk to Cumaill, he'll be glad you've returned."

Nerran, the last appointed Paladin of Lesganagh in Danastaer, nodded. "We'll wash up and see to Braigh and the others first."

"Do that," Kildanor said.

He had just reached the bottom of the staircase when he

heard Ealisaid shout after him. He turned around, and saw the Wizardess hurry down the steps, her two guards just a few feet behind. What did the woman want of him now, he wondered, and asked when she reached him.

"I just remembered something," she panted. To him it was obvious the sorceress was not used to physical work.

"Aye?" he asked, curious.

She looked at him, eyebrow cocked. "You could treat me with a little more respect."

"Why? You're free but still under guard. The end justifies the means; that's the only reason you are still around. Yes, you did help with this Ralgon character, but remember you also killed a dozen people and destroyed two buildings. Wanton destruction earns fear, not respect." The woman's arrogance made him angry. Maybe she wanted to help, but he had seen what Phoenix Wizards were capable of, and unlike Cumaill Duasonh he would not trust a weapon he could not control.

"I made a mistake!" she hissed.

"Mistake?" he snorted. "Accusing the wrong person of theft and finding out afterwards who it really was and preventing the wrong person from losing a hand, that's a mistake! If thrusting apart two houses and magically dismembering two families is what you count as a mistake, I don't want to know what you call a grave error! The Baron has need of your abilities, that's why you're free." He paused when he saw his words had the desired effect. "Well? What did you remember?"

Ealisaid struggled to regain her composure then said, "We forgot the dog…"

Kildanor didn't even hear her finish whatever she had been saying but ran through the guardroom into the dungeon and down the corridor until he reached the abandoned cell. It still reeked of piss and feces, but that hardly mattered. Behind him, he heard the captain of the guards approaching. The man stopped as Kildanor kneeled on the floor to inspect the area surrounding the cot. "Sir?" the guard said.

He straightened and looked at the man. "Fetch me a lamp, will you?" Formalities weren't his strength, especially in situations like this.

When the man returned, Kildanor took the lamp and began to search the floor again. "You haven't cleaned out the cell."

It had been delivered as a statement, but the captain answered, "No, sir, it's just criminals down here. This place ain't meant to be comfortable, sir."

"He's right, you know," another voice added.

"Ralgon, is that you?" he asked, finally discovering what he was looking for.

"Aye," the former mercenary answered. "And your friend's right. A cell shouldn't make a prisoner feel comfortable."

"Say, man, do you own a dog?" he asked as he pulled forth the mummified remains.

"Me?" the captain said.

For a moment, he had forgotten they were not alone. Kildanor shook his head. "No, Ralgon." To the guard he said, "Leave us."

"As you wish," the warrior replied and walked away.

"So, do you own a dog?" he asked again, still in the cell, inspecting the canine corpse. He was no expert in things dead, knew how to kill but usually, aside from maybe burying or burning bodies, he didn't bother to stay and watch a corpse decompose. This dog had been dead for years.

"Aye," Ralgon said. "She's called Dog." He laughed. "Silly name, but she doesn't mind. Why?"

This animal could not have been alive last night. Its fur and skin were so brittle; both fell away in the places he touched. Kildanor remembered the mutt that had led the horse into Dunthiochagh; she had spoken to him. And she had been with Ralgon when the man had returned from the dead. A little worse for wear, true, but it had been moving, eating, and, looking very much alive. This creature hadn't drawn a living breath for many years. Was it the same animal?

"Does she speak to you?" he asked. "I know it sounds stupid, but I heard a voice when I met her leading a white horse through the city gates."

His question was answered with silence.

"Ralgon, still there?"

"I am," was the reply. Kildanor was about to repeat his question when the former mercenary spoke again, "Yes, I heard a voice, sometimes when I looked at Dog... I tried to ignore it... I've heard voices before, why should this have been any different? When... when Hesmera died... I heard voices then. They spoke to me... I still dream of them... nightmares. But... I didn't... couldn't let the voice, any voice, talk to me again."

Was this man utterly insane? The Chosen felt as confused as Ralgon surely was. No wonder he had seemed so at peace when he'd died. What could he do? What should he do? Should he do anything at all?

The former mercenary talked on, "You know, voices spoke to me whenever I got real angry, or when I killed someone in battle, or when I was drunk... gods know I haven't touched alcohol in ages. I heard them again, before I awoke in this cell, they called me, told me I was... I can't remember."

Kildanor straightened. The demons had been talking to him? What had this ceremony in the mountains been about? What had the men tried to gain by sacrificing Ralgon? Had part of their ritual done what it was supposed to do? Why did he turn up now when the land was at war?

"I can't remember what the voices told me... I never remember, but now..." Ralgon fell silent again.

"Now what?" Kildanor prompted.

He heard the prisoner draw a deep breath. "I remember what Dog said... that my time... that I still had time... that I must remember..." Again, the man paused. "Damn!"

"What?"

"The voice... Dog's voice! I heard her while I was in the dark place."

"The dark place?" Kildanor asked. "What are you talking about?" He stood, walked out, and headed for Ralgon's cell.

The former mercenary sat on his cot, elbows on his knees, his hands holding his head. "What are *you* talking about?"

CHAPTER 53

Drangar hadn't had time to think about all that had happened. His mind was a blur. The gorge in the Shadowpeaks, the dark place with voices fighting over him as if he were cattle on the market, his torment by the bloodied demons, the journey into the past, it felt as if there was barely a thing any sane person would believe.

He looked up and saw the man he'd been talking to. Short-cropped hair, clear, thoughtful eyes, and the tired look of someone who had spent too many nights without decent sleep. "The guard was very respectful," he said. "Who are you?"

"Kildanor, Chosen of Lesganagh."

Drangar groaned. The past would always come to haunt him, it seemed. "I guess you know my name?" he said.

"Aye. What is this dark place you were talking about?"

He brushed his hair back and tucked strands behind his ears. "I could use a bath." How could he talk to this man, this Chosen, if he didn't understand any of what he'd gone through? He looked at Kildanor, but the man didn't move, eyes locked on him. Drangar exhaled. "Listen, mate, for however long I've been in this new cell, I've been trying to figure out what has been going on… I don't think you'll understand."

"Try me," the warrior of Lesganagh replied.

"Very well," he said, stood, and began pacing the little room. It wasn't more than four yards across and less than two paces deep. Cells weren't meant to be comfortable. "I think I died, but I didn't come to the Bailey Majestic, I never made it to the Scales of Lliania. I was in," he said, thinking, "in a place of darkness." He looked around. "Much like this place, only there was no floor, or ceiling, or anything. I drifted, or something. I felt someone washing me, I think, and I heard the Hymn of the Sun. Then there was this voice, threatening, vicious bastard I'd say. I don't know, he tried to... I don't know... I felt threatened by him, and he pulled me toward him. Then I felt at ease—sheltered you could say—and another voice shouted at the first one. This one was... I know this makes me sound like a lunatic, but the voice sounded like Dog's, like the voice I'd heard on occasion. They were fighting, and Dog's voice struggled and lost, and I felt drawn toward the fiend-light again."

"Fiend-light?" the Chosen interrupted.

Drangar didn't know how many times he had walked the few steps between the two walls that separated his from another pair of cells. He didn't care either. He looked at the Chosen, frowning.

"The threatening voice was hidden behind some sort of light, and a net, like a fishing-net. I really didn't want to go there... fiend-light, felt fiendish." He scoffed and resumed his pacing. "Well, there came another voice, and she said the sunargh, that's what she called the creature behind the curtain, had to obey the rules, or some such thing. That new voice was different from Dog's, in a way.

"Then I fell from the dark place, and found myself held by those cat-things." Even now, as he spoke about his experiences, Drangar felt he was retelling a nightmare. But he had gone through them, of that he was sure.

"I saw the demons," Kildanor said.

Drangar whipped his head toward the Chosen. "You did?" he asked. This man had seen them; it wasn't a nightmare!

"Aye, the cat-things are demons."

"I thought they were defeated during the war," he said.

The tales of Traksor's victory over Turuuk and the battles in Danastaer had been fed to him on a regular basis when he was a child. "How can they be demons if they were defeated? They're gone from the world..." He halted in midsentence. "The Sons," he whispered. "They were right!"

"Sons?" Kildanor asked. "What Sons?"

"The Sons of Traksor."

Life held symmetry. Kildanor had always believed this, but that the Sons of Traksor were mentioned in the ramblings of a man who had been dead surprised him. He remembered the missive, the warning the Sons had sent north before the invasion had begun. The warning Jathain had intercepted. Drangar Ralgon knew of them. The man's familiarity with them was obvious from the ease with which he mentioned their name.

"What do you know of these Sons of Traksor?" he asked.

Ralgon stiffened. There were some bad memories associated with the name, Kildanor was sure of that. "I was raised by them," the prisoner said. "Ran away from their nonsense when I was fourteen."

"What did you mean when you said the Sons were right?" He knew this line of thought was sidetracking him, but he was interested.

"They say the demons will return and they will be there to fight them."

"Why would anyone want to sacrifice you to them?"

"Sacrifice me to the demons?" Ralgon sounded incredulous.

This question had plagued him ever since the five Demonologists had gone up in flames. Maybe the victim would know. "Aye, the men who ambushed you had prepared a demon-circle to sacrifice you."

Ralgon seemed surprised. "Damned if I know..." then he paused. His left hand rubbed his mouth and chin as he stared into the distance, thinking. "Did the Wizardess tell you what I've told her?"

"Not really. She just said I should fetch an Upholder and that she believed you."

What Ralgon told him now was strange and frightening, and the Chosen didn't know what to make of it. Until the report came to the part where the ghost had taken the prisoner to observe the mysterious group planning the drug induced murder. At this point Kildanor held up his hand, halting the prisoner's tale. "They wanted to break your spirit?"

Ralgon nodded, "Is it possible that the two events are connected? What if the Demonologists wanted to sacrifice me even then and failed? It wasn't the first attempt on my life at any rate."

A mercenary would see many killings and many people who would want to end his life, but he deliberately said "attempts", which implied intent beyond the regular slaughter of battle. "How many?"

Shrugging, Ralgon replied, "I don't know. A handful each year."

"When did these failed murders begin?"

"Shortly after I left the Eye."

"The Eye?" Kildanor didn't like feeling as if he were an ignorant pupil.

"The Eye of Traksor, the fortress of the Sons," the former mercenary answered.

He took the information in stride and continued voicing his thoughts. "So, we can assume the Sons protected you until you ran away?"

"That would be my guess as well."

Too many things had already been said, and Kildanor had to know if Drangar Ralgon was telling the truth. "I'll fetch an Upholder," he said and rushed out of the dungeon.

Upholder Coimharrin wouldn't be happy to see him, and with Nerran's riders cleaning up Eanaigh's Church he could hardly blame him. The news of Caretakers, adherent followers of the Ban, being killed by the Paladin of Lesganagh and his Riders had quickly spread through Dunthiochagh.

"Good day, Upholder," he said when the priest entered the antechamber of the Lawgiver's Court. No town was without a Court of Lliania, and he had to admit that the massive scales, symbol of the goddess, gave weight to her priesthood. No deal was legal without her priest's blessing. Coimharrin, rumor had it, was one of the few priests considered worthy of being named Lawpasser, but as long as the old one in Harail was still alive, the man had to be content with the position of judge in Dunthiochagh.

"Ah, yes, what a splendid day. Bloodshed in the streets, in the House of Health, Eanaighists dropping like flies," the Upholder grumbled.

The Chosen could imagine how the man felt; he had probably felt the same way during the Dawnslaughter. "My lord," he began, but Coimharrin held up a hand.

"The Eanaighists began this nonsense, again!" the priest ranted. "As if that legal abomination of thirty years ago hadn't been enough, now the fools dared arrest people without either the Baron's or my consent."

The statement caught Kildanor by surprise. "Sir?"

"The bloodshed began when those oafs tried to arrest Paladin Nerran and his... gang," Coimharrin said. "They have the right to police their own, but they can't detain others. They don't have that right!"

"But..." he began, only to be interrupted again.

"That foolishness three decades ago? They struck like thieves, assassins. They only claimed legality after the deed was done, a quite convenient fact, don't you think?" the Upholder asked. "But the Lady's Scales know every soul," he said absentmindedly, and regarded Kildanor. "Well, son, what do you want?"

This turn of events came unexpected, and Kildanor took a deep breath to gather his wits. The Upholder actually approved of Nerran's actions! "Well, sir," he began, feeling slightly out of place. He was older than Coimharrin, by at least forty years, but the priest wore the aura of confidence like a cloak, and wielded his knowledge of law and justice like a weapon. "You really think the Dawnslaughter was wrong?" he couldn't help but ask.

"Think, son? I don't think it was wrong, I know it was wrong. But what can you do? When there's no plaintiff, you don't have a trial. They were very thorough."

For a moment he didn't know what to say.

"So, son, you didn't come here to discuss the finer points of sword-point-law with me."

"No, sir, I need your help."

"The Chosen making deals now?" Coimharrin scoffed. "A divorce maybe? No? Spit it out, son, never heard of you lot being tongue-tied!"

He felt himself blushing. For a century no one had made him feel like a bumbling farmhand. "I need to know if someone is telling the truth," he finally said.

"That simple, eh?" the Upholder seemed disappointed. He turned and walked into the antechamber. Kildanor followed.

Instead of heading out onto Boughaighr's Alley, however, Coimharrin strode toward the house next to Lawgiver's Court. Confused, he followed, into the building, a small foyer, and then into a homely kitchen. A young woman stood next to the hearth, stirring the contents of a pot.

"Father, why didn't you tell me we have a guest for supper?" the cook said.

"Guest?" Coimharrin asked and looked around. "Oh, you want to eat something, son?"

"No, sir," Kildanor replied.

The Upholder helped himself to a bowl of porridge and added some butter and bacon. "Good, more for us!" he exclaimed and began to eat.

"Shouldn't we be going, sir?"

"Going? Where?" the priest asked, his mouth full.

"To the Palace, sir," he said, feeling as if he was talking to a doddering fool.

"Is it urgent, that truth business? Life or death, that sort of thing?"

"No, sir."

"Good! Let me eat in peace, son. Have some porridge if you're hungry."

Kildanor sighed; it was going to be a long day, again, but he quickly discovered he was hungry.

CHAPTER 54

Jesgar wasn't sure whether he should just enter his home as if nothing had happened, or if he should knock. Ten days had passed since his imprisonment, and part of him knew Ben would be furious. Another part kept hoping his brother would be more worried than angry. As he rode closer, he heard someone working the forge. It almost felt like nothing had changed, but the fact he rode a horse would remind his family he was a different man.

He guided his gelding to the back of the house. This was his home as well, and he would not tie the mare to the front like a common visitor. The steady beat of the hammer, interrupted by the hissing of iron lowered into the barrel of water, hardly slowed when he halted in the yard.

"Need new shoes?" Bennath's voice drowned out the hissing metal. "If so, come back tomorrow!" The hammering resumed.

Jesgar dismounted and immediately the sound of his brother's work ceased. Ben's soot-tinted face poked out of the smithy. He had been afraid of disappointment, but instead his brother's face showed a mixture of surprise, amusement, and relief. "Ah, little brother, you're alive," the older Garinad said, white teeth piercing the soot in a broad grin.

This he hadn't expected, and he was even more taken aback when Ben seized him into one of his bone-crushing hugs. After being in the saddle and among Nerran's Riders for days, it somehow didn't feel as tight as it used to. Jesgar smiled and returned his brother's affection. "Good to see you too," he said.

Ben released him, took a step back, and inspected him. "You look well," he finally said, tousling Jesgar's hair.

He felt as if he'd been transported back almost ten years to when his big brother had seemed like a moody, yet benign giant. Of course, he was older now, but Ben could still make him feel like that youth. Maybe to him, Jesgar would always be this boy. He looked at his sibling. "Lots of fresh air."

Bennath shook his head and snorted. "Go on in, Maire should have supper ready. I'll be with you soon." He turned and headed back into the smithy. On the threshold he glanced back at him. "Good to see you," he said then resumed his work.

For a moment, Jesgar couldn't do anything but stare at the smithy's empty doorway. Ben had never treated him like this before. It felt more like the reunion of two friends than the return of the prodigal son he had feared. Had he ever been an embarrassment to his family? At times it felt like it. Ben had never been happy with his work with the hammer, and he had always felt useless in the smithy and the household. Yes, he'd been good at carrying coals, refilling the barrel, working the bellows, but any fool could do that.

Still pondering his brother's unexpected welcome, Jesgar entered the house. He had never been much of a cook, but he was a good eater, and could tell by the smell wafting out of the kitchen that whatever Maire was preparing was delicious. Ben had agreed on sharing the workload, but when his wife had sampled her husband's first, and thankfully last, attempt at cooking she had chased him away from the stove.

"Mommy, I'm home," he said, as he stepped through the door. It had been ages since he had called his sister-in-law mommy—Ben had slapped that habit out of him—but now it felt right to call her thus.

A fierce slap was her reply. His left cheek stung almost as much as his legs had a few nights ago. The right cheek followed, as Maire's hand made the return trip to her side. "This used to be funny when you were a boy!" she snarled. "And before..." she fell silent.

"Gods, I'm sorry, Maire," he stammered, realizing how painful this reminder of several stillbirths had to be for her.

His sister-in-law shook her head. "Don't. You meant it as a jest, I know. Still, the slaps should remind you in the future."

She then drew him into a long, bone-crushing embrace.

He hugged her tightly. "I missed you."

Maire stood on tiptoe and kissed his cheek. "As I did you," she said and took a step back. "You're leaner."

"Courtesy of porridge and several days of riding," he replied. Seeing her astonishment, Jesgar added, "I've been as far south as Dragoncrest."

She drew him to the big table and pushed him onto a chair like she had done when he could still have been pulled and pushed by her. He came along willingly, happy with the bit of familiarity. Maire was like the mother he'd never known and after the arduous journey, he enjoyed being coddled. "Tell me all about it," she said as she went about the kitchen.

"Well, I rode with Nerran Ghonair, accompanied him on an inspection of the fortresses," he said as his brother's wife placed a mug of heated wine before him. He took a sip and continued. "Our journey took almost a week and... listen, can I tell it when Ben's here? I don't want to repeat the stuff."

Maire agreed, and soon his brother entered, washed hands and face, and joined them in the kitchen. Supper was served and now, with all three of them together again, Jesgar really felt like he had come home.

The talk turned first to his journey—he told them what he thought was safe to be told—and then what had happened during Jathain's revolt. It seemed that word certainly had spread, but most folk knew only the rumors that had circulated in the taverns. When Ben asked about the influx of troops that had entered the city by nightfall, Jesgar related to them his encounter with General Kerral and his band of survivors. The General had gathered the remnants of the various warbands that had scattered when Harail had fallen, people who refused to surrender to the Chanastardhians.

"He's a little loud for my taste," he said at the end, and knew for him to state such a thing, the man was really noisy. Jesgar was, like his brother, not a demure man, and his comment was rewarded by a bellowing laugh from his brother and Maire rolling her eyes. He looked at her and saw her head shaking with a mixture of resignation and amusement.

"You must've gotten along just fine with this Kerral then?" she asked as she refilled her mug.

"Not really," he said.

"Yeah, right," Ben threw in.

"I'm serious! You learn modesty when you're with the Riders," he said. "On the road you're on your own, and with Chanastardhian outriders haunting the countryside you've got to be careful, especially at night."

"Little brother, you don't expect me to believe that for one moment, do you? You couldn't stay silent for more than a few breaths if your life depended on it."

"Ben," Maire whispered, putting a hand on her husband's arm. "You should..."

But her attempt to prevent another Garinad fight came too late. Jesgar stood and glared at his brother. "You have no idea what you're talking about! You wouldn't even hear the trumpets of the gods if they were playing a march next to your thick skull! You've been half-deaf for the last decade because of your constant hammering! How would you know how quiet I can be?"

He was furious. Sure, Ben had kept the family warm and well fed, but like their father before, he had been too busy to care for anyone emotionally. That had been Maire's duty, much like it must have been his mother's before her.

"Had you gotten your head out of that furnace, you would've known I barely slept in my bed at night."

"Boys!" Maire tried to intervene again.

"You selfish bastard!" Bennath Garinad shouted. "I worked night and day so you could live like you did! Without me you wouldn't have been able to ever carouse through the night!"

"I hardly ever did that!" he retorted. "I had better things to do!"

"Like what?" Ben ignored his wife's attempt to soothe his temper. Jesgar had seen things like that happen before. Ben loved Maire and he would never hurt her, but when the older Garinad's temper flared, nothing could stop it. Aside from...

"I worked!" Jesgar growled. "I worked at the Library!"

"Doing what?" Ben asked, his voice sounding calmer.

"Whatever needed to be done! Carrying pisspots, washing linens, scrubbing floors, that sort of thing!"

Now even Maire looked surprised.

"And you buggered off whenever I needed help with the forge?" Ben asked.

"I did not!"

"In all fairness, love," Maire said, taking a firm hold on her husband's arm. "He did help us most of the time!"

"So, what did those Librarians pay you?" grumbled Ben, slightly quieted by his wife.

"No money, if that's what you think," Jesgar replied, bracing for a new outburst.

"What?" Ben roared. "You carried shit for them and they didn't give you money?"

"Wait, love."

"Wait for what? My lousy little brother worked for them priests and they didn't pay him? Next he'll tell me he also sucked their cocks!"

Jesgar didn't believe his ears. The next moment he was up on his feet, hands balled into fists. "You... I...," he stammered. "They taught me to read and write, you idiot! That was my payment! Letters! I didn't want to end up like you! I helped you in the forge because I knew you needed the help, but I never wanted to be a smith! I'm sorry, Ben, but the smithy is your dream, not mine!" He stormed out the kitchen, ignoring Maire's and Ben's shouts. He would come back, certainly, but for now he wanted to be alone with a few mugs of ale, maybe a brawl, and surely a woman.

The Tankard wasn't a big tavern, nor was it clean, but it served the best ale in Dunthiochagh. Since it was in the seedier part of town, not many merchants or nobles frequented it. Jesgar had been to the Tankard several times before, but never with such a clear goal in mind. Sure, he had had a drink or four, or watched drunken lowlifes demolish each other and the furniture, and he certainly had met fine lasses here as well, but he wanted to get pissed, bash a few heads, and get laid. After the first few stouts he wasn't quite sure if he should fight now and fuck later or the other way around. After a few more he decided drinking was the best pastime.

Then he made a new friend.

Dalgor was, he was sure, a fine fellow, and he said so repeatedly. He didn't know much about his new best mate, but he ordered more beer and paid as well. He talked with his new best mate; later, Jesgar wasn't so sure if...what's-his-name... spoke as much as he did, but that seemed perfectly all right with him.

When he got out of bed—he had no idea how he got there in the first place, but then he barely remembered anything except the good time he and his new mate had had at the Tankard—he remembered he would meet Dalgor again tonight. Everything else was a haze; he greeted Maire and Ben, ate a meager breakfast, and was off to the Palace.

CHAPTER 55

It was well past dusk when Kildanor and Upholder Coimharrin entered the dungeon. On their way down Trade Road the priest had commended the actions of Nerran's Riders. "Sometimes justice lies at the tip of a sword, son. When words and reason can't help anymore, you know?" He was still talking about the finer points of justice when the pair reached Ralgon's cell. Kildanor, lamp in hand, lit the way until finally the mercenary was illuminated. Coimharrin stopped his monologue and stared at the prisoner.

"I'll be damned," he whispered.

The Chosen was confused, and he said so, "You know him?"

Coimharrin shook his head. "I don't think so, but he has the same eyes as someone I knew once."

Ralgon looked at the priest. "Really now?" He shrugged and turned to Kildanor. "Is this the Lawman?"

Before he could answer his companion said, "I'm Upholder Coimharrin, son, and the Chosen here asked me to see if your tales hold some truth."

"Truth is a matter of perspective, as you well know," Ralgon, much to Kildanor's surprise, replied. The man wasn't only a murderer and mercenary, but also a philosopher.

"Yes, yes, quite right you are, son," agreed Coimharrin.

"Nonetheless, you said something about a journey into your past, and the Upholder is here to verify your story," Kildanor interrupted. Maybe his tone was rude, but he didn't want the old man distracted by discussions about truth and what it meant for every soul. "Upholder, please focus on the matter at hand."

The priest turned his head and frowned. "The boy's right,

Chosen. Even if I confirm that he is telling the truth, it is only his truth, his perspective. I can't tell you if what he says is genuine truth."

Kildanor frowned, "It doesn't matter if it's only his truth; we need to know what is going on!"

"Gods protect me from impatient men," Coimharrin said.

Ralgon chuckled. "Chosen," he said, looking at him. "For the idiots who began the Dawnslaughter back in the day, their truth was that Lesganagh's priests were evil, so what they did— at least to them—was right and just. Put one of them before an Upholder and he'd tell you it was true. So, anything I'd say would still be clouded by whatever doubts you have."

"Listen to him, boy, he's got the gist of it."

"So, you're saying I should believe him anyway?"

Coimharrin shook his head. "No, you just have to judge for yourself if you do." The priest hesitated and looked at the prisoner. "He seems quite together, not really bound to hallucinate"—at this Ralgon scoffed—"so we can assume what he'll tell us will be his relative truth."

"What about the fact that he came back from the dead?"

Coimharrin's head whipped about and he looked at the prisoner. "What are you saying?"

Ralgon said, "Don't look at me; I don't have a clue either! By all rights, I should be quite stiff and rotting."

"He returned from the dead?"

He nodded. "Aye." How could he explain to the priest what he didn't understand either?

"You should ask a Caretaker," Coimharrin muttered. "This is a bloody miracle, health and all that, and I'm certainly not in the healing and nurturing business."

"I don't want you to tell me why he's come back!" Kildanor snapped. Had he known this would turn into a philosophy session, he might have accepted Ralgon's tale immediately, just to spare himself this senseless blathering. "I want you to tell me if his tale about seeing what happened in the past is true!" Before the Upholder could reply, he continued, "Can you tell me if this man has really seen the past? And if so, is what he saw mere fabrication or fact?"

"I'm no bloody oracle! But I can tell you if his tale is a lie, not whether it is the utter truth, I'd need more witnesses than him."

Exasperated, he let out a sigh of relief. "That's all I ask of you, Upholder."

"Very well," Coimharrin said and turned to Ralgon. "Let's hear it then." The priest muttered a brief prayer and looked expectantly at the prisoner. "Go on then, time's awasting."

"So, you're telling me he is innocent?"

Kildanor looked from Cumaill to the Upholder and waited for the priest's reply. Even after hearing Ralgon's tale a second time, it still sounded more like a nightmarish fiery tale than an account of the past, but Coimharrin verified the story.

"Aye, Lord Baron." The Upholder's deference toward Cumaill surprised him; so far, the man had treated everyone as a child. "His tale is no lie. And no divine voice told me otherwise. He wielded the sword that killed this woman, yes..."

"So, he's guilty?"

The Chosen also had had problems comprehending the finer points of the verdict, but now, after a long elaboration on the topic, he understood.

"No, milord, he isn't, unless you would also accuse a rope of committing a burglary."

Kildanor thought Duasonh made the same face he had worn in his confusion. "No, of course not," the Baron said.

It was time to intervene. "What the worthy Upholder is trying to say is that Drangar Ralgon was, at the time of the killing, not the master of his own body. Someone else held the strings."

"Who?"

"He doesn't know, and neither do we," Coimharrin said, quite reasonably in Kildanor's opinion. The priest was surprisingly uncomplicated. "I was asked to verify the boy's tale, and so I did. If I could find a culprit merely by listening to some statement, I'd be somewhere up there with the gods meting out due punishment. The Lawgiver's Scales judge people by their deeds when they enter the Bailey Majestic, but she doesn't tell anyone how to live. She merely gives us laws."

"What Upholder Coimharrin is trying to say is this:

judgment is given by the goddess in the afterlife, based on her laws. She's impartial, and it's our job in this world to find out who's guilty," Kildanor intervened.

"So, we release him," Duasonh said.

"Sure, I don't see why not?" the priest replied. "Unless you also keep daggers and ropes in your dungeon."

Seeing Duasonh's eyes dancing with mirth had become a rarity these past days, and he was glad his friend was still capable of humor. The Baron walked to the door. "Tell the jailers to release Drangar Ralgon," he ordered one of his guards; then he shut the door again. "Anything else you would like to discuss with me, Upholder?"

Coimharrin frowned and remained silent for a moment. The only time Kildanor had seen the priest quiet was when eating, so he was surprised at the prolonged silence. "Well, milord, there is one thing," he finally said. The priest apparently interpreted Duasonh's lack of reply as permission to speak on. "Releasing the sorceress from captivity is your right, certainly, but there have already been objections."

Kildanor, who had had this argument with Duasonh before, knew what the reply would be. What he didn't expect was Cumaill's attempt to appease.

"Upholder Coimharrin, I am aware of the controversy regarding the Wizardess Ealisaid's release, and I assure you that if things were different I would also have executed the woman after the crimes she committed. But with war engulfing what's left of our country, I'll not throw away a weapon like her..."

"Can you control her?" the Upholder interrupted. "The destruction she has already caused is, in all likelihood, just a taste of what she can do, should we anger her. The law demands her to stand trial for her crimes, milord."

"I know what the law demands!" Duasonh retorted. The Chosen could have warned the priest of this reaction beforehand. After all, he had heard words in a similar vein before. "I also know the law is what I say it is in times of need!"

"Certainly, sir, that's your right." Coimharrin's face didn't hint at any emotion, so Kildanor figured the priest had expected this outcome. "However, milord, the atonement for the crimes is merely postponed. When all of this is over, be assured that I will press charges against her."

"Let's hope we make it through the coming siege, otherwise this talk isn't worth the breath we've just used."

"Very well then," Coimharrin said, bowing before he left.

After the door had closed behind the Upholder, Kildanor looked at Duasonh. "If people have already started talking, the affair with the witch might turn against you quickly should one of her spells misfire." Even though he liked the woman's attitude, he felt certain she was barely out of her training. This didn't mean she was incapable of magic, but pupils such as she had caused the most havoc with spells that went awry during the early days of the Heir War. Luckily, they had perished quickly. The Wizardess might be better versed in her knowledge, but that did not mean she was as adept in the practical use of magic.

"Then she best not make any mistakes!" Duasonh growled. Cumaill seemed tired after the exchange with Coimharrin, and Nerran's return had probably done its part in wearying him.

"Damn, mate, you need to rest," Kildanor said.

"I know," said the noble and slumped down on one of the chairs. He was about to say more when the door flew open and Nerran entered.

"Bloody Scales, Cumaill, you look awful," the Paladin said. "Get some rest." Before Duasonh could reply, the warrior went on, "That lad I was telling you about is here."

"Lad? What lad?" Duasonh said, straightening in his seat.

"Oh, good eve, Kildanor," Nerran said as he saw the Chosen. "Fancy meeting you here. I got some news for you." To the Baron he said, "That royal pain in the ass... that general."

"Kerral?" Duasonh said.

"Aye, that's the one. He brought some of his troops into the city already."

"How many?"

As important as this conversation was, the Paladin was in storytelling mode, and Kildanor knew that nothing short of a well-aimed blow to the head would stop the man.

"He left a good five hundred outside, they want to slow the Chanastardhians approach," Nerran said.

"How many warriors are in my city?" Duasonh asked, slapping his hands onto the chair's armrests.

"Oh, there were more, but I think I told you that, he left some in the fortresses..."

"I know! How many additional mouths are mine to feed?" His anger brought some color back onto the Baron's cheeks. "And don't give me the bloody numbers of those the castles have to feed, just those that will need supplies inside Dunthiochagh!"

Either his friend would go to bed soon, Kildanor thought, or he would find the strength to plow on through the tasks ahead of him. Cumaill looked tired, but he knew the city needed its lord, and a bit of anger was already helping. He decided to interrupt. "What news is there for me?" he asked.

"Kildanor!" the Baron barked as he stood.

Nerran looked to the Chosen, mischief glimmering in his eyes. Obviously, the Paladin understood what he was trying to do. "Oh, I meant to tell you before, but forgot, what with those fifteen hundred warriors following me from Dragoncrest. Your fellows got to the fortress, but there are only sixteen of them, I think."

Kildanor frowned and began to pace in the room, right in front of the Baron. "Hmmm," he said then turned back to Nerran. "Did Galen mention when the others would come?"

The Paladin scratched his head, seemingly oblivious to Duasonh. "Let me think."

"Think on your bleeding own time, outside my office!" Duasonh yelled. "Fifteen hundred new warriors inside the city? Fifteen hundred mouths to feed?"

The Paladin winked at him and faced their friend. "Ah, Cumaill! Glad to see you're awake," he said with a broad grin. Even Kildanor couldn't keep a straight face.

Duasonh, despite his anger, smirked. "You bastards!"

"No, born and bred to a true family," Kildanor said.

"Me, too," Nerran added. "Not his, though." He pointed at the Chosen.

Duasonh sat back down again. "So, you were making fun of me with fifteen hundred warriors added to our garrison?" he said, relieved.

"No, not really," the Paladin of Lesganagh replied. "Don't ask me how, but this Kerral gathered more than two thousand lads and lasses to his banner over the past week and a half."

"Two thousand?"

Maybe he hadn't paid much attention to the first part of Nerran's speech, Kildanor thought. "There're some before the city, and some were left to reinforce the garrisons in the fortresses," he said.

"How is the clearing of the farmsteads coming along?" Duasonh asked. He stood and leafed through the pile of reports cluttering his table, pulled out a sheet of paper, and read. After a few moments he paused. "Most of the outlying farms are expected to be bare the day after tomorrow. Did these troops take supplies with them?"

"You best ask the general, mate," Nerran replied.

CHAPTER 56

"So, Dragoncrest's warleader really offed Jathain?" Kildanor whispered to Nerran. "And hung his corpse on the outer wall?"

The Paladin inclined his head, but remained silent.

They were in the audience chamber, standing to left and right of Cumaill Duasonh who was besieged not only by the regular sycophants, but also by angry innkeepers and brothel-owners. Apparently General Kerral had requisitioned several buildings for his warriors.

"Think he'll start throwing out people?"

Kildanor snorted. "The question isn't 'if' but 'when'."

"General Kerral is within his rights to requisition quarters for his troops," Duasonh almost shouted.

"But he has to pay for them!" whined a fat and greasy weasel of a man. "He can't just take the rooms and not pay!"

"This chap has no idea what requisitioning means," Nerran whispered.

The Chosen suppressed a chuckle.

"Do you know what it means to requisition something…" the Baron frowned at the innkeeper.

"Herve, milord, Herve Enrick, sir. Proprietor of the Dancing Lady, sir," the man replied.

"Lousy place to stay at, if you ask me," Nerran whispered.

Duasonh took a deep breath and asked again, "Do you know what requisition means, Herve Enrick, proprietor of the Dancing Lady?"

Kildanor admired Cumaill's patience. For a while now, these men had complained without seemingly taking a breath.

Once again, he was glad not to be lording over anyone. How the Baron managed to stop himself from hanging all these people on the spot he didn't know. Had it been up to him, he would have ordered the complainers to keep their mouths shut or dance on the gallows.

"No, milord," Herve Enrick said.

"It means that by law a warleader of the King's army is within his rights to take what he needs, within reason, for his men to be in fighting order!"

"But sir!" another innkeeper added. This man Kildanor knew. A well-respected, wealthy citizen everyone called Dreamy Duncan. "We lose business." Now the Chosen knew why the man had got the nickname.

"If Dunthiochagh is captured, gentlemen, you'll lose more than merely your business!" Duasonh snarled. "Next!"

"Milord," a short, bald man said as he stepped to the front. "Alarnai of Dunth Street, milord. Proprietor of…"

"I know who you are, man," Duasonh said.

"Of course he does," Kildanor whispered.

Nerran leaned closer. "Aye?"

"Had to drag Gavyn and me out of there last year, remember?"

The Paladin grinned. "Aye, that bet he lost."

"Bet?"

"What is your complaint?"

"They may requisition rooms and such, but they still have to pay for the boys and girls they fuck," Alarnai said. Then he blushed, "Pay for services rendered, sir."

Nerran winked. "He claimed he could be as intimidating as me," he whispered. "I dared him to get you two out of Alarnai's place."

"He got us out."

"Dead drunk the three of you. You all had to be carried out, lad, I swear on my sword."

"Indeed, they have to pay for that," Duasonh said. If he had been paying attention to the conversation his friends were having, he didn't show it. "They also have to pay for booze and food beyond porridge."

Kildanor looked from brothel owner to Cumaill and then at Nerran. "Did he pay for the booze he needed to get us out of there?"

Before the aging warrior could answer the double door was flung open and an impressive looking man pushed his way through the guards. "Let me through, idiots!"

"Kerral?" the Chosen asked.

"Kerral," Nerran replied.

"Quite full of himself, eh?"

"Gods, you have no idea."

"Lord Baron, I am General Kerral of his Majesty's Army, and I demand to speak to you."

"He wants to speak 'to' not 'with'?" Kildanor said, astonished at the man's audacity.

"This lad usually speaks to people; he isn't one to discuss things," Nerran replied. "Why the Scales do you think we rode into the city half a day before him?"

"The King is dead, man," Duasonh replied. "You might have been general of his army, but in this city, you follow my orders. Do I make myself clear?" General Kerral stood still, as if struggling with the very idea. "Furthermore, your warriors will pay for every whore, every mug of ale they drink, and every slice of meat they have to their porridge. Understood?"

"But sir!" Herve Enrick protested, again.

Kildanor knew what was coming and Duasonh didn't disappoint. "Your grievances end now, innkeeper! Get out!" Enrick and the others shuffled out of the audience chamber. The Baron turned to his two friends. "I'd appreciate a restraint of muttering now, if you please."

Nerran glanced to the Chosen and gave a little shrug. "Milord," the pair said in unison.

"Sir," Kerral began, "my warriors have marched long and are tired; they are merely looking for some fun."

"Fun they'll have to pay for, general."

"We hardly made it out of the Chanastardhians' way, sir. Most of my warriors have little coin left. How shall they pay for whores or booze?"

This man really worried about the wellbeing of his troops.

Kildanor was genuinely surprised. There weren't many of the King's warleaders who cared for the men under their command. The way Kerral dressed was also uncommon for warlords from Harail; his armor was piecemeal, not the typical plate and mail one would expect, and neither was his surcoat adorned with the crest of a noble house. A common warrior raised from the ranks? That might explain the man's lack of lordly behavior. "What House do you hail from?" he asked.

Duasonh threw him a questioning glance and then turned to the general.

"None, sir," Kerral replied.

"Elaborate," the Baron ordered.

"Not much to tell, Lord Duasonh. I was hired by Dame Bethia of House Grendargh."

"Bethia?" Nerran said. "The poor lass died last month."

"Aye," Cumaill said.

"Killed by her own servant," Kerral confirmed. "Or so we were told."

"She once told me she didn't trust most of those court-bastards," Nerran said. "Poor lass must have been aware of the treachery long before any of us were, Cumaill. Think that's why she was killed?"

"Could be." The Baron leaned forward and stared at Kerral. "If you were Dame Bethia's creature, general, how come you were not demoted or thrown out immediately?"

At this the warlord smirked. "Clerical error, milord."

"Explain."

"Lady Grendargh suspected something, at least that's my guess. Apparently, my commission was sent on a long journey, sir. I was attached to my warband with preliminary orders awaiting ratification, which just arrived three weeks ago."

Some people hadn't been as corrupt as he had thought. He had never liked Bethia Grendargh; to him she had always seemed too enthralled by intrigue and gossip. As minister of war she had been impeccable, he remembered that much.

"General Kerral," Duasonh said. "Why did she make you warlord? Were the two of you lovers?"

The warrior snorted. "Scales, no!"

"Speak, then."

"Very well, sir. My father, well, it's like this, sir, my ma never told me who my da was; just a customer she said. My ma's a serving wench, sir."

"Go on," the Baron said when Kerral paused.

"Aye, sir. Well, turns out that guy who sired me was Dame Grendargh grandnephew, Kohal. Far-flung part of the House, really, but quite active, if you know what I mean. Anyway, I'm a bastard scion of House Grendargh. This doesn't mean a thing, really, because Kohal won't never admit having a bastard boy, but Dame Bethia had gotten wind of the matter and managed to hire me."

"So, you lay no claim to the family name?"

Kerral shook his head. "Why bother, milord, I'm fine as is, and even if I did, no one would support me. Scales, even Lady Bethia didn't. She gave me the job as general, which is enough for me, really."

"You were quite successful in evading the Chanastardhian army, laddie," Nerran said. "So old Bethia must've known you're a decent campaigner. Seen much action?"

"Some, sir."

"I've been remiss in my manners, general," Duasonh said. "You know Nerran Ghonair, Paladin of Lesganagh, and this is Kildanor, Chosen, my aides, advisors, and friends."

Kerral nodded to Kildanor, and then answered in more depth. "I've been a mercenary for most of my adult life, sir, traveled here and there and fought in a few places."

"And your success against Mireynh?"

"I knew it!" the warrior exclaimed, balling his hand into a fist. "Sorry. Well, you know how it is with old dogs and tricks, don't you?"

"Aye," Nerran drawled, "most don't learn new tricks."

"Yeah, that's it, the same with the old buzzard. Campaigned under him a while, a few years ago. Figured some ways out of his old traps in the past couple of years."

"Good," Duasonh said as he stood. "Get all your men settled, general. You will obey the three of us in all matters regarding the defense of the city; should we take the field and pursue

Mireynh, you'll be in command."

"All warriors, sir?"

Kildanor wondered what his friend had in mind, and he was anxious to find out. But he held his tongue.

"Aye, all of them. But before you depart..." The Baron rang a bell and a few moments later a servant entered the room. Unhurried, yet at a brisk pace the man approached Duasonh's chair and bowed.

"My liege?"

"Glendon, see to it that the newly arrived troops receive half a dozen barrels of..." the Baron turned to Kildanor. "What's that clear stuff with the stinging taste called? You know, the one distilled from barley and such."

Before he could reply, Kerral supplied the answer, "Broggainh, milord? Very kind of you, sir. I assure you they will be happy about your gift."

"You said most have no money left. We all agree warriors must be of good spirit. Ration it, there might not be a source left once Mireynh gets here."

"Six barrels of Broggainh to this man's troops right away, sir," Glendon said and hurried out.

"Very well, milord." Kerral saluted. "They will appreciate it. By your leave," he said, turned about, and left the audience chamber.

Duasonh turned to Nerran. "He's quite amicable, don't you think?" he said, satisfied.

"Well, you put the man in his place the moment he came through that door, mate."

"Even battle dogs can learn new tricks," Duasonh said. Then he turned to the Chosen, "What about Ralgon?"

"Oh, I gave him a cot in the barracks, didn't want to let him loose on the world just yet."

"Well then, I have to see our witch."

CHAPTER 57

Nineteenth of Chill, 1475 K.C.

The cot he had been given was more comfortable than that in the cell, and Drangar also enjoyed breathing fresh air. Prisons were no inns, as he had so aptly reminded the Chosen, but he was glad to be free. Not that he was certain he deserved it. Knowing he was innocent didn't wash away the terror of watching himself hack Hesmera to pieces.

For a while he stood at one of the barracks' windows and watched the Baron's warriors practice defensive maneuvers in the courtyard. The killers were long gone, he knew, but with all the new knowledge it was difficult to keep still. Two years of solitude and now he couldn't stand the complacency. He had to do something, anything.

Drangar slipped into his coat, surprised to see that someone had mended the cloth, and headed out into the inner bailey. As he closed the door, two warriors who had been loitering nearby stood and watched him. Even though the Upholder had proclaimed his words truth, Baron Duasonh still thought him dangerous. If he was honest with himself, Drangar didn't blame the man. He'd have sent people to watch himself as well, had he been in the Baron's place. The Palace's walls were strong. He had seen them before, during his city watch days, but now, with the Chanastardhian army only days away, he appreciated the thick walls even more. At least they would hold back the enemy for a while. Leaning against the gatehouse was a young man. Drangar felt an odd tingle running down his spine as he watched the man. Despite his obvious size, the younger man didn't wear the garb or the colors of a warrior, and although he seemed out of place, he bothered none of the men-at-arms. The former mercenary let his gaze wander across the practicing troops, his attention, however, still on the young man. He felt he was being watched.

"The demon you know," Drangar muttered and headed for the gatehouse. He knew where he wanted to go. It was maybe just a glimmer of hope, but he had to begin somewhere. The Chosen might be able to help, but he didn't want to bother Kildanor or one of the court officials. They'd spent too much time with him as it was. He didn't want to burden anyone with what would likely be a trivial matter to them. Finding Hesmera's grave, however, was not simple for him. A quick glance over his shoulder assured him the two guards were following as he entered the barbican.

The activity in the outer bailey was almost the same as it had been in the inner, but here, in addition to the practicing warriors, several smiths busied themselves with fixing blades and armor, and the creation of new weapons. Drangar had been in enough battles and sieges to know the routine and headed straight for the drawbridge and onto Trade Road. It felt good to walk; he wasn't tempted to saddle Hiljarr and ride through the city. Kildanor had assured him the charger was being well cared for, which was all that mattered.

His thoughts drifted to Dog, and the woman who had taken him into the past. They had shown him Dog's mummified corpse, and he had accepted the canine's death. He was as puzzled by the animal's sudden demise as Kildanor and the Caretakers. The corpse had been of an animal dead for well over a decade, and Dog had been around just the day before when the Chosen had let her enter his cell. Her skin had been brittle, and by accident he had broken off one of her legs. He still couldn't believe it was that of his companion. An animal he had known for the past two years. How could she appear like she had been dead for years when he most certainly knew the beast had been alive just two weeks ago?

The watch station in the Merchant Quarter hadn't changed

over the past two years, and to his surprise Drangar felt a sense of homecoming. Strange, he thought, it had been here in Dunthiochagh that he had experienced some of the most joyous moments of his life as well as the most horrible one. Would Glaithan still be here? Or Rob? He turned to look at the guards. His senses were honed by years in the field, but without the experience of having seen himself in the past, he would not have paid as much attention to his surroundings as he did now. There, at the corner, almost hidden by the building's shadow, stood the brawny young man he had seen earlier. Why was he following him and who was he?

"I'm gonna talk to the guards here, chaps," Drangar told his escort. "Come in, or wait outside, I dunno how long this will take." They didn't reply, but followed when he entered.

As with the exterior, the front office hadn't changed a bit. It was still cluttered with all sorts of books and papers piled on one large writing desk, the pole arms hanging in their rack on the far wall, and the duty warden leafing through a report. As the door closed behind the three, the watchman looked up from his paperwork. To his surprise Drangar recognized Rob immediately.

"Yes?"

"Hello, mate," Drangar said, forcing his voice to sound jovial. He was overcome by emotion, at once both pleased and terribly afraid. Rob would know of Hesmera's death and his own suspicious disappearance.

"By the bloody gods!"

"Aye, them too."

"Drang? Is that really you?"

"In the living flesh, mate."

Rob looked at the two guards and then back at him. "Don't tell me you did it..."

"I'd be the first to ask for a hanging."

"And those?" Rob nodded in the direction of his guards.

"Can't blame the Baron for being careful."

"But you just said you didn't kill her!"

How could he explain what he didn't fully understand and would Rob believe him even if he could? Drangar knew he had to come to terms with the past, gut wrenching as it was, but it was not the same guilt he had felt for the past two years.

"When you left without a trace there were rumors. All your stuff was gone, but I didn't believe for one moment..."

"It was my hand that held the sword," Drangar said.

"So, you did kill her?" Rob sounded confused, angry, frightened.

"It's a little more complicated than that." Had he lost his chance to convince his former friend? He was barely able to convince himself half the time. "Someone manipulated me. Poison." Seeing his friend begin to object, he continued, "I know it sounds like some weird tale out of a nuthouse, but it's the truth... as far as I can tell. Upholder Coimharrin verified it. Scales, two weeks ago I wouldn't have believed it myself, but it's true."

For a long moment Rob remained silent. Then he asked, "Poison? Who?" Drangar recognized how his friend's investigative mind took over.

"I don't know," he answered. "The trail has been dead for two years now, and that is literally."

He saw the next question forming in the guardsman's mind, a question he had asked himself time and time again. He said, "I just know they are dead. I'll explain later, when I understand more. Trust me."

"I do," Rob said. "So, what do you want if you don't want to follow a dead trail?"

"I need to know where Hesmera's grave is."

"I'll be off duty in a little bit. I can take you there."

"I appreciate it, mate." He really did. He took a look out the window and scowled.

"Something wrong?" Rob asked.

"I don't know." The brawny man he'd seen just a moment before was gone. "I was followed here by this chap. Tall fellow, brown hair, shoulders like a smith." He shrugged. "He's gone now."

One of the guards cleared his throat. "Excuse me, sir."

Drangar smirked. "I ain't no 'sir', Sean. What is it?"

"A thief was caught and released two weeks ago or so, from

what you said, this fellow could be he."

Duasonh had him followed? Weren't two guards enough? Determined not to let his anger dictate his actions, he took a deep breath and turned to Rob. "I'll be here at dusk."

"Right you are. I'll be waiting." After a moment he added, "Maybe we can get the old gang together, like the old days. What say you?"

"The old days are gone, mate; maybe some other time." His escort preceded him, and at the door Drangar turned back and said, "Didn't mean to be so harsh, Robart. I'll see you at dusk."

Outside, he quickened his pace back to the Palace. Now his anger ran free and drove him onward so that his two guards barely managed to keep up, but he didn't care. He wanted to do speak with Kildanor as soon as possible.

"It's all right, Cumaill," Nerran said. "I gave the lad a couple days off. He was real exhausted, what with the riding and all. You know how it is."

Duasonh nodded, but Kildanor could sense the Baron was upset. So far no one had managed to find Jesgar Garinad, and given Drangar Ralgon's recent vision of the past, with strangers that followed him and caused him to kill his lover, he could hardly blame the mercenary for being upset.

"Where the bloody Scales is he?" Duasonh said.

"I think he wanted to see his brother," Nerran replied.

Duasonh waved for the servant. "Send someone to Garinad Iron Works; it's a smithy in the Merchant Quarter. He's to ask about Jesgar Garinad's whereabouts." To Kildanor he said, "Isn't that where Ralgon went after he gave you an earful?"

The Chosen nodded. "He wanted to meet an old friend and then visit the grave of his woman."

He felt sorry for Ralgon. He couldn't imagine what it was like to wake from a nightmare only to find reality was even worse than the dream. He had been to the house two years before, when word of the murder had reached the Palace. The woman had been chopped into pieces no bigger than two of his fingers held together. The watch had handled the investigation, and he had again been too busy with other affairs to follow the case.

Now, two years later, it was solved. In a very unlikely way, but solved nonetheless. No one was the wiser, for this answer just shoved more questions down the throats of everyone involved, but with the Chanastardhians so close, there wasn't the time to dwell on these things.

There was a knock on the door; a servant opened it, and in strode the witch Ealisaid. She was still clothed in plain tunic and shirt. With all her possessions seized by the city to reimburse the victims of the destruction she'd caused, she didn't have much of a choice.

"Ah, there you are," Duasonh said, sounding more jovial than Kildanor had heard him be in a few weeks. "Come on over and join us. Please."

Like the fare for everyone in Dunthiochagh, the supper was simple. Rationing had already begun, and Cumaill had placed the Palace's pantry under firm control. Kildanor agreed with the command, his stomach, however, did not. Porridge was nourishing, certainly, but too much of a good thing was still too much. It had been decades since he had lived on warrior's fare, and the only course he really appreciated was the fruit they were served for dessert.

Duasonh's reason for extending the invitation to Ealisaid was still for Nerran and himself to guess; the Baron hadn't revealed it yet. Neither Paladin nor Chosen broached the subject, and it was obvious from the Baron's precise questioning of the witch that Duasonh was equally uncertain about his motives.

"Bugger this!" Nerran shoved away his plate and looked at Cumaill. "What's all this business with her being here?" he asked, pointing at Ealisaid. Subtlety had never been one of his strengths, and his brusqueness now demonstrated this facet of his personality. Kildanor hid his smile behind a napkin.

"As I said before," the Baron began, "I want to use every weapon in my arsenal. Even with General Kerral's warriors adding to our numbers, the Chanastardhian army is still at least thrice as the size of ours."

"That if not more, mate," Nerran said. "Some scouts report Mireynh's forces outnumber us six to one."

"I know the figures," the Baron replied. "But I guessed this includes the supply train, camp followers, and such. If not, they still have to cross the walls."

"They just have to starve us out, Cumaill," Kildanor said. He didn't like being the cold voice of reality, but raising false hopes, he knew, never helped morale.

"You want to surrender?" Duasonh growled. "Besides, as far as our scouts can tell Shadowpass is open."

"An error he will remedy soon," Nerran said.

"So far, the river remains a barrier, and the hinterland remains free. To cross the Dunth he would have to send his army either east through the hills, or build barges," Kildanor added. "The river hasn't turned to ice in almost a hundred years."

"I know, old friend. Winter is coming, and even if Mireynh has his siege fortresses up and running by the time the first snow falls, he still has to house his warriors, man the castles and barriers, dispatch troops to cut us off from the north, and keep his troops happy. I think he's counting on a quick victory, possibly even open gates, or some such. Look at how Harail fell. He may expect resistance, but he still thinks there's a traitor here. We can use that to our advantage."

"How?" Nerran asked, but Kildanor could guess what Cumaill had in mind.

"I thought maybe we can get Mireynh to believe the doors are open to him," Duasonh said. "Not during the day, of course, but..."

"At night," the Paladin finished the sentence. "Bloody brilliant, except for one or two tiny problems. First: how do we know the signal Jathain was supposed to give Mireynh? And second: once the gates are open how do we close them again?"

"Your late cousin's rooms were destroyed by fire," Kildanor said. He paused and scratched his stubbly chin. An idea was forming, but as the thoughts tumbled through his mind he doubted the suggestion would be welcomed.

"We know that," said Nerran, "what's on your mind?"

His idea was beyond insane; no one would allow a priest of Jainagath to call back the traitor's spirit. "Never mind."

"Come on, lad, spill it."

"I know this face you're making, mate," said Duasonh. "You have one of your harebrained ideas. Let's hear it."

Kildanor grinned. "You know me too well, but if you think Nerran's little cleansing of the Church of Eanaigh caused an uproar, I doubt you like what I have in mind."

"Now that sounds exciting," the Baron replied.

The Chosen looked over to Ealisaid. She had remained calm, but her face displayed various emotions. He thought he saw doubt, resolve, and fear. His gaze wandered over to Nerran, whose jovial manner had suddenly changed to confusion.

"You can't be serious," the Paladin said.

"Serious about what?" Duasonh demanded.

"Lad, there's a reason why the afterlife shouldn't be trifled with."

He sighed. "I don't see another way. We need to find out what the signal for Mireynh was."

"But to ask a Deathmask for help..."

Kildanor looked at the Baron who sat back in his chair, deep in thought. "What do you think, Cumaill?"

"Is there another way?"

"Not that I know of," the Chosen replied.

"What about the taboo?" Nerran muttered.

"It's not like we would be asking one of the Deathmasks to turn the dead Jathain lose on the world."

"Deathmasks?" Ealisaid asked. The three men looked at her. "The order still exists?"

"It's not like they can die, eh?" Nerran said. "Yes, they still take care of burials and stuff, and they vowed not to raise a single person back to life again."

"Aside from their dead," Duasonh added.

Kildanor knew what bothered Nerran. "Don't tell me you believe this nonsense!"

"Of course not," retorted the Paladin.

"Then why so worried?"

"Have any of you ever dealt with a Deathmask?"

"Only when someone had to be buried," Duasonh replied before the Chosen could. He nodded. Ealisaid did the same.

"You take the corpse to a Deathmask and pay him... her... it."

"That's not dealing with one of them, lads and lass. You pay the Deathmask and that's that, but have you ever tried to speak with the dead?"

Kildanor and the other two shook their heads. "Have you?" he asked.

"Aye, I have. Cost me part of my sanity, but aye. And before you ask when, where, and why, I tell you to bugger off. It's none of your business!"

The Chosen realized Nerran had contacted his parents to find out who was responsible for their murder. "Well, it's either that or try to guess the signal, so I say we talk to a Deathmask."

"You talk to one, sure, go ahead. The next time I see one is when I have to bury another lad," said Nerran

Duasonh looked at Kildanor. "Will you go?"

Kildanor shrugged. "Guess I can ask for a favor. The Deathmasks should honor the request of one of the father's servants."

"Well, lad, they honored mine as well."

"Not to be insulting, but you're a servant of the Church, Nerran. There is a difference."

"Whatever," the Paladin grumbled. "What are we going to do should our mighty Chosen manage to squeeze the necessary information from the traitor's spirit?"

"That depends on our Phoenix Wizardess," said the Baron. "Lady Ealisaid, I've read about what your kind could do. First, will you fight on our side? And second, can you do as I'll ask?"

The witch had paled during the conversation. Obviously she had thought about such a proposal before, but the consequences still frightened her. "Lord Baron, of course I will fight for my home," she replied. Then she cleared her throat several times, yet more proof of her nervousness. "I am not sure I can wield magic as effectively as a full-fledged Wizard, but I certainly will try." She swallowed once then continued, "What do you want me to do, milord?"

Kildanor had no idea what Cumaill had planned, but since his friend appeared as giddy as a schoolboy, he was certain it was something nasty for the Chanastardhians.

"Well, let me ask a question first," said the Baron. "How well can you cast... images... illusions?"

"Easily," Ealisaid replied. "What do you have in mind?"

"Oh, merely the entire southern wall devoid of warriors and the slow opening of the gate," Duasonh said merrily, clapping his hands and giggling. The Chosen wondered if his friend knew what he was getting into.

Nerran, having obviously recovered from whatever memories plagued him, gasped then slapped his hands onto the table and began to laugh. "Bloody brilliant! That's really bloody brilliant, lad!"

"If she can do it," Kildanor said. He liked the plan, and hated to be the voice of caution, but somebody had to be. The witch had said she hadn't completed her training and lacked confidence after the incident that had gotten her imprisoned in the first place.

"Well, Wizardess, can you accomplish this?" Duasonh scrutinized her. There were only a few people in Cherkont and Boughaighr who could endure the Baron's stare for long. The Chosen had seen established merchants cringe under this glare, a trait Cumaill had inherited from his father and grandfather. Kildanor had witnessed Bodhrein Duasonh, Cumaill's grandfather, stare down a delegation of elves right after the Heir War, so he knew the Baron would not blink for a very long time.

Ealisaid tried to reply, but her mouth merely opened and closed again and again. Kildanor caught a glance of Nerran shaking his head in delight. He shared the sentiment; this cat-and-mouse game was amusing.

"I can try," she finally said.

"Trying is like emptying a chamber pot against a storm," Nerran grumbled. "You get nothing but shit and piss."

"I will do it."

"Good..."

"However, my Lord Baron, I need to prepare things, and for that I will have to use magic. Thus, for your plan to succeed, you need to lift your ban even before the enemy arrives."

Kildanor saw Duasonh's face sag and couldn't help but say, "Oh, don't tell me you didn't see that coming!"

"Curious," Nerran muttered. He turned and saw the Paladin gaze after the Wizardess.

"What's that?"

"Oh, just that our lad over there seems to be quite smitten with her," the other replied.

"And she likes the attention."

"You're serious?" Cumaill asked.

"Aye."

"You, Culain," Duasonh said, and the guard came running.

"My Lord?" the man saluted.

"Should she ask, I want you to assist the Lady Wizardess in whatever way she deems appropriate. If she doesn't ask, you will guard her door nonetheless, understood?"

The young man bobbed his head, grinning like an idiot.

"I didn't quite hear that, son." Now Duasonh was being a right bastard; Kildanor couldn't suppress a chuckle.

"Yes, sir, my Lord Baron," Culain said, saluting. At the door he almost stumbled over his feet.

"Give the lad a break, you old bastard," Nerran said, chuckling.

CHAPTER 58

"Thank you," Drangar said and bowed to the cemetery's Deathmask. "I think I'll find the grave."

"She'll rest easier now you're here, sir," the priest of Jainagath said, his voice muffled by the thin brass mask that hid his features and gave the priests their name.

Would Hesmera really know he had been at her grave, he wondered. Had she forgiven him when he couldn't? Was she in the Great Hall of the gods, feasting with the dead?

"Yes," the Deathmask said.

Early in his life Drangar had learned not to question a priest's ability to know, and the Deathmask's answer reinforced this lesson. He turned to Rob. "Would you mind waiting here? I want to be alone with her."

The watchman shook his head. "Of course not."

The cemetery was not for villeins, and most freeborn. Nobles cared for their dead vassals with little more than a sack for a coffin and a few shovels of earth for a grave. Most freeborn could not afford more than an urn for their deceased's ashes, which was put into a hole next to hundreds of older urns. If the allotted space in a cemetery was full, the remains were dug out, the ceramic reused, and the ashes given back to the earth, fertilizer for the fields.

Here, however, things were quite different. Marble statues lined the paved walkways, grass and shrubs were well tended, and clearly marked flowerbeds occupied the spaces surrounding marble memorials. Next to the massive crypts, the final resting places for the rich and noble, were two-yard-long slabs of stone let into the earth, graves of valued but poor freeborn. Most of these stones, like the statues guarding the crypts, were chiseled into the likeness of the deceased, and Drangar couldn't help but wonder what Hesmera's marker would show. Oil-lamps lit the way, held by marble arms, if the statue was human, or teeth, if the sculpture represented an animal.

The night was cold, as well it should be. Winter was coming, and he felt the chill more pronounced than he had in the past two years. Sure, his clothes were different, but although he could almost see frost forming on blades of grass, it couldn't be as cold as the water he had washed in, even in the midst of winter. As he neared Hesmera's grave, Drangar finally knew what it was to grieve, forgive, and let go.

Before him a marble sarcophagus rested on a small mount decorated with flowerbeds. The hill was circular and the plot was divided into three parts by winding paths of yellow stone. Lesganagh's symbol as Hesmera's people knew it.

Drangar looked at the tomb; one end of the coffin was engraved:

Hesmera
Warrior
Woman
Friend

For a moment, he didn't know what to say or do. Then he walked up one of the paths, his knees trembling, and as he neared the top he saw her likeness chiseled in minute detail into the marble lid. She lay there, unlike the other frescoes and statues, not in stately robes, but in plate and mail, sword pommel underneath her chin, hands clasped to the weapons hilt, eyes forward. Her hair seemed to blow in a breeze and her lips curved in the smile he loved.

Drangar knelt, put one hand on the coffin's lid, and waited. He wanted to remain here, close to her; he wanted to... "Love," he whispered, "I'm sorry. I didn't know. I had no hand in it." He shook his head. "It sounds stupid, I know, what with me wielding the sword and all, but I... I think I wasn't even inside my body when it happened. I can't really explain it. You were there; you saw me, you saw the sword. Gods, I swear I will find those responsible and make them pay."

Peace, he felt calmer than ever before, and knew he had been forgiven. It was as if Hesmera had heard him from the gods' great abode in the heavens and told him she forgave. Drangar clasped the lid. "I miss you," he whispered, but what he really meant was that he was ready to forgive himself as well. The guilt had stopped raging after the spirit had taken him into the past, but now it was gone. He stood, unsure what to do now. Bow? No, that didn't feel right. His vow was made; he would find those behind the killing and make them pay. His tears had sealed this promise over the last two years.

"Good bye," he said, turned, and walked down the winding path. The trip back to the cemetery entrance went fast, and he didn't feel as cold as before. Had he been afraid? He thought a few moments then nodded. Aye, he had been afraid. Afraid his heart would shatter, and join his already fraying mind in an even deeper abyss. Instead he was free. The past was the past, aye, but now he knew what it was, and could look back without ghosts rising up from the mists.

Rob was standing a few paces away from the Deathmask. Drangar couldn't blame him, the priests of Jainagath made everyone nervous. His business with the cleric wasn't done. This man, if it was a man, would know who had paid for Hesmera's grave.

Hesmera's grave. It came easier now, the thought she was dead. It no longer filled him with regret and self-loathing. He was not responsible for her death! He would find those who were, and make them pay.

"It seems you have found what you were looking for," the Deathmask said. "To find peace one must face the past. Loved ones gone ahead to the Bailey Majestic, they're waiting, they're patient, and give us peace when we need it most."

"Aye," he replied. "I have one last question."

"Yes?"

"Who gave her the burial she deserved?"

"The Ladies Neena and Leonore Cahill, sir."

He turned to Rob. "Know them?"

The watchman nodded. "I'll take you there tomorrow."

Drangar turned back to the Deathmask and bowed. "Thank

you, kind sir. I wish I had money to donate, but, alas, my purse is lost. When I recover it…" He fell silent, unsure what to say. Even the apology that came to mind sounded empty.

The priest shook his head, "You don't have to donate anything, ever, sir."

Arching an eyebrow, he shrugged then bowed again. "Nonetheless, you have my thanks."

"Very well, sir. Good night."

They left the graveyard, and Drangar had to hurry to keep up with Rob. After they had rounded another corner, Rob finally slowed his pace to a walk. The former mercenary felt different, not carefree, but certainly freer than he had in ages, and he was famished. They found a tavern, the Citadel, and sat at an unoccupied table.

"I hope you don't mind paying. I'm really broke." He didn't like to ask for charity, never had but the alternative would have been to return to the Palace, and for the moment he preferred the company of an old comrade.

Rob chuckled and said, "Mate, that's what friends are for. Today it's fish for supper at home, and you're the perfect excuse for my not being there."

"Married?" Drangar asked, surprised. "When? Who?"

"About a year ago. The lass who did laundry for us."

He thought for a moment; it was hard to recall names from a time he had tried to forget. "Meghan? That's the only name I can remember."

"Meghan, aye."

"Beautiful lass! Congratulations!"

A serving woman came and took their orders. The selection was limited due to rationing, and both settled for meat, bread, and turnips. When Drangar ordered milk, Rob frowned. "Still no booze?"

He shook his head. "I'll never touch another drop! Even if I didn't kill her, alcohol makes me do strange things. I don't ever want to go down that road again."

"Suit yourself," the watchman said. "I'll have an ale."

The woman left and returned shortly with their mugs. Rob looked at him and raised his drink. "To old friendships."

He returned the toast, "May we walk those dark paths together." It was odd, he thought as their mugs clunked against each other. A month ago, he would have sat in his cabin in the wild, listening for wolves, the only two beings to talk to a dog and a horse. It had been a long time; he'd almost forgotten how to make conversation.

Fortunately, Rob spoke after having a long pull from his tankard. "So, what will you do now?"

He took a sip of milk, wiped his mustache, and brushed his hair back. "Honestly? Aside from talking to Hesmera's friends, I have no idea." Rob's frown made him laugh. "This isn't typical watch-work, mate. Any traces the assassins might have left are gone by now. I don't know where to start."

"Tell me again of this dream of yours."

When he was done with his tale, Rob said, "We could try the house."

"Which house?"

"That hovel you talked about."

"You know how tenants change in places like that. Same as with the booth on the marketplace. Any traces are long gone."

Before Rob could reply, their supper was served. The watchman sampled the meat. "Not bad, but…"

"It needs more salt," Drangar finished the sentence.

"Indeed!"

Both laughed, and Rob waved the waitress over and ordered the salt. Drangar had to admit the meat lacked some, helped himself to a bit, and then joined his friend in devouring the supper.

Neither of them spoke. The former mercenary was lost in thought, trying to find any angle from which he could set out after the murderers. As he had told Rob, he couldn't. Any traces were gone, which left him with only one possible solution. "I need to catch the next bastard who tries to kill me," he muttered through meat and bread still in his mouth.

Rob swallowed his mouthful and looked at him. "You're crazy. No, wait, let me rephrase that: you're fucking crazy!"

"It's the only way."

"You're going to sit there and wait for some bastard to slide a knife into your gut?"

Drangar shook his head. No, they wouldn't come after him with a knife. He could barely remember what had happened in the Shadowpeaks, but knew the murderers were not keen on just killing him. There was more to it. "They won't just knife me down, mate."

Rob took a pull from his beer and frowned. "What? They gonna slice and dice you first?"

"No," he replied, brushing back his hair. "They need me for some sort of ritual."

"Ritual? What the Scales are you talking about?"

"They almost managed to off me, in the Shadowpeaks." He tried to recall what had happened. "Poisoned me, then got me to a... a circle with a fire... only when the Chosen showed up did they slice me open."

"So, you intend to let them poison you again and then, while you're under the venom's effect, you try to capture them instead? Good, that's gonna work!"

"Of course not! I'll need some people to ambush..." Drangar fell silent and looked across the room. There, at the other end of the taproom, sat Duasonh's thief! "What the fuck is he doing here?" he growled.

The bastard occupied a table with another man who had his back turned. From the look of his face, the youth had spent quite a while drinking, and Drangar was torn between staying where he was and ignoring the man, or shaking the bloody truth out of him.

Rob turned to find out what he was looking at. "That's the fellow who's spying on you, eh?"

"True enough," he growled. As he rose from his chair, he felt his friend's firm hand on his right arm.

"Don't, mate," Rob hissed. "You can give the lad his thrashing later."

"I just want to ask the bastard some questions."

"You can ask him later; do you think he'd even remember his mother, judging from the mugs before him?"

The thief looked rather pissed, Drangar had to admit. Even if he managed to grab and beat the man, he doubted the spy could be more senseless than he already was. He sat back down. "Bloody Scales." He had no idea what the man was up to, but he was certain it didn't bode well.

CHAPTER 59

Ealisaid sat on her cot and stared at the far wall. She had no idea if she could deliver the magic Baron Duasonh demanded. Certainly, she was proficient in casting illusions, but never before had she attempted to control a space as vast as the city's defenses. Intent on the wall, she stood and headed for the door.

In the corridor beyond a pair of guards still watched over her. She couldn't blame the Baron for being cautious, it was only prudent, and part of her feared her victims' families would still avenge the deaths, despite the verdict. It also reminded her she still was a prisoner. As her eyes adjusted to the dim corridor, she noticed to her delight that the guard on the left was the same man whom Kildanor had pointed out earlier, the one who had regarded her with such longing intensity. The cute one.

"Join me for a moment," she asked him.

For a moment, the warrior glanced about like a cornered rabbit. Then he said, "Have I offended you, ma'am?"

Shaking her head, Ealisaid stepped aside. He entered the room, frowned, took a step back, and looked at the far wall. "Where's the cupboard? And the window?"

She felt elated. The first success. Now for the difficult part. She had to maintain her focus. "Shake me, do anything to distract me."

"Ma'am?"

"Just do as I ask, please."

The warrior obeyed. He grabbed her by the shoulders, shook her, pinched her, and tickled her. She squirmed under his tickles, but her focus didn't waver, the illusory wall remained.

"Good! Now surprise me."

For a moment the guardsman just stood there, pondering what she wanted him to do. He blushed, frowned, started to say something.

"Surprise me," Ealisaid encouraged.

He shrugged, and then he did surprise her.

As she returned his kiss, the image of the plain wall vanished. The man had indeed done as she asked. For a moment she was unsure of how to proceed. On the one hand she had to continue with the illusions; on the other hand, she didn't mind kissing him. She freed herself of the man's lips, felt a blush creeping onto her face, and said, "Good, please stay. I have more testing to do."

The warrior stared. "More... testing?"

"Yes." Ealisaid looked about the room and thought she was ready for the next... test. She concentrated on the image of a small vale in the Shadowpeaks. When the picture was firm in her mind, she made the room change.

Surprised, the warrior took a step back and looked around, but her hands remained on his waist. "What the Scales..." the man stammered.

"Relax, we're still in the room," she said. If she could maintain the illusion while the guard kissed her, she would be one step closer to Duasonh's goal. Not that this was the only reason she wanted the... testing to continue. It had been far too long, figuratively and literally, and she yearned for comfort. "Now distract me."

The warrior didn't have to be asked twice. Even though she felt giddy and more than a little excited, Ealisaid turned a great portion of her attention to the imaginary vale surrounding them. She opened her eyes. Of course, the first thing she saw was the guard's angular face. Beyond him was the little waterfall that fed the pond just as she remembered. She wanted to see more, discover how well the image was holding against this pleasurable test. Leaning into the guardsman, she turned him, kissing his stubbly jaw line so that his face less obstructed her view.

The warrior, not knowing her intentions, merely reacted

and began kissing her neck. For a moment the imaginary tree line fogged over as her body responded to the gentle bites on her collar. Her deep breath became a gasp as she tried to retain focus. The illusion was what mattered, not her roused lust, she told herself. Her body was taking over. Ealisaid forced her hammering heart to slow down despite her yearning. The imaginary vale stopped wavering and again the illusion was perfect.

With regret she pulled back from the guard, panting, and unsure of her desires. She wanted the walls around the gate to appear empty, the gate open, but she also wanted this man whom she had just met.

"What's wrong, milady?"

"Nothing."

"I... apologize. I thought you wanted me to distract you."

She couldn't stop the giggle. "I don't even know your name."

"Culain, milady."

Again, the giggle. It was followed by a grumble. She felt like an innocent girl again, and wasn't sure whether she liked it or not. Seeing his scowl, Ealisaid stepped forward and put a hand on his chest. "You're doing well, Culain." A mischievous grin formed on her lips. "This is an exceptional distraction."

The warrior chuckled. "Aye, milady. That it is." He frowned. "Do you want me to leave?"

"No!" she said. She felt herself blush again as she continued, "There's more testing to be done. And call me Ealisaid. Please."

"As you wish," he replied with a bow. "What are you doing here anyway?"

"You mean aside from behaving like a maid in spring?" she asked, the blush slightly receding.

"Aye."

"I need to see if I can maintain a big illusion whilst being distracted."

"That's all?" Culain frowned.

"Primarily, yes, but I do like this distraction." She leaned forward and kissed him. "I like it a lot."

When they pulled apart again, she saw Culain smile for the first time. It was easy to fall into his green eyes, and for a moment all she wanted was to stare at him, drown in his eyes. No one had really treated her kindly ever since she had blasted into this new world, and this man seemed like an anchor to hold her. She kissed him briefly then looked at the vale that still surrounded them.

"Either we have to retreat to a bigger space or this room will soon appear very packed," she said.

"I also have to get back to my post," Culain added.

"Can't you just ask for a replacement?" Ealisaid couldn't believe herself, but she pouted. She hadn't thought it possible to find solace in this world, but here her peace of mind was in the form of this rough warrior.

"Hmm..." Culain stood before her, his hands in hers. "You said you need to make complex images, right?"

"Aye."

"Could you let me stand guard outside with Domnall while maintaining this vale, maybe a few birds, a bit of rain, and trying to stay focused?"

Again, she giggled. "You're bad."

"Just tryin' to be helpful, milady," he replied with a curt bow. "I swear I'll do my best to distract you."

"You'd better," she said, beaming at him.

The moss they lay on felt real, as did the gentle rain that drizzled down. Her focus, what little remained of it, was sorely tested. Culain kept up his promise. Bites, kisses, gentle licks eased the scratching of his stubble on her neck, face and shoulders. Ealisaid huddled against him, enjoying his breath on her skin. At times she felt helpless against her desires, but Culain's reminder to concentrate pulled her toes back to the ground time and again.

As her excitement rose, her focus fell, and when his hands undid her bodice the illusion flickered for just a moment. Immediately Culain stopped his advance. Ealisaid took a gasping breath, steadied herself and the images around them.

"Too much distraction?" he whispered in her ear.

"No," she said, leaning against him.

If Domnall had seen his fellow warrior's image waver, she couldn't tell, all remained silent outside. Her breathing hastened when Culain's hands slid over her skin, and she fought to retain her focus as he found her breasts.

"Birds now," he whispered.

She could almost feel him smile into her hair. Biting her lip as he pinched a nipple, Ealisaid conjured songbirds into the trees around them. It came so easy, the magic. Nothing had to be forced, unlike what she had done in her house, and the street. Even though part of her was distracted and aroused by the warrior caressing her; the man's gentleness was like a balm. As she felt his touch, sometimes soft sometimes rough, she felt the magic flowing through her in a way she had never experienced before. Magic, it seemed, was more than raw power; it was emotion, desire, love.

Somehow Culain did what no one else had done before. Ealisaid felt more at ease with herself and the magic she had been taught to master. Maybe this was what the hibernation was supposed to do? To become enveloped by the strength magic truly was. She turned to him. "Don't stop now," she said a smile on her lips. Whether her plan succeeded or not, she would find out in the morning.

Culain's hands probed lower, his touch at once tickling and light as a feather. The magic followed her feelings, rose when she did. She fought the urge to mount him immediately, resisted the desire to force events into motion. Magic had to be nudged, not pushed. It was enough to feel and anticipate, and expect, for the knowledge that things would happen was almost enough.

Almost enough. When his hands reached her womanhood, she felt a barrier break. It was natural to just turn and reach out, to kiss, caress, and love, and the magic did what she desired it to do.

The cemetery should already be closed to the public, but Kildanor knew the Deathmask would be there. Jainagath's priests hardly left their posts, so why should this one be an exception? Only during the midsummer and midwinter celebrations did the clergy members mingle with mortals. They didn't eat, drink, or sleep, and it was rumored that the undying Deathmasks consumed the blood of the dead. He knew such tales were wrong, but the priests' appearances gave rise to much speculation. Gray robes, boots, hood, and the featureless mask seemed to be their sole attire.

The Chosen neared the ornate gate and the rather subdued temple that huddled against the cemetery wall. Standing in the arched entrance, he saw from a distance, were Drangar Ralgon and a man of the watch. They were talking to the Deathmask. He didn't want the man to think he was spying as well. Young Garinad's strange behavior had already roused the man's anger and he didn't want to add to it.

After a quick exchange, Ralgon left the others standing in the pale light of the gate's lantern while his companion fidgeted near the Deathmask. The watchman was clearly uncomfortable, and Kildanor could hardly blame him. Deathmasks were unnerving, even to him. It wasn't the first time he wondered whether the priests were truly undead, living corpses. Some people were frightened by the thought of walking and talking dead, but to him undeath was merely another state of being. Deep down, Kildanor felt a kinship to the priests of Jainagath. Neither of them could die naturally, which made both, Chosen and Deathmasks, alike.

A movement to his left halted his musings. Thankfully lamps attached to walls and posts lighted the streets here, and he discerned Jesgar Garinad's huge form hugging a building's shadowy entrance. What the Scales was he doing? Neither Nerran nor Duasonh had ordered Ralgon observed; the Upholder had cleared the man; his innocence was fact.

He decided to interrogate Jesgar, crossed the street, and stood before the spy in a matter of heartbeats. If Garinad was surprised, he didn't show it; he didn't react at all. What was going on? "Jesgar?" the Chosen asked, but the young man acted as if the street was still empty. Intent on whatever happened at the cemetery gate, the thief didn't even notice Kildanor's hand. Waving didn't get his attention, and neither did the gentle shaking of arm or shoulder. Something was decidedly wrong with the lad.

Movement at the cemetery caught Garinad's attention, and he moved closer to the gate. Kildanor followed. He heard

Ralgon's question and the Deathmask's reply, and once Jesgar had heard the names "Neena and Leonore Cahill" the spy took off at a quick pace.

For a moment he didn't know what to do. Should he follow Garinad or should he proceed with his task? It only took a few moments to decide, and so he remained near the cemetery, out of view of the gate. Jesgar had picked a nice spot for his eavesdropping. He remained in the shadows after Ralgon and the watchman had left the area. His thoughts were leaping from the upcoming interrogation of a spirit to Jesgar's strange behavior. What was going on?

"No!" Kildanor hissed. "Jathain's spirit, the defense, that's what matters, the boy can wait." He doubted Garinad was a threat; the youth was harmless. Jesgar had to wait, Jathain's information was more important. Yet there was this strange lack of awareness; it seemed as if the youth was sleepwalking. He'd have to talk to the sorceress about this.

Finally, he left his shadowed hideaway and approached the cemetery gate. As soon as he reached the archway the Deathmask stood before him. Jainagath's priests were silent, he had to admit that.

"Greetings, Chosen."

"And a good evening to you."

"Humor, how... nice. An attempt at levity," the Deathmask said. Before he could reply, the priest continued, "Are you prepared to pay the price, Chosen of Lesganagh?"

"What price?"

"Withdrawing even the lowest soul from the halls of the gods is costly. You know even the lowest have a purpose, their task is everything to them. Unlike those who feast and celebrate, those who can easily be distracted, the serving spirits need to be ensnared, lured.

"Some spirits are easier to catch than others. The lure is emotion, love, fear, despair, anger, hate. Which feeling is necessary depends on the person you want to call back. The one you seek to interrogate is most likely a spittoon, or if he is lucky a dancer. The price for him is high. He won't help you voluntarily, so your sacrifice is for his capture and the torment of his soul. Are you willing to pay the price, Kildanor of the Chosen?"

He frowned. "My master is your master's lord and father. There should be an exception!"

"Why?" the Deathmask asked.

"I am Chosen!"

"Death makes few exceptions. Do you want the soul of Jathain the traitor before you and willing to answer your questions, yes or no?"

"What will you take?" He hated this lack of control, wished there was another way.

"There is none."

"Get out of my head!" he snarled. The Deathmask remained silent. "What say you? Answer me! What will you take? What do I have to give you to ensnare Jathain?"

"Whatever is necessary."

A cold shiver ran down his back. The priest's reply was meaningless. What did it take to capture an unwilling soul? "What will you take?" he asked again. "What is this price?"

"Memories, feelings," was the reply. "To capture any soul, you need to use bait. For those who celebrate with the gods it is simple: feed them love and they come. For the maggots, the filth, those of whom Lliania's Scales did not approve the lure is different. I can explain this again, if you want me to, but the price will be the same."

"You won't take my memories?"

"No, merely feelings, dark emotions for dark souls. It's simple, Chosen. Symmetry in life and death."

"Very well, you leave me no choice." His feelings made him who he was; his anger fueled him in battle. Now he had to surrender all he had left of the past, and he wasn't even sure he could get the answers needed from Jathain's spirit. What would the priest take? Would it be something that made him Kildanor? Who would he be after the summoning? There were very few things that could still make him afraid. This, the danger of losing his memories, was one. In essence he was his past. Would he still be the same? "I'm afraid," he admitted to the Deathmask and himself.

"To fear is to be human, Chosen." He was about to protest when the priest continued. "You are human, even if you are loath to admit it! And you will remain who you are, maybe more so. The gods know the answer. Are you willing to pay?"

"Yes."

"Good," the Deathmask said, turned away from him, and walked toward the skull-adorned chapel.

Kildanor, feeling glummer with every step, followed.

His return to the Palace felt strange, almost as if his body was not his own. The Chosen didn't know what the Deathmask had taken. He didn't feel any different, in essence, but something was gone. His memories were intact; he could recall his youth. He and his brothers, Ethain and Ganaedor, playing in the fields and woods that had surrounded their farm. Nothing seemed missing, but some parts were as if he knew of them, as if he had read them in a book. Danachamain he remembered as a good man who had gone off and fallen to some magic. The Heir War, a conflict of wizard against wizard in which he had fought. The demonic invasion that had followed the Wizard War, in which he had defended the fledging nation of Danastaer. It all was there, he knew what had happened, knew of battles, friends who had died. If the Deathmask had taken any price, Kildanor couldn't remember. What counted was that Jathain had told him the signal to the Chanastardhians.

For a moment he thought of young Garinad, but tracking down the errant spy had to wait. The information he had now would at least give pause to Chanastardh's advance. He whistled a tune as he walked down Shadowpeak Street, enjoying the chill night air like he always had.

Duasonh's study was uncommonly cold; not as cold as the air out in the open, but compared to the warmth that usually permeated the place, it was quite chilly. "You rationed the firewood as well?" Kildanor asked as he entered.

"Aye, says he wants the people to know he's with 'em."

He spotted Nerran huddled in layers of blankets near the fireplace. "You're a Paladin, man. Show some dignity!"

"This place is still warm, lad. You should see our quarters. Cumaill had the staff close down all fires, except the kitchen and this miserable excuse." The aging warrior pointed at the feeble glow. "Besides, not everyone is as young as you. Bah, you know what I mean, so sod off!"

"Where is he?" Kildanor walked to Duasonh's chair. He plopped into the seat and put his feet up on the table.

Nerran turned and frowned. "He ain't gonna like that."

"He has to cheer up some," he replied.

The Paladin squinted then sat up, a few layers of cloth falling away from his shoulders. "So, you paid the price, eh?"

"Aye, can't recall what it was though."

"Took me years to figure out."

"And?"

"I don't grieve my parents' death anymore."

"Oh," Kildanor said.

"It's not as simple as that. If you don't grieve, you can't really feel angry, which in turn makes revenge sort of pointless," Nerran explained. "What drove your wagon?"

He thought for a moment then said, "I don't know."

"Makes life simpler, yet takes something you need, or think you need. I don't know."

The Chosen frowned. "So, you didn't kill the Eanaighists out of vengeance?"

"Nah, I'm at peace with what happened to my parents; that's life, whole circle and all. And before you ask again, I did what was necessary. Buggers were fucking things up, and right now we need the Lord of War more than turnips, eh?"

Ethain, Ganaedor, his brothers, he remembered them, could recall their betrayal, but there was nothing, no pain, no hatred, just the cold facts. He didn't care one way or the other; his brothers were lost to him, like his parents, his sister, all were gone. He was Kildanor, Chosen.

Nerran winked at him, "Your worry lines are gone, lad. Guess he took a whole bit away from you. It won't return either, no worries there."

Duasonh stormed into the room, halted the Chosen's answer, slammed the door, and growled, "Get outta my chair!"

Kildanor abandoned the seat and leaned against the bookcase. The Baron sagged down and heaved a heavy sigh. "What the Scales is this Garinad person thinking?"

"What's that?" Nerran said. "What's he done now?"

"Nobody knows."

"I saw him near the cemetery tonight," Kildanor supplied. "He was watching Ralgon."

"What's his business with Ralgon?" Duasonh snarled.

"Didn't you send some lad to see him, Cumaill?"

"Aye, he wasn't in. His brother and sister-in-law said he'd been out drinking all night. Drank himself silly, they say. Couldn't get anything coherent out of him."

"He seemed pretty together when I saw him."

"You didn't stop him?" the Baron asked.

"Wanted to. He took off when Ralgon left the graveyard."

"Why would Jesgar go after the Scythe?" Nerran scratched his beard.

"Scythe?" Kildanor and Duasonh asked in unison.

"Yea, you know, that's what they called Ralgon. Cumaill, can you get the bloody servants to put more wood in the fire. I'm freezing! Anyway, the lad mowed down his opponents, like, you know, a scythe."

"Another bit of useless information," the Baron muttered.

"Aye, but does your man have any better?" Nerran grinned.

"No, and he left the Garinad smithy after nightfall to report. He's back there now." Duasonh turned to Kildanor. "What about Jathain?"

"I know how he was supposed to signal Mireynh."

"Splendid! We can lay the trap."

"If she can do it, lad," Nerran added.

Duasonh was about to reply when their room transformed into a lush garden, complete with rosebushes, gurgling wells, songbirds and a few fruit trees. "What the bloody Scales?" the Baron uttered and looked around, astonished.

"I think the lass can do it," Nerran replied, grinning.

CHAPTER 60

Twentieth of Chill 1475 K.C

As the sun's first rays broke through the canopy of clouds, a scout sped toward the main body of Mireynh's army. Anne Cirrain looked at the High General and smiled faintly when he gave her what he believed to be an understanding wink.

He was happy with their progress; a forced march was exhausting, but it could not be denied that the warriors were anxious to do battle. Dunthiochagh, he hoped, would certainly offer the first real resistance in this, so far, rather uneventful campaign.

Preliminary reports indicated that, in stark contrast to the main body of the Danastaerian forces, which had scattered in the first assault on the once thriving kingdom, Baron Cumaill Duasonh was prepared. A large force of his troops was supposedly gathered in Dunthiochagh. Some of Duasonh's warriors were still manning the bastions in the army's back, but Mireynh wasn't overly worried. Several scores of warriors each sealed off the fortresses; none would harass their rear.

What bothered him were reports that ragtag groups of once routed warbands were flocking to the Baron's banner. Two royal flags flying alongside Boughaighr and Higher Cherkont's colors on top of Dragoncrest Castle supplied ample proof of this. The other strongholds only flew the standard of the twin baronies, and with sixty warriors blocking Dragoncrest's only exit they didn't have to worry about either the Chosen or whatever remnants of Lerainh's army were hiding behind the massive walls.

Duasonh's troops were rested, but Urgraith Mireynh was no novice at leading warriors. At night he ordered extra rations of ale and wine, keeping morale high. Happy warriors were good warriors. Despite the cold that penetrated even the thickest coat, the songs the warriors sung as they marched with the drums' loud thump providing rhythm showed that his army truly was in high spirits.

Mireynh looked at Anne Cirrain who sat comfortably and confident in her saddle. He still couldn't believe such a woman came from a rebel family; truth be told, he doubted the High Advisor's word that House Cirrain's uprising was due to their traitorous nature. Her manner with warriors and warleaders alike was respectful, and almost everybody liked her. Still, his orders were clear: permit no message to her or House Cirrain's warriors, and take her hostage should circumstances require it. Much like his army, he liked the woman, but sympathy for a rebel noble would only result in his own family's execution.

"Report!" Cirrain glanced at the scout as the man brought his horse to a halt in front of the two.

"The Baron's scouts have located us, sir!" The man petted the neck of his exhausted horse, and looked at Mireynh. "Our vanguard was unable to catch all of their lookouts."

"No matter," the High General said. The traitor was still inside Dunthiochagh, and come nightfall, once the gate was taken, Duasonh would have to surrender the city. If not, the men were itching for a proper fight. He had been assured the South Gate would be open and the walls manned by warriors who'd then abandon their posts. Besieging a half-taken city would be easy.

Urgraith Mireynh looked at his adjutant and smiled grimly. "They are warned now." Turning to the scout, he asked, "Any horse?"

"Only scouts as far as I could tell, sir."

Again, he looked at his aide. "Any sightings of heavy horse nearby? I don't want to be caught between hammer and anvil. The setup is perfect for it."

"No, sir," Anne Cirrain said. "None."

"That doesn't mean anything," he muttered. "How long until we reach the city?"

"We are bound to reach the Dunth-plain before noon, sir," another warleader said.

"Good," the general said. He rubbed his left hand across his face, and closed his eyes, thinking. Then he looked at his warleaders. "Slow down the pace; if we arrive on the plain in the afternoon it's early enough."

"Yes, sir!" the nobles shouted, turned their steeds and hurried to carry out his order. Only Anne Cirrain and the scout remained.

"Go get some rest, son, you've done well. See that your horse gets rubbed down and has some hay. I expect you back for duty at noon." Mireynh waved the man away and looked at the road ahead, watching as his warriors changed their pace. The thunder of the drums altered as well, and soon even trumpets began to play a slow, lamenting tune. The warriors sang along and for a moment the general thought himself in a temple with thousands of voices forming an immense choir.

He turned his attention to Cirrain. "As soon as we reach the plain I want several parties to scout the area around Dunthiochagh. We have to cut them off. Have them look for suitable sites; if need be we will set up fortresses along each road. Also," he added, "have them look for fords in the Dunth to the east. There's only one road leading out of the city that way, and we must block every access, if need be."

"If need be, sir?"

"Aye, my guess is we won't have to use any of them, but circumstances may change." He looked at the troops passing him. "Best be prepared, eh, Cirrain?"

"You think we'll take the city tonight?"

"At least half the city, if the traitor does his job, aye," he replied, confident.

"Traitor, sir?" the woman asked.

"Do you think we would've taken Harail in a day if their defenses had not been weakened?"

"But I thought..."

"I don't like them?" He felt his smirk turn into a pained mask. "I don't, and the one helping us here will be executed once we have the city, same as in Harail."

"Sir?"

Gods this woman was dense. He liked her, but at times she just lacked the understanding of what it took to win. "This is war. We fight to win, remember that, Cirrain. Everything is allowed, so I use the traitors and then get rid of them."

She swallowed, nodded, her gaze remaining on him. "Very well, sir. Scout out the places and then what, sir? The ground likely is frozen," the woman said.

"Then we'll wait. If we need to build the castles, so be it, but until we know for sure, have people take note of places with strategic value. Mark them on a map and that's that."

"And should we need to build them?"

"Have them light enough fires to melt the ice!" the High General snarled. "If we start a siege, you're responsible for the thawing. We already have some wood, but I want more trees cut down. You see to that!"

"Yes, sir," the warrior-woman replied and rode off.

"They're set," Mireynh muttered as he scanned the plain below. His horse stood on a hill near the forest that surrounded most of the southern Dunth-plain. Wrapped in his fur-lined winter coat he observed the walls of Dunthiochagh. The river had done its best to envelop the grass with swirling mist that seemed to thicken as Lesganagh's Orb sank toward the western horizon.

Duasonh's troops stood on the ramparts: a bristling barrier of spikes that lent the stones an extra layer of menace. Behind those lancers and swordsmen, he suspected archers. In front of the open gate he could discern several armored figures on horseback. One of them held Baron Duasonh's standard, the falcon, while the other four waited with empty hands. They were expecting to be treated with respect, and he would honor them with this formality.

Anne Cirrain had returned to his side and looked at the assembled riders. "Guess it's time to look into our enemy's face," she said.

"Aye," Mireynh replied, urging his horse into a light canter. "Time to demand surrender, boys. Come on."

His black clad escort fell into place, their horses' coats as raven as the riders' armor. One of them carried the royal colors: red dragon before silver mountains on black. Their faces seemed as unchanging as the obsidian hearts attached to their cloaks. He didn't even know their names, didn't talk to them most of the time, and truly didn't give a damn whether they lived or died. His brown gelding and Cirrain's gray mare were like islands of color amidst the massive black steeds. They outnumbered the Danastaerians six to one, but Duasonh's archers more than evened the score.

As he came closer to the wall, he saw that this southern stonework was higher and in much better repair than its counterpart in Harail. Mireynh guessed that the rampart's depth offered enough space for at least two lines of archers with enough room to maneuver for another half dozen in the rear. It would be tough to storm this wall if he had to. If the city's defense was as formidable all along the curve of Dunthiochagh, it would become a long siege. But so far, every traitor had executed their part.

They neared the gate and stopped a dozen paces away from the riders. He had no idea what Cumaill Duasonh looked like; according to rumor the Baron wasn't the most fashionable dresser, but to his mind all the Danastaerians in front of the gate were dressed in rags, even the standard-bearer.

"Pretty damn cold to start a siege, eh?" a fat man with salt and pepper hair said.

Mireynh was surprised; the man's tone was very relaxed, almost casual, even in the face of the massive army that slowly assembled near the tree line. When the four other men began to chuckle, he realized that his face had given away his astonishment. He scowled. "I am Urgraith Mireynh, High General of Chanastardh. In the name of King Drammoch the Second, I demand you surrender your city!"

"What? No terms?" a younger man asked. By the look of him, he was barely out of his teens, but when he looked the youth in the eye, he saw age.

"You need to name terms, High General," an older man said. "You know, like that you'll spare our women and children and all that. It's the proper form."

The Danastaerians snorted with mirth.

"Are you mocking me?"

The chubby man shook his head, still grinning. "No, good man, we aren't mocking you. We're far too frightened to mock you; you certainly have us at a disadvantage, what with your army out there in the cold and us in here."

The younger man turned to the speaker and said, "That is mocking, actually."

Mireynh could barely contain his anger; these bastards made him look like a fool. He wanted to extend the common courtesy offered to every enemy, but the Danastaerians made this time-honored custom into a laughing matter. "Will you surrender your city?" he barked.

"What if we won't?" the older man asked.

Gods, how he wanted to rip their faces off! The nerve, these sons of whores poked fun at him even in the face of his army. "If you don't, I will let my men off the leash and they will plunder, kill and rape!"

The fat man chuckled. "Kill then rape? Gods, your warriors are hardy men indeed!"

"Insult me, if you will, make fun of my heritage, if you must, but don't insult my warriors," he retorted.

"You said they'd kill and rape, lad."

He looked at the speaker, a man barely older than he, he suspected. "Guard your tongue, man."

"Ah," the youth said, "don't mind him, he calls everyone lad. Besides, he is right. You stated there'd be killing first and then rape. So, you have to kill women before laying them?"

The fat man held up his hand. "At least they'll do it with women, not goats."

"You bastards! No mercy to anyone within Dunthiochagh!" he growled.

"Good," the fat man said, his humor gone in an instant. "We ask for none, and you will receive none! You are a crude man, Mireynh; you don't just ask for surrender, you promise to spare whomever. You didn't, and even if you had we would have spat in your face, with more pomp and etiquette of course, but the answer would've been the same. This city withstood the Heir

War and the Demon War when other places, including Herascor, were reduced to rubble! If you think you can storm these walls, burn the gates, and kill its people, then Dunthiochagh asks you to try. There's a mass grave waiting for your warriors! Now, go. You're fouling the air!"

The man's manner had changed from joking lout to nobleman in a heartbeat. Not even Drammoch carried authority the way this man did. He was impressed, terrified, but also furious. Furious at the fat man, the Baron most like, his own error at forgetting the rules of war, and at the jokes they had made. He also worried how his troops would take to insult.

"Fucking bastards," he growled and turned his gelding. Snorting horses and the steady beat of hooves indicated his followers rode back with him, but he didn't care. He wanted Duasonh's head on a pike before the night was over. The insult would be turned into a weapon. His troops loved him, respected him. He treated them fairly, and this abuse was directed at them as well. "Cirrain!" he shouted.

The noblewoman rode up and kept pace. "Sir?"

"Extra booze for the men, not too much, but enough to make them… more receptive, understood?" They would be frenzied when the storm on Dunthiochagh began.

"Aye, sir!"

CHAPTER 61

The South Gate grated shut behind them.

"Nice speech," Kildanor said. He looked at Duasonh and shook his head in amusement. "Think he'll grow careless?"

"If what Kerral told us is true, he's already foaming at the mouth."

"Well, lad, he did look very purple when he rode off."

Kildanor chuckled; Duasonh looked very pleased with himself as he glanced at Nerran. "I don't think he'll be so foolish as to send his entire army to storm the gate at once, but he probably has all of them ready to follow in."

"So, you think the lass can actually deliver?" the Paladin asked.

After what he had seen last night, the Chosen didn't doubt the witch could create the illusion. It had taken them quite a while to leave Duasonh's office, and they had the bruises to prove it. Once they had entered the corridor the images had vanished, and when they had entered the Wizardess' chamber she had been lying in the arms of one of the guards commanded to watch over her, utterly spent. Cumaill had been furious, but had calmed once Nerran had made it obvious that the warrior had still looked over her.

At least she'd had fun casting that spell.

"Aye. Mireynh will be even angrier in the morning, trust me."

"Oh, I trust you," Nerran replied.

"That's all I ask for."

"Lord Duasonh!" Kerral's voice came from the rampart. "It worked."

"What's he doing, General?"

"They're handing out bottles!"

Duasonh looked to Nerran. "What's that good for?" The Paladin shrugged. "Well?" the Baron asked General Kerral.

Ever since last night Kildanor had wondered whether he should be at Cumaill's side when the attack began, or if he should monitor what young Garinad was doing. Now he had reached a decision. It didn't matter if he was on the battlement, even on a good day his archery was pathetic, and at night he'd be lucky to hit a barn from ten paces. Sure, it didn't matter, one just had to draw back and let go at a decent angle, but he had a feeling that whatever Jesgar was doing might not be in the boy's best interest.

"It's an old ritual of Mireynh's, milord. He gets them slightly pissed and then angers them with some slight, imagined or real. Your little speech provided him with better material to rave about!"

If Jesgar was following Ralgon there had to be a reason. Actually, he knew the spy followed Ralgon. He had seen Garinad lurking near the cemetery when the not-so-dead man had talked to the Deathmask.

"When do you think he'll attack?"

"Whenever he sees the signal, I reckon."

"Cumaill?" He had to tell his friend.

"All should be ready by midnight," Duasonh shouted and then turned to the Chosen. "Yes?"

"I won't be with you on the wall tonight." Before the Baron could ask any questions, Kildanor continued, "You've Nerran up there with you, as well as yon general, and let's not forget the witch."

"What will you do?"

He had expected Duasonh to refuse, to argue, but once again his friend surprised him. "I'll look in on what young Garinad is doing. Ralgon saw him in a tavern yesterday, talking with some hooded man."

"Did you talk to him?"

Nerran grumbled, "Give the lad a break, will you, Chosen? He's been through a lot, I'm sure he doesn't do anything harmful. He's a good lad."

He sighed. "I know he is, but this carousing and following, not to mention his lack of memory of what he's been up to, I don't like it."

"Lack of memory?" Duasonh asked.

"Sir!" General Kerral's voice interrupted his reply.

"What?" the Baron shouted back.

"He's sending out riders!"

"Probably to scout for places to build siege fortresses," Nerran muttered. "Does this general know nothing of sieges?"

Duasonh shrugged. "I'll join you up there in a while, mate. Will you look after the chap?"

"The lad'll be safe under my wing, Cumaill," Nerran said, dismounted, handed the reins to one of the squires accompanying them, and headed up the stairs to the battlement. "You'd best take good care of her, or I'll have your hide, lad," he told the young man when he was halfway up the stairs, pointing at his mare.

Duasonh turned to the would-be knights. "Get back to the Palace, arm yourself, and come back here."

"Yes, milord," the two men replied in unison.

"You do know how to handle a bow, eh?"

"Yes, milord."

"Good, now off with you."

"Whose are they?" Kildanor asked.

"The blond one is Giles Huwill's oldest, and the other chap is heir to House Tremay."

"Any ties to Chanastardh in those Houses?" Kildanor asked.

"No, theirs are good families harking back to old Janagast."

"Any other nobles we need worry about?" He was concerned that some aristocrats not involved with Jathain's attempted rebellion would favor living under Drammoch's rule rather than staying independent. There were enough families that had emigrated south after Halmond had conquered the three realms.

"A few, but we'll see. You said something about a lack of memory. What did you mean by that?"

"Seems young Garinad has no idea what he has been up to the last two nights, maybe more. That's what his brother's wife told a man I sent there this morning."

"Too much boozing?"

He shrugged. "I have no idea, but I don't like it."

Duasonh's mind was at work, Kildanor saw. The Baron's eyes were slit as he gazed off into the distance. He thought it best to remain silent while his friend worked out whatever he was pondering. Finally, Cumaill focused on him. "Didn't this Ralgon character say he had been poisoned by something and then his body was used to kill his lover?"

This was a possibility he hadn't considered. Too many other things occupied his thoughts, and although Ralgon was upset, the wellbeing of the man was not his priority. Yes, Jesgar's behavior was odd, but that an enemy of Ralgon's was in Dunthiochagh and might use the spy to work some mischief hadn't occurred to him. "Aye, he said that. You think young Garinad might be under a spell?"

"Possibly," Duasonh said. "See if you can find the boy, and stop whoever is behind this. If there is anyone behind it. Could just be that our spy is just following his hero."

He arched an eyebrow. "You think that's a possibility?"

"I doubt it. That Ralgon saw Jesgar with some man without Jesgar taking note of Ralgon seems to indicate the opposite." Duasonh focused again on the warriors manning the battlement. "Good thing we have the Wizardess."

"I still don't trust her," Kildanor countered.

Cumaill furrowed his brow. "So far she hasn't broken her word to me."

"So, you'll be here?" Kildanor asked, switching the topic.

"Where else should I be, mate? I don't rule to hide behind strong walls when danger nears. This is my home!"

"Aye, that it is," he replied. "Good luck for tonight."

"Thanks," the Baron nodded his dismissal and walked up the stairs to join Nerran and General Kerral.

The inner bailey was busy. The quartermaster distributed sheaves of arrows, shields, even some spears. Off to the far side some warriors were practicing their archery. The men and women stood, barely two feet apart, in double rows of twenty, quivers tied to their belts. On a warden's command, they drew and nocked arrows, aimed, pulled the string taught and, at a second order, let fly. Each missile found a target, and Kildanor saw that all five straw-wheels sprouted eight arrows. He paused to watch; a second group stepped forward, and the process was repeated.

Something else caught his attention. In the shade of the keep a lone man went through the motions of basic swordplay. The man, unlike regular troops, was not equipped with shield and sword. Instead, he held the wooden practice sword's handle in a two-handed grip, the blade raised above his head. It seemed as if the swordsman was uncomfortable, awkward with the weapon. The arms were too straight so that any slash would be carried with only a fraction of the force a proper Eagle's Guard stance normally yielded. An uneasy cut later, the man saw his error, changed his footing and the angle of his arms. Now the stance resembled the Eagle's Guard, and he slashed again.

Resuming his now-corrected position, the man, obviously not a novice in swordsmanship, went through a series of cuts, thrusts, and parries until he returned to his original stance. Each of his movements seemed as if he reacquainted himself with both weapon and the routine. Still, the weapon was not meant for two-handed fighting, and even when he adjusted his left hand to grip the pommel, blade and fighter seemed at odds with what was clearly meant to be achieved.

Kildanor crossed the courtyard and joined the man. Surprised, he finally noticed he had been observing Drangar Ralgon. The former corpse was frowning in concentration as he went back into Eagle's Guard and began the routine anew. He had thought about suggesting that Ralgon pick up fighting again, if only as a means of self-defense, but the man had come to the conclusion himself. By the look of it, hair matted and sweaty, trousers and tunic showing stains of exertion as well, he had been at it for a while.

For a moment Kildanor could see the man Ralgon must have been before the murder of his lover: determined, focused, and utterly unrelenting. Again, he went through the routine of cuts, thrusts and parries, and then the automatic return to the original stance. If only half of what Nerran had told him about Ralgon was true, the Chosen was glad to have never met the man in combat. The former mercenary halted in mid-swing and turned to face him.

"What?"

Kildanor shook his head. "Nothing. Practicing the old moves, eh?"

"Figured I best be able to defend myself."

"So, you have been thinking about why these attacks were made in the first place?"

"Aye," Ralgon replied and resumed Eagle's Guard again. He slashed and blocked. "Found the bastard spy?"

"No, but we are looking. Something is definitely wrong with him," Kildanor said.

The former mercenary turned his head and managed a smile. "I appreciate your help. I really do."

CHAPTER 62

"Are you going to follow me throughout the night?" Drangar looked at the Chosen as he stopped in front of the watch-house. Rob would finish his shift soon. Sword-practice made him realize there were muscles he hadn't used in a long time, but he enjoyed the ache in his arms and legs. Had anyone told him a year ago he'd be shadow-fighting through most of the day, he would have called them crazy. Warriors were married to battle, and he had always said fighting was second nature. If there was anything he had managed to forget in the past two years, it was the moves.

The Chosen halted beside him. "I want to make sure the boy won't do anything stupid."

"Think I can't handle a youth?" He didn't know what to make of Kildanor. Sure, without him he might have fallen victim to the Demonologists—why they wanted to sacrifice him to these foul creatures he still had no idea—so he was grateful, but the Chosen reminded him of claims made during his youth that he was blessed by Lesganagh, another thing he would rather forget.

"Oh, I'm not worried about that. I want to know what the Scales is going on with him."

"Do as you like," he said and waited on Rob, the Chosen leaning against a wall a few yards down the road.

"You fight with a two-handed sword?" Kildanor broke the silence after a while.

He turned his head to look at his companion. "No, too clumsy. Good for chopping down horses, though. Why?"

"You seemed uncomfortable with the sword."

Sword and shield, the preferred weapons of the Sons.

Drangar had never liked to fight this way. Sure, he could if he had to, sometimes the extra protection a shield offered was needed, but it again served as a reminder of his time in the Eye where he'd learned what it felt like to be shunned, feared, even hated. "Not uncomfortable; I prefer the bastard sword. Shields are for the wall. I hated the wall."

Luckily, Rob left the building before the Chosen could reply. His friend seemed to recognize Kildanor and gave a brief salute before shaking Drangar's hand and pulling him into a hug. "I see you survived," the watchman said.

"Aye," he replied. "Let's be off." He pointed at the Chosen and shrugged. "Hope you don't mind the escort."

Rob shook his head and smiled. "Not at all, it's an honor, Lord Kildanor."

They walked in silence. Rob led the way up Hill's Road, across the Dunth onto Miller's Strip, and onto Shadowpeak Street. Drangar remembered some of the buildings from the dream-journey, but knew he wouldn't have been able to find Neena's home on his own. He saw Kildanor glance back every now and then, but whatever the warrior was looking for seemed not to be there.

As they entered the Nobles' Quarter well within Old Town, with buildings of varying opulence to their left and right, he began to ponder what he had tried to avoid thinking about all day. What would he say to Hesmera's friends? How should he explain what had happened? Certainly, mother and daughter would think him the murderer, and he could hardly blame them. Had he not thought of himself as a killer for the past two years as well? "Rob?"

"Hm?"

"When Hesmera was found and I had disappeared, did you think I was guilty?"

The watchman halted and scratched his neck. Drangar remembered this gesture his friend did whenever he felt uncomfortable answering a question. "I would've also," he said. "Had I been in your place, that is."

"It was kind of hard not to, Drang," Rob said, turning to look at him.

"I know. I thought it myself."

"You're worried how her friends will react."

He nodded.

"Explain the entire affair to them the way you told it to me."

"How long has it been since you worried about something like courtesy?" Kildanor asked.

Drangar looked at the Chosen, but remained silent. How long had it been? He could hardly remember when he had been in a situation where etiquette was required. Back then he had said what he thought, not bothering with the niceties of court and society. He hadn't even known about Hesmera's friends until he'd seen Neena and the others. Had she kept this side of her hidden from him? Probably. He had told her more than once how he despised sneering, backstabbing nobles. "I've been speaking my mind ever since I ran away," he muttered. "But I do remember how to do small talk and all that."

"You better," Rob said. "The Cahills are one of the oldest families."

"Cahill?" the Chosen asked, clearly astonished. "That's where you're going?"

"Aye," he replied. "The Lady Cahill and her daughter were friends of Hesmera's."

"They're also quite easygoing, compared to some of the old lickspittles crowding these mansions," Kildanor said. "Don't be a pig, and all should be fine."

"Pig?" Drangar said, frowning.

"You know, don't be too much of a mercenary, show some courtesy, and let go of some of that stoicism."

"I'll try," he said.

The Cahill residence was old, yet in remarkably good repair. Unlike other villas, the place had a crenellated curtain wall and a rather stout-looking steeloak gate. Next to the entrance was a bell pull, which Drangar used at once.

After a few moments, a small window inside the door opened and a pair of grim, blue eyes scrutinized them. "It's bloody late. The master and mistresses don't receive visitors, beggars, or merchants at this time. Come back tomorrow."

Drangar cleared his throat and said, "Be so kind and convey this to your masters: Drangar Ralgon, lover to the deceased Hesmera wishes to speak to the Lady Neena."

The guard snorted. "Doubt that'll make a difference, but I will tell them." The window slid shut.

"Well," said Rob, laying a hand on his shoulder, "I left the wife alone last night, can't do so again. Wish you all the best, Drang." The watchman saluted the Chosen. "Good night, Lord Kildanor."

"Night, Rob, and thank you."

They watched Rob leave, and when the chill penetrated their cloaks both Chosen and Drangar started to pace.

"I will stay outside, Ralgon."

"I thought so," he replied, relieved but also frightened at the prospect of facing Hesmera's friends alone. He was about to thank Kildanor for watching his back, when the gate creaked open.

"The Lady Neena will see you, sir," the green-clad guard said stiffly. "Please leave any weapons with me."

"I'm unarmed," Drangar replied.

"Very well," the guard said, and he thought he could detect a trace of suspicion in the man's voice. The servant locked the gate, then passed him and headed up the paved way toward the mansion. "Follow me."

They entered through what could only be the servants' entrance, but he didn't mind. He had always felt more at home with villeins and hard-working freeborn than with nobility. House Cahill's kitchen was bigger than most inns he knew. Marble-topped tables dominated the center of the room, and there were several ovens on each wall. Few cooks or scullions were busy at this time; instead a dozen armed men and women stood between him and what could only be Neena Cahill, Hesmera's friend. Their weapons pointed his way.

She barely looked as he remembered her. No longer blushing maiden, Neena had matured. Her hair was still the long tangle of locks worn open, but in her eyes he saw bitterness. With the exception of himself, she had likely been most affected by

Hesmera's death. What little color she had drained away when she saw him. Drangar couldn't blame her.

"So, you have returned?" Gone was the girlish laughter, her voice seemed harsher.

"Aye," he replied. There wasn't much else he thought of saying at this moment.

"Did you..." She was still grieving. "Did you kill her?"

"Would you believe me?"

A trace of hope crept into her eyes. "I want to."

"Why would I want to kill the only person that made me feel loved?" he said, unwilling to say more. He couldn't stop. "She told you I had never been in love, and that's true. Most of my life I have never felt truly alive. Like I was going through the motions, but never really belonging. When I met her all this changed. I would've killed myself before I'd harm her." He took a deep breath. "Lady..."

"Just Neena."

"Neena, I... I... for years I lived with the knowledge she was dead, thinking it was me who killed her. Damnation, I wanted to take my own life more than once!" Drangar felt his voice rise, saw the woman and her guards tense, and calmed down immediately.

"I don't believe you," young Lady Cahill stated.

Only one thing could show her the truth, and so he rolled up his sleeves and held out his arms so she could inspect the scars. For a moment, the guards tensed, and Neena gasped as she saw the places he had cut himself. "I swear by all the gods, it wasn't me who killed her. If I lie let Lliania strike me down."

He wanted to tell her the truth, wanted to tell her what had happened two years ago, but not before all the guards. "This is a private matter, Neena. Tie my hands if you must, but I won't bare my heart before your servants."

She must have understood his meaning and nodded, in much the same way Hesmera had done. "Bind him, then leave," she told the guards. "And ask my mother to join us." To him she said, "Hesmera was her friend as well, she deserves to know."

Soon after, Drangar sat with the Cahill women in the same

chamber he had seen them in with Hesmera. The mood, however, was different; the laughter that had apparently lined Leonore's face was a thing of the past. Like her daughter, she still grieved. Drangar knew their pain all too well, but as he told them what he had seen in the past, his sorrow was once again overshadowed by fury and determination. "I will make them pay," he said as he finished.

Neena and Leonore Cahill sat in silence, regarding him. He saw how they digested all he had revealed. Occasionally mother would whisper to daughter, but he remained still, they too had to come to terms with what he had seen. At one point, Leonore's gaze fixed him, her brow furrowed. "You hope Neena knows something of these false tradesmen, don't you?"

He nodded, was about to answer when all the lamps in the room, as well as the fire, went out and they were plunged into darkness. As he rose, moving backward to reach the wall, glass splintered, and Neena cried out in alarm.

CHAPTER 63

With Culain at her side, Ealisaid felt confident like never before. Her hand in his, they entered the Baron's office. Inside were Duasonh, seated on his chair, a younger man with short-cropped blond hair, and Paladin Nerran. Duasonh looked up when she entered and smiled.

"Have a seat, Wizardess."

"Thank you, but I'd rather stand."

"As you wish."

"And?" Nerran said in his usual gruff manner. She had never really encountered this man without him being bad-tempered. Followers of Lesganagh weren't known for their politeness, she knew, and after meeting Kildanor she had expected a Paladin was just as bad. Then again, the sun was nothing if not direct.

"Can you do it?"

"Do what?" the blond man asked.

"We intend to lure the Chanastardhians into a trap," Duasonh said. "General Kerral, how many archers are under your command?"

The warlord scratched his stubbly scalp. "About four hundred, milord."

"And how many carry a bow, aside from these archers?"

"They should also know how to shoot," Nerran interjected.

Duasonh glared at the Paladin, but turned it into a knowing wink. She had seen them play this sort of game before. In her time outside the dungeons, it had become apparent they were close friends. Duasonh could be as gruff as Nerran if the situation required it, but at this moment both seemed to enjoy teasing General Kerral.

"All of them, sir," the younger man replied.

"Very well," the Baron said. "And what are you doing here, Culain?"

"Is she really a wizard?" Kerral interrupted.

"Aye, she is, lad. Listen now, gawk later," Nerran snapped. This time Duasonh merely nodded.

The Baron cleared his throat and repeated the question.

"My Lord Baron, I'm assisting the Lady Ealisaid, sir." She squeezed his hand and gave a brief nod of encouragement.

"She has guards. Why are you with her?"

Ealisaid knew this was a secret council, but Duasonh had given her free hand on how to proceed. "He is my escort, and strength, my liege. Without him there won't be much of an illusion when the time comes."

"So, you were the chap responsible for me bumping into a cabinet that looked more like a shrub, laddie?" Nerran growled. "Had some fun, eh? Can't say I blame you." He laughed and muttered, "Lucky bastard."

"Why thank you, sir," she said with a mock bow.

"Enough of this," Duasonh scoffed. "Lady Wizard, what do you mean when you say this man is your strength? I've heard tales of people being drained of their life-force to feed a wizard's spell, are you using him as a means to empower your magic?"

To her left, Ealisaid saw Nerran stiffen. The Paladin's hand inched closer to his sword. "No, milord, this isn't what I meant. He is my strength, yes, but only insomuch as a husband is his wife's strength. With him I'm confident in myself and my magic."

"Good," Nerran chuckled mockingly. "She may keep him."

Even though she knew who and what she was, the Paladin's comment hurt. Before she could snarl a reply, however, Culain spoke, "Lord Nerran, I am neither a villein, nor a slave. Your wit has a place somewhere, but here it isn't appreciated." To Duasonh he said, "My liege, I ask permission to stay with Ealisaid for as long as need be."

The glare the Baron sent Nerran's way was earnest. "If I find out this is just so you have a toy-boy, I'll have both of your heads." He faced her. "Well?"

"No, my liege, he isn't. Without his aid"—at this Nerran hiccupped artificially—"I would not have been able to do what I did last night."

"Very well," the Baron said, "stay with her, Culain. You will, however, not merely stand on the wall to stare starry-eyed at her. You will carry a bow and shoot, make yourself useful, understood?" This was not what she had hoped for, but there was nothing to be done about it.

"So, what's the deal with this trap?" Kerral said.

"Right," Duasonh replied. "We know High General Mireynh expects aid from a traitor inside the city. This traitor is dead..."

"Rightly so," Nerran interrupted.

"The traitor is dead," the Baron continued, again glaring at the Paladin. "But we know their plan. At night the South Gate should have been emptied of all guards, except those loyal to said traitor. The walls were to be manned by more collaborators, so that when the gate is opened none could raise the alarm. The Chanastardhians would have taken half the city without much resistance."

"You want the sorceress," Kerral pointed at her, "to make Mireynh believe this ploy is still working."

"Smart, lad."

Duasonh nodded. "Aye, that's the plan. Of course, the gate will still be closed, fully manned, and the walls brimming with archers."

"Mireynh won't send out his full army," Kerral pointed out. "He'll send a strike force to secure gate and wall. When this is done he'll send more troops." It was apparent this man liked to boast. "So, the only thing you will achieve with this is to eliminate one of his elite warbands."

"He'll send in the elite?" Duasonh asked.

"To take an essential position and hold it? Fuck yes!" The warlord was as rude as Nerran.

"Then we take them down, fine by me," the Baron said. "Are you sure you can do it?"

She nodded, this time Culain squeezed her hand. "Aye, my liege, I can do it."

Duasonh was about to say more when the door opened, and

a warden poked his head in. "Milord, one of the scouts."

"Send him in," Duasonh commanded.

A horseman entered. "Sir!" The man stood at attention. He was clad in leather and fur, and stank of sweat and horse. "The Chanastardhians are two miles away from the plain!"

The Baron rose. "Warden, coordinate with warleader Kaltairr, see to it that we get more wood inside, there's still plenty to the north! Nerran, fetch Kildanor and my squires, and make sure each of them looks ready for war, we'll see Urgraith Mireynh very soon, I think." He turned to her. "Lady Wizard, rest, if you so require. Be ready by nightfall."

Each of them rushed out of the office. Soon she would have her chance to prove she was valuable to the city.

In Culain's company the day passed quickly. She could have prepared, meditated, practiced concentration exercises, but his presence was all she needed. With him, through him, Ealisaid had performed magic in a way she had never been able to do before. Even with her inner fire, she doubted she could have created the illusion that had enveloped the entire keep. The baileys and walls had remained unchanged, if the servants were right, but the bulk of the Palace, every room, had been turned into a glade.

From the reports the inhabitants had given, each area, from the smallest closet to the great audience chamber, had become part of the glade she and Culain had shared. In her mind she must have pictured their place as part of an even bigger space. Ealisaid wasn't sure how this had happened; she wasn't even sure if all the various rooms strung together would compose an entire valley. It might have been that she had created replicas of their vale in various sizes.

Not that it mattered. She felt confident she could mask the archers and let the enemy see what she wanted them to see. There was only the matter of figuring out if she could create an image that worked only in one direction. When she had cast her spell with Culain she had seen everything he had. Could she alter the illusion so she was unaffected while her lover saw what she wanted him to see? She had to try.

"What're you thinking about?" he whispered in her ear.

"I want to try something."

"What's that, dear?"

Ealisaid sat up and looked down at him. He yawned and stretched his arms above his head, touching the wall behind the bed.

"Do you trust me?"

Culain couldn't hide his surprise. He then rubbed his hands across his face like she had seen him done before when he was thinking. "Can I trust you?" he finally asked, humor gleaming in his eyes.

She scrunched up her face then leaned down to kiss him. "Aye."

He grinned. "Then I do trust you." Her concern must have shown, for he sat up and put his hands on her shoulders, staring at her. "What do you have in mind? Nothing that will harm Baron or city I hope."

She managed a smile. "You just worry about Duasonh and the city?"

"Oh, and myself of course," he added with a chuckle.

Her playful slap caused both of them to laugh. "What about me?" she pouted.

"Well, I do worry about you, too. So, what is it you want to have me for?" She made a face. "Other than *that* I mean."

When was the last time she had felt so giddy around a man? "I need to try something new." His grin broadened, and she hurriedly continued, "No, no, no, not that... well, also that, but later!" She felt the blush when Culain laughed. "I want to create an illusion you can see, but I don't," she added, squirming in his hands as he tickled her.

Culain dropped his hands to his side. "Go ahead," he said, his face earnest.

In the evening they stood on the southern gatehouse. Winter's icy grasp seemed to get a firmer grip every day, and both of them wore heavy cloaks to ward off the cold. To their left and right, all along the wall, stood archers. Many of these men and women were regular warriors who normally fought on foot; only every third was fully trained, Culain had explained. But aside from the warriors there were also citizens on the battlement, people who, at times, knew the craft of archery better than the warriors.

She appreciated his effort to explain, but didn't really care to consider the upcoming bloodshed. She herself had killed a dozen people or so, by accident as she had to remind everybody, including her lover. Ealisaid dreaded the willful killing that would happen in the dark of night.

"Where's Duasonh?" she muttered. After their meeting, she had, of course, been busy, yet she had expected her liege to give some last moment instructions. The plan was as good as it could be, but still...

Culain must have detected her nervousness for he pulled her into a gentle embrace, kissed her hair, and said, "Don't worry, dear, he'll come."

"What if I..."

He placed two fingers on her lips. "Don't worry; you will work your spell flawlessly!"

"How do..."

Again, his digits blocked her words. "I know, all right. You are a great mage, eh?"

His encouragement relaxed her. She looked up into his eyes, kissed his fingers. "Aye," she whispered. In this new world he was her mountain, her solace, her anchor who'd hold her no matter what, and she was grateful for his existence.

"Now look at those lovebirds!" Even in the relative silence of anticipation along the wall, Nerran's voice seemed to boom across the stonework toward them.

The Paladin walked ahead of Duasonh and General Kerral, clapping the shoulders of a few archers, nodding to more. His battered surcoat bore the sun and sword crest of Lesganagh; he wore it over a chain shirt, and a sword was at his belt. Even he carried a bow; she noticed the fletching of his arrows poking up from behind his back.

Duasonh was as friendly to the assembled warriors. He stopped to talk to some, gripped their forearms in a warrior's greeting, and shared a few laughs with his troops. His armor was caergoult, boiled and hardened leather molded to fit the wearer like a second skin. He too had a sword belted to his massive girth. Dunthiochagh's falcon embroidered on his tabard, cloak and even etched onto his armor. Yet, while even General Kerral was holding an elegant longbow, the Baron carried no such weapon.

Duasonh walked up and greeted them with a brief nod. "At high moon the walls will clear."

His statement surprised her, and she couldn't guard her face quickly enough to suppress the emotion. "The walls will clear?" she echoed.

"Aye, lass," Nerran replied in Duasonh's stead. "They have to believe our traitor has succeeded."

Culain gave her shoulder a gentle squeeze. "Don't worry, dear, you can do it."

"But won't they see that the faces are not the same?"

"No," Duasonh said. "They won't send anybody close enough to see individuals. They would be too close for our archers, and the surprise'd be spoiled."

"You sure you can do that, lass?" the Paladin asked.

She gave herself the leisure of thinking it over before she nodded her assent. "Aye, the Chanastardhians will see the wall clearing." She chanced a look left and right. There sure were a lot of people on the wall. "Won't they worry about this many warriors?"

"Can't see most of them, milady," Kerral said. "You can arrange a score of men to look like three score. Mireynh knows this, but he will see the walls being abandoned."

"Let's wait then," Nerran said. He looked around and asked, "Anyone got some Broggainh? I'm cold."

The assembled warriors chuckled and shook their heads; even Ealisaid couldn't help but smile.

Culain held her, whispering into her ear. She barely heard his words, so focused was she on her task of creating the illusion. Unlike her earlier experiment with him seeing the illusion while she didn't, she now had to see the image, and then maintain the mirage of an empty wall.

"They're stirring," her lover whispered." The Chanastardhians can see the walls clearing, dear!" She felt him release her, to pick up his bow.

Timing was everything. The illusionary warriors could not merely vanish from the wall, they had to move realistically. There had to be sound as well, the scraping of boots, the chink of weapons, and the like. Noise carried, especially in the dead of night when almost everything was asleep. Culain kissed her cheek. "You can do it, Milady Wizard." Ealisaid looked up and down the wall. Did the warriors move too slowly? Was their retreat authentic? Again, she felt his lips on her cheek, her temples, and her forehead. Again, she let the magic flow as it may, as reality might have been. There was no need to summon her inner strength.

She could do it!

Now! The illusory warriors had cleared the wall. Part of her focus maintained the empty ramparts, while she concentrated on the gate itself. She heard imaginary hinges creak as the steeloak portal swung open. Now a figure, illuminated by the shine of his lantern, stepped into the gap. He began to wave the lantern in the prescribed pattern. Once, twice, then he stepped back into the gate's shadow, extinguishing the light.

At first, she could see nothing, then, in the pale light of the moon, she saw figures shuffling across the plain, onto the road, toward the gate. The bowmen, unseen to her, waited. Culain was as invisible to her as Duasonh, Nerran and the others, but she felt him standing near, bow at the ready.

The Chanastardhians were close now. Ealisaid heard the creak of steel and leather which, despite being muffled, was quite audible. They were at the gate!

"Now!" Nerran shouted.

She heard arrows being nocked, drawn and released around her, saw enemy warriors fall, but couldn't see the sources of their deaths. Her illusion worked so well that not even the missiles fired by the bowmen became visible to either her or the enemy. For a moment she felt elated, this was magic! Her magic! She had cast a spell—a sequence of spells really—she had thought herself incapable of.

Then she saw how much damage the bowmen were inflicting on the confused warriors milling about in front of the gate. The bodies lay on the ground, some deathly still, puncture marks in chest, neck, face, legs; others were twitching, pinned to the ground by their wounds and the feet of their panicked comrades. An enemy warleader had the presence of mind to order his warriors to raise shields; and still the Chanastardhians were trying to get through a gate that in reality was closed.

She heard that same man order retreat, saw the warriors obey, and still heard Duasonh's troops let fly their arrows. More warriors were felled. Now the Chanastardhians were running.

There was the distant sound of arrows. Ealisaid looked toward the enemy encampment. Atop a hill were archers. The Chanastardhians were shooting at their own troops! She was so surprised her focus vanished and she saw the people around her once again.

Nerran's eyes widened in shock as a second barrage of Chanastardhian arrows sped up into the air and came down in the enemy's own lines. "I don't believe this," he muttered. Then a third volley was fired into the retreating footmen. The remaining warriors died during this last assault. The enemy returned to their tents as if nothing had happened. She saw various groups of people vanishing into the woods. "The siege has begun," Nerran sighed as the sound of trees being felled echoed across the plain.

"What..." she stammered, unable to summon the strength to speak, so deep was her horror.

"I have no fucking idea!" Nerran snarled, disgust plain on his face.

Duasonh shrugged as if to dismiss the matter. "Look lively, lads!" the Baron shouted. "There's much work to be done! Get those catapults fixed! We need more!" He pointed to a few warleaders. "You, Runnaidh, you'll command the escort for the lumberjacks! Blarney, Candles, Keep, organize patrols on this side of the river! You know what needs to be done!

"And pray to Lesganagh!"

He found himself huddled against a grandfather tree. For a

moment he didn't know who or where he was. He didn't even know how he had come to be there. "Who am I?" he muttered, staring at the marks scratched into the tree's bark. There was blood among the cuts; his fingers ached. He looked at his digits, his nails split and torn, blood crusted on the tips. "Who am I?" He touched the tree. Why had he scratched the grandfather like a lunatic? "Who am I?" he said again, hoping the answer would come, hoping that someone would answer.

Lloreanthoran.

He remembered.

Elf wizard, sent back from the hated home the elves of Gathran had created after the Wizard War. The Aerant C'lain, the Stone of Blood, gone, everything was gone. Bright-Eyes, his familiar, dead. The spirit of… whom? What was that name again? Da… na… cha… main… The syllables came haltingly.

Danachamain. Who was Danachamain?

He had escaped Danachamain, run blind for… how long? It was dark, a while after dusk if he chanced a guess. How long ago had his entry into the Aerant C'lain been? Running, running, running was all he could remember. Something must have released him from the fear the apparition had unleashed within. Lloreanthoran focused his senses inward.

Nothing… there! To the north he detected the molding of magic, the gentle nudge of a mind shaping what was into what could be. It was an inexperienced mind which relied on the feelings of another to change reality. Was this what had drawn him out of his stupor? A barely trained mind using magic the likes no one had seen in the land for a century.

With a determined push, he thrust into his spiritform and looked north. Who was this sorcerer? The world folded underneath him as he concentrated on the source of this change, and when he reached the border of what once had been Gathran, he saw the novice's signature flickering high above the city of Dunthiochagh. The spiritual imprint was unique to every caster, with one exception. A century ago he had seen many of these beacons whenever he traveled the realm in spiritform. His symbol was nothing more than a bright, green leaf, but the humans had all been imprinted with the same sign, a phoenix, like the one he was seeing now.

Impossible! They hadn't left anybody alive. Yet it was there, fading in and out, like a dying, or kindling, flame. The caster might not even know there was a signature above him, in the spiritworld. A poke on his shoulder snapped his consciousness back into his body.

"You wasted enough time, staring and screaming gibberish," a somewhat familiar voice said.

It took a moment to get his bearings, but then he saw the incorporeal being that floated beside him. "Lightbringer," he said, and bowed.

"Better than kneeling and wetting yourself, I suppose."

How could she manifest her spiritform this way? The thought hadn't even crossed his mind back when she had visited him the first time, but now he stared at the Lightbringer.

"You could just stand here and wait for the snow to fall, or you could do something that actually honors the little squirrel's sacrifice."

"Where have you been?"

"Busy. You?" she said in a mocking tone; then held up her translucent hand and muttered, "No more questions, you know what's at stake here, so you best get going, lost enough time as it is. Head south to Kalduuhn, find the Eye of Traksor, the monks will help you locate the books and the Stone."

All Lloreanthoran could do was nod.

The next moment Lightbringer had vanished, and he set off to the south, to find the Eye of Traksor, whatever it was.

CHAPTER 64

"So, what shall we do? Wait for the signal?" Anne asked. She wasn't used to large-scale assaults, sieges, and treachery, and didn't like Mireynh's casualness on the matter.

"Trust me, the signal will come," he muttered. "Say," he glanced at her, "how many volunteers do we have?"

She looked at him, astonished. "You want to send the Danastaerians as the spearhead?"

Mireynh's shoulders went up and down as if he cared little. "Why not?"

"They'd face their countrymen."

"They joined us knowing they'd have to fight, did they not?" he said, hatred plain in his voice. It was almost as if he said "Let them die; I don't care; if they take the gate even better." Instead he growled, "I'd rather have had them butchered on the field when they faced us, but they pleaded for mercy, traitors to their country, their families. Let's make the circle complete."

A shiver ran down Anne's back as she heard the High General's words, but she nodded grimly. "Four hundred, sir."

"Good, once I give the order they are to advance and take the gatehouse, understood?"

"Yes, sir!" Anne answered. No matter what happened, Chanastardhian blood would be spilled last. She turned her horse and sped toward the troops that had volunteered to fight for Drammoch, a ragtag group of Danastaerian men and women who had fled their own flag to escape death. Dispirited when they first faced their countrymen, they had grown bolder in the folds of Mireynh's command.

Though she didn't like traitors, the cold-hearted order she

was bound to deliver sickened her. This wasn't honorable. But neither was turning traitor. The High General's hatred for turncoats was well known, but sending those people to the slaughter was beyond cruel. This was war, she reminded herself, trying to rationalize Mireynh's order, wanting to see some sense in this approach, trying to stow away her disgust in the deepest recesses of her mind. Danastaerian blood would flow, so why not on both sides, she tried to convince herself.

"Heads up!" the turncoats' warleader shouted and the warriors assembled in a tight-standing square. "Orders, milady?" he asked, looking at her as she halted her horse.

"Yes," she said matter-of-factly. "You shall be first inside Dunthiochagh. Upon the High General's signal, you are to advance and take the gatehouse. Good luck."

"But, lady," the man said, "that's suicide."

"You have your order," Anne muttered. "Carry it out!" She felt sick and couldn't stand facing the warleader any longer. Quickly she turned her horse and let it canter back to the High General's vantage point.

When she reached Mireynh, he was talking to the leader of the First Bows, a hardened veteran of several campaigns. "Understood?"

"Yes, sir!" the man snapped and returned to his troops.

"What good will archers do, sir? The gatehouse will be undefended."

"None of your business, Cirrain."

"Yes, sir," she replied. Then she waited.

The night was getting cold. Anne rubbed her gloved hands to keep some warmth in her fingers, and still they waited. Then, just like the High General had promised, a light came from the gate, left to right, then up and down. One man of Dunthiochagh had done his best to let the city be taken.

Mireynh turned to the group of flag-bearers. "Signal the advance!"

The young men bearing the banners started waving them, swinging the poles widely, signaling the Danastaerians. The warriors marched forward, heading toward the gate. No sound was heard, apparently the turncoats had used the time to muffle their armor; there was no clink, no scrape, only the dull, almost inaudible thump of boots. In the clear sky, the moon illuminated the scene, and once Anne had brought some distance between her and Mireynh's tent and the accompanying fire, she saw the huddled mass of warriors hurrying forward. They reached the gate and… halted?

What the Scales was this? Why didn't they enter the city? Were Duasonh's troops blocking the gate? Was this a trap?

The first warriors went down, dying, but who was killing them? The wall was empty! Why were they dying?

Anne heard the Danastaerian warleader order his men to raise their shields. While doing so the warriors without shields tried to find shelter beneath their comrades'. And still the warband stood before the open gates. Still men and women fell. Who the Scales was killing them?

She saw more go down, screaming, blood gushing from shoulders and necks. Others dropped their shields in shock as if the wood offered no protection. What were they defending against? What should they protect the warriors from? There was no archer in sight!

"Retreat. Retreat, fools," she whispered.

Apparently the Danastaerian leader had the same idea, because all of a sudden they marched backward, shields high above them. Still warriors fell, blood spurting from faces and arms, and chests and throats. Still no one was shooting! People were dying because of wounds no one had caused. Anne didn't understand what was going on; even the nobles around her were confused.

"The bastards failed us, shame us with their inadequacy! Chanastardhians would never run! Archers!" Mireynh shouted.

Anne's head snapped around. She saw the First Bows at the foot of the hill. The bowmen nocked arrows, drew, aimed high, and let go. A cloud of missiles sped into the air and descended on the retreating troops. Now, the cause of the wounds could be seen, and Anne watched in horror as her countrymen, people she thought in her heart were decent fellows, decimate warriors sworn to serve King Drammoch. Mireynh's single word had done more damage to her faith in the High General than anything he had done before.

The street was silent, the moon was full, and Kildanor was bored and cold. For a while, after Ralgon had entered Cahill Manor, he had waited in the shadow of another mansion, this one not as venerable. The chill didn't bother him at first, but as time crept on, first his feet then his legs went numb. How the warriors on the battlements survived this cold he didn't know, but as he began pacing he also started to envy their resilience.

At first, even when walking back and forth, Kildanor had worried about stealth, but the longer he walked and nothing happened, the more careless he became. "Stupid idiot," he cursed. "Should have stayed in the bloody Palace, but no." He had decided to escort Ralgon in case Garinad was up to no good. The Chosen rounded a corner and swung back to return to the gate when he saw a shadow move across the Cahill's curtain wall. Had he been able to he would have also slowed his heartbeat, but all he could do was remain still.

The shadow flickered across a wall adjacent to one of the lamps lighting the street. Suddenly, he was glad he had decided against wearing his heavy winter boots. He padded toward the spot where he suspected the intruder and saw him walking down the road, skirting the guttering lanterns the nobles had demanded put up in their streets. One of the lights allowed him to discern the intruder's shape.

Garinad! He was spying on Ralgon! Kildanor followed the stray spy, but despite his knowledge of Dunthiochagh, in the pale moonlight he soon lost his bearings. The streets looked alike, but when Jesgar entered a tavern, the Tankard, the Chosen once again knew where he was. The pub was close to the western slums, near the warehouses, close to where Jesgar had spied on Jathain's smuggling operation. What he couldn't figure out was why the young man had come here.

A quick glance through the window showed a taproom packed with off-duty warriors and a few tradesmen; he didn't see Jesgar. He couldn't afford to lose the youth again, entered the place, took a longer look around, and finally saw Garinad at a table in the far corner. So far, he had been undetected, and he wanted to keep it this way. When a drunk vacated his spot at the bar, he slipped into the opening.

"What's yours, mate?" the aging publican asked.

"Pint of bitter, please," he replied.

"One silver leaf."

"What? I can buy an entire barrel with a leaf!"

"Could, mate, could. The rationing and them warriors make prices go up," the man said, foaming mug in one hand while the other was stretched out. "Take it or leave it."

Taverns and inns must do smashing business, but he didn't begrudge them their fortune. Sure, the price was outrageous, but such was the nature of things: more demand, less supply, higher prices. He fished in his bag for a leaf and placed it in the bartender's hand. Then he held his mug and took a long pull, his eyes once again on Jesgar's table.

A while later—at the rate this was going he would be broke after a few bitters—a man in a brown hood entered the tavern and pushed his way toward the far wall. Was this the same chap Ralgon had spoken of? The new guest sat down opposite Jesgar, his back to the entrance. Obviously, the man wasn't worried about anything untoward happening behind him. Both men leaned forward and Jesgar began to talk. As the conversation went on, the hooded man ordered one pint after the other, most were for young Garinad while the chap still had his hands wrapped around his first mug.

"No wonder he wakes up remembering nothing," Kildanor muttered. "The boy drinks like a horse."

The conversation came to an end, the hooded man handed the serving maid a handful of coins, clasped Jesgar's hand, and gave the spy an affectionate slap against the temple. Jesgar's reaction seemed very odd. The young thief stood, a vacant look in his eyes, and headed for the exit, uncaring of the shouts and shoves he received from some of the patrons.

His first impulse was to follow the boy, but if anyone was a danger to both the spy and Ralgon it was the other man. Jesgar would, in all likelihood, go home and sleep, with everything of this night forgotten by tomorrow morning. Given the spy's consumption of ale he'd be incoherent anyway, and the lack of attention to his environment reinforced the Chosen's notion. The key was the hooded man.

Kildanor drained his bitter and left. If Jesgar had told the man about Ralgon's whereabouts, Cahill Manor was the man's destination. Was it possible this person was one of those who wanted to sacrifice Ralgon to the demons? He'd covered his face, like those bastards in the Shadowpeaks, and he certainly was looking for Ralgon. The longer he thought about it the more convinced he was this man was a Demonologist. If his way led him back to the Cahills, any doubt he might have would be eliminated. There was naught to do but follow.

If his new friend suspected any pursuit, his pace would have changed. The man wandered through Dunthiochagh as if he had not a care in the world, and Kildanor found it easy to keep his target in sight.

They crossed Old Bridge, the Chosen always a few dozen steps behind. Mist, frozen on the cobblestones, made footing treacherous, and he slowed. His mark went on, as if the frost-rimmed stones did not bother him.

At the Palace, the man turned right into Shadowpeak. Here, Kildanor's steps were little better than stumbles, but soon, as they got farther away from the river, his soles had more traction. He quickened his pace, could still see the man, but...

There! The chap hurried around another bend. The Chosen sprinted and reached the corner a few moments later.

He chanced a quick glance into the crossing street, and recoiled. The hooded man stood directly in front of him, stepped forward, and fixed him with his shadowed face.

"Do not interfere, Chosen!" the man hissed. As he spoke his hands completed a gesture and light blinded light him.

Pain seared through his head, lancing inward from his eyes as he tried to open them. His lids fluttered in expectation of another blaze, but the alley was still. "Bastard!" Kildanor growled. How long had he been out? The night sky was almost the same; it couldn't have been that long. Sitting up, he felt the paving underneath his cloak. The temperature was barely different from the stones around him; the stun had lasted only a few moments, but that was more than enough time for someone who could use magic. Cursing himself, he stood. He had been careless; Demonologists used magic the same way as every son of a bitch Phoenix Wizard. This guy was good at what he did, otherwise he would not have been sent on this mission alone.

Ralgon was in danger.

With his presence revealed, stealth mattered little, and he ran down the alley. Cahill Manor wasn't that far. Not much further! How did this bastard know he was Chosen? His attire bore neither Lesganagh's orb nor any other badge that revealed his allegiance. None of the people inside the pub had identified him either. So how had this man known what he was? It didn't make sense. He rounded another corner and saw the curtain wall ahead.

Glass shattered, women screamed, and he had no more time to think about how the Demonologist acquired his knowledge.

CHAPTER 65

Kildanor was frantic. He didn't even consider the bell pull. Judging by the sounds of turmoil coming from inside Cahill Manor, no one would have answered it anyway. It had been a while since his last climbing of a wall, and the one surrounding the residence looked formidable. He took a few steps back and launched into a swift run. When he was a few feet away from the barrier, he jumped. His arms shot up and he managed to grab hold of an outcrop. Muscles tensed as he pulled. He felt his hold slipping, fingers hanging on to the rock. Now his slide halted, even when he let go with his right hand to reach out for the top of the wall.

Thankfully the crenellations were merely decorative. No sentinel patrolled the barricade, and he found enough purchase to let go with the other hand and pull himself up. Muscles cramped, he took a moment to massage the ache away and then was down on the trimmed lawn, moving toward the manor.

Despite the general uproar within, a servant must have heard his banging on the door, for the main entrance swung open. The Chosen did not wait for the man to question him, but ran through the opening into the hallway and stopped amidst the chaos of servants and guards running about the place. Most of them were on the stairs, heading up. The others looked at him askance. He could only guess at his appearance; his tunic was probably torn.

"Why do you stand there gaping?" a stout man of middling age shouted. "Get up there and find out what's going on!" Kildanor had seen Lord Úistan Cahill only a few times, several years ago, but now that he had a closer look he saw the man hadn't changed that much. "You, Chosen!" the nobleman snapped. "This has something to do with you?"

He sketched a bow and said, "No, Lord Cahill, but I'm here to help nonetheless."

"Good. Up you go, and help my people. Stop whatever it is."

Kildanor didn't even bother to reply; stairs, guards, and servants seemed to sweep past him as he rushed up the steps. On the first landing he stopped. The demonology he'd felt before was now mingling with something else. What was it? It felt familiar, but for a moment he couldn't identify it.

The people behind him hurried by, he saw them glancing at him as they went. Why did this other presence feel so familiar? It was as if... no, that seemed unlikely. Yet, it was too similar to what he'd felt when his fellow Chosen had perished and Orkeanas had sacrificed himself for their escape. Could it be possible? He continued his ascent, every step reinforcing the impression that demonology was being used in addition to... Lesganagh's might.

The Demon War had seen rise to many strange things. Priests of Lesganagh had summoned demons of their own to battle what Danachamain had unleashed in Honas Graigh. He hadn't been there, hadn't felt the powers at work, yet he was certain he could distinguish between the gift of the god and demonology.

The guards, he saw as he reached the uppermost landing, were trying—and failing—to force their way through a door. Whatever magic was being used, it was happening behind that door. He still couldn't shake the feeling that Lesganagh's might was intermingled with demonology.

One of the guards called for axes, and a pair set off to fetch the weapons. "Steeloak, Lord Kildanor," explained the man, the arms-men's leader he figured. "Bloody hard to get through on the best of days."

"Aye," Kildanor said. "May I?" he asked as he walked forward. Not waiting for a reply, he put his hands against the door. Yes, the magic came from here.

Demonology was now prevalent, the residue of godly power almost gone. He heard raised voices, shouts, but no words.

There was a surge of…

He woke a moment later, lying on the floor; the confused faces of several guards looking down at him. "Gods!" he cursed. That much vile power he hadn't felt in almost a century. The circle in the Shadowpeaks had been mild compared to this! "We need those axes!" he shouted as he stood.

"My wife and daughter are in there!" Úistan Cahill thundered. "Out of the way!"

He saw the aging nobleman shove his way through the assembled guardsmen, in his hand a massive broad bladed battleaxe. Who was he to deny the lord of the house the honor to destroy his own property? He stepped aside.

Lord Cahill stepped in front of the door and chopped the two-handed weapon in a mighty downward swing. The impact reverberated through the corridor, yet only a small piece of wood chipped off. "Thrice-damned quality workmanship," Úistan Cahill swore in a very unlordlike manner. His next swing had the same effect. The noble turned to Kildanor, "Want a hack at it, son?"

The Chosen couldn't suppress his amusement. Why didn't Cumaill spend more time with this man? "Certainly," he said and received the heavy weapon. The axe's weight was unlike any he had wielded before.

Lord Cahill must have seen his frown, for he guffawed, "This is a man's weapon."

"A very big man's weapon, milord," he replied, chuckling.

"Aye, that it is. Now get going," the noble commanded.

Surprised, Kildanor obeyed. Like Cahill, he couldn't use the haft's full length, so he put as much strength as he could summon into the swing. A considerably bigger splinter came lose. "Again, son!" the noble shouted, and he obeyed. There! A big chunk of wood splintered inward. He could see into the room. What he saw shocked him.

Inside the square chamber a glowing circle of light with beams acting as a cage illuminated the entire scene. Behind the bars stood Ralgon, fingers aflame, hair reduced to ash. The man struggled to escape his prison, growing leaner by the heartbeat. Opposite, in direct line with the doorway, stood the hooded man muttering what could only be a summoning spell. The demonic energy swelled, seemingly rising to ever-higher levels, and Kildanor trembled, whether out of rage or fear he knew not. One thing he did know, however, was that this man was trying to summon a demon, using Ralgon as a sacrifice.

He chopped again at the door. "Damned Demonologists!" he shouted. He had to break through!

Lord Cahill, using a maul, supported him, slamming the weapon's considerable weight against the wood. The noble did not ask what caused his agitation.

Then, suddenly, the presence of demonology vanished, leaving only traces of magic behind. Kildanor seized the chance and threw himself against the door. Metal screeched, tore, but the door hardly budged. Something was still blocking it.

"Neena!" Úistan Cahill's voice boomed next to his ear. "Leonore! Clear the way!"

There was some scraping and grunting as the women pulled away whatever stood in front of the door. Kildanor moved to enter, but was pushed aside by the lord of the manor. He followed. The women were safe, weeping as they clung to the nobleman's broad shoulders, held tight by him.

The turret room was a battlefield. Its two windows shattered, furniture broken and aflame. The outlines of a summoning-circle were still visible, the burning remnants flickering in the quickly chilling room. Inside the circle, clothes, skin and hair badly burnt, knelt Drangar Ralgon. He stared at something in his left hand while muttering "You bastards, why?" again and again.

Lord Cahill quickly assessed the situation and barked orders to the throng of people. "Get water and blankets! They're freezing!"

Kildanor liked this man. "Take both of them out of here!" he added, leaving mother and daughter in the care of a pair of maidservants who stared wide-eyed at the destruction. The women were led out of the ruined room as if in a trance. Neena Cahill's gaze wandered over to Ralgon. She started to move toward him, but her father's strong hands took hold of her shoulders and guided her out.

As he watched the women leave, he heard lord Cahill's sharp intake of breath. He turned and looked the direction the noble was staring. "Impossible," he muttered.

Amidst the chaos he had paid little attention to Ralgon; aristocrats had priority over a former mercenary. Now he had the time to spare.

When he had seen the man the first time, albeit as a mutilated corpse, Ralgon had looked slender, but well nourished. Now, the naked, huddled man, his hair burned away, looked ill. The fire had barely injured him; aside from the loss of all hair, Kildanor saw no wound on him. What worried him, and Lord Cahill, was the pallor and malnourishment.

Ralgon was barely more than skin and bones, and he didn't even realize something was terribly wrong with him. He just hunched over the trinket he held in his hand, rocking back and forth, muttering to himself.

CHAPTER 66

It wasn't as if a gust of wind had blown out the lamps or extinguished the fire Drangar realized. No, all light had vanished! Neena and her mother let out surprised shrieks and he straightened in alarm, stood, trying to get his bearings. "This darkness is wrong," he muttered, tense. There was a fourth presence in the room. "Ladies, I need my hands. Cut the bonds, please." The women must have felt it as well because they whimpered in fear. How this person had reached the room from outside, Drangar didn't know; they were in a turret room dozens of feet above the street.

"Perceptive as always and all tied up, bastard!" a voice said. "Makes it so much easier!" The voice was everywhere, resonating from walls and inside Drangar's mind. Footsteps rushed forward and he heard a stool being shoved aside. There was a whoosh of air as something or someone appeared next to him and vanished again. Muffled screams followed.

"I hope you like being reminded of being helpless, bastard," the voice taunted. "Such nice women you got here, the young one so unlike your dead lover, eh?"

Drangar turned. Where was he? Why did this voice sound so familiar? He tried to locate the man, fear surging up, not for him, but for Neena and Leonore, who struggled against the unseen enemy. He was afraid of losing both Cahill women; they were his last link to the past, his last chance to find the murderers. His wrists were still bound behind his back.

He chuckled. "Bloody idiot," he cursed himself aloud. Here, within this room was one of the killers. This man could tell who was after him and why they wanted to kill him. "Who the fuck are you?" he shouted, desperate to buy more time. A tug at the rope, both arms strained against the knot. Muscles protested against the unusual action.

A mad giggle echoed from unseen walls. "Look at you, won't you? The sorry fate of the one Lesganagh blessed, who was always so strong and so gifted."

Whom had he slighted in the past? There were many, but most of them were dead. A relative maybe? His blessing was no secret, but he had never gone about bragging. "Let them go!" Drangar had to make the intruder let the women go free, and he had to get out of this rope. There! His tugging worked! He felt the hemp give a little.

"How was it to feel so helpless, so alone, bastard?"

Someone hammered against the door, but he felt only he could free them. If the assailant could be defeated in this bloody darkness at all. Finally! The rope snapped, but the friction had taken its toll on his wrists. His fingers felt wet. If he died tonight a little blood would hardly matter. Groping about around him, he got hold of a stool. "Maybe I'm not as helpless as you think, murderer!"

"Murderer? You call me murderer? You little shit!"

Let him talk, Drangar thought. All he needed was to pinpoint a spot to throw the stool.

"Forgot that little village down in Rantarr, now, did you? What was it called?"

"Little Creek," Drangar growled. How did this bastard know such things?

"Ah, yes. Nice work down there, worthy of you, Scythe! The entire village! And you call me a murderer?"

"Let them go!"

"I haven't even started killing anybody, yet!"

There! The foe had to be there! Drangar threw the stool and heard it shatter against the far wall. "Missed me!" the voice mocked. "You know what, bastard? Maybe I'll kill you first and then have my way with the ladies," taunted the intruder. Why did the voice seem so bloody familiar? "I'll treat them better than you did that dark-haired slut."

"She was no slut!" shrieked Neena. In the darkness it

sounded as if the younger Cahill woman was struggling with the assailant, but only for a moment. A grunt followed by a resounding slap and the struggle was over.

"I don't like hurting women!" the voice said. "But I'll do so should either of you wenches piss me off again!"

"Let them go!"

"Ralgon!" He recognized the voice as Leonore's. "Save us, I beg you!"

"How can he when he can't even save his own worthless hide, eh, bastard?"

Who was he?

"Just imagine, bastard, me drawing a sharp blade across the young one's throat, killing her silently while you are surrounded by darkness, hating yourself for your inability to help her! Brings back memories, eh?"

Drangar growled in anger, clenching and unclenching his bloodied fists. He couldn't locate the voice and now the women's noises were also coming from every direction. He trembled with frustration.

Not again; his mind reeled. He refused to allow this! His anger focused. He wasn't helpless, hadn't been helpless ever since his journey into the past. "Memories of traitorous wretches too afraid to face one man! Memories of cowards choosing to kill an innocent instead of doing the deed themselves! I've seen sheep with more courage than your lot!"

He heard the sound of a dagger being unsheathed. "Damn you, fiend! Leave them alone!"

"Oh, but I do like to play, and I take the word fiend as an insult from one such as you!"

He didn't know whether it was Neena or her mother whose whimpering was echoing from the walls. "Leave them alone! Take me instead!"

"Oh, please, do you really think I would spare them after I am through with you? You must have more sense than that!" That voice, cruel, calculating, he knew he'd heard that lilt before, could almost link a name, a face to it. Who was he? Why did the voice seem so familiar?

Fury overwhelmed him, fury at his own inability to help

the women, fury at his past and the enemies that had caused Hesmera's death. No, he was not responsible for her death, but he would be responsible for Neena's and Leonore's if he didn't do something. Anything!

He grabbed a chair and raised it above his head, ignoring the taunts. "How nice, the fool wants to play some more!" Drangar threw the chair in one direction, he couldn't tell which. The roar of splintering glass filled the room as the chair smashed through a window. Drangar heard the unseen assailant scream in pain, followed by a woman's wail of fear.

For a moment he fought the red veil of anger that threatened to wash over him; he would not lose control as he had in Little Creek—he had forgotten the village's name! The Fiend would not win this battle, he would not allow it! If he let his fury dominate, Neena and her mother wouldn't be safe from him either. He struggled, desperate to maintain control, felt this rage seeping into his soul.

"No!" He had to keep the Fiend at bay; the meditations must have been good for something. On the battlefield his fury had saved his life time and again; maybe he could channel it into saving Leonore and Neena Cahill now. He took a deep, steadying breath and ignored the assassin's taunts.

Could he control the Fiend?

He had to guide it, let the fury be his servant not the other way around. Like a red curtain, the anger seemed to envelop him; he pushed back. It tingled like a sliver of lace might; the urge to rush blindly forward was there, but unlike all those times when the bloodlust had taken hold of him, this time he prevailed. The curtain became like a frame, gilding his sight; it still drenched his soul with fiery blood, but he could control it, had to control it. Drangar roared, closed his eyes, opened them again and could see the room as it was, still illuminated, one window smashed by the chair he had thrown and the forced entry of the man who had both women collared with a glittering band. The blood that had seeped out from his wrists was gone, only a thin red mist remained. His wounds closed as he watched. What was happening?

The hood his opponent wore hid the man's face, but he

remembered at once the person who had sat with the spy last night. The Chosen had been right, none of Duasonh's men had sent the youth after him; it had been this man. Who was he? Drangar peered into the hood but couldn't discern anything.

He pivoted as if still searching for his opponent, trying to keep the foe in the belief he was still affected by the magical darkness.

The intruder then shifted his gaze from Drangar to the women and moved his hand in well-practiced motions, ignoring the deep cut he had received, probably by Neena. A desk slid across the room in front of the door whose lock slid shut and melted, barring every route of escape.

"Now the bitches will die," the man said, sneering at Drangar. He raised both his outstretched hands and formed a circle with his fingers and thumbs, muttering words that seemed strangely familiar.

"No!" Drangar charged the attacker.

Irritated at his sudden move, the assailant stopped his spell work—it had to be magic—and raised his left hand to his chest, quickly dropped it down, and vanished from the spot he had just occupied. Unable to halt his attack Drangar smashed into the wall.

"Too slow," the man taunted as he reappeared next to the broken window, his voice quavering slightly.

The impact with the wall proved almost fatal, but by sheer force of will he remain conscious. "Damnation!" he cursed and turned around, fiercely blinking away the motes of light that flickered before his eyes.

"Damnation indeed," the assassin sniggered and prepared the ritual again, faster this time. "I think I'll take care of you first," the man sneered. "You'll have to wait, ladies," he added with a nod toward the cowering women. A jet of flame rushed toward Drangar, forcing him to dodge aside, away from the inferno. Whatever the fire touched was set aflame, tapestries, carpet, his clothes.

Drangar twisted into a ball, rolled onto his back, and extinguished the flames. The smell of burnt hair and skin intermingled with the smoke that now filled the room. A quick look at Neena and Leonore assured him they were somewhat safe; he crouched low and watched the man's next move.

Who was he? Even the quaver in his voice reminded him of someone. Was he a wizard like this Ealisaid person? The bastard certainly knew magic.

A few uttered words caused a fiery circle to appear within the room, surrounding him. Drangar sprang forward, straight for his opponent, but smashed into an invisible barrier that burned his skin. Tears of pain and frustration welled up as he watched the man draw closer. He knew this man! Why couldn't he remember? The cold voice, the almost feral snarl. "You don't belong here, bastard," his attacker said.

A memory lingered in the back of his mind but refused to step forward. The barrier was thorough; his probing fingers didn't detect an opening. He didn't care about the burns, already smelled the charred meat, felt the pain coursing from his fingertips down his arms.

The man stepped closer, his robes shifted slightly and for an instant Drangar thought he saw a medallion hanging around the man's neck. Confusion and anger welled up again, and he felt the fiend, his fury, which he had thought was finally under control, rising.

"Now the circle is complete," the assassin said, chuckling humorlessly. "Quite literally."

Still Drangar struggled to control his rage. It had helped him overcome the magical darkness. Could it help him overcome this barrier as well? There wasn't much left to lose, his fingers were slowly being devoured by the circle's flames, Neena and her mother were helpless, leashed to the wizard by magic, Hesmera was dead because... he refused to let the suspicion rise fully inside, he couldn't be sure just yet. Gently he let his fury envelop him, not the uncontrolled wine-induced madness he had experienced before, not the bloodlust-fueled rage of battle; no, this was as if he poured out all the anger, fear, self-loathing, grief into a dam, through the breach, to feed a stream steadily.

He held this fury on the edge, felt his grasp on reality crumble, saw the magical collar around Neena's neck flicker and fade. The bastard didn't have much control after all. Neena rose carefully, her eyes met his and then moved over to the enemy. The young Lady Cahill edged toward the one remaining chair, completely ignored by the assailant whose attention was focused on Drangar. The assassin chanted, sung, words too weird for him to comprehend. It almost felt as if he was praying. No, suspicions he might have, the glimpse of a medallion that might or might not be there fed them.

Instinct and reason battled inside his mind; from one moment to the next he didn't know which side would take control. For now, he could hold his rage back, but a part of him wanted to rend the bastard apart, feed his entrails to his dying body! The Fiend within roared, urged on by the slowly dawning realization this was merely the last of a string of assassins sent by... no, he refused to believe this! His consciousness battled the Fiend, and through the haze of pain he felt a change happen to his fingers. Drangar chanced a quick glance to his hands. The burns were mending! He looked back at the assassin, and from the rim of his vision saw Neena, mouthing two words: *For Hesmera.*

He blinked once, twice. He understood what she intended. The bastard was chanting, his hands moved in complex patterns, tracing and retracing complicated lines in front of him.

Lines of gleaming hot light sprang up from the circle, closing in on each other above his head, forming a cage of white light. His body shook with rage, but Neena's mentioning of Hesmera had brought reason back to Drangar's mind and he regained control over the Fiend. His anger finally controlled by his will, his conscience.

Eyes still focused on the mage, Drangar felt his strength ebbing away, sucked into the circle around him. Tendrils of light leapt up from his body, away from him into the cage.

Soon.

Neena had moved up behind the stranger and raised the chair above her head, poised to strike. As if it was nothing the man turned, looked at her, and then as calmly as he had turned to face her he returned to his position, leaving her as she was.

Drangar saw the noblewoman tremble with effort as she tried to look into his eyes, saw her fear and determination battling something inside her. She was spellbound, he realized, his stomach clenching. He thought fiercely about what to do, his strength ebbing with every heartbeat.

A great boom resounded from the door. Someone was trying to get in. Again, the entrance shook under the force of the assault. It had to be Kildanor. Dimly he heard the Chosen of Lesganagh curse, "Fucking Demonologists!" The wood creaked, part of it splintering away, but he doubted the Chosen would be in time. The door was too thick.

Bile rose in his throat. The fiend begged, taunted, promised that only with it in control could he save them. For a brief moment, he battled with himself, then let go. He would not allow this man to kill the women. Or him!

Straining against the forces that drained his body and soul he shouted, "Hesmera!"

As he screamed from the top of his lungs, felt how his fury ripped free of its leash. He stormed forward, crashed into the barrier of light. The searing heat and pain were nothing. He could not be held, could not be tamed, nothing would ever stop him!

His shout had the desired effect; Neena snapped out of her trance and brought the chair down on the assassin's head. Luck was with the enemy. He twisted aside and evaded most of the blow.

Kill, kill, kill, the fiend roared inside of him. Again, and again he smashed into the barrier. Nothing could stop him!

Kill, kill, kill! The roar went on and on. A detached part of Drangar's mind felt the searing, the burning in his shoulder, felt how his hair burned off his scalp, feared what the fiend might do when the wall was breached. Already the barrier seemed weaker but he also noticed how even the rage that fueled him ebbed away.

Neena pummeled the mage with her fists and feet as Kildanor struggled to overcome the door.

Kill, kill, kill, the hiend howled. Drangar felt the wall shatter. They were free. They? Almost meekly the fiend seemed to halt. It was as if his fury was looking back at him, looking for the way. He was still in control! For the first time in his life he was really and truly in charge. The mental leash was tied quickly, but not too tightly. Drangar felt his knees buckle, but the fiend pulled him forward. There would be no stopping this time, he knew.

He lunged for the wizard and got hold of his throat. "And now you will speak!" he roared, his face twisted with anger. He raised his other hand, balled it into a fist. The assassin's hood fell off.

Drangar hesitated, staring at the revealed face in disbelief. It couldn't be true! He refused to believe it! "No," he wheezed.

"Oh yes, Ralchanh, oh yes."

Ralchanh, the name he had discarded fourteen years ago, the name he had dismissed, and the name that was his by birth. Here, in his trembling hands, was Dalgor. Cousin Dalgor, the bullyboy. Dalgor the Bastard, he had called him. The child that had always treated him like vermin from the beginning, who had spat in his hair, thrown mud into his food. "Why?" Drangar whispered. He felt his hands shake uncontrollably, his voice hoarse, his breathing labored. "Why?" He refused to believe it.

The assassin twisted out of his grip. The chain holding the medallion in place halted his attempt for a moment, and with a flick of his head he snapped the links.

Before Drangar could react, the man held his left hand out, pulled it downward, and vanished. Drangar looked at the place where the man had been just heartbeats before, blinked, gazed at Neena as she hurried to her mother's side. Then he stared again at the amulet.

"Why? You bastards why?" Drangar mumbled again and again. "Darlontor, why do you want me dead?" he whispered.

Why did they want him dead? He didn't understand. What had he ever done to them? What reason did they have to kill Hesmera? He looked at the amulet in his hand and felt himself fall into a darkness that was worse than the endless night he'd been trapped in when they had tried to kill him. Why would they go to all that trouble to kill him?

He felt a hand on his shoulder and looked up. "Why?" he asked, tears running down his face. "Why does he want me dead?" His knees buckled, slammed onto the carpeted floor.

He didn't even feel the impact, his eyes wandering back to the trinket in his hand. "Why?"

The how didn't matter anymore. He knew they had means at their command that most people in this age only dreamed about. He did not know the reason for the killing, but he finally knew the source of all his misery. There was no doubt now. He looked at the proof—the medallion's face engraved with the coat of arms of the Sons of Traksor.

CHAPTER 67

Trudging through frost-rimmed Gathran was hardly effective. Was he already on Kalduuhnean soil? Lloreanthoran didn't know, and where by Lliania's bloody Scales could he find the Eye of Traksor the Lightbringer had asked him to find?

Walking would not get him there, wherever "there" was. Where should he start? Which city had a library that could possibly hold the information he needed? Ma'tallon, the capital of Kalduuhn! It had survived the Heir-War and, he hoped, the Demon-War. As it was the capital, it had had one of the biggest libraries, attended by venerable priests of Traghnalach. If the city and the library still existed, the priestly historians and scribes would have at least a fraction of the information he needed. Whispering, he hurried through the chants and gestures of the teleportation spell and disappeared from the small clearing.

A heartbeat later Lloreanthoran stood on a hill outside the city. The sight of Ma'tallon caught him by surprise. A century ago the city had been a sprawling rectangular block of walled in houses and mansions. Now it looked more like a massive tower.

The whitewashed walls still demarked Ma'tallon's limits, but it seemed as if the humans had expanded not horizontally, but vertically. Above the marble of mansions, villas, and temples, there loomed another layer of city, built right on top of the roofs, and one or two more layers on top of those. Massive stilts, latched onto walls and several of the lowest buildings, supported the framework holding everything aloft.

He stared in disbelief. Elven magic had once built the city, the first town in which former slaves and former masters lived together. Nothing could break down both buildings and walls.

Yet, instead of expanding beyond the massive stone edifices, like other cities had, it seemed as if the rulers had decided to go up.

Walking closer, Lloreanthoran saw stairs and pulley-driven lifts connecting the various layers of Ma'tallon. Wheels, very much similar to those on mills, driven by wind, pumped water into the upper levels. Unlike what he had expected, the higher the city went, the more desolate it looked. Nobility and clergy, it seemed, was earthbound, while the lower classes—did they still distinguish between villeins and freeborn?—lived higher up. He now saw, the upper levels barely had railings and handholds, so that accidents were quite likely to happen.

To the humans, life remained cheap.

As he neared the northern gate, he pulled up the hood of his cloak. It would do no good to be discovered. Elves had left these lands long ago; his people's exodus was only the last in a long line of retreats. The elves of Kalduuhn had moved into a more remote area, still living in the world, but apart from it. Human wars had hardly abated in the centuries before the Heir-War, and even to the vengeful elves the constant warfare and moving of borders had become tiresome.

Ma'tallon was a reminder of what had connected the two races ages ago: master and servant, much like the elves and those who had enslaved them.

The closer he came, the more details did Lloreanthoran see. The layer on top of the original city was less decorated, but still respectable. It also had an unbroken railing surrounding its limits, a sturdy steeloak fence almost half a man's height. Above that, things looked more decrepit. No more handholds, functional houses belying the buildings they stood upon, and even further up, sheds that looked only remotely better than some of the tents that had been set up next to them. Waste, it seemed, was tossed into chutes leading to the ground, where it was gathered by somebody to be towed off. Also, the people most removed from the ground seemed most prone to stumble and fall to their deaths.

Yet children were climbing all along this latticework, up and down, playing a death-wish version of hide and seek. Lloreanthoran stood and stared, amazed at the skill of these young humans as they darted about the framework.

"They're called lattice-children," a passing woman, bent by age, explained. "Ma'tallon's very own version of the gutter-youths found in other cities." She shook her head, muttering, "One of these days it'll all come down."

He wanted to ask her something, but she had hurried onto one of the departing lifts, carrying a score of people up.

Was this how humanity treated elven leftovers? Ma'tallon looked, at least at its foundation, very much as he remembered it. Much like Honas Graigh before the Wizard War, stone had been called up from the bowels of the soil to form walls and houses. Only after the rock had cooled had artists hammered frescoes into the stone. The interiors and roofs were stone as well, making them appear like children's toys when viewed from above.

At the gate, a bored pair of guards gave him a cursory glance. Apparently, they were satisfied for they let him pass without question. Inside the city the bright, crisp autumn day was replaced by gloom. Flames flickered in lanterns, and a little sunlight entered this stuffy underworld through the gate behind him and from a few breaches in the frames holding up the higher layers. It almost felt as if he was back in the Aerant C'lain.

Almost.

The moment he passed through an alcove onto one of the main squares, the atmosphere changed. This was a marketplace, he noted to his astonishment. Back when he had last visited the city this once sky lit area had been host to theater groups, philosophers, all talking and playing to whomever was interested. Now there was a massive pillar in the square's center. Four huge tree trunks had been put together to keep the wood and plaster ceiling high above his head up in the air. Attached to the wooden column was a wide staircase leading into the next level. On those stairs, each wider than a medium sized boat, was a booth of some merchant or other. The steps themselves were firmly embedded into the wood, and supported by metal poles that seemingly reached from the ground all the way up to the ceiling.

Lloreanthoran stopped and stared, unable to tear his eyes from this magnificent piece of human architecture. He tried to grasp the skill and manpower it must have taken to build this pillar, let alone the upper tiers of the city. The air was still stuffy, but now a myriad of scents surrounded him. Smoked meats, pies, vegetables, fruits, cured leather, there even was a smithy built right under the staircase! From the look of the workshop, the owner had managed to make the shack fireproof, and even as the woman beat a piece of gleaming iron into shape, the sparks flew up and were swallowed by the forge's ceiling.

He was still staring when someone pulled at his right sleeve. Irritated, he looked down and saw a young boy dressed in the garb of a Librarian staring up at him. Certainly, the God of Knowledge and Sky would know of his arrival, and inform his priesthood. Still, he was surprised to see the Chief Librarian had sent a boy to fetch him.

"Are you...?" the lad fell into an uncomfortable silence, his eyes trying to pierce his hood's darkness.

In the gloom it was impossible to see his face, and he was glad about that. "I am Lloreanthoran," he replied, knowing full well the boy had wanted to know something completely different. "And you are?"

"Danthair," the boy said. "I understand things!" he declared, his small chest filling with pride.

Knowing the little Librarian could not see his features, Lloreanthoran allowed himself a smile. So, the Chief Librarian had sent his replacement to escort him to the temple. "I am certain you do," he said.

"Shall we?" Despite his apparent youth, Danthair exuded the authority of a well-learned sage.

"Certainly." Taking one more look at the massive pillar and stairs construction, Lloreanthoran followed his young guide across the plaza and into an even more shadowy side street which, he was informed, led right to the Temple of Traghnalach. They headed for the entrance, and he allowed himself a brief pause to marvel, for the first time in well over a century, at the simplicity of the construction.

Every wall was kept simple, no sculptures adored the plain

pillars that held the overlapping roof, and in contrast to other human and elven temples no fresco or picture indicated that this was a house of worship; apart from one thing: a pair of hands holding an open book, the symbol of Traghnalach carved from the finest marble, rested on top of its flat roof.

They hurried through the entrance and Danthair pushed on, deeper inside. Lloreanthoran recalled the temple's layout, and remembered they were heading to Chief Librarian's room. It wasn't. The chamber, he remembered as the administrative heart of the temple, had been turned into a scriptorium.

Through the open door Lloreanthoran saw a score of priests hunched over their writing desks, scribbling meticulously. As Danthair turned away from the room, the child glanced back at him, saw his obvious confusion, and smiled. "We changed it a few decades ago," he explained. "Like the King himself declared that nobility must shoulder the common man, Chief Librarian Grannath decided to dedicate his office to recordkeeping; a smaller office suffices, he says."

Had man surpassed their former masters in wisdom, Lloreanthoran wondered. Not that there was much wisdom in the elves of Gathran these days. He followed the young priest. They were now closing in on a very plain looking door. No ornament, not even a sign adorned the wood, and just before they arrived, it swung open, revealing an elderly man.

"I thought I would never see the likes of you again," the man croaked, his voice parched from age far beyond that of any human he'd ever encountered.

He scrutinized the speaker, a huddled semblance of a man. Danthair sketched a quick bow and left. This had to be Chief Librarian Grannath. The priest's age stunned Lloreanthoran. This man looked older than it seemed possible for a human. His skin was pallid, brittle, and appeared ready to break any moment. Despite his obvious ancientness, this human was still perceptive and aware of his environment, and he had most certainly discerned his origin, by his posture. "Who are you?" he asked, merely to confirm his assumption.

The old man chucked, "There, there, shouldn't I ask who you are, elf?"

"How did you know what I am?"

"As if you didn't already know the answer, pointy ears. You people move like no human ever could, and your haughty bearing is even more perfected than any of the lesser nobles, lesser human nobles that is."

"So, who are you?" Lloreanthoran inquired again.

"Ah, ah. Now, aren't you a great example for your race's arrogance? You entered my home, so you answer my questions first." The old man took a deep, rasping breath. "Now, where were we? Oh, yes, who are you and what are you doing here? Especially the latter interests me, and while you're at it tell me how you came from beyond the Veil of Dreams?"

The last question caused him to lose composure. "What?" he blurted out, not comprehending how a human could know about his people's secret hiding place? Their refuge.

"Ah, now I've got your attention, eh?" the old man sniggered, then the look on his face turned thoughtful. "Hey, I do remember you, elf. You were the concerned one, the seeker as my old master called you. He used to make fun of you because you came here sometimes to unearth some knowledge your kinfolk didn't know yet."

The elven wizard became even more confused now. He had always prided himself on having an almost flawless memory, but this old man proved him wrong. He could not remember him.

"Lloreanthoran, correct? You're Lloreanthoran."

"Yes," he mumbled, dumbfounded. "Yes, I am," he said then, more forcefully, as to remind himself who he was. "And who are you?"

"You may, and I am Grannath, Chief Librarian," the old man said, smiling an almost toothless grin. "And how may I help you, Lloreanthoran? On second thought, we shouldn't talk about whatever it is out here in the open, so please follow me." He turned around and walked slowly into his office. Looking over his shoulder the Librarian found Lloreanthoran still standing at the same spot. "You're going to grow roots if you keep standing there, and birds will nest in your mouth if you don't shut it."

Finally, he regained his senses and followed the wizened, old man, still pondering the revelations. Some humans knew about the elven refuge. Was his race threatened by this knowledge, or would this help him convince his brethren to leave their created home and return to Gathran? Maybe, this was just something Grannath knew because of his proximity to his god, and the old man had kept it to himself.

They were in a small room, its only furniture a huge table and several, cushioned chairs. "Have a seat, mage. It might not be much, compared to what you're used to, but it is all you'll get, so you might as well appreciate it, and from the look of your clothes you've been sleeping on the floor."

Numbly, Lloreanthoran sat down on one of the chairs and looked at Grannath. "How is it that you still remember me? The last time I have been to the library was well two hundred years ago."

"Ah, a good question, although not the most important one on your mind, but it's easy to answer. When my master and predecessor died, I took over as High Priest and Chief Librarian, and Traghnalach blessed me by giving me more time to learn and help him guard and guide knowledge. And, well, here I am, a bit gray around the ears but still alive and doing what my god wanted me to do." The old librarian smiled at him, making the elf fear that his brittle skin would finally be torn asunder under the stress. "Also, finding a successor is somewhat difficult."

"I am here on a very important mission, and to accomplish it I need to know as much as possible about the Demon-War," he said after a brief silence. "Forgive my abruptness on this, but if you knew what had transpired days ago, you'd understand my lack of interest in idle talk."

"The Demon-War, eh?" the old man chuckled. "So, you elves finally want to pick up the pieces of the mess you left behind? A little late for that, but the time you choose to undo your mistakes isn't of my concern. Before I start recounting the entire war and possibly wasting your time and mine, I would like you to be more specific about what you want to know."

He concluded that the old librarian knew more about the hidden shame of the elves and his people than he had thought possible but this man was, after all, the High Priest of the God of Wisdom and Knowledge. His own information regarding the time of the Demon-War was slim, mainly based on what Bright-Eyes had told him and his own deductions, so it was best to ask for a short wrap up of the war before asking his specific questions. "I need to know what generally happened in the Demon-War, how it was started, and how it ended."

Grannath looked at him for a moment and then closed his eyes. "The Demon-War, eh? Or shall we call it the elven initiated mess?" he chuckled. "Well, it all started with your people leaving Honas Graigh and the shattered remains of your kingdom to hide behind the Veil of Dreams, as you call it. You took almost everything with you, and the one thing you forgot, you had quite literally wanted to forget over the last few centuries."

Grannath drew a deep breath and looked at Lloreanthoran shifting uncomfortably on his chair. "As it was, Chanastardh had invaded what was still standing of the three kingdoms Gathran, Dargh, and Janagast Shortly afterwards, those realms were given to Halmond of Greyrock who was crowned king of Danastaer, named after Halmond's chief advisor Danachamain."

Lloreanthoran flinched when he heard the familiar, nightmarish name, but Grannath ignored his unease and went on. "Danachamain, the little twit, wasn't satisfied with the advent of a new kingdom, he wanted more. Knowledge, power, you name it, he wanted everything. And he suspected the key to all this lay in Honas Graigh." The old man looked at him, and shook his head. "Ironic, isn't it, you left the world because of the havoc humans had wrought and yet left the biggest danger behind."

"The Tomes of Darkness," Lloreanthoran whispered, even though he knew those vile books had been responsible for the demonic war, the fact that humans were aware of the elves' failure, and that it wasn't just one person's or a certain group's mistake, but the failings of the entire populace of Gathran, was almost too much for him to bear. "You humans must despise us," he finally said.

"Oh, no, we don't despise your kind, but most here, who never venture to other parts of the world, view the elves as a part of a past that should best remain that way."

"But the Heir-War," Lloreanthoran stuttered.

"Now this particular war was bad, but, you must understand, it was only a small group of humans who started it and this fraction has been obliterated; people didn't have anyone left to blame. In the Demon-War case," he muttered, his scrawny hands wiping across his face. "Well, let's put it this way, you people unwittingly left the tools behind when you fled into your dream domain, and for those who know about it, which are still many, you are the initiators and cause of this war." Grannath raised his hand before Lloreanthoran could intervene. "And even if you say that such things were never meant for human hands, one must ask oneself why you left it behind in the first place. Out of sight does not mean out of mind, at least not in case of the Tomes of Darkness and the Stone."

It astonished Lloreanthoran to agree with this wizened human. At the time of his people's Grand Departure, the scars and fears of the Heir-War had been too fresh and the horrors of what had happened had preoccupied the minds of every single elf. The Tomes of Darkness had, since they were stored in the Aerant C'lain, simply been forgotten. It was the elves' mistake to leave them behind, far worse that his ancestors hadn't destroyed those books after the initial contact with the realm of demons and the brief, but violent, battle that had ensued to force the demonic hordes back into their own lands after the Stone of Blood had opened the portal. The elves back then had believed all knowledge to be sacred.

"I... I have to... agree," he finally said. "The books should never have survived into this age; we should have destroyed them a long time ago."

"And risked that some foolish Phoenix Wizard started to dwell in the same area again?" Grannath asked mockingly. "Knowledge once discovered and retained is quite difficult to discover again, and if it is, the people who discovered it in the first place could halt any further destruction." He smirked. "Well, that might be the ideal situation anyway, and today no one really bothers with such things anymore, especially your people. But your ancestors weren't like that. The Aerant C'lain had two purposes, in case you didn't know."

Two purposes? Lloreanthoran became even more attentive.

"The first was to store those books and keep them from harm, or better yet, to keep anyone else from harm by not allowing anyone near them. The second, and this is the one everyone has forgotten about, was to prevent anyone from rediscovering the knowledge held within the Tomes of Darkness. Basically, that meant, should anyone discover the mysteries of the demonic again, the Aerant C'lain would smite this person down, well, not the building but the magic within the building's structure." Again, the old man grinned. "Astonishing that the elves of old weren't the scheming misers we know, isn't it?"

"But how could this Danachamain gain access to the Aerant C'lain when it would have slain him for rediscovering the knowledge?"

Grannath chuckled again, clapping his hands. "Now that's an easy question to answer. The protections were for people discovering the knowledge through research, not for someone who read what elves had found out ages ago. Your ancestors foresaw a great many things, but not that their heirs would leave their ancestral homes. The Forbidden Chamber wasn't sealed and it was not guarded against people entering; for all we know your forefathers wanted people to study the dangers in order to fight them. When you elves left, you left the biggest and most dangerous arsenal behind: The Tomes."

"My people made a grave mistake, I know," Lloreanthoran agreed. "And I am here to correct this error."

"Well, good luck then," Grannath snickered.

"You can spare me the sarcasm, before you is one elf who does care," Lloreanthoran spat.

Leaning back in his chair, looking at him, Grannath sighed, "It's sad to see that only one has the courage and sense of responsibility, even after almost a century, to actually come down here and try to clean up a mess his entire people are responsible for, don't you think?"

"Who gave you the right to judge?"

"Oh, I don't judge, I just state what should be going on in your mind as well," Grannath replied calmly.

Hanging his head in resignation, he had to agree, his people had escaped the world so they weren't forced to adapt to the changes the Heir-War had wrought. They still were the bickering, intrigue loving people they had been one hundred years ago. "You are right, my people's values are twisted," he finally said.

"But I am not here to give you a lesson on morals. You needed to know something specific," Grannath said, changing the subject immediately. From being the teacher lecturing a helpless pupil he turned into the librarian ready to help one who searched for knowledge. "What do you need to know?"

"Are there remnants of Danachamain's followers who might still roam the face of the world?" he asked, astonished at the speed the priest changed subjects, glad the lecture was over.

"I should think so, otherwise the Sons of Traksor would be foolish to stick around after all these years," Grannath replied.

"You have no specific information in that regard?" Lloreanthoran leaned forward, folding his hands, looking anxiously at the High Priest.

"Before his death, Danachamain was given the power to hide his doings from the prying eyes of the gods, and thus even Traghnalach can't see what he or his followers were and might still be doing."

"You mentioned the Sons of Traksor," the wizard said. "Who are they?"

"Oh, that is easy to answer. Tral of the Royal House of Kassor, heir to the Kalduuhnean throne, had been exiled because of his love for a woman born a commoner and thus unsuited for marriage. He went into the wilderness of Gathran, taking the name Traksor, and lived there until the Demon-War. When the hordes of fiends stormed the lands, he was visited by Lesganagh and given a sword with the power to drive the demonic hordes back. He gathered many outlaws living in the woodland into a small warband that faced the demons, but it was he alone who sacrificed his life while defeating the mightiest of them, the Archdemon Turuuk, and thus winning the Demon-War. The remnants of his army formed an order, the Sons of Traksor, dedicated to countering any demonic moves in this part of the world. They are dedicated to Lesganagh, naturally, and are under his protection, as far as I know. If you seek more answers you might as well ask them."

"Where can I find them?" the elf asked.

"They rule a fief that covers the northern reaches bordering to Danastaer, and their center of power is the Eye of Traksor; they pay their taxes duly and take good care of their villeins. If you have further questions you might as well ask them." Grannath rose and smiled at him.

"Two more questions, your worship."

"Yes?"

"How do you remember all this?"

"Oh, well, I remember everything. Why do you think I was chosen as High Priest," Grannath chuckled. "And the other?"

"Might I peruse the library? I would like to learn more about what has happened in the last century."

"Certainly, what knowledge we may share is yours, wizard."

Lloreanthoran bowed. "Thank you."

"Now, off you go; I'll find out if you succeed.".

About the Author

Ulff Lehmann has spent quite a while waiting on his Midlife Crisis, and decided he won't go there. For the past two decades he has been developing the stories he is now publishing. Born and bred in Germany, Ulff chose to write in English when he realized he had spent most of his adult life reading English instead of his mother tongue, and brings with him the oftentimes Grimm outlook of his country's fairy tales to his stories. A wordsmith with a poet's heart, Ulff's goal is to create a world filled with believable people.

According to his friends, his place is utter chaos and filled to the brim with books, CDs, and DVDs. In an earlier part of his life, Ulff turned his love for music outward, singing in two bands. Nowadays the only singing he does is in concert with his shower, and it thinks his voice is still acceptable. His passion for movies led him to begin Movie and TV studies at university, begin being the operative word. He didn't finish. Instead life pulled him this way and that until he finally understood he was a storyteller.

Curious about other Crossroad Press books?
Stop by our site:
http://store.crossroadpress.com
We offer quality writing
in digital, audio, and print formats.

Enter the code FIRSTBOOK
to get 20% off your first order from our store!
Stop by today!